PRAISE FO... ...

"*Equus* is a delight, with a unique take on an old subject. There's a nice range of mood and subject, but the overall theme is well-explored and central."   —Jaym Gates, ed *War Stories*

"All the stories in this collection are good. Each author has a completely different take on where the animals live and how they behave. It makes the stories surprising and unique. If you like fantasy, magic, or horses, you'll love this book."   —Journey of a Bookseller

"This was a wonderfully eclectic anthology, with practically any stripe of fantasy a grown-up weird horse girl could want on offer between the covers."   —T.R. North, short story author

PRAISE FOR THE MAGICAL MENAGERIES ANTHOLOGY SERIES

"*Corvidae* evokes the majesty and mischief of corvid mythologies worldwide—and beyond our world—in a collection that is fresh and thoroughly enjoyable."
— Beth Cato, author of *The Clockwork Dagger*

"With fifteen talented writers and a subject that is both evocative and memorable, Rhonda Parrish's new anthology, *Scarecrow*, is no straw man. Like any good scarecrow, this anthology is truly outstanding in its field. Don't be scared to pick this up and give it a read."
— Steve Vernon, author of *Tatterdemon*

"The call of SIRENS is quite powerful indeed. With a variety of stories, crafted with care, you will delight in the tales that the many authors weave throughout this fantastical anthology. It will lure you in and not let go."
—Tara Platt, author *Zartana*

Titles in the Anthology Series
Rhonda Parrish's Magical Menageries

Fae
Corvidae
Scarecrow
Sirens
Equus

EQUUS

Edited by

RHONDA PARRISH

Rhonda Parrish's Magical Menageries

Volume Five

World Weaver Press

EQUUS

Published by World Weaver Press, LLC
Albuquerque, NM
www.WorldWeaverPress.com

Cover layout and design by Jonathan C. Parrish.
Cover images used under license from Fotolia.com.

First edition: July 2017
ISBN-13: 978-0998702209

Also available as an ebook

CONTENTS

INTRODUCTION
Rhonda Parrish –1

STARS, WINGS AND KNITTING THINGS
J.G. Formato – 5

EEL AND BLOOM
Diana Hurlburt – 19

A COMPLETE MARE
Tamsin Showbrook – 39

NEITHER SNOW, NOR RAIN, NOR HEAT-RAY
M.L.D. Curelas – 59

RUE THE DAY
Laura VanArendonk Baugh – 71

RIDERS IN THE SKY
V.F. LeSann – 93

ABOVE THE SILVER SKY
Dan Koboldt – 114

A MOTHER UNICORN'S ADVICE TO HER DAUGHTER
J.J. Roth – 129

LADIES DAY
Susan MacGregor – 131

THE BOYS FROM WITLESS BAY
Pat Flewwelling – 149

THE HORSE WITCH
Angela Rega – 171

ELI THE HIDEOUS HORSE BOY
Michael Leonberger – 186

DIFFERENT
Sandra Wickham – 208

TO RIDE A STEEL HORSE
Stephanie A. Cain – 220

THE LAST RIDE OF HETTIE RICHTER
Cat McDonald – 230

WE US YOU
Andrew Bourelle – 245

SCATTER THE FOALS TO THE WIND
Chadwick Ginther – 260

LIGHTLESS
K.T. Ivanrest – 279

A GLORY OF UNICORNS
Jane Yolen – 299

ABOUT THE AUTHORS
301

ABOUT THE ANTHOLOGIST
307

RHONDA PARRISH'S MAGICAL MENAGERIES
309

DISCUSSION QUESTIONS
311

For Beth

EQUUS

.

INTRODUCTION
Rhonda Parrish

I've always loved books—they were a temporary escape, a source of freedom, for me for as long as I can remember. When I was younger, I primarily borrowed them from the library, but I also had a small, perpetually growing, personal collection. Most of them had been purchased second-hand from musty old shops with names like, "The Rabbit Hutch" or "Marshall's Attic" but some rare few were purchased new from a Scholastic book fair at my school. And they were almost always softcovers. Hardcover books were an incredible luxury and I owned only a very few until recently.

My first ever hardcover book was a copy of The Black Stallion by Walter Farley. It still have it. It is inscribed:

Merry Xmas Rhonda
Love Mom
1984

1984 means I was eight years old when I received it. Eight years old and crazy about horses. I never owned a horse—oddly enough they tend to be even more expensive than hardcover books—but from Kindergarten to grade three I spent every lunch hour and recess playing 'Unicorns' with my friend Linda, and every Friday I'd sleep over at her house and we'd ride her horses. Her real horses.

A couple years later we moved and I made a new friend—Miranda. Miranda also had horses—Raven Chick and Mr. Tuxedo. We called them Raven and Tux (or Tuxy) for short, and I spent a lot of weekends at Miranda's farm. Weekends that always included some horse time.

While our mutual love of horses wasn't the only thing that informed my friendships with Linda and Miranda, horses were one of the reasons we were friends. Horse people attract other horse people—even beyond childhood. To this day a great many of my best friends and favourite people are horse people.

And of the horses themselves, what is the attraction?

I can't speak for anyone else but for me it's a whole lot of things. Physically they are gorgeous, gorgeous creatures. They've great, dark, gentle eyes that might just be the origin of that whole 'windows to the soul' idea. And they are so strong, so clever, so amazingly intelligent—yet they let us ride on their backs. Their spirits are wild, and they are freedom made physical.

There was a lot I wanted to escape from when I was younger, and what could possibly be a more romantic escape—more freeing—than galloping off into the sunset on the back of a horse?

Given how often horses, books and imagination had provided an escape for me (separately as well as in different combinations with one another) how could I possibly resist the idea of making the final installment in the Magical Menageries anthology series about horses? I could not.

And though horses are magical in their own right, I did grow up on a steady diet of pretending to be a unicorn, and watching Pegasus, Newton (and little Toot!) on the 1960s cartoon, "The Mighty Hercules". Later I fell in love with The Last Unicorn by Peter S. Beagle and… well, I'd best not start a list or this introduction could get a wee bit long. The point is, why limit the anthology to just horses when I could throw open the doors and include all kinds of equines?

I didn't have a good answer to that question either, which is why in this anthology you'll find stories of horses, and unicorns, and flying horses, and Sleipnir, and demon horses, and… you get the idea.

They are all here, waiting to gallop you away new worlds, new adventures with them. And the two things they all have in common is that they include an equine creature and an offer of freedom.

When I was re-reading these stories during the production process the themes of escape and freedom came up again. And again. And again.

I hadn't consciously chosen freedom-themed stories for *Equus*, but as it turned out, that's what I ended up with.

And given my history with horses and escape, I couldn't possibly be happier. Things worked out perfectly.

~ Rhonda

STARS, WINGS, AND KNITTING THINGS
J.G. Formato

I didn't tell him the news until I'd placed the last raisin in my oatmeal. The wise and wrinkled happy face I'd created was quite encouraging. "Marcus," I said, waiting for acknowledgement and eye contact. His eyes were still mostly contacting the *Wall Street Journal*, so I cleared my throat and dinged my spoon on his mug. Announcement style.

He emerged from the paper and frowned at the ripples in his coffee. "Why'd you do that? I was reading."

"Were you?" I asked, genuinely curious. I always thought his morning paper was like an adult security blanket. But instead of making him feel safe and loved, it made him feel all grown-up and professional. Ready to join the Rat Race. Reading it for fun was a totally different story and not nearly as endearing.

"Of course I was, Annie. Now, what were you going to say?"

"I think the house is haunted."

"You think the house is haunted?"

"Mm-hm."

"Why?"

"Because I saw a ghost." Why else would I think the house was haunted?

"Where?"

"In the backyard. It was kind of swooshing all around by the swing set."

"So, really, you think the *backyard* is haunted." He looked very pleased with himself, like he scored a point or something. All those years of law school must have really paid off.

"Okay, fair enough. If you want to pick nits, I think the *backyard* is haunted."

"What did it look like? Your ghost?"

"It was white, of course. And shimmery. Oh, and it had wings."

"Like an angel?"

"No, not like an angel. Angels don't haunt people's backyards."

"Of course." He smacked his forehead—but in a smartassy way, not an oh, duh kind of way. "When did this even happen?"

"Well, it was before you got home, but it was still pretty late. You had a lot of paperwork, huh? Anyway, I couldn't sleep, so I got up to look at the stars and relax—"

"You were wandering around the backyard in your pajamas? What if somebody saw you?"

"I wasn't wandering around the backyard in my jammies. I looked out the window. It's see-through, you know."

"Oh. Okay. So you saw it out the window?"

"Yeah."

"The swooshing winged ghost?"

"Yep."

"Annie, I'm pretty sure you were dreaming." He glanced at his watch. He needed to leave in exactly seven minutes if he was going to get to work exactly fifteen minutes early.

"Ah, but that's where you're wrong. I knew you were going to say that, so I took your slippers from their spot by the bed, and I put them in the tub. They were still there this morning. Dream slippers would never come true."

"You did that? They got soaked when I turned on the water." He groaned. "Why'd you do that?

"Well, I had to prove I wasn't dreaming. And besides, slippers are pretentious."

"Slippers are not pretentious. Slippers are useful. And why didn't you just move something of your own?"

"Because my stuff's always lost." I grinned at him. "But your stuff being moved—that's an anomaly."

"Alright, babe." The conversation ended abruptly before I could make him late for being early. "We'll talk about it some more when I get home. Maybe get an alarm system or something. And try to eat something, you haven't touched your breakfast," he said in a fatherly tone with an equally fatherly kiss on the forehead. Gross.

I'm not going to touch that breakfast. I hate oatmeal and raisins are withered souls. As soon as he leaves I'm having S'mores Pop-Tarts dipped in Nutella.

It gets boring fast at home. There's nobody to talk to, and I miss the smell of nail glue. And there's way less colors here. Marcus and I decided on a monochromatic classy look for our home, but I think the rainbow polish wall at Top Nailz is much prettier. It's shiny and busy. I probably shouldn't have quit until I actually had a baby that I could stay-at-home-mother.

We're supposed to be making one, but I usually forget to try until it's too late and I'm on my period already. It might be better off trying for an orphan. Or maybe I can stay-at-home-mother the ghost. Ghosts are usually lost souls, and that's kind of like being an orphan.

It (He?) (She?) was nowhere to be found in the yard that morning. That was to be expected, though, since it was daytime. I slipped onto the swing and tightened my hands around the thick chains. The swings were always my favorite in elementary school. They didn't require a very high level of interaction and the motion added momentum to my imaginings. Eyes closed to the rising wind, I created my own reality. One where a shining Pegasus with powerful wings flew me far from this land, all the way back to where I belonged.

No one was around, so I went for it. The running start, the pumping legs, the eyes screwed shut—I'd never forgotten the way. I could still lose myself on the swings.

But not for long. Nausea kicks in way quicker at 30 than it does at 8.

I jumped, landing ass-first on our professionally manicured grass. My eyes drifted back open, a little reluctantly, but they knew it need to be done.

A lone white feather rested beside me, just left of my pinky. It caught and threw the sunlight like a grounded disco ball and glittered a greeting. It wanted me to pick it up.

It looked like my diary feather. In fact, it was identical to the one I've used as a bookmark in all of my journals, ever since I was a little girl.

It better not be my diary feather because that means Marcus has been reading all my business. On the swings. Which is not only rude, but weird.

Clutching the feather, I ran back to the house and up the stairs, two at a time. My diary was still in its secret spot—the bottom of the magazine basket. It had seemed like a pretty good spot up until now. Marcus would never touch my *Cosmos* and *Redbooks*, let alone dig around in them.

I heaved a loud and dramatic sigh of relief when I saw the familiar quill sprouting proudly from my journal. I opened the book to last night's ramblings and pulled out my oldest, dearest possession. It looked just like the brand-new backyard feather.

I think it's not a ghost that visits the backyard.

I think the not-a-ghost and I must go way back.

When Marcus gets home, we do not "talk more about it" like he said we would. And I don't show him backyard feather—he doesn't even know about diary feather. It was party night, so we partied. But not very heartily. Because it is a Marcus-people party.

At Marcus-people parties, we eat half-bites of tiny foods and we drink half-sips from tiny wine glasses. Sometimes I put out a pinky. It just seems like the right thing to do.

At Annie-people parties, we eat Ruffles and French Onion dip and drink dark beers.

Marcus-people parties are goal-oriented. We are there to network, to climb, to be so damn charming that they can't help but raise Marc from his lowly status as a paralegal to that of attorney. Perhaps one day—even—dare we say it? *Partner.*

Annie-people parties are Annie-people oriented. We are mostly there to get drunk, make fun of each other and watch *Real Housewives.*

We don't really go to Annie-people parties anymore.

But I do get to watch Real Housewives. And tonight I made contact with the Alpha Wife. Marcus looked up from his mingling and eye-contacted me, telegraphing his hope and trepidation. *Be nice. Be normal. Her husband owns the firm.* His thoughts were really loud—and also really rude. When am I ever not nice and normal?

Alpha Wife is lovely, even if her nails are a boring pink-and-white and her hair flips up like it's the '50s. Her name is Althea and she is a knitting enthusiast. So enthusiastic was she that I didn't even have to be nice *or* normal. All I had to do was nod and admire her handiwork.

Althea was pulling a blanket shaped like a mermaid tail out of a gigantic patchwork bag, when Marcus and Gina moseyed over. Gina is the other overly qualified paralegal with ambitious fingers permanently crossed. She is lovely, too, even if her nails are too red and her skirt is so tight I could make out the pattern of lace on her underpants.

"Now that is adorable," Gina gushed. Then she turned to Marcus and punched him on the shoulder. "You need a big boy one to cuddle up in while you read over documents. I can just see you all curled up in bed, your fins waving." She giggled throatily and grinned up at him. She smiled at me, too, inordinately pleased with her witty (not really that witty) banter.

Never trust a big butt and smile! The immortal advice of Bel Biv DeVoe sprung immediately to mind.

"What?" Marcus, Althea, and Gina exclaimed in unison. Marcus in horror, Gina in amusement, and Althea in utter confusion.

I then realized that the lyrics to *Poison* had not only sprung to mind, but to mouth as well. I'd quite literally and loudly sang out my thoughts.

"Nothing. Nothing." I shook my head. "I was. Um. Listening to my best of the '90s mix tape earlier. You know, while I was, doing some…Pilates? So, like, that song's been in my head all day. Anyway, what were we talking about? Knitting is so cool. Everyone needs a nice, toasty mermaid tail to slip their feet into."

Or their head.

The journey home was like riding a glacier. Freezing cold and really slow. And also pretty hard. I don't know if Marcus was more appalled by my lack of social prowess or my deep and secret love of early 90s hip hop, but I'm definitely feeling like feral child again. Like, I don't even belong indoors, let alone parties like that.

"Sorry," I said, by way of a conversation starter.

Hunch-shouldered, white-knuckled, road-rage silence.

"Is it really that big of a deal?" I tried again. I mean, Annie-people would have just laughed. And I can't imagine Marcus-people don't have *way* more important things to think about than little old me singing to myself.

"You embarrassed me, Annie. I don't why you always have to be so weird."

"I'm not that weird." He used to think I was funny. He used to think the quirkiness was cute.

"That crap's not normal, admit it. Normal people just say 'Hi' or 'Nice to see you again.' They don't sing inappropriate lyrics at their husband's colleagues."

I wanted to say, 'Oh yeah? Well, normal husbands don't have inappropriate colleagues.' That seemed like a good comeback. But I was still iffy on the magnitude of my wrongness, so I shrugged and fell back on a weak, "Sorry."

"I'm sorry I can't count on you." Oooh. Burn.

Marcus pressed the automatic garage door button and pulled in so fast I thought we were going to break through the back wall. The second he stopped the car, I ran out, tucking into an Indiana Jones roll beneath the slowly closing door. I rounded the house and reached the backyard as it screeched and thumped against the ground, metaphorically sealing me out.

Good. I hope he goes right to bed and sleeps off the douchebag. As for me, I planned to sleep outside under the stars like the big weirdo I am and wait for the owner of the feather in my pocket. Maybe he/she/it can tell me where I'm from.

Marcus doesn't know this—I didn't know it myself until a year ago—but I really am a little bit of a feral child. My mom wasn't my bio-mom, and her final act at hospice was to confess this to me. It was a very poignant scene, but terrible timing. I would have preferred about twenty years earlier or never.

She called me a foundling, which is much more romantic than a feral child. She was hiking with her mom, early one summer morning. They stepped into a clearing in the woods and saw me, my pale skin and hair glowing against the emerald grass. No blanket, no diaper, no clothing. My only possession was a shimmering feather in a chubby baby death-grip.

They were lonely and a little bit bored, so they decided it would be fun to adopt me. But nobody ever figured out who I was or where I was from. Or what in the actual hell I was doing buck naked in the middle of the woods.

The feather had to be a clue. It's always meant something to me, even if I didn't know what. I loved that thing like other kids loved their blankies, I carried it everywhere until I was six and it was promoted it to its place of honor in my journal, where all the secret things go. I decided it wasn't anyone's business but my own.

I laid down on the ground to wait for a sign or a visit. The grass tickled my calves and bare shoulders, and I sunk down further into the earth, flattening the blades. Gazing up into the night sky made me realize how long my eyes have been down.

Pegasus came immediately into focus. The brightly starred square and trailing plumes gave way to his powerful equine body, shimmering wings, and hooves. His strength was comforting. Ever since I was small, he'd always been my favorite.

There's supposed to be a foal, too, peeking out from behind its father's long face. I've seen it in books—Equuleus. But I've never actually been able to find it. Maybe tonight would be the night. Squinting, I searched for that sweet little bundle of stars, but only darkness flanked the constellation. Pegasus looked lonely.

Hours passed and so did sleep. I started to regret my bitter campout, but not enough to go inside. And besides, I didn't have my key.

My reddened eyes distorted the stars until they were rips in the night sky. I heard a song one time that said something about stars being the holes to heaven. I loved that idea—that the stars are little tears in the fabric of our world that give us tiny glimpses to what lies beyond. It'd be nice if some of that heaven dripped down.

Sighing, I closed my eyes. That was enough staring down the sky for one night.

A hot wind rolled over my face and cascading softness brushed my cheek. Silvery tendrils fell about me, covering me with a moonlit glow. I brushed the mane away and looked into eyes as deep and black as the spaces between the stars. He whinnied softly and shook out massive wings that enveloped the sky and eclipsed the stars. He was here—not my ghost, but my Pegasus.

I jumped to my feet and reached for him, every fiber of my body screaming to join him. To climb up on to his back and beg him to fly me home. I wrapped my arms around his neck, and the muscles rippled against me like water. His glowing ivory flesh wavered, brightening and darkening in my grasp, as he moved between the tangible and the intangible. I held his undulating form, whispering nonsense and wishes into his silvery pointed ears.

But, as we all know, the more you try to hold on to something, the faster it goes away. Pegasus faded in my arms and I was left hugging myself, with nothing but a pale feather in the emerald grass.

Marcus came home early from work with a present. It made me wonder a little bit if he'd ever actually met me, but I thanked him anyway.

It was a big bag like Alpha Wife Althea's, filled with little bundles of yarn in every color of the rainbow. Normally I like lots of colors, but this looked like a gnome's barf bag. I told him so, and he rolled his eyes.

"Don't be silly. Anyway, I thought it'd be a great hobby for you. Althea really enjoys knitting."

"And if I did, too, then I'd have lots of normal things to say at parties." No answer. "Does Gina knit?" I asked.

"Gina works."

"I used to work. I could go back to work. A job would be a good hobby."

"Painting on people's fingernails is not a real job. And we've talked about this, you don't need to work. I've got everything covered—"

"So, are there, like, needles in here?"

"Of course."

"Good."

Coming home early meant going back late, so Marcus went back to the office or whatever after dinner. I went upstairs and found the knitting bag slumped on the bed, spilling its colorful guts. The needles glittered defiantly at me, long, sharp, and useful. I had no idea what to do with those bitches. I picked them up like chopsticks and picked at noodly threads of yarn. I put my hair in a bun and stuck them crossways through it. I spun them like miniature batons until I accidentally poked myself.

I was going to Google how to knit, but then I didn't want to anymore. Instead, I stabbed my pillow, thrusting the needle deep into its unsuspecting puffiness. The fabric made a muffled popping sound with each puncture, sighing its displeasure.

Little bits of white fluff welled up from beneath the black satin pillowcase and bled through. Marcus thinks black sheets are sexy. I always thought they were kind of try-hard, but I liked how the pillow looked with its ivory innards pouring out of it. I wrapped the knitting needle around bits of fluff and pulled them through until I'd sprouted a three dimensional constellation. The fabric of the pillowcase gave a shadowy backdrop, like the midnight sky.

I stuck the knitting needles in my back pocket and strolled down to the backyard.

The grass was hot and sweaty. It seized my bare arms and legs with a hundred damp little fingers. My heels sunk into the soil between patches of green, anchoring me to the earth. I locked eyes with the sky and Pegasus brightened. He twinkled a greeting and I smiled up at him. I'd like to think my teeth were just as dazzling as those glimmering stars.

Equuleus, the foal, was nowhere to be found. That's okay, though, I had a theory about that.

The stars shone down, through the velvet cover of night.

Wayward beams forced their ways through the pinholes in the night sky. These constellations were hints from heaven, pictures from another world, and messages from those that lived beyond. The light from Pegasus unfurled from its fixed places, dangling like long, ragged threads. They dropped closer and closer to me, until I was surrounded by long glowing strands. I could just about touch them. Instead, I held up a knitting needle and wound a thread of light around it. The glowing, ethereal yarn clung to it like a snake on a branch, coiled and ready.

Headlights flooded the yard with crude, artificial light as Marcus rounded the corner. My star thread evaporated beneath the glare. Bummer.

I slid the knitting needles into my back pocket and sprinted through back door and up the stairs, two at time. I dove into bed and curled up in a ball, letting out soft, intermittent snores. He didn't even look my way—just hopped into the shower. Which is good, 'cause it gave me time to hide the raggedy crime-scene pillow.

I have gotten better at pulling star threads. Within moments of looking at the sky, I can pick out the glowing fibers straining against the dark curtain of night. They press heavily against the little rips, forming pictures and figures. I'm working on the threads of Pegasus. Each night, I wind them around a knitting needle, one by one, drawing them closer to the earth. They fall around me in a tangled web, grazing my skin with a burning static. Soon I'll figure out how to knit that glittering mess into something I can hold. That's what he wants.

Marcus called. He's "working" late again. I actually heard the air quotes this time, but he doesn't know that. I think he thinks I'm stupid, but really I'm just glad he's "working" late. The later the better. I can't work on my knitting when he's here.

I stole away to the backyard and sat cross-legged in the grass. Tonight, the star threads from Pegasus dropped and surrounded me, without any prompting or tugging. They waved in the breeze, caressing me with warm, shining tendrils. It was like being tucked into a deep-sea anemone, the bioluminescent deep-deep sea ones I saw on the Discovery Channel. As above, so below, I guess.

I pulled the knitting needles from my back pocket and seized two of the sparkling threads. With a satisfying series of click-clicks, I knit them together in nice even stitches. Just like the nice old lady on Youtube did with her yarn. They were remarkably cooperative. The burning strands twisted over, under, and through each other, blistering my fingers as I gave them shape.

Within moments, a large wing covered my lap. A shimmering, white-feathered wing. I ran a finger over the feathers, ruffling them slightly. One loosened and dropped to the ground. As it did, the weight of the wing lightened and it faded from view. All that was left was a glowing feather in the shadowed grass.

Marcus didn't come home last night. I figured I'd better call him in case he was dead in a ditch somewhere. Gina answered. I know it was her, 'cause she's the only one I know that has a legit deep, raspy, sex-kitten voice. Such a stereotype she is. I hung up, glad to know that Marcus was *not* dead in a ditch somewhere.

Later, I texted him and told him he didn't have to come home at all if he didn't want to. I could use the time alone.

He didn't text back, so I assumed he'd taken me up on my offer.

"I'm ready to go home now," I announced. I was tired of the dim sadness that flanked Pegasus. He looked so lonely.

Star threads fell about me, like strands of Rapunzel's hair. The radiant fibers were too thin to climb, of course. I was going to have to knit them real. Seizing the closest threads, I worked them beneath my needle, stitching and purling and all that knittery stuff until a solid shape began to form. My hands cramped with the fever of my work, and the heat of the star threads scalded my fingers. But when I saw the strong equine head take shape beneath my hands, I bit my lip and pushed through the pain. Hours I stood, knitting the stars, just as the Fates weave their tapestry.

A soft whinny let me know I was done.

Pegasus stood before me. This time, he was solid and present—not a ghost or a vision. I hugged his neck, feeling the caress of soft fur beneath my cheek. When he shook out his wings, they shaded the moon.

I glanced up curiously, and saw only a dark patch of sky where his constellation had been.

"Can we go home?" I whispered, my lips brushing the velvet of his ear. He nodded and tossed his glittering mane, stamping the grass with silver-tipped hooves. I was psyched, but also completely baffled as to how to climb aboard such a stallion.

He snorted in amusement at my hesitation and knelt forward. I climbed onto his back, nestled between his soft feathery wings and wound my fingers through his mane. Within seconds, we were flying—soaring towards the emptiness in the sky at a breakneck speed.

I wasn't scared. I knew this speed. I'd been looking for *this* speed my whole life, ever since I was the odd little girl on the swings. It was the speed designed to smash that emptiness and break through to the world beyond, leaving nothing but the soft remnants of our light in the rips. I just needed Pegasus to get there.

Astride his light, we confronted the darkness. Our bodies were the battering ram that beat down the barrier between this world and the next. The black veil of sky shredded beneath us as flesh dissolved to light. We pressed on through the tightly drawn fabric of night, squeezing through the rips and tears that are the only gateways to the world beyond. I was back where I belonged.

No one could miss Equuleus now. My happiness blazed forth, illuminating my constellation's holes to Heaven. Peeking out from behind Pegasus's strong head, I looked down and saw Marcus wandering around our backyard. I twinkled a good-bye wink at him, and I'd like to think he winked back. Or maybe he just had something in his eye.

EEL AND BLOOM
Diana Hurlburt

Three strange horses stood outside the house on the day the corpse flowers bloomed.

They were strange in that I didn't know them by sight but they were normal old horses, warmbloods of some variety, not limerunners—water-bred, strange by nature. The piebald snorted as I came up the drive, the chestnut blinked, and the gray eyed me, one eye brown and one milky blue. I suspected he wouldn't like to have people on that blue-eyed side. Voices floated from the front windows, my mother's lost amid lower ones, men's voices, and I stopped before opening the door.

"I don't like the sound of that," one man said, and another added, "Thinking to out-smart us, she is," in a strange, coarse accent. They fell to squabbling, a mess of chatter about the night's race, every other word caught in the gap-boarded walls.

As my mother's voice responded, the wind picked up, chiding my eavesdropping. It whistled through the Australian pines, the tongue of it hard against the windowpanes and carrying a scent—not rain or exhaust from the highway a quarter mile west but something heavy and rotten, some dead flesh I didn't feel like dealing with. It was summer, not butchering season, and I wanted spring water in my nostrils, hay and horse sweat, not death.

The door bumped open and hit me in the chest, and I stepped aside as three men came out. Whatever the dead animal was, wherever the carrion lay, it was less important than the business the horses' riders had been here about. No one came to see my mother this close to sunset because they wanted to.

Each of the men looked at me as they passed, which suited me not at all.

I watched them trot down the road toward Tampa, the horses' hooves stamping crescents into the dirt. The gray had a nice long gait. God usually gave horses with a blue eye something extra to make up for it.

"You smell that?" Ma cooed when I came into the sitting room. Death-scent was all through the house now, bad enough that I wanted to close the windows, though the heat probably would have been worse. She rocked in the chair my grandfather had left before running north, her feet firm on the hooked rug. "That's swamp money in the air, girl."

I didn't know what she meant, and there was no sense in wondering, because she was about to tell me anyway.

She rocked slower, the cadence of the runners creamy to my ear, planed wood smooth on wood polished by years of feet and lemon oil. She nodded in unison with the chair's movement. "The corpse flower, my Bea—oh, it seeded long before either of us was born, it's more legacy than anything else on this property." She spat to the side, saliva and tobacco landing neatly in the tin pot placed at the base of the tall bookshelf for that purpose. "What did I say when your grandmomma took me into the back garden and pointed at the tallest plant I'd ever seen and said 'Mira, this plant above all else'? Why, I thought she was crazed, everyone else did too, but—"

Ma tapped the two good fingers of her left hand on the rocking chair's arm. Her lips closed up tight, studying me. Then she said, "You best ride crafty tonight, Bea."

That put my back up. I didn't like when people talked about a race before it was run.

"No no, girl, none of that look of yours. No. Now." She straightened in the rocker, glaring. Her blue eyes were about as uncanny as that of the gray horse. "You know I'm no gambler, God forbid, but I don't believe the Lord frowns upon dealing with those who do. For the good of my family! It's a hard life we've set for ourselves out here."

We've set, she said, as though I'd had any say—or, for that matter, as though she had.

"That bloom will make our fortune," Ma said. She waved a hand through the air, heavy and ill-smelling and physical, wafting it toward her face. "You wrinkle that pretty nose all you like, daughter mine. It's called corpse flower for a reason. And before you get petty, know this: it ain't because the scent is bad, it's because the pollen…the living parts…that crumbly bit of nothing raises the dead."

She laced right hand through left, five fingers wrapped around two good ones and a scarred mess of palm, and smiled at me. She said, "You beat them at their own game, or three trappers walk out of Springfed with more power than any soul's got a right to."

Hair went up along my neck. Trappers they were called, though they seemed more like carrion birds to me. The death-scented flower out back would suit them fine. They traveled, sometimes on the highways and sometimes on the corpse roads; they had a knack for showing up when Molly Sullivan's great-aunt died and left her a bracelet of rough, dark hair, or when Ben Lopresti went fishing in Low Springs and dredged out a silky's token in his net. They never had the wrong currency for a purchase, whether it was lips pressed to a bit of paper with a certain name in it or cold cash.

"Word is our flower ain't alone." Ma seemed bothered by this, like she'd thought our acreage was special for its exotic bloom. "Word is there's a few more here and there…a garden in New York City, if you can credit it, some rich man's aviary in Charleston. The seeds were brought off boats from God knows where—wasn't we lucky men thought my grandmother beautiful enough for rare gifts—and now they're blooming, the trappers said, all t'once."

The scent in the air had not yet begun to turn sweet to my nose, but I imagined when Ma breathed in she smelled money.

"I've planned this," Ma murmured, her eyes straying to the window. "I purely loathe the thought of some no-account trappers muddying my plans simply because they heard—why, it's unconscionable, what they did to Mr. Greeley to get that note. The pollen's been his long years past, the oath in my mother's writing, but can I blame the poor man? Word is they sank a five-spot at his gate and smiled wrong at his woman." Her eyes came back to me, harder than before, winter sky and rare frost. "You understand me? They got that note in uncanny hands."

I understood less her concern over who might get the pollen. That she should dig up some civic-minded worry now—but then her family was clannish, always had been, and trappers were outland. Inherently untrustworthy.

"Now," my mother said, calm as though we sat over tea. "You go start making movements toward riding hard tonight, Bea."

I went, but before I headed for the barn, I snuck around the side of the house. When I heard the porch door shut I went a little way further and saw my mother wander into the back yard. She stopped at the foot of the corpse flower and ran her hand up its stem. I hated to watch her fingers, pale on the purple, mottled flesh of the flower. It seemed obscene, the corpulent stalk and its aroma, its heavy, open blossom. Carnal, suggestive where her ruined left palm was death. Even in her girlhood she'd never been a dab hand with limeys as I was.

I left her to it and went to fetch Eel.

The air was cleaner north of the house, the monstrous flower's aroma losing some of its wrench to manure and hay. A flower blossoming in our yard, one in a rich man's greenhouse in South Carolina, another in a city garden in New York, and who knew how many others, the world over? My arms were chilly in the damp summer heat. If Reverend Anson caught word of this, his sermon on Sunday would be hellfire and omens, the Book opening, the world ending.

Something bothered me more than the thought of the reverend's face poppy-red and sweating above his collar. My mother was a liar, this the whole town knew, slick-tongued and false. There was no point in lying to me—I knew full well she was a gambler through and through, it was in our blood—but I couldn't figure what she might've thrown into the pot to set against the corpse flower's pollen. No trappers worth the name would gamble to walk away with nothing.

I hoped she hadn't offered Eel. It wasn't like I couldn't get another limerunner should I need to, but I was fond of Eel. We worked well together, and he didn't give me half the lip Coral did. Sometimes I thought he kind of liked me.

He looked at me across the small, stream-backed pasture, and I let him, let him remember why I was there. His coat shone under the late sun, sleek and liver-dark, a faint red gleam of vestigial gills. Once he was used to me again I tacked him up with the small saddle limerunners could be taught to tolerate and slipped on his halter, flexible bay bound with braided moss, and we jogged out onto the road. His hooves left demon prints next to the normal half-moons of the trappers' horses. A nice jog was just what we needed, him to warm up so we didn't have to spend too much time on the track with the others, and me to lose myself in the movement, let Eel carry me away from the house and the scent of the corpse flower.

The racetrack was five miles west, just south of the cemetery between Springfed and Odessa. I clocked Eel in my head, more out of habit than anything else; his outsized legs covered the distance in forty minutes or so. The sun chased us into town. Road traffic grew thicker the closer we got to civilization, people honking now and then as though we were too close to the pavement, in someone's way, bothering them at all. It took more than an Oldsmobile horn to spook Eel, and more than snotty townspeople to irk me. They liked to pretend dismay at limeys, chattered to Town Hall about banning the races, but I saw them at the track all the same.

When the racetrack gates came into view I drew Eel up and hopped off, then led him the rest of the way by his halter. We'd timed it right, walking beneath the big curly sign that said *The Grove* just as the sun sank behind the barns. There were still a few trainers and jockeys around, men whose eyes slipped over me as though Eel was walking himself. Most of the men who ran or rode Thoroughbreds had no time for limerunners and those who sat them.

Had I a mind to play horses, I wouldn't have bet on theirs.

We didn't use the stables; there was no need for the quarantine barn, because limerunners didn't fall ill and couldn't communicate illness to normal horses, and no reason to try to obtain stalls in the other barns, because limeys had to be turned out near water, bedded on moss, and stabled on calcite floors. It was generally accepted that even had we wanted to stable limerunners at the Grove, someone would've kicked up a protest.

"Hey," said Tim McDonough when Eel and I reached the fence. I kept Eel well away from Tim's limey Corker, who had a tendency to bite first and ask questions not at all. Tim spat a wad of chaw onto the concrete on the far side of the fence. "Heard tell your momma's got a big bet riding on this one." He laughed at the look on my face. "News travels faster than Eel, looks like. Might wanna work on that before the race."

My middle finger let him know what I thought about our chances.

"Not very friendly," Tim said mildly. Corker's head snaked out toward Eel and Tim tightened his grip on the bridle. "It true that weed y'all got out back smells like shit on a stick?" He chuckled again. "Guess as long as it brings Miss Mira some cash. It or you."

About the only thing I was good for was bringing Ma cash, whether in bills or wet and cloven-hoofed.

"Might as well warm 'em up," said Tim. He led his limey out onto the track. After a moment I followed, though Eel was good and warm by now. I watched Tim mount up, the motion effortless; one minute his boots were flat on the dirt and the next he was aboard, no space between the two. There was no point in being jealous. Some folk looked pretty on a horse and some didn't, and I didn't look pretty anywhere, on horseback or at the grocery store or in the skinny bed in Tim's apartment without a stitch on. Then again, people came to gawk at the limerunners. No one, as Ma pointed out now and then, was there to see me.

No one cared how nice the rider looked, as long as the horse won.

The railbirds of the day's races had given way to nightbirds. Tim and I trotted, the limerunners spaced well apart and even-pacing, and Eel felt calm enough beneath me that I looked to the fence. Crowds were drawing in, gossiping about the new postmaster in town, rumored to have a color television, sniping one another for frivolous bets. Folk filled space along the rail and claimed benches on the concrete apron. The Grove didn't allow the upper stories to be used for seating during limerunner races, nor access to the tote board. Gambling on limeys went hand-to-hand, off-track in theory and under-the-table in practice. Exotic wagering had a different meaning at night.

"That little girl'll do it, mark me," someone called to someone else as we trotted around the clubhouse turn. I didn't see the man, nor who he was talking to, but the air felt heavier, as it did when chancy bets were being placed. My eye skipped along the fence—Maria de Carlo the abortionist, Trotter Henry and his bullyboys, Caesar Charles with wallet in hand, ready to lose his paycheck and maybe his soul—counting off familiar faces and a few strange ones, a girl a little older than me with air on either side of her, and three men lounging.

I didn't get a chance to see if their faces matched those of the trappers who'd been to see my mother, because Tim yelled and Eel shied. There was a riderless limerunner bolting toward us.

Feral limeys were dangerous enough; borderline-tame limeys without a rider were worse. Either way, I knew as the limerunner crashed into Tim and his mount that the porous rock beneath the track was about to be drinking blood.

Tim catapulted off his horse like one of the carneys over in Gibsonton had shot him out of a cannon. I left my eyes on him long enough to check that he'd rolled under the fence, and then I grabbed Eel's mane and dug my heels into his sides. A ruckus blew up along the rail, people shouting for help and some putting money down. As Eel galloped toward the backstretch, a couple of outriders on ponies passed us heading the other way. I didn't envy them their job. Breaking up a pair of tussling water horses was dirty work.

"Bad for business," someone observed from the makeshift gate when I slowed Eel on the dirt. The man turned so that the sunset no longer lit him from behind, and I saw that it was Faran Humphrey. If he didn't quite run the limey game in these parts, well, the bigwigs at the Grove didn't hate him, either. He grimaced at me. "Who's that beast belong to?"

I shrugged. I could guess, and I figured he could too.

"I'll have Matt Hancock's hide." Humphrey waved as one of the clockers came up. "Where the fuck is that boy? He looking to get banned from this establishment?"

This establishment, he said, like there was any other game in town.

Humphrey and the clocker fell to gossiping. I held Eel tight between the beams of the gate we used to line everyone up. Limerunners never cottoned to iron, so the standard starting gate was out. I didn't know who had figured out that a sort of latticed lean-to, like something you'd put up for a sixteen-year-old girl's birthday party in the back yard, worked best. Oak supports on either side, roofed with bay and moss threaded through, and up to a dozen limeys lined up snapping their teeth at each other. I had been expecting six competitors today. Looked like we were down two.

Tim came limping up, favoring his left knee. His face could've pickled eggs. "I find Matt Hancock, he'll be pissing blood for a week. The hell was he thinking?"

Everyone had questions for Matt Hancock, it seemed.

"Listen, Bea," Tim said, leaning on my shoulder. He smelled like tobacco and horse, not the honest musk of warmbloods but limey-rank, a drop of blood in spring water. The warmth of him and the scent worked on me like they always did. "Bea—I don't like this. People are talking, and I…Christ, I needed that money. And for next week—you think you could—you know I'm no hand at hooking 'em."

He was shamefaced. I was less interested in his embarrassment over needing me to catch him a limerunner and more in what people were talking about. I nodded, then tilted my head toward Faran Humphrey and the clocker. A few more riders and their mounts were trotting up to the gate, while Humphrey had his head together with the clocker and Kathleen Montgomery, who handled the more genteel bettors. Tim snorted.

"Yeah. I wouldn't like to be Matty when Humphrey gets his hands on him. Say, you don't think…" He paused, like I was going to finish the thought for him. Sometimes even Tim forgot. "Them trappers your momma went in with. What if they're trying to—to winnow out the field?"

I thought about it. Ride with the same batch of failed bankers' sons, grove boys, and weekday fishermen for long enough, and the odds are obvious. Even had Matt Hancock walked up with a half-broken limey fresh from the water, he'd have been the favorite. Whoever the trappers were running, they wanted to win. I wished my mother had told me the exact terms of the bet. I held up my left hand, rubbing my fingers together in the signal that meant *gambling*.

Tim's eyes jumped from my hand to my face. "Bea. She ain't told you?"

Someone laughed just behind my shoulder, and Hank Fremont said, "Get it while you can, Timmy boy. Bea's not long for this track."

Usually it was helpful, how expressive my face was. Made it easier to communicate with people. Just then I hated what I knew my eyes were doing, my lips. Tim wasn't looking at me anymore. Hank laughed again and kept walking, his limerunner mincing over the raked sandy dirt. I hated Hank Fremont on a good day. This was turning out to be a bad day.

"You gotta lose, Bea," Tim said. His voice was low, slipping beneath track-chatter and the wind and the distant rattle and roar of cars. "Miss Mira…I don't know whether she's drinking or what, you'd know, but you don't—I can't believe she ain't told you."

She says ride, I mouthed to him, my fist coming up on *ride* to emphasize it. She wasn't here at the track and she wouldn't be tonight; she placed her bets with Kathleen Montgomery and sent Lemmy, our hired boy, to collect the winnings or pay out. She had never seen me win. She wouldn't leave our property if a hurricane was coming, and she had the corpse flower to think about besides.

And she hadn't told me to win, exactly. Riding crafty didn't always mean riding to win.

"They got your momma and Mason Greeley between wind and water." Tim reached for my shoulder and Eel's teeth snapped just below his elbow. He yanked his arm back, glaring at the water horse. "You win, you go with them. You lose, they take that—whatever it is they want off that stinkin' flower. Look, I don't know what all. All I know's you gotta lose."

So it wasn't Eel Ma had bet, then. That was why the men had looked at me on the porch. I supposed I could be useful to the trappers; I was generally counted the best around at catching and breaking limerunners. If they stuck around Springfed I'd make them money, and if they took me away I'd make them money too, racing at the Bushnell track or in St. Augustine, or the little ring just far enough away from Hialeah for propriety. Maybe they wouldn't ride me at all. Maybe they'd pitch me into the cypress flats and prairies and tell me not to come back 'til I had a limey they could sell for speed or teeth or hide.

I didn't care to countenance other options for use by trappers.

"We'll fix it so—" Tim said, and stopped. He rubbed his hands on his jeans. Blotchy freckles bled together when he wrinkled his nose. "It'll be ok. We'll figure something out."

I was glad Eel was feeling ornery. I didn't want Tim touching me just then. He didn't often get like this—protective, superior—he didn't usually act like he was doing me any favors. If there was any figuring to be done, I'd do it myself. Mainly I was annoyed Ma hadn't warned me, that she'd let me hear it from Tim, from Hank Fremont.

I could wish I were more surprised that she'd pull this, but our family ran on commerce, not love, and Ma hated nothing more than a debt unpaid.

"Get that nag in the gate," Faran Humphrey snapped, coming up on Eel's left, just far enough away. "Sun's about set. McDonough, with me."

"Sir?" Tim said, playing dumb, but I saw his brown eyes gleam. Sure, he'd think about me, 'til there was money to be made.

"Hancock's backers will compensate you for the limey," Humphrey said. I felt bad for rolling my eyes at Tim. He had his mother and brother to take care of, after all. "Munro's poorly. You'll take over the mount."

"Yessir," Tim said, and stepped to the side as I swung up on Eel. I didn't look back when we trotted for the gate, but I kept my ears peeled for sounds that meant Tommy Munro's limerunner wasn't taking to its new rider.

Munro, doing poorly. I looked down the row of water horses and men, jiggering the chess pieces in my head. Matt Hancock and his limey out of commission, Tim's Corker not racing and Tim aboard a mount he didn't know. Munro absent. Three outland trappers fronting I knew not who. My mother backed against the barn, unable to lose the corpse flower and plenty able to lose me. Folk who bet on limerunner races were even more brainless than those who bet on Thoroughbreds; the payout was juicier than anything at Hialeah. The pawn-man Mr. Greeley, to whom the corpse flower's pollen had been promised, held shifty bets, and Kathleen Montgomery the town clerk held cash, and the only person who went home scot-free and richer at night's end was Faran Humphrey.

Eel wriggled beneath me. He had a slink to him even standing still, a sly motion that had given him his name. I gathered his mane in both hands, just tight enough to make him pay attention. He eyeballed our neighbor through the bay slats, and I watched Tim and Tommy Munro's limey slip into the last post. I wasn't at all convinced Tim riding that limey—a fresh one, a female I didn't recognize—was a good idea, but Humphrey wouldn't countenance being down three runners. Bettors liked a big field. Better chance of blood.

"No moon," Will Cypress observed. He spat onto the sand beneath our mounts' hooves. I didn't like to notice it, but the saliva landed on the edge of Eel's shadow as it faded with the sun. "Big race, huh, Bea?"

Everyone knew. It made no difference. I ran over the men in my head, flexed my fingers in Eel's mane and pretended I was touching the other water horses' coats and nostrils and hocks. I didn't want to go away with any trappers. I didn't want Mr. Greeley's shop in flames from a fired hex piece, nor the house down around Ma's ears from the trappers' wrath. It was hard to blame her for trying to wiggle out of this. It was only her out there if Lemmy and I weren't around, and her sharp tongue might've kept me in line but wasn't enough to stand up to three men with Christ-knew-what in their saddlebags.

I waved to Will and when he looked at me again I held my right hand up, moving the fingers slowly, showing him *gambling, three men, whose horse.* He frowned, tongue poking out over his bottom lip. Then he mouthed *Jasper* and shrugged. He looked sore about it, like it was some personal offense. Miccosukee men had strict ideas about fair play.

Jasper Huss. I liked him less than Hank, slightly more than leeches or malaria. He rode dirty on the best occasions, and this was no good occasion. I thought again of my mother's words. *Ride crafty. Ride hard.*

Me losing didn't necessarily equal Jasper winning.

The last stripes of sunlight disappeared from the sky and night came plummeting down. Track lights bloomed, garish, eye-searing. Every spectator became a ghost and the limerunners' eyes lit red, like gators' eyes in the cypress swamp a bare quarter-mile to our north. The loudmouth Northern boy Faran Humphrey used as a race-caller was talking, but my ears turned elsewhere, seeking Eel's pulse and the breathing of Sandy, Will's limerunner, and the unfamiliar girl beneath Tim. I sank inside myself, shut the doors that housed Ma and Mr. Greeley and Tim and the trappers, and sought loopholes. Cracks to be driven wide, weak flesh in which to sink teeth.

The starter's bell sounded, its deep, echoing boom a world away from the high-pitched shrill of the Thoroughbred track bell. In the same moment, without so much as a wink of warning, the sky opened up. The dust-lit air of the track became rainlight, the lamps spaced along the outer rail sputtering and hissing. Eel leapt forward. His neck pumped and strained against my hands, and I leaned in, forcing my weight down to check him. Sloppy track was no concern for limerunners; in fact it was a blessing, or would've been, had not all limeys been mud freaks by birthright. If the sudden slick surface let Eel run faster, well, it was helping his fellows, too.

The first turn in a Thoroughbred race was where jockeys began talking, wasting breath on chiding or encouraging their mounts, calling insults and threats to one another. Limey riders had nothing to say on that first turn, nor in the arrow-straight lane into the chute. The only people on the track not talking, us riders. The first turn signified nothing but that your mount was still going. The wire might've been yards away, but we still had miles to run before passing beneath it, the shape of the race somewhere between a classic Thoroughbred mile, a human triathlon, and the wild hunt limey riders ran down in the Everglades. The cheers and howls of the bettors followed us up the chute and into the woods, the flat accent of the race-caller sinking into bark, muffled by pine needles and sand underfoot. The rain, I could tell, would be a cloudburst and then naught.

A body slammed into us, and my right knee wrenched. Will and Sandy had started off on our right down the track, but once in the woods there was no semblance of order. As long as the limerunners stayed on the path, fair was fair. No lanes, no protocol, nothing but race-riding. Wan moonlight flashed on Hank Fremont's teeth as he pressed his mount close to Eel, and I decided right then that whoever won, it wouldn't be Hank. It was time to go to work.

I slipped down Eel's side, my legs wrapped hard around his barrel and the rest of me flopping, loose, one arm hooked through his mane, to grab a twisted root. It tore at my palm as Eel bolted forward, and the root rippled up, tangling in the hooves of Hank's limey.

The yelped "Dumb *cunt!*" meant my mean trick had worked. I didn't look over my shoulder when the pressure of the faltering limerunner left our side.

The woods were as familiar as the stone bench in the back garden at home, or the squat pine-board school where a succession of teachers had been sure they'd be the one to get me talking. Despite Ma's bet—despite the trappers and the scent of the corpse flower not yet washed from my nostrils by rain—I felt better than I had all week. When all was said and done, this was what I was good for, good at. If I could've been in the woods all the time, in the low, dense hammock where water horses thrived, I would've.

"Bea!" Tim hollered, somewhere off to my left. "*Bea!*"

I lay down along Eel's withers, his neck hot and wet beneath my hands. I wasn't sure what Tim was shouting about, but better not to be a target. As I shrank down something whipped across my cheek. A stray branch, innocent, or a purposeful smack from another rider, it hurt all the same. The path broadened as it turned toward the river, wide enough for three limeys to run abreast. Jasper and Hank flanked me; I let up on Eel's mane, twisting my fingers in the way he hated. His muzzle snapped sideways, greedy of freer movement. Water horse teeth were nasty, unnatural as Reverend Anson said, glaring down at Ma and me from his pulpit; they were no prey animal's teeth, for limeys were not prey. Eel's sank into the cheek of Hank's mount, barely missing the throat latch. When I saw blood well I snatched him back in hand, dragging his head up, and concentrated on the river in front of us.

As Eel's chest hit the surface and water washed over my legs, I glanced back. Hank stood on the shore and his mount half-knelt, its front knees buried in sand, and blood darkening the thin river tide.

"You bitch," Jasper said conversationally as we swam the limeys. "Figure you'll win thataway? There's tricks you can only play once."

It was easy to imagine Eel's teeth in Jasper's throat. I'd seen a limerunner kill a man.

"Some kinda score to settle," Jasper continued. The river lapped my waist, warm as blood. The tide was negligible at this point in the Tocobaga. No one, not even the hungriest bettors, wanted to see what would happen if the limerunners were turned into a rapid river, what the current would do to their pulses. Jasper's seat on his mount was firm, his hands steady. I hated to see it. "How you believe Tim'd keep you around? Fish-mouthed whore." He leaned just far enough over, keeping his elbows well away from Eel's head. "Men like to hear a woman scream. So what're you good for? How'm I supposed to know you like it?"

Talking distracted people, I'd observed over the years. They focused on the sound of their own voice. If Jasper loved the way his words fell like spring hail, well, maybe he wouldn't notice me plucking a strand of trailing amaranth from the water. I crushed the flowers just a bit and tucked them into my belt.

The far shore grew larger in my sight. I counted off the new odds in my head. Me and Jasper, more riding with us than most people had figured on; Tim and his wild-card girl; Will and Sandy. All else being equal, I would've preferred not to do to Tim what I was about to.

Eel's hooves hit sandy river-bottom and dug in, his flexible feet grabbing for purchase. He and Jasper's limey were running before their riders' legs had cleared the water, the most difficult part of the race, for my money. I'd fallen off that way more than once, the water's drag and the mount's speed a bad combination for balance. I darted a look over my shoulder as Eel picked up pace. For this to work, I needed Tim closer than he was. But if I lagged back, Jasper would get the lead, and that was no good either.

I let Eel have his head and he slammed forward. I threw my weight to the left and he veered into Jasper, clipping his limey's heels. The forest pressed in around us again, oak fingers reaching for loose hair. Eel and Jasper's limey tangled, snapping at one another, and my heart galloped. If Eel could just stay clear—if Jasper's mount wasn't too vicious—if Tim would just hurry his fool ass up—

The wet roan coat of his limerunner flickered on my periphery. I dug the strand of amaranth from my belt and tossed it over the rump of Tim's limey when she pulled up on our right, then rolled Eel's mane up tight between my hands. The scent of amaranth on a girl limey's hide would hit Eel, too, he sure wasn't immune. But I was expecting him to berserk, and Jasper wasn't.

Jasper's mount flailed sideways, no longer interested in sinking his teeth into Eel. He dove for Tim and the girl, and dumped Jasper in the process. For that I was grateful; no one liked to be between a male and female limey when the male had an idea.

Gleaming coats collided, black and pale roan, and more yellow teeth than I cared to look on. For the second time that day Tim went sprawling, and Will's mount stepped on him as they came up.

The crunch of hooves on ribs hit the air like a shot. My heart clawed up into my throat, but I kept Eel moving. Jasper's cursing followed us while Eel ran down behind Will and Sandy.

The trail narrowed again, tree roots sinking away and smoothing out the closer we got to the track. Will rode silently, his attention on the water horse. My face was wet, from the river or sweat or tears, I wasn't sure, and the only sounds were the night sounds of a forest and the hot breath of limeys laboring.

When the track lights appeared ahead, Will called, "You know, I ain't heard why these bastards go crazy for love-lies-bleeding."

I'd heard, or at least I'd heard Mr. Greeley's nephew Ronnie hold forth on the topic. Ronnie of the bottles and jars, caretaker of the pawn shop's back room: He had a theory for everything, figured taking a few science courses at Flagler made him a regular alchemist. *Amplifies them natural phero-mones, Bea,* he'd told me once, watering the amaranth his aunt kept in a hedge along the front porch of the shop. *Why, it's just like a lady putting on perfume.*

I'd forgotten, somehow, the common name for amaranth. *Love-lies-bleeding.* I hoped they would be fast about getting Tim out of the forest.

My arms were wrecked, muscles strained noodle-weak and about useless. Riding a limerunner was hard enough from the get-go, them not being a species naturally given to domestication. Racing one was that much harder, keeping it on the straight and narrow, guiding it, holding it from savaging its fellows. Riding one as I had, nastily and with motives beyond winning…I didn't like tonight, didn't like what I'd let Eel do, what I'd made Jasper's mount do. I felt like coffee grounds used twice, my mouth just as sour.

We galloped back onto the track and passed beneath the wire half a length behind Will and Sandy.

The cacophony that greeted Will's win told me everything I needed to know. My eyes slid to the three men on the rail, the disgust dragging at their eyes and their mouths muttering. I wasn't too worried about them coming for me. Eel was sweating and shuddering, but there was enough of him left to get between me and them. It sure wasn't my fault they hadn't thought of putting in a contingency, what would happen if neither Jasper nor I won.

Curses and catcalls and questions followed me as I turned Eel toward the gate. I was usually the safe bet, after Matt Hancock. Those who somehow hadn't heard the gossip were flabbergasted, annoyed, out money or goods. I was slightly more concerned about the townspeople; I had to live with them every day, after all. I didn't bother waving to Will or Faran Humphrey or Mr. Greeley, who was about the only spectator looking half-pleased. My concern was Tim, whether his limey or Jasper's had savaged him, whether the kicks from Will's had done too much damage—

A figure, familiar as life yet alien in this setting, caught my eye. My mother stood a little way off, her eyes fixed on me and Eel. Whether guilt or morbid curiosity had driven her to the track tonight, I didn't much care. It hadn't been love, that was certain.

"My girl," she began when I led my limey over, "it was what seemed best. Goodness, if only you'd seen those—heard them talk, such oaths as would turn the preacher's ears blue. I knew—" She shook a finger. "Oh, I had faith in you, Bea. Didn't I know you'd find a way? And now the pollen will go to Mr. Greeley, it's only right. Such a debt owed."

She removed something from the pocket of her church dress. The lace edging the kerchief told me it was one of her nice ones, one of the Irish-woven hankies intended for my hope chest, before everyone had agreed there would be no need of one. "Still and all, I know he can't be expecting something for nothing. Carry that to him." She pressed the knotted kerchief into one of my hands, holding my wrist for a minute. "My Bea. What a miracle, a sharp little thing like you. Who would've thought...?"

She spoke sweet now and then. My mind was having trouble with the words, exhaustion and sorrow clouding my ears. The sounds which should have carried meaning seemed out of sync with Ma's mouth. A soft kind of rage grew, throbbing in my skull like a headache from sun exhaustion. Ma, the small god of our homestead, surrounded and equivocating, and me the only tool to her hand. Me, nodding and riding and ruining my reputation. Me, using Tim as Ma had used me.

The kerchief in my hand sat like a fishing weight, the pollen within slivers of lead.

I thrust Eel's reins into Ma's hand and stumbled away, blinking to clear my vision. Mr. Greeley was clear enough by the fence, his face expectant, but at the last moment my feet swerved toward the ambulance blocking the gates. The doctor stood with Mrs. McDonough and Faran Humphrey in the open gates of the track, and a stretcher stood there too, mounded with a sheet-draped form. An arm drooped beneath the sheet, limp against the stretcher's frame. Tim's freckles were visible at a distance, ink blots on death-pale skin and blood smearing his elbow. My mind much preferred Tim's arms in other modes: veins standing up with the effort of holding a limerunner, bare and relaxed alongside mine in white sheets.

"Bea!" someone called, and I saw Mr. Greeley waving. Then it was *Bea* from all sides, faces blurring together with one popping out now and then, Will's eyes dark and reproachful or Kathleen Montgomery's mouth wide and red. The track still swarmed with gamblers, questioners, folk who'd seen a thing and wanted to talk about it.

Sometimes I stood in the shallows of Low Springs or braced against a cypress, and let a water horse swim from me. Sometimes there was a choice; sometimes, between bills owed and blood to be paid, there was room for mercy.

I went up to the stretcher and pulled the sheet aside. I didn't know how the corpse flower's pollen worked, didn't even know if my mother was telling the truth about its properties. The handkerchief sat light in my palm after I tugged it from my pocket. The pollen drifted over his face, waxen and rigid, lips slightly parted, until the specks were barely distinguishable from his freckles.

I wondered if I should kiss him, like a fairy tale princess. I wondered what debt it was we owed Mr. Greeley in the first place, that such a power as this would cancel it, whether it was true my grandmother had asked him to have her husband run out of town. I wondered what Mr. Greeley would do to me in a minute, how I'd make it up to my mother without a stack of cash—and I wondered whether any of the other limerunners had dragged themselves out of the woods, if I'd ever race again or if even this, my lone skill and shabby claim to livelihood, would be taken from me—and the only answer I found was that it needed to be me Tim saw, when he opened his eyes again.

A Complete Mare
Tamsin Showbrook

Family, I reflect, as my big sister Pen scrabbles at the stable door, is overrated.

"What the fuck are we going to do now, Vez?" She wipes her forehead on her arm, rubbing chaff into her eyebrows, then slumps onto the nearest bale and buries her head in her hands. "Shit," she mumbles. "Mum's gonna kill you if we ever get out of here. This is *your* fault. I'm supposed to be avoiding stress. And what about Saqib? My baby needs its dad."

She rubs her belly. Eight months gone. She's right, she doesn't need this, but she's always been a bloody drama queen. Five years ago, when I found out what I am, she was straight on her mobile to her mates chatting shit about it and when her mobile stopped working—when *all* mobiles stopped working—she threw it against a wall.

I ignore a distant scream from outside, tongue another grain out of the barley stalk I've been working for the last ten minutes or so. "Whatever. Least we're safe."

"So *you* say."

A grass seed must've wormed its way into my t-shirt: my chest feels like someone's tickling it with wire wool. I pull my collar wide, brush at the spot, but there's nothing there. Pen's shoulders have started to shake as though she's sobbing. Shit.

"Pen, we're gonna be okay. This is my safe-house, remember? Onkel promised."

"He's not *my* 'onkel.' I'm not the freak…"

That's true. I am Verity Marshall and I am part Norse deity. Say it enough at support groups, it gets easier.

"…And you're really going to trust someone who spends eternity bullshitting?"

He really does, the bastard.

"…That door's the same one we came through to get in, why won't it open now?"

Gods, she's not going to shut up? I halt her flow. "I've got a clean line—nothing but Sleipnir blood got in the mix. I'm not a Jumble. He'll be protecting me because he knows if me and the rest of his descendants go, that's curtains for him too." He also told me he might need me for something, but he can fuck right off if he thinks I'm sticking my neck on the line for him.

Penny gives a bitter laugh. "More likely he's trapped both of us so we roast nicely before them outside get us. Bet he's watching us cook right now." Apart from the beach-ball shaped lump under her t-shirt, she looks like the pictures of her very mortal dad: thin and tall, pale gold eyes, mouth like a razor slash, wild hair.

I don't. I'm descended from a line of shape-shifting horses Onkel set going several thousand years ago. What idiot god pisses Odin off, then tries to solve the problem by turning into a mare to distract a stallion from its work and gets knocked up in the process? Loki, that's bloody who. So he as she-the-mare gives birth to this eight-legged, four-headed horse, Sleipnir, who Odin then claims as his steed. Sleipnir's descendants break up marriages for kicks. Or that's what Mum and Pen say. My dad charmed Mum in a club on one of her mates' hen dos, the bastard. She cries when anyone mentions it.

Like I say, family is overrated.

Loki said I was to call him Onkel; he says all his descendants call him Onkel. As well as trying not to think about the fact that a lot of people now want me dead because of my heritage, I try not to think too much about how Sleipnir mated with a mort, because that must've been what happened.

I've still got human form—others weren't so lucky when the bloodlines activated—it's more…sturdy, I get called, but with "graceful lines." My neck even has this arch to it and my eyes are *huge*. I hate them, but there's been a couple of people I've had to avoid on the estate because they keep telling me they're amazing and then they just stare: gormless full-mort prats. They stare even more at my hair because it's silver and dead straight. Tried dying it with beetroot from the garden once. Didn't work. Nothing works. Mum cut it short last year, along with Pen's, because the lice got bad again: too many of us living in the main Hall. Grew back. Overnight.

Lice are hardly the biggest problems though. The Hall's in a ropey state. And the rest of Castle Howard. And Yorkshire. And—you get the idea. Better here than the south, I suppose. Though that's always been true, if you believe the rumours. I never got to London before it was levelled. Wanted to see Big Ben and Buckingham Palace, go on a red bus. Oh well. Seen a lot of other stuff, I suppose. Mum says it's "hardened" me and she hates that I never got to finish being a kid. Sometimes, she stares at my face, dead intense, like she's searching for something. She finally told me what it was last weekend: fear. I'm too "detached," apparently. Like some big house in the middle of nowhere. Like here.

"I get scared," I told her.

"You don't show it. Having no fear isn't healthy."

"I just don't show it like Pen *always* does."

Now, Pen groans. "Can't you just kick the door down, you stupid mare? You've got four legs and four arms, fucksake."

If I had hackles, they'd be up—and there are folk with hackles—Fenrir's lot. You don't mess with *them*.

"Don't call me that, and anyway not at the moment, I haven't." I lift up my shirt and show her the buds where my extra arms sometimes put in an appearance. They're sore today, them and the nubs at my hips, which means I'm due on. Explains the comfort eating too. I pluck another ear of barley from the bale I'm sitting on and pop it in my mouth. Two seconds later, I spit it back out as something crashes against the back wall. "Proper battle out there now."

Pen fair leaps across the stable to press her ear to the wall but she doesn't shout out. We both know better than that.

They used to keep Thoroughbreds in these stables. And workhorses. But there are none of either in here anymore. Food took precedence over transport a few years ago. Mum made me eat some for the iron. Dried strips it was, like that American stuff—jerky. Did me no good; I threw up after. I tried to tell her it was basically cannibalism, but she wasn't having any of it, especially since the limb thing had just happened, and it wasn't like now. I only lose a little blood now each month when they emerge, my body knows what it's dealing with. The first time, well… I remember the pain and waking up and a pile of ruined sheets in the corner of the room, but not much else.

I'd like to point out at this juncture that my dad didn't know he was part deity when he and Mum conceived me. He most likely knows now, just like everyone does. "Dei-trippers" the media called us when the Shift occurred: that magic moment when everyone's heritage was revealed. And I'm not just talking Norse. You name the god type, their distant relatives are now very aware of what they are. Dad's ancestry may just account for his god-like behaviour: descend from on high, shag a mortal, fuck off back to your parallel plane of existence and watch the tiny-people drama unfold.

Pretty dramatic today.

I've lost track of what the factions are all fighting about. You can try and follow it when news bulletins get through, but I don't know if the reporters understand it themselves. The only common factor is the descendant-killing. We're like Pokémon—gotta catch us all! if you want to destroy the root. There's rumours some original Roman god carked it a couple of months ago. Immortality only goes so far, it turns out.

I get up off the bale and press my eye to an old cable hole in the stable wall. Outside, the air's dense with smoke, but trampled in the mud a few metres away, I can see a body. Literally, a body, oozing red into the murk of the yard. The head and limbs have been torn off— probably eaten as part of some ritual. Fenrir's lot do that as well.

My stomach's roiling now, but that's okay, I've got used to not listening to the bits of me that'll slow me down if I let them.

An almighty bang sounds from the door, which ripples inward, before bouncing back.

Pen bursts into another round of tears and hugs her bump. Fucksake.

"What are you crying about?" I ask. "It's holding. Told you, Onkel's charmed this place."

"How long?" she sobs. "And what about Mum? We should've gone back to the Hall when all this shit started."

My insides twist. "Shut up."

"But—"

"I said, shut the fuck up. Mum'll be fine. She'll be in the safe-room under the cellar."

The door heaves inward again, the wood warping. It splinters. Just a little. And there's a definite sag as it returns to its normal position. Shit.

A voice like hoar frost snarls outside, "What's in there? Can you tell? We need to find the child before the Yarburgh contingent arrive. I have it on good authority it's here. *I* want that snivelling shitbag's head under my foot and his immortality ripped from the fucking fabric of the universe by sunset."

"Yes, Ma'am," another voice replies. "I'll do a closer check."

I hear loud sniffs, and a pattering like the feet of thousands of huge ants over the walls. Something dark, shiny and metallic skitters across my peephole and I start backwards.

"Anything?" the first voice asks.

"No, Ma'am, but I think this is the work of an Original."

A too-long silence, then, "Which one; him?"

"Hard to say, there's so much happening."

Pen whispers, "What faction is it?"

I shrug. "Could be Hephaistians—they've got metal search bugs. You're right, we need to get out of here. They're looking for a little kid; we need to let the others know."

"Shit, there's only five on the estate since the last raid!"

"I know. Listen, we'll wait 'til this lot clear off—*if* they clear off—and I'll try and break us out. Just don't go into labour or anything daft, okay?"

If Pen had been pregnant at sixteen and ready to pop at seventeen five years ago, everyone would've thrown their hands up and rolled their eyes and made comments about young mothers and the state of society and education. *We* threw a party when she and Saqib announced they were expecting. A big one.

A couple of people have told me I should choose someone and try now that I'm sixteen but I'd rather be locked in an overflowing septic tank for the day than try it with a bloke, even to give humanity a few more years.

The battle noises are moving northward, across the fields. The crops. Bastards. Last winter was tough and it's harvest time now. Everything was ready to be brought in. I'll be okay: I can survive on grass if push comes to shove, but some of the folk here, especially the full-morts, might not make it.

Outside, the group shifts. They don't test the door again, but there are mutterings even I can't hear. This is one time I wish Onkel would show up and be all badass, but it looks like I'm fairly low on the scale of favouritism. He's never told me exactly how many newly discovered relatives he has scattered across the globe, but I'm willing to bet it's quite a few.

The footsteps of the group outside are fading away and the explosions nearby have stopped too. I rub at the prickly patch on my chest again. Hope it's not something new.

"Come on then!" Pen gestures at the door. "Do your…whatever."

"Not there. They'll look for signs of that if they come back." I pull a bale aside where I know the brickwork's in bad shape. "Here. We'll have to crawl. And I can't promise this place'll be safe next time."

I plea silently to Onkel and give the wall a hard backward kick. The shockwave flings me across the barn. Shaking my head, I haul myself to my feet and return. The wall's bent outward a little a least, but it's not enough and I punch it. Pain and frustration trigger my extra limbs; they tear out of my hips and my ribcage as I'm flung into the air again. My t-shirt, already fieldwork-stained beyond repair, adds four splashes of blood to its colour palette and thank Gods I wore a skirt today.

With my back to the wall again and still gasping from the fierce burning in my joints, I jump, and Pen wide-eyes me as I kick all four legs against the same spot. The bricks give way and a fierce red glow and smoke begin to twist in through the gap like something out of a bad horror movie. My aim's definitely more accurate than the last time I sprouted. Everything still hurts and my chest is itching even more, but job done.

I go to scratch, but my brain can't decide which hand to use and I give it up as a bad idea. No new sounds issue from outside, just the distant rumble of crop destruction. I can pick out the slightly sweeter scent of wheat and oats burning and my mouth becomes as confused as my hands: dry one second, salivating like a good 'un the next.

Having tested the hole to make sure Loki's field is broken, I kneel down and inch out into the red gloom, extra limbs tucked tight at my sides. It's like being some kind of human-spider-horse hybrid. You can see why all those superheroes in the old comics stop at the powers of just one animal. Any more than that and it just becomes an unholy fucking mess.

Pen remains silent as she struggles through and gets to her feet. A series of skidmarks from the mud have raked across her bump; it looks like some wild thing's taken a swipe at her. She's breathing hard, her eyes are glazed and she looks grey. Is she on the verge of passing out? I point in the direction of the Hall, put a finger to my lips and take her hand, give it a squeeze. Most days, I feel like the big sister.

"Face forward, yeah? Eyes off the ground. There'll be... Well, there could be folk we know."

She just nods.

My ears twitch forward automatically in the open air, listening for anything suspicious. Hate that. Useful, but I hate it. Just a bit too horse-ish. Like the whole grass thing. Folk've told me it doesn't show, but I'm sure they're just sparing my feelings.

As we skirt the north wall of the yard, I keep my eyes off the ground, where I know there'll be dead and dying. After the cacophony we've endured for hours, the quiet's a shock. Sweat rolls in waves down me; it was a hot August day even before the battle started. I need water. We both need water. Pen lets out a tiny yelp.

"What?" I hiss.

"Kelly."

I don't look. Kel's a full-mort and we've been in the same dorm together for three years, one of the old royal suites. Really liked her. I was hoping... I swallow hard, but I don't look.

"They've burned her eyes out, Vez, and her chest—she—"

I don't look. "She dead?"

No reply.

"Keep moving, Pen."

My vision's blurred with tears. Kelly, fucksake. I hope we *do* meet up with whoever did it, because I'll kick their sorry arses into another dimension.

"Why here? We weren't doing anyone any harm."

The itching in my chest has turned into a burning and there's a pressure too, where the halves of my collar bone meet. Great. Either I'm having a heart attack or this is definitely something new.

We need to get through the old Boar Garden and in through the south wing of the Hall. The once-was topiary dotted about what were pristine lawns and are now vegetable plots, is ragged with neglect and heavy with dark ash. As we pick our way across, most of the drooping bushes look like huge ravens, flapping through the smoke towards us. My ears jerk forward. Someone's coming. The sound takes on a form, a shadow setting the smoke to a swirl around itself as it gets closer. Pen grips my hand tighter. We've nowhere to run. A familiar voice drifts with the smoke. "Penny?"

Pen yells as Saqib emerges from the mist, and runs—as well as she can in her state—to throw her arms around him. Pangs run through me as I think about Kel again. I shake them out.

Saqib's thin face is more drawn than usual when he and Pen finally separate. His hand rests on her stomach a moment.

"Is Mum okay?" I whisper.

"Yeah," he replies. "Yeah, she's fine. A lot of people aren't though. Where were you?"

"Stable block. Onkel's charmed it so I'm safe in there. His idea of a sense of humour."

Saqib rolls his eyes then jerks his head in the direction of the Hall. "Come on, we'd better get back inside. They might have left people behind."

"Who were they?" I ask as we set off again at a brisk trot.

"All sorts. I reckon they've got one Original in charge, but they all had different powers. They weren't really after us; they were toying." He blinks. "Some of the things they did to the bodies... Our jumbles managed to give them a run for their money, but they only left because they were bored, I think."

"No, they were looking for someone: a child."

"Oh. Oh, so that's why...they got three of the kids. I don't know about the others."

We all go into shock at the ice-cold facts for a moment, then Pen mutters, "Fingers crossed." And then she looks at me, brow wrinkled, because I'm rubbing my chest again.

I'm not imagining it, there's some kind of lump there. Fuck.

Saqib notices too. "What's up?"

"Nothing, I've just—there's something there, but I don't know what it is."

"Most likely an extra head," Pen says, grim.

"Thanks a bloody bunch."

"Well, good ol' Sleip had four, didn't he?"

"Not helping."

We're at one of the functioning Hall doors. Saqib turns the doorknob, pushes it open.

Genuinely shocked, I hiss, "Why didn't you lock it when you came out?" That would have seemed petty before the Shift, but now it's the rule: always secure whatever you can as much as you can. So something's wrong; Saqib's one of the most security conscious of us all. I grasp Pen's hand, bring us both to a halt.

"What?" she asks.

"He wouldn't forget."

Saqib turns, eyebrows raised. "What is it?"

"You don't forget. To lock the door. You don't."

He sighs. "Damn, knew I'd miss something."

And he cracks open.

Literally, cracks open; sheds his skin and flesh as Pen lets out a scream and a thing unfolds from the centre of the mess. It's all glistening spine at first, then torso, limbs, a tail emerge. The whole thing's skeletal; the eyes in its monstrous skull are two pits of nothing so deep and dark they could suck you in and spit you out halfway across the universe if you looked too long. On top of the skull, a mass of whip-like bones twist and writhe.

It turns its full gaze on us and Pen stops screaming, freezes, her skin greying even more.

"Pen?" I grab her. She feels cold, but her heart's beating wildly.

"She can't hear you." The creature's voice is like two slabs of granite grinding against each other.

"What have you done?" More alarm bells ring inside me. "What—Was that Saqib? Did you—or did you just make yourself look like him?"

As the monster's otherwise toothless mouth spreads and opens to a grin, two sets of enormous fangs unfurl. "I can count the great Atë among my forebears—may her path be lined with the bones of the righteous. Your friend proved very amusing before I dispatched him. And satisfying after that."

"So he's…" Shit. "Where's everyone else?"

The creature raises its hand, the fingers of which are tipped with huge straight claws. It strokes my cheek and gives me a look of what might be pity.

"Sleeping below," it replies. "I was hoping to take you there for a look. Fear makes adrenalin and adrenalin adds a piquancy I can't describe. Your sister would have been quite the gourmet treat. Not you though. We have other plans for you."

Now I need to vomit. The sensation in my chest becomes a purer pain and my brain buzzes with questions about what these "plans" might be, but more importantly…

"Where's Mum?"

The grin widens and its owner leans forward to hiss in my ear. "Don't worry, we didn't waste her. We won't waste anyone. It's not often we find so much food in one place. Our leaders let us eat our fill and later, when the smoke has cleared, we will all return, eat the rest and tell stories of our glorious battle by the light of the heavens."

A gorgonite. That's what this is. Whatever it says about its heritage…a touch of Medusa, maybe. Definitely. I mean, look at Pen. Look at her… Stop crying. Look at Pen. Look at your sister… Mum's gone? Everyone's gone? What does this thing want with me? I hurt so much inside I'm starting to wonder if my own body's going to be ripped open.

The creature cocks its head. "Fascinating. We'll keep your sister alive, for now, I think. It always helps to have a bargaining chip in these circum—"

Its voice is drowned out by a scream. My own. I don't know whether it's my voice or the feeling of my chest splitting open but it's the only thing I can hear. Falling to my knees, I lean forward and let my four arms take the strain of whatever's forcing me open. I can see something emerging and then, like someone's thrown a switch, my eyes stop working. The impression of what I last saw is still there, but even that's fading. I'm conscious of being grabbed by the scruff of my neck, lifted up, and then the switch is thrown back on and my vision powers up as I swing back and forth in the gorgonite's grasp, my feet catching on the path every few running steps.

What I see is crazy, though. No human brain is built to see 360 degrees all at once, but that's what I think I'm seeing—the fug of smoke, the side of the gorgonite, the Hall and the garden and behind us and to the side and—and I have to shut my eyes because it's too much. My shoulders ache like they're supporting an extra weight and, dreading what I'm fairly certain I'll find, I raise my hands and press my four palms against four heads. They're all human, but there's four of them. Front, back, left, right. I can feel the rush of air on all of them now.

I have never hated my ancestors so much.

What's the good of four heads? Because apparently, I can't switch between them. It's not like a bank of security cameras. And I need to see if the gorgonite's got Pen in its other hand. Maybe there's a dominant head, the first one, the forward-facing one. Maybe if I focus really hard, I can—

The gorgonite's picking up speed and the burning crop smell is getting stronger again. I experiment, opening one eye in what I hope is the front head. No good, I'm just opening one eye in all the heads and again, the sensation overwhelms my brain. But I have caught the idea of a blackened field and a crowd in the distance.

"Enheph!" the gorgonite booms. "I believe I have found what we were seeking."

It comes to a stop but keeps a tight hold of me. A thud sounds close by. I risk a peek and just about register the crumpled form of Pen lying in the charred stalks.

The ground shakes with the approach of heavy footsteps, and a clank of armour rings through the air. Then silence until something very loud bursts into laughter.

"What a sight!" it splutters. "What a sight!" Tremors run through me as the thing slaps the gorgonite on the back. "You have done well, Keith."

For a stunned split second I feel like joining in with the laughter. Keith?! I suppose everyone had a name before all this. Still, there's possibly no other name that says, *I'm a huge fuck-off gorgonite capable of petrification* less than Keith.

Then the voice seems to shout up at the sky, "Loki, my old friend, see what your mischief has caused. Thousands of years in the making too. Where are you? I want you to witness me crush this abomination, your last one. I want to see you die. Are you too much of a coward to show yourself?"

My limbs are starting to feel flu-heavy: must be dangling from the fist of a gorgonite.

I try to shake myself out, get the blood going, and the ease of movement surprises me. But when I press my hands together, straining to lose the pins and needles, there's a loud clack.

No.

I try again and sure enough, what I hear isn't the soft clap of hands but the hard crack of bone on bone. There are fingers, but they're huge and when I flex them they feel like I imagine a crustacean's armour must feel on its body. Hooves. I have hoof-hands. Oddly, it's this of everything that's happened so far that tears it for me. I think about Kelly and trying to hold her with hoof-hands and hurting her without meaning to, and my eyes swell with heat behind their lids. Then my brain somehow thinks it's also a good idea to make me wonder how the hell I'll wipe my bum and how Mum would kill me if I left the bathroom in a state and I burst into manic laughter that kills the conversation between Enheph and the rest of the group.

As I bring myself back under control, there's a horrible silence then a thud of feet that are probably ten times the size my new "hands" will ever be. Enheph—because I'm certain that's who it is—gives off so much heat, I start to pour with sweat as he leans in close to inspect me. My skin's toasting, blisters bubbling up. I hear a spitting sound, then a sizzle from my left arm and a breeze where his saliva's burned through my jacket.

"Laugh at me again, abomination," Enheph's voice rumbles, "I'll do that to each of your four ugly faces. Are we clear? Open your eyes and look into those of your master. I'm going to break you, then I'm going to put bits in your mouths, halters on your heads, and a saddle on your back, so you should accustom yourself to obeying me."

Bastard. I open my eyes more because I'm curious than anything else. What I can make out of Enheph's face resembles a jumble of glowing lumps of steel. At the outmost tips, where the air's cooling it, the metal shines silver. Heat drives my eyelids back down and Enheph chuckles.

"I control you, I control Loki. Maybe I'll ride him too." This brings a chorus of laughter from the rest of the crowd. "The gods should not have spread themselves so...thin over the years. They will be held accountable now the tide has turned."

"How do you know?" I ask. "That I'm his last descendant. How can you?"

"Oh." The chuckle deepens. "We are very organised. We have records."

"Who are your ancestors then?"

"All Gorgons, Titans. Things formed by the darkness for the darkness. The oldest of the old. And a wide variety. We answer to no one but ourselves. Humanity is a god-fashioned annoyance. I left mine behind as soon as the Shift occurred."

"What did you do? Before?"

"I spent much of my time at Her Majesty's Pleasure. Violent tendencies. I had a disturbed upbringing."

"Haven't we all. Boo fucking hoo." I can't believe I've just let those words out and, clearly, neither can Enheph. That's the Loki genes at work. I blame them for the detentions when school still existed.

The gorgonite doesn't drop so much as hurl me to the ground, and my limbs splay around me. One of my lips split as well. Bothering to work out which one really isn't my top priority, I'm more concerned about the grit and charcoal now clogging my nostrils and the wet in my groin which I know without checking is fresh blood.

"Get up then, abomination!" Enheph roars.

Hauling myself to my four feet, I struggle to balance on what must be full hooves—last half-decent pair of Converse fucked then—and try not to let my neck (necks?) bow under the weight of my heads. When I risk opening my eyes, I can make out the group conferring a few metres away. They're all huge. Keith's breath further clouds the already thick air around me.

Where's Pen? My eyes go into overdrive as it all gets too much again. I panic, quell an urge to scream, squeeze them tight shut.

There's a cracking sensation inside, and I recall a walnut being shelled, Mum teasing me the nut looks like a brain and me feeling sick as I fumble it out and break it in two. Then I reopen my eyes and I know Pen's lying behind me, at Keith's feet.

I know this.

I can see it.

The same way I can see that some dude in the group in front is grinning broadly, slapping Enheph on the shoulders. The same way I know a crow has just taken flight from a hedgerow on the west side of the field and a fox is staring at the group from the eastern side. Behind him in the distance, dark grey smoke still pours from the Hall and gardens. And I can take it all at once. All of it.

Pen is the same colour as before, but her bump is twisting like the baby's fighting its confines. I don't know if any of Enheph's bunch have noticed, but the fox seems interested. It's not staring at the group, its eyes are fixed on Pen and me. All eight of my ears flick its way. It raises a paw and licks it, checks the claws.

"Lokiiii!" Enheph's bellow cuts through. "Where are you, you son of a bastard pretender to the heavens?"

An urge builds, deep in my gut, to charge forward and knock him and the rest of them down like so many skittles. My shoulders bunch, new muscles hardening. My fists, if I can still call them fists, tighten with a sound like shifting gears. I have to *do* something. Sleipnir was the finest horse in all Norse history, fucksake. And I'm just stood waiting for someone to cut my head off or disembowel me or whatever these guys are planning.

The fox is trotting. Towards us. Some animals have no sense.

Keith notices, lets out a dead-waking roar, but his glare doesn't turn the fox into a garden ornament and still it trots, oblivious.

"Enheph!" he calls. "Look!"

Enheph rises into the air and comes crashing down inches from me. I want to stamp his head from his neck and use it as a football to take out the others. Two of my hooves paw at the blackened ground and my teeth grind unbidden. I will *not* foam at the mouth though. There are limits.

The fox sits, with perfect posture, tail curled around its front paws, and I can make out a scar running from its right eye to its jaw.

On the northern side of the field, the crow has settled in the hedgerow. Its eyes are on me and on the fox, I'm certain. And I'm also certain I catch one flashing ice blue through the smoke.

Enheph's glowing eyes narrow. The fox lifts its muzzle, sniffs the air, snorts ash.

"What are you?" Enheph growls.

Unperturbed by the rumble the monster's voice has sent through the ground, the fox draws back its top lip, snaps at a passing moth. A pair of dusty wings twitch past its lips and down its gullet and a tiny burp pops into the air. The way things are, that moth better not have been Hope.

Give me some credit, little one.

The words echo in my heads and I have a lightbulb moment.

Onkel?

The fox yawns, nods.

I try not to frown. *Where the fuck have you been?*

Why... The fox's tail twitches. *...the fuck did you leave the safe place I made for you? We could have avoided all this...unpleasantness. You're officially the last, you know. You're all that's left of me now.* He looks me up and down. *Ignominy. It hardly seems fair.*

Who are these people?

Agents of Atë. Chaos to their core. Your sister is all right though. And the child. We still have a fighting chance.

Enheph advances on Loki. He doesn't move, apart from a flick of his ears. Behind me, Pen's stomach twists again. What the hell is in there? Saqib was a full-mort.

No.

The fox's eyes are huge, cartoon innocent.

What did you do? I hiss at Loki.

Your sister was such a ripe fruit. And when I took Saqib's form that night. Well... She hardly needed persuading.

My head buzzes. *You're telling me...*

Desperate times, desperate measures. I need more descendants. But I fear the new one will arrive too late. All the new ones will arrive too late. Bodies. Pah.

That finishes off any restraint I had. I somehow launch myself, not at Enheph, but at Onkel, whose ears spread flat against his head before he vanishes, and my hooves find only hard-baked earth. Bastard. I've learned a trick though: don't think about it and I can move, and move well.

No one can get near me because I can see everything. And if they do get near me, I kick and buck with legs that are somehow longer, that must be making me at least ten feet tall. And I clamp and tear with four sets of teeth that pull limbs and heads from the bodies of Enheph's crew. I am a thing of terrifying fucking beauty.

By the time I'm done with them, the smoke's cleared and the sun's bleeding into the horizon behind the rolling hills of the Yorkshire Dales. On the ground, Pen still lies, her skin slowly turning back to its usual colour, her breathing less shallow. She won't know about her baby till she wakes up. She won't know about me either.

My body hasn't changed back like it usually does. I have a feeling it never will, but I quite like this. I like the sensation of raw power in my limbs and knowing that I can take on the worst of the worst and win. Doesn't stop me from throwing up at the sight of what I've done though.

A crow descends as I'm wiping the last of the bile from all my lips, and begins to peck at the remains scattered around me. As I regain control of my breathing and I'm able to focus on something other than revenge, thoughts of Mum flood back and I burst into tears, stamp at the ground. Why the hell couldn't Onkel have protected *her*?

"Because it's not his way." A man dressed in funereal black is standing where the crow was. He holds out a hand. "Odin. Pleased to make your acquaintance."

My laugh rings hollow across the wide open space. "And where were you a few hours ago?"

He seems to flinch. "Many places. I'm sorry for your losses; there was nothing I could do. I do however, need your help. That display was impressive to say the least and I am...not what I used to be. This war is pointless, and no one can win. But we can get through it together if we stay sharp, negotiate, co-operate. Atë will consume us all otherwise."

Pen sits up, stares around, clutches her belly. Then she looks up and sees me and screams until she realises. "Vez?"

I nod. All four of my heads.

"Shit." She heaves herself to her feet. "Mum?" Her face crumples as she sees the answer on mine.

Onkel glides back up behind Odin.

"Fucking coward!" I yell. "Can't even appear in your true form."

Odin sighs. "He's trapped this way for now, at least until the child is born. Too weak to change back."

"What now?" Pen asks, hugging herself. "I mean..." She points at the Hall. "Where? And what child?"

Skilfully avoiding her question, Odin continues, "I have a settlement near Durham. Well hidden. I can take you there and we can plan our next move."

Pen looks up at me. "Vez? What d'you think?"

I take in the view, the beauty of the open countryside past the bodies and the burnt earth around us and a voice deep down inside me shouts loud. It shouts that this is the place for me. Grass as far as the eye can see, when it grows back. Space to move and yell and kick at the sky. And more importantly, it whispers impishly, it'll really piss off those higher up.

See? Family. It's in your bones; you can't escape it.

"I think," I tell Odin, "we'll take our chances here for now. I don't fancy being anyone's trusty steed and I don't think you can make me. But I can take care of my sister, if she wants me to."

Pen nods, slowly.

Scowling, Odin turns to Loki, "See what you've wrought?" He faces us again. "I cannot promise any help if you stay here."

"I think we'll do just fine without, thanks. And if we don't, well, that's meant to be, isn't it?"

Odin's face is a picture of silent outrage, but he recovers himself, manages a laugh. "Good luck, child. I won't return, but I can guarantee this idiot will." And he and Loki head for the northern edge of the field.

"Gods, *you're* the idiot," Pen groans at me. "There's no medical equipment, hardly any food. It's all right for you with your bloody hay and oats." She shivers despite her flippancy.

"Women have given birth without medical equipment for thousands of years," I say, restraining my own urge to shake with the cold left in me now the adrenaline's gone. The clean-up's going to be horrendous. All those people. Everything. "Stop being such a fucking wuss."

She studies the ground. "We should see if we can find Mum. If they didn't... We should try and find her. And then we should get ready. For the baby and...everything."

I paw the churned earth with my hooves, one after another, leaving neat grooves. "Let's get started."

Neither Snow, nor Rain, nor Heat-Ray

M.L.D. Curelas

London, England, 1900
Five days after the Martian landing

No one had been alarmed when the first Martian vessels landed, pocking the ground like open sores. They'd only been mildly concerned when the cone-shaped ships vomited forth the spindly, tripod machines. It wasn't until the trains stopped running that panic had set in. Then the tripods had come with their Black Smoke and heat-rays.

Emma swiped the oiled cloth over the bridle again, checking carefully for any cracks in the leather. She would maintain her equipment, as a conscientious and accomplished horse-woman, despite her lackluster feelings about her assignment. Emma had heard that scientists were working around the clock, designing weapons to combat the Martians and their damnable tripods. In the meantime, the fragmented government and military were organizing an evacuation out of Chelmsford. Most of London had fled the city, Emma's family included, but despite her family's wealth and standing, Emma hadn't been allowed to leave. She'd been— conscripted, she supposed.

A rustle of hay and a velvet nose pressed against her neck announced the arrival of the reason for her conscription. Emma's death grip on the bridle relaxed, and she reached up to stroke the cheek of Beezus, her mare.

The Martians had disrupted communications. Nothing worked, not the telegraph machines nor the new telephones. Messengers were needed. Messengers on horseback, because human runners were too slow and easily killed by the Martians and their Black Smoke. But horses were scarce so when the general had sighted Beezus, a fine hunter, with a skilled rider—her—they'd been pressed into service on the spot, no matter that she was a girl, a civilian, and a daughter of good family.

And now she and Beezus would be part of the messenger team sent out to the docks—integral to the coordination of the Navy escort for the evacuee ships, or so she'd been told. Emma scowled. Her revolver would've been of better use helping her family travel to Chelmsford than giving messages to a boat.

The mare snorted against her neck and started mouthing her hair. Emma laughed. "Enough of that." She pushed the horse, and Beezus obligingly pulled her head back into her stall.

Emma rubbed the mare's nose. "Can't fool you, can I? Yes, we're going out." When Beezus nodded her head, Emma wagged her finger. "Business. Not a pleasure ride."

Beezus huffed.

After checking the mare's water and hay, Emma resumed her equipment check. It was the mare's nervous whinny that halted her. She caught sight of Beezus' wide, rolling eyes and cast a furious glare at the stable door.

"Stay out there!" she yelled. Scowling, she set down the saddle and shut the top half of Beezus' stall door. Maybe that would block the pungent scent of that Moreauvian fiend enough for Beezus to calm down.

Emma opened the stable door, grabbed the arm of the man standing there, and tugged him around the corner of the building toward a garden shed—it wasn't safe for anyone to linger long outside, in case of Martian patrols.

The soldiers had watered down the grounds, washing away most of the deadly Black Smoke, but Emma could see traces of the black grit in the flower beds. She stayed clear of those areas, just in case.

Once inside the shed, she crossed her arms over her chest. "Well?"

He grinned, revealing white, pointed teeth. "Don't you have an office in the barn?"

She sniffed pointedly. "I can't have my barn reeking of predator. You upset Beezus."

His grin slipped a notch. "They're used to me, up at the house," he offered, chuckling nervously. "Still can't believe they're stabling horses in the ballroom."

"They're preserving my modesty." Emma couldn't help smiling. Here she was, wearing trousers, a revolver belted around her waist, and the general was concerned about her sleeping in the same building as the soldiers.

The Moreauvian pulled a message tube from his pocket and handed it to her. "A map and a copy of your orders."

She took the tube, made no move to empty it. "Thanks." As if the map would be useful, with the polluted landscape and destroyed landmarks.

He seemed to understand. "It has tripod locations marked. Or where they seem to be patrolling, anyhow."

Emma nodded.

He held something else to her. A sweat-stained glove. "You'll need this too." When she hesitated, he clarified, "Your *horse* needs this."

Emma reluctantly accepted the smelly item. Oh, no. She shut her eyes, counted to ten. Re-opening them, she stuffed the glove in her pocket and upended the tube. She scanned the parchment, already knowing what she'd find.

...to aid in the successful completion of the mission, several messengers will be sent, following separate routes. They are as follows...

She skimmed the list, finding the name she sought at the bottom.

Henry Fletcher, Moreauvian

Bad enough that he was acting as a sort of aide-de-camp. She didn't need the Moreauvian monster on the field in addition to the Martians. Emma rolled up the paper and stuffed it back inside the tube. She did not look at Henry Fletcher.

"All the messengers need an item of clothing, in case we encounter each other—"

"I understand," she snapped. "I have to finish preparing for the ride." When Fletcher didn't move from the door, she said, "Don't you? Have to prepare?"

He shook his head. "I don't need a horse." He paused. "I…can move quite fast…when I need to."

She had a good idea of what that meant. Even the lowliest of chimney sweeps had heard of Dr. Moreau and his…experiments. She didn't want to hear the details of what Henry Fletcher could do. She gestured to the door. "I have to saddle my horse."

Fletcher sketched a bow and stepped to the side, allowing her to venture out into the gloomy day. "Good luck," he called.

Beezus hated the stink of the glove, and shifted uneasily as Emma fastened it to the saddle, moaning.

Emma stroked the mare's shoulder. "He can't smell much worse than a dog, can he?"

Beezus snorted, wagging her head.

"Well, then." Emma whispered into the horse's ear, "I don't like it either, but we'll make do."

Beezus bobbed her head. Emma smiled, resting her forehead against Beezus' neck, breathing deeply of the horse's scent, feeling her heart slow. They would get through this—Black Smoke, Martians, and Moreauvian ally be damned.

Emma inhaled deeply, taking some peace from Beezus' solid presence. She tugged on the bridle's buckles one last time to ensure a secure fit.

Satisfied, she led the mare outside. A small group of soldiers huddled in the yard. There was no sign of Henry Fletcher, or any other messengers. One of the men, the general, approached her.

"You have your orders?" he asked.

Emma nodded. "Yes, sir."

"Right, then." He waved a boy forward, who boosted Emma up on her saddle.

"God speed," the general said and thumped Beezus on the shoulder. "Off you go."

Although the dense Black Smoke eventually sank to the ground, the air was still smoky from decimated buildings and vegetation. People, too, probably. She groped for the message tube containing her orders and the instructions for the fleet and squinted through the haze.

This section of London was desolated, the people long since fled or killed and many of the houses smoking, empty shells. A few, like the one the military had commandeered, were more or less intact. They didn't look inhabited, but then, it wasn't wise to do anything to attract the attention of the tripod patrols. Especially—Emma shuddered—since she'd heard that there were worse fates than death to be had from the tentacles of the Martians.

Going through the city center would be the quickest route, but the most hazardous—too much rubble obscured by the haze and therefore too risky for Beezus. They would, instead, skirt along the edges of the park and then cut over to the docks. There would be less cover for them, but Beezus was a fine runner. Her speed and nimbleness would get them past the tripods, where human runners and mechanical motors had failed.

It was so quiet that Emma wondered if the Martians had stopped patrolling in this particular area. She guided Beezus around a coach abandoned in the middle of the road. The horses in the harness were dead, sloppily and hastily butchered. Chaos and violence had overcome the people quickly, even in this respectable part of London. Emma grimaced, recalling the confusion yesterday as her family had forced their way through the streets, her father striking people with a riding crop to keep them from climbing atop the laden carriage.

A crash to her left startled her out of her musings. Emma glimpsed a tripod from the corner of her eye and hunched over Beezus' neck, asking the horse for more speed. Their best defense against the tripods was distance. The Black Smoke and heat-rays could not be defeated or deflected, only outrun. Beezus leapt forward as a spindly metal leg stabbed the earth where they'd just been.

Zig-zag, Emma thought, communicating her directions to Beezus through subtle touches of her heels, hands, the reins. The mare responded lightning fast, almost instantaneously. The resounding clangs and stomps of the tripod followed them, not able to catch up despite its long legs, not quite, but—

Zot.

A tree turned to ash on their right as they jigged left.

The heat-ray. Emma's mouth went dry. Probably better than canisters of Black Smoke, but still not good.

Zot.

Emma stood up in her stirrups, her head alongside Beezus' neck. She was calm. There was her, there was Beezus, and there was the road in front of them. The buzzing of heat-rays was no more bothersome than a fly.

"Cart!" she yelled. Beezus' ear flicked, but she'd already seen the obstacle. Her muscles bunched, and Emma adjusted her seat as the horse jumped the over-turned cart.

Beezus came down fine, no stumbles, and Emma was already communicating a course direction as the cart disintegrated behind them.

Emma glanced over her shoulder. The tripod didn't seem to be gaining. Would it let them escape? Find easier prey, or—

Emma steered Beezus off the road into the trees as a second tripod erupted from the houses, a heat-ray blasting holes in the road.

Emma gulped. They'd have to slow down, sacrificing speed for the cover of trees. Beezus pushed through a clump of bushes, and Emma nearly sobbed with relief as the mare's hooves came down on a well-maintained bridle path. Beezus picked up her pace, her stride lengthening, and the noise of the tripods faded.

These trees were faring well, still leafy and green—healthy—and with none of the powdery residue of the Black Smoke. It was tempting to stop, to rest, but she didn't dare. What if the tripods decided to follow her into the park? Distance. Distance was her best defense.

Gradually, the trees thinned and then ended abruptly, abutting against a once-elegant house which now lay in ruins. Smoke spiraled in the distance. Through the miasma, Emma could see dark, irregular shapes. Houses, perhaps, with their roofs blown away.

Beezus shifted and whickered softly. Emma patted her neck. "Hush, my lovely. Let's get our bearings."

Emma pulled out the map. Buildings would be next to useless, but surely the park...? She located it on the map and grunted with surprise. They had come farther than she'd thought. The road before them would lead to the docks—the Navy. If they were even there.

These ships, she had heard, had been called from the North by telegraph before the Martians had disrupted communications. They might not have arrived yet. And if they had, they might have been discovered by the tripods and burnt to ash with the heat-rays, or the crews killed with the Black Smoke.

She sighed, staring glumly at the road. The most sure way to reach her destination; the most sure way to be found by tripods. She peeked behind her. The park was silent and green. No Black Smoke, no rotting corpses, no foulness. She and Beezus could scrabble there for a while. The Navy and the Army could fight the Martians, figure out ways to counteract the Black Smoke and heat-rays. It was *their* responsibility, *their* duty. She and Beezus would sit this out. They would be safe.

But her father was on the road to Chelmsford, along with hundreds, maybe thousands of people. The Navy needed to be there to guard the retreat and to do that they needed to be told where to go. She stroked the butt of her revolver. She couldn't be with her family, but she could still ensure that they escaped the Martians.

Emma patted the mare and urged her forward. "We'll see it through to the end."

Beezus' eager strides ate the road, and it wasn't long before the odor of the Thames reached them. Sewage. Fish. Rotting humans.

Many of the buildings were husks, the air full of smoke and dust and grit, the hazy sky making it difficult to gauge the distance to the actual docks. Bodies littered the streets and sidewalks, trampled, rather than victims of the Black Smoke. She didn't want to imagine the horror and chaos of yesterday's evacuation. A glimmer of white shone through the haze and her heart jumped in her chest. Sails!

As she directed Beezus toward the sails, a dark form darted into the street in front of them. Emma blinked. Another rider? She whooped with excitement. Another rider had survived the journey!

The second rider also veered toward the glimmer of sails. Emma bent low over Beezus' neck. They would arrive together, triumphant, and see the ships off to Chelmsford where the evacuees waited.

Flooded with elation, Emma nearly missed the tremor that shook the earth.

Beezus didn't.

The mare canted sharply to the left. The ground burst behind them, spewing rocks and dirt. A Black Smoke canister? Emma kept her mouth shut tight and prayed for Beezus to run faster.

Peeking underneath her arm, Emma could see the low-hanging cloud of Black Smoke. And beyond that, the tripod navigating the narrow streets between buildings. She gulped. It was stepping *over* the buildings. But it had to sacrifice speed for the shortcut, since it could only move one spindly leg at a time, ensuring solid footing before initiating its next step.

Emma turned forward. Beezus could outrun it and the Black Smoke, she was positive. But…with a tripod so close, they wouldn't be able to watch the ship take sail. In fact…in fact, they would have to charge the tripod after delivering the message. She and Beezus playing decoy while the ship made way.

Emma gulped again, laying one hand flat against the mare's neck. They would do it. They wouldn't—couldn't—falter now, not with so many relying on them.

Maybe, she thought, and the tightness eased in her throat, maybe with the other rider, she and Beezus could peel away now, lead that monstrous machine a merry chase in the park, and give everyone a better chance at survival.

Her fingers tensed on the reins, and Beezus' ears twitched, waiting for the new direction.

Zot.

A hole, in front of them.

Zot.

A building, engulfed in flames, spewing ash.

A rock struck Beezus and she squealed, weaving sideways.

"Don't fall, don't fall, don't fall," Emma chanted, hauling on the reins to help the mare recover her balance.

Beezus' stride smoothed, and Emma drew her to a halt.

"We're lucky its aim is so bad," she panted, slapping the mare's shoulder and leaning to one side to check for a wound.

Zot.

A horse screamed.

Emma jerked upright and gasped. The other messenger was…gone. His horse—

Gagging, Emma drew her revolver and fired. The terrible shrieking ceased, and Emma dug her heels into Beezus' side. Beezus bolted forward, and Emma holstered her weapon before concentrating on guiding Beezus through the debris- and corpse-ridden street. They could still make the ship, a promise of hope gleaming in the gray, smoky air.

A second tripod appeared among the buildings and strode down the street toward them.

"*Damn* it!" Emma yelled.

The shock froze her brain for a moment, but the sails beckoned. They could dash behind that abandoned carriage, dodge into the alleys…use the buildings as shields. The alleys probably connected and formed their own crooked and narrow pathway to the docks. Before she could put the sketchy plan into action, Beezus neighed and rushed straight for the Martian tripod.

"No!" Emma yanked on the reins. "Beezus, no!"

Red light blazed on the hull of the tripod. Emma shut her eyes.

Zot.

Squealing…metal?

Emma's eyes snapped open. Beezus was still running like hell for the new tripod. Emma threw a glance over her shoulder. A hole smoldered in the body of the first tripod; its legs wobbled. With another scream of distressed metal, it toppled, crashing to the earth with a resounding thud.

Tingly with shock, Emma looked again to the new tripod, the one which had destroyed its comrade.

"Beezus, how did you—?"

A portion of the tripod slid open. A human, not a tentacled Martian, popped into view.

"Make for the ship! Hurry, before another of the damned things arrive!"

Emma squinted. "Fletcher? Henry Fletcher?"

The Moreauvian messenger waved. "I'll keep watch!" he shouted. "Hurry!" He ducked into the machine and the door slid shut.

With no further obstacles, Beezus ran between the spindly legs of their unlikely savior, Emma too stunned to do anything but provide basic guidance.

Emma watched the ship make way, tears streaming down her face. With luck, *Thunder Child* would rendezvous with the evacuation fleet.

She leaned against her mare's shoulder. "Sorry for doubting you, my lovely," she murmured. "I won't do that again."

Beezus snorted and bobbed her head.

"That was some riding," said Henry Fletcher, stepping up beside her.

Emma wrinkled her nose at his musky scent and laughed. "I just hung on. She did all the hard work." She hesitated. "Listen, Fletcher, I'm sorry for being so rude earlier. Thank you for saving us. For saving Beezus." She proffered a hand.

He gripped it and gave it a firm shake, and she noticed for the first time that his fingers were tipped with thick, pointed claws.

"Think no more of it," he said.

Emma smiled. "We're returning to headquarters now. Will you— will you accompany us?"

Fletcher looked surprised and his cheeks reddened. "I would be honored to, under ordinary circumstances, but I have a feeling our Navy will need some help with the evacuees. And I can provide formidable support."

"Oh, of course," she said, squashing a surge of disappointment. "That's a brilliant plan. I'll inform the general." Impulsively, she kissed his cheek. "Good luck, Fletcher."

"And to you," he said. "Farewell, Beezus." He stroked the mare's forehead, bowed to Emma, and hurried to his tripod.

Emma watched as he scaled the tripod legs with, she presumed, his claws and clambered into the body. Once it had stalked off and she could no longer see it, she grabbed Beezus' bridle.

"We've a ways to go before we can rest, my lovely," she said, guiding Beezus toward the park.

She had to report to the general. What she'd seen and done today would prove valuable for the military and the scientists. Aiding the evacuees was just the first step, she realized. The next step would be eradicating the Martian invaders. Messengers would be needed.

She and Beezus would be needed.

It was their duty.

RUE THE DAY

Laura VanArendonk Baugh

Galyne ducked and the spear passed over her. She came up gripping the short wide sword better suited for close quarters and drove it upward beneath the cuirass of the man in front of her. Her left arm hung weakly, blood running over her dangling fingers. She tried to look around, to gauge the state of the battle, but there were three more enemy soldiers closing on her.

There was no way she could have heard a snort or hooves behind her over the clash of metal and the battle cries and the screams of the wounded, but somehow she sensed it, and she whirled away and down to her knees as Nova leapt over her and drove into the center fighter, shouldering him back and to the ground. The mare collected herself and half-reared, turning to the soldier on the left and sweeping her horn to drive him back. The remaining soldier thought to attack the unicorn from the rear, but Nova sprang into the air and kicked out in a perfect capriole, her hooves catching him full in the chest.

Galyne rose and put a hand on the mare's shoulder, as each of them scanned for new threats. No one rushed them, and with the unicorn watching Galyne could take the extra time to look across the field and read the flags and banners. Yes, King Menshir's troops were holding the field solidly, with only a little raggedness along the front. They were holding.

Galyne found the stirrup and used the pommel of Nova's saddle to pull herself up one-armed. "Back," she called, her hand pressed flat against the unicorn's muscular neck, and the mare wheeled and galloped through the ranks, stepping nimbly over the fallen, dodging fights in progress, and once veering slightly to thrust her steel-capped horn between the shoulder blades of a Scapian soldier who was spearing one of Menshir's wounded.

They passed into the eerie space behind the fighting, where the noise of the battle carried plainly even as men and women stood and spoke as if lives were not being lost a stone's throw away. Some treated the wounded, some gathered equipment, some shared maps and advice and orders.

Galyne slid from Nova's saddle as the mare came to a halt. Trainer Isabel looked in her direction, her usually-stern face concerned at seeing them return while the battle yet raged. Galyne tried to shake her head—so far as she knew, Nova was largely unharmed—but the effort dizzied her. Nova bent her neck to press her muzzle against Galyne's chest, her horn carefully angled over Galyne's shoulder.

Isabel said something and pointed, and two grooms started toward Galyne and Nova. *What a bother,* Galyne thought as she pressed her good hand to the hot gash on her upper arm where her light armor was torn away.

One of the young grooms—Melane—reached her. "That's a lot of blood. Give me your weight, and let's get you to a physician."

Galyne tried to shake her head again. How exhausted she was, once out of the fighting itself. "Nova."

"I'll see to her myself," Melane promised. "But she won't get much care while you're leaning against her."

"Cheeky," muttered Galyne. "Insubordinate."

Melane did not care. Galyne let the girl pull her away from Nova and toward one of the physicians' circles scattered to receive returning soldiers. Nova nickered and followed, her head beside Galyne all along the way.

"Galyne?"

She wasn't accustomed to anyone calling her in the barracks, and certainly not a male voice. She tugged her belt through the buckle, one-handed the tongue through the proper hole, mildly cursing the sling on her left arm, and went to the door. "I'm here. This way."

It was indeed a young man who stood at the end of the barracks corridor, looking awkward. "I didn't know which room was yours," he confessed.

"And so you decided to shout?"

"I thought—if I went to all the doors—I mean…"

Fresh meat, she decided, and poorly trained. "First," she said, "this is a house of virgins, yes, and you should be mindful of your conduct. But it is equally a military house, and thus your conduct should be mindful of proper protocol, which does not include shouting down a hallway for a superior."

He stiffened. "I'm—"

"Second, as I am that superior, you should address me as Trainer Galyne, at the least," she continued.

His jaw clenched, and he assumed a parade stance. "Trainer Galyne, I apologize," he said. "I am Rue, reporting for duty."

Galyne closed her door behind her and came down the hallway toward him. "What duty is that?"

"I'm assigned to you and the stables, ma'am," he answered promptly. "In that order."

"What?"

"There's worry the Scapians might send someone secretly to infiltrate the war stables," he said. "I'm a—a guard, of sorts. For you."

"What?" She was repeating herself, but what he said was laughable. "You do know I am a soldier in my own right, yes? Even before we factor in the fourteen hundred pounds of fully-trained war unicorn?"

"I have Trainer Isabel's orders, ma'am. And with respect, you're wounded, and there's no unicorn here in the barracks, ma'am."

Galyne sighed. "I'm going to the stables now. I suppose you can come along."

"Yes, ma'am."

He was probably in his mid-twenties, like Galyne herself, which was old for a novice groom but perhaps more typical for a guard. A bodyguard, she realized. She stifled a smile.

He caught it and mistook it. "I am sorry for my inappropriate conduct before, ma'am."

"Oh, stop," she said. "Another *ma'am* dropped here and I'll trip on them. Trainer Galyne will do when you need to address me by name. Are you really a bodyguard?"

He nodded. "Though I am to help in the stables as well."

"We can use that, at least," she said.

The stables were not far from the barracks which served them. Someone had vandalized the sign. Again. Beneath the stern *War Stables* a line of sloppy blue paint advised, *Virgins only beyond this point.*

"What's your name?" she asked.

"Rue," he said. "Yes, really, before you ask. Like the plant, not the regret. My parents didn't really think it through." He looked at the sign. "Are they—is every—does it really matter? If you're..." He trailed off, looking uncomfortable and awkward.

She took pity on him, for both his silly name and his embarrassed question. "Yes, all the handlers and trainers are virgins. It does matter. But the vandalized sign is petty."

He followed her into the first barn. "Then it's all right if—"

She suppressed a smile. "If you're not? Yes, you can come into the stable—with me or another trainer, and only following our instructions. Do not approach any of the unicorns on your own, and if we tell you to move, then move. Immediately. They're big, they're faster than you think, and if you wait to ask if they're serious, it'll be too late."

Rue looked a little panicky, so she added, "But don't worry too much. Most of the regular army are not virgins, and the unicorns fight alongside them. You aren't likely to get into trouble if you keep your hands to yourself."

Rue nodded and crossed his arms, hands tucked inside. Galyne looked forward and hoped her amused smile did not show.

She went first to Nova's stall, of course. The mare whickered and extended her head over the half door, and Galyne cradled it and rubbed her forehead about the base of the horn. "Hello there, my lovely lady."

But Nova was pricking her ears and *whuffing* at Rue, who stood well back in the center of the aisle, trying not to look like he was keeping his distance. Galyne slipped a leather halter about the mare's head, buckling it over the poll, and opened the half-door. Rue took another step back. "Is it safe?"

"She's a war unicorn," answered Galyne flippantly. "Of course she's not safe."

She had seen a unicorn put a horn through the right breast of a townswoman who had insisted on petting him, though she had been told repeatedly to back away from the animal. Some people could not understand that they were not exceptions. But as long as Rue kept his distance and Galyne kept an eye on Nova's body language, he should be fine.

"Let me see you, girl," Galyne said as she went over the mare's body and legs. The grooms were to watch for any nicks, swelling, or other signs of injury or disease, but no trainer left such care solely to others. She ran her hands down the sleek neck, over the gleaming shoulder and the ugly knot of scar tissue, down the foreleg.

"What happened there?" asked Rue behind her. He was leaning to peer into the stall from a distance. "Her shoulder?"

Galyne returned to the scarring. "She took a spear," she said, smoothing the tension from her voice. "Last year. It went deep, pushed in by her own momentum. It was a miracle it missed her heart."

"Wow."

"She shouldn't be alive," said Galyne, "much less still fighting." She caught the head which turned to her, extending the horn over her shoulder. "Yet here she is."

"Heads up," came another voice, and Rue jumped forward as a man led a bay unicorn behind him. The other trainer gave Galyne a friendly nod as he passed and continued down the aisle.

Rue stared a bit too long after them, and Galyne prompted, "Yes?"

"Um," he said, and his cheeks actually were turning a faint pink. "Um, I didn't know there were male trainers."

Galyne couldn't help herself, she laughed aloud. "There can be male virgins, too. And male trainers."

Rue frowned. "Why would they…"

Now Galyne snorted. "Because they want to be trainers. They want to work with unicorns. And they don't let someone else's foolish standards or false superiority stop their dreams, and so they don't bow to mockery or scorn."

"I didn't say—"

"You didn't have to; we've all heard it often enough to know how it goes. And the guys have it the worst." She grinned. "But it tends to end pretty quickly. It's hard to mock a man too much for his supposed weakness when he's standing beside a big unicorn trained to kill people."

Rue nodded once.

Galyne gestured. "I need to take Nova out to work. I suppose you're following?"

Nova flattened her ears at Rue as he backed away, and Galyne shortened the lead, just in case. The mare wasn't usually testy, but they were often wary of strangers in the stable. She would let Nova work out her nerves in the practice pen.

"Come on," Galyne called down the corridor. "They're pulling another unicorn today. I have to be there, and that means you have to be there." She turned and started away.

Rue dutifully followed her at nearly every waking moment, even waiting outside the privies. It was irritating, but he was so apologetic about his trespasses that she forgave him and even found herself looking for him when she emerged in the mornings.

Rue caught up with her and slowed his jog. "Another unicorn?"

"To train," Galyne said with exaggerated clarity. "Because unfortunately it doesn't look as if the Scapians are going to go home soon."

The Scapians were a stubborn enemy. It was common knowledge they could not field a force to match the war unicorns and were gradually losing to them, and it was common rumor that they would counter not with direct battle but by sending assassins to eliminate the unicorn trainers. There were a number of new guards about the barracks and stables, but only a few injured trainers had their own personal protection, as Galyne did Rue.

There was a small group gathered on the beach, half-ringed about a woman of perhaps forty, dressed in fitted skirts with her hair drawn back severely. Trainer Isabel, stablemaster and head of all the royal trainers, stepped close to speak with her, and Galyne thought they might have been sisters.

Then Trainer Isabel stepped back to join the half-circle. "We are ready when you wish."

The sun dipped against the ocean. Rue stepped close to Galyne, keeping his eyes on the sorceress as if he did not trust her. Sorceresses had that effect on people, especially at first.

The woman spoke strange words in an awful voice and raised her bare hands against the wind and sea. She stood immovable on the wet sand, deliberately weaving her hands as if to pull the wind like wool or candy.

And then, as another wave rolled to break against the shore, Galyne saw a horse's form in the waves, its mane rising and falling with the waves' crests, though there was no flesh-and-blood horse there. The dread woman on the sand called again, and the head broke above the water, an ivory horn piercing the air.

The unicorn was the color of night upon the ocean, its mane and tail like foam lit by moonlight. It rose majestically from the waves and stepped onto the packed sand, arching its thick crest as if aware of its own powerful beauty. It paused before the woman who had summoned it from the elements and raked the sand with one magnificent hoof.

"Reaver," said the sorceress simply, and the beast bowed its head in gracious acknowledgment. Trainer Isabel stepped forward, extending a halter of worked silver and gems, and the unicorn tossed its head, sending spray over the women, and then extended its neck to accept the halter.

"How does she do it?" Rue whispered.

"It's a request," Galyne said. "She invites a unicorn from the elements, but it is always the unicorn's choice. She grinned. "You don't argue with a creature of magic who has agreed to fight on your behalf."

Reaver, gleaming with seawater and his new silver halter, walked away with Trainer Isabel. Galyne's eyes followed them. "I hope I have a chance at him," she said. "He's gorgeous."

"Like everything to do with unicorns," Rue said, and there was a note in his voice which should not have been there.

Galyne looked at him, but he was watching the sorceress and Trainer Isabel, and she did not ask him to explain.

It was awkward to always stand by and watch someone else work, so after ten days or so Rue began helping Galyne with some of her training tasks, especially those which required two strong arms as hers was recovering well but slowly. Nova did not like him too near, but she appeared to have reluctantly accepted his presence, and so he could carry grooming boxes or drag jumps and training dummies as needed.

The first time he saw the training dummies used left him speechless. He knew, like everyone else, the war unicorns were trained for battle. But he had clearly never observed a fully-trained unicorn perform an elegant capriole, leaping into the air and striking backward with enough precise force to detach the dummy's head and send it careening into the wall beyond.

Galyne had to prompt him to fetch the wooden head and try to refit it on the dummy. "If it won't go back on, don't worry about it," she called. "It wasn't a good strike, anyway."

That surprised him. "What?"

"Better to go for the chest, where it's harder to miss if he dodges. Armor won't save him from a direct hit."

Rue looked at the crude and dented head in his hands. "No, it won't."

Galyne dressed Nova for battle, to practice in the weight of armor: the chamfron, fitted over the horn to shield her face, the criniere for her neck, the peytral for her chest—though it could not always prevent a spear coming from underneath, as they knew too well—and the flanchards and croupiere for her flanks and hindquarters. Finally the steep-tipped coronel set at the end of the horn, lending a honed edge to the natural power and thrust. It was a heavy set, but Nova worked frequently in it and had the strength and endurance to perform even in its weight.

Afterward, however, she needed thoroughly bathed to clean away the dusty sweat. Galyne could leave this task to the grooms, but it was good to care for the mare herself, and anyway it was a more pleasant task in the summer heat.

Rue stayed near as she sponged the mare. He watched her work, arms crossed, unable to help directly but bringing her a refilled bucket before she asked. Finally he blurted, "So, you'll do this—forever? Without...you know, without love?"

Galyne laughed. "Not without love, just without sex."

"But..."

She shook her head at him. "Haven't you ever loved something? Loved someone? Loved a personality more than a throb in your pants? This is what I choose, and I love it, and I have no regrets."

"But you don't even know what you're missing."

"I'm not entirely ignorant," she said, raising a stern eyebrow. "I've seen the sheep and the goats and the dogs, you know. And half the taproom, on a winter's night when there's no planting in the morning. I know the gist of it. And it's a few minutes of sweaty, squirty hugging against a lifetime of working with the most amazing creatures I know. Look at Reaver—such a glorious creature, entrusted to my care and training. No, it's no sacrifice at all."

Rue shook his head. "You're dedicated."

"Yes," she said simply. "And don't say it like it's a bad thing. There's more to life than an itch in the crotch."

He looked down the path away from her. "My itch can get pretty insistent."

She snorted. "The apothecary probably has a powder for that."

He threw a sponge at her, which she ducked, and Nova tossed her head in mock alarm as they laughed and sought soft missiles.

It was possible to see the Scapian advance, if one climbed high enough on the mountain behind the city. Rue and Galyne squinted into the distance to discern the tents and cooking fire smoke against the horizon.

"Why don't they go home?" asked Galyne, surprising herself.

"Leave us alone? It's a trade route. It's money. It's not worth all this."

"It is to them," Rue said. "And it is to us, too, or else we'd let them have it." He shrugged. "People will do a lot of things for money."

Galyne took another drink from the skin Rue had brought. It was heavily watered tea with a fruity taste, different but refreshing. The climb had brought out a light sweat, and the mountain breeze was perfectly cool against her skin.

"Thanks for coming up here with me," Rue said. "It gets very close in the barracks."

"Military quarters aren't known for spacious accommodation," agreed Galyne. "It's good to get out once in a while."

"I didn't know if they would, you know, let you."

"What? My arm's healing well enough."

"I didn't mean that."

"Oh. No, of course we can go out. We're virgins, we're not fragile statues or gems to hoard. We made a choice and if we change our minds, we can retire instead of sneaking around. We couldn't sneak, anyway; the unicorns would tell on us." She laughed and thought she sounded just a bit drunk. Which was funny, because she was drinking fruity tea, but maybe it was because she liked Rue.

She did. Not *that* way, not all the way that way, but it was different having him around. And he liked her, she could tell, and that was very flattering for someone who was more used to mockery for her strict choice.

Rue was still worried about their outing. "But the Scapians?"

"Are over there." She pointed at the distant army. "The perspective or height made her feel strangely unbalanced, and she took another drink. "Besides, I have my personal bodyguard with me."

He frowned at her. "Are you okay?"

"Yeah, I'm fine. Weird dizzy spell or something, maybe from the climb." She shook her head, as if that might do something to help. It didn't. "I might be losing condition faster than I thought. Stupid arm."

He rolled his eyes. "It's a good thing you're pretty, to make up for the dumb." And he hit her.

The blow caught her in the temple and her vision blurred. She tried to step back with it, recover and raise her arms, all the movements trained to unconscious fluency in a professional fighter, but even her good arm felt thick and slow. Her feet moved but did not stay beneath her, and she fell to the rocky meadow.

He went down with her, pressing, pushing, pinning.

No no no no no no

Her injured arm was not strong enough to throw him off, and all her movements came too slowly. The realization that he had drugged her came slowly too, and she was pinned by the shock and hurt atop the drug. "Rue!"

He laughed. "Yeah, I knew you'd like it if you gave it a chance. Keep calling my name, girl."

Her limbs were growing heavier even as her fear burned hotter within her, and she felt her movements slowing further. She could not feel which way was up as she looked at Rue and the sky. She could not fight him off.

She could not stop him.

He left her on the rock-strewn grass. He spoke to her as he re-tied his trousers, said something to which he clearly expected a response. She wasn't sure what words he used.

"Hey! Are you listening?"

She did not answer. It was hard to concentrate.

"Pretentious bitch." He spat on the ground. "You weren't even that good. Glad I'm getting paid for this."

Galyne stared at the sky, the white clouds, the blue space, the sky which looked just the same as if nothing had happened.

Rue left her lying there.

She lay still and watched the clouds move across the sky. The sun had crossed her and started toward the Scapian camp before she began to cry. Slowly the deadening pressure faded from her mind, and what replaced it was worse.

She rolled onto her side and wept.

Not me. Not me. Not me.

The words ran through her, poured out of her, punctuated her ragged breath. *Not me.* She hadn't meant for it to happen, hadn't wanted it, hadn't stopped it. *Not me.* She couldn't work with it, couldn't go to Nova or Reaver or any of them.

Not me.

She could not go back to the barracks, could she? But where else could she go? She carried only a few coins. All her possessions were in her room. She had to return, even just to collect her things and to go and—

—and to tell Trainer Isabel that she was going. She could not vanish without an explanation. Trainer Isabel deserved to know one of her trainers was leaving.

For some reason this brought fresh sobs and she cried anew at the thought of telling her respected superior that she was going. That she needed to go. That she could no longer work with her beloved unicorns.

She choked and cried and pushed herself off the ground.

The walk down the mountain was cool and lonely. When she reached the town, the market was already starting to clear for the evening, and few gave her more than a glance as she passed. Still it somehow felt as if they *knew*, as if they could see it and turned away out of avoidance rather than busyness.

She went directly to Isabel's office at the end of one of the stable buildings, but she could not make herself knock. She stood outside, heart racing, throat closed against air, squeezing her eyes closed.

"Galyne? Come on inside."

The muffled voice made her jump, and she opened her eyes and stared at the door. Then she fumbled at the latch—fingers thick now with fear and shame rather than drugs—and went inside.

"Finally," said Trainer Isabel. "I saw you through the window. There's no reason to stand outside and work yourself into a lather. I know why you're here."

Galyne's heart froze. "You do?"

"I do. And I'm sorry to lose you, but I understand. You're certainly not the first."

Galyne stared at her, unable to breathe, unable to speak. "I—I'm sorry. I didn't—I didn't want—"

"I suppose we should have expected it, putting guards so close with our trainers, but it seemed a risk we needed to take."

Galyne began to cry.

"Now, there's no call for that," Trainer Isabel said, not unkindly. "Brandon and Erda were sad to go as well, when they decided together. It's a change, sure, but you knew it would be. Time to go forward and—"

"How did you know?" Galyne sobbed. It seemed suddenly important.

"Know? Rue came by this afternoon and told me."

Galyne's knees went weak. "No..."

"I was surprised, I'll admit. I didn't expect it of you. But—"

Galyne reached to the wooden chair before Isabel's desk and grasped the back for support. "What did Rue tell you?" she whispered.

Isabel hesitated. "That you and he had become lovers and that you wished to leave the stables."

This was worse, this was somehow worse, and Galyne could hardly force the words. "He lies."

Isabel frowned.

"He—" She could not say the words.

Isabel pulled a cable on the wall and went to the door. She caught it before it could open fully, blocking any view of Galyne, and instructed, "Bring me the guard Rue."

"That's ridiculous," said Rue. "It's beyond ridiculous, it's offensive." He faced Galyne. "If you think you can keep your position here by this, you're wrong. You've already lost your virginity. You can't get it back by sacrificing me."

Galyne shook her head, feeling as if she were drugged again. "That's not why I'm saying this."

"Then why are you saying it? You told me you wanted me. I believed you. Now you lie and say I did something awful."

"*You* lie! You *did* do something awful!" She began to cry.

Rue pointed at her. "You're a trained soldier," he said. "How would I be able to force you without at least a few bruises?"

"You hit me," she said. "Here."

"You fell on the mountain path," he said, his eyes wide and hurt. "You laughed and said you were fine. And you are a soldier, aren't you? I couldn't hit you once and incapacitate you, and not without doing a lot more damage."

"You drugged me."

"Now it's a drug instead of force? And I suppose you have evidence of that?" He threw up his hands. "This is ridiculous." He turned to the two town guards who waited silently beside the door. "I came here in good faith, and I find town guards waiting to arrest me because a wanton girl wants to change her mind and keep her job. Can I complain against her sullying my name?"

One of the guards shifted. "I don't know about that. You'd have to talk to a magistrate."

Rue looked hard at Galyne. "Maybe I will." He looked back to Trainer Isabel. "I've had enough and I think I've made my point. Is there anything else to this, or can I go now?"

Galyne looked at Isabel, hope and fear welling in her and spilling from her eyes, shaming her again.

Isabel sighed and nodded once, gesturing Rue and the guards from the office. They did not look back at Galyne.

Galyne stared at Isabel, feeling her mouth gape but unable to care. "How—do you believe him?"

Isabel sighed again. "It doesn't matter if I believe him," she said. "What's done is done, and makes no difference to my responsibility here. However it came about, you are no longer qualified to be a unicorn trainer, and I must let you go and find a replacement."

Galyne could not move, could not speak, stunned for the second time that day by a blow from a trusted friend.

"Go back to the barracks for tonight; we'll release you in the morning. And you already know, but stay away from the stables. It may be upsetting to the unicorns to note the change, and that will affect their bond with their new trainers."

Galyne only shook her head. *Nova... Reaver...*

Isabel pressed her lips together, and Galyne could tell she was fighting tears, too. She did not know what to think, but she was upset because Galyne was upset. "Go on, then. I'll see you in the morning."

Will you believe me then? Galyne asked silently, but she knew it did not matter. Isabel was right. How it had happened or what people believed was irrelevant to the unicorns.

She went out into the twilight.

The royal stables were surprisingly lightly guarded. The complex itself was gated and patrolled, of course, to keep anyone from creeping inside to set fire to the stables or work other harm. But once one reached the buildings themselves, there were few eyes or gatekeepers. Fully-trained war unicorns tended to be their own security.

So no one saw Galyne, wrapped in the striped woolen blanket she had kept about her since first returning to her room, carry her fire-safe lamp toward Nova's stall.

Trainer Isabel was right. The unicorns would be unsettled to find one of their trusted own suddenly something other than what she was. Even now she was moving fast down the aisles, passing stalls before their occupants could wake and recognize her.

But Galyne could not just walk away from the stables without looking back. She would miss all of them, but Nova especially. Nova had come for her when she was wounded in battle. Nova would not turn away from her now—would she?

If she did, Galyne did not know what she would do.

Without the unicorns, what would she be? A soldier, yes, but one trained to fight alongside war unicorns, not in the regular infantry. She might find a place in a support squadron.

And watch forever the beloved unicorns she could no longer handle working with a different trainer as Galyne went through foot drills at a distance.

She pushed the thought savagely away. There would be time for plans later.

She slowed as she neared Reaver's stall, and the big sea-dark unicorn was already awake and watching her approach. She hesitated, shifting the light to spare his eyes, and extended a hand toward him.

He laced his ears back along his neck and tossed his head with a squeal. The heavy half door shook with the resounding impact of a front hoof.

She drew back, her breath catching in her throat. Reaver was new, he did not know her so well, he was not familiar with night visitors or the lamp—

But they were all excuses for her ruined presence.

She almost did not go on to Nova's stall, but her charges were stabled together and she was already there.

Galyne set the lamp down in the center of the aisle, casting shadows over the stalls and grotesque parodies of unicorns on the rear walls of the stalls. Nova snorted. Galyne faced her, remembering the townswoman who had tried to pet the unicorn, remembering the bloody horn and the woman's scream and the panicked run for a doctor.

She had worked her entire life toward becoming a unicorn trainer and then becoming a better one. Rue had taken her integrity, her work, her *life* from her.

She reached for the latch and let the heavy protective door swing open. "Go on, then," she said. "Tell me."

Nova snorted from the back of the stall, the whites of her eyes visible in her dismay. Her ears alternated between flattened and pricked, and her breath *whuffed* through her nostrils. She pranced in place and then stepped forward, gingerly, as if the floor might shift beneath her.

Galyne felt the floor was unstable beneath her as well. She clenched her fists and made herself rigid so that she could not flee.

Nova gave a little squeal and lashed out with a foreleg, but it came nowhere near Galyne. Then the mare took another step and extended her neck, stretching toward Galyne from the greatest possible distance.

Her soft dark muzzle was so close, nostrils flaring wide and snorting out the offensive scent of her defilement. Galyne could reach out and touch it, feel the velvet warmth one final time. But fear kept her frozen in place, waiting.

Nova stepped forward, lifting her head high and dropping it so that her throat rested on Galyne's shoulder. She pulled, forcing Galyne to stumble into her muscular neck and chest.

Galyne stood frozen, hands against the sleek warm hide, and then she leaned into the mare. "You…"

Nova nickered and sang the low song of an equine greeting.

"Do you understand?"

The woman's voice made Galyne spin, her heart pounding. It was the sorceress, the woman who might have been Trainer Isabel's sister, the one who drew unicorns from the sea and sky.

"What are you doing here?" Galyne demanded defensively and pointlessly. The sorceress had more right than she did at this moment.

The woman came down the aisle with slow, even steps. "I thought you might come," she said evenly. "Isabel told me there were accusations…"

Galyne did not want to discuss this again, not now and maybe not ever. "And you came to watch if the unicorns would reject me? Would kill me?"

"Not exactly." The sorceress nodded toward Nova. "Do you understand what she says to you?"

"I know she has embraced me when she should not have."

"It is true she has embraced you, but it is not true that she should not have."

Galyne stared at her. "But—but unicorns accept only virgins. I know it matters, I've seen—"

"It matters," the woman agreed. "But not in the way you think it does."

"But I'm—I'm not—I'm not a virgin, not now."

"You are what you do. You are not what is done to you."

Galyne stared at her. Nova's head pressed heavy across Galyne's upper back. Galyne's hand slid across the mare's shoulder and ran over the knot of scar tissue. Her heart seemed to jump in her chest.

The sorceress nodded.

"But what about Reaver? He…" The words hurt, to describe how he had thrown his head and struck at her.

"Yes, Reaver. What did you expect? He is new, and if you had come any night with a lamp in the middle of the night, he would have been skittish and wary. And what has been done to you—of course he knows, and he is repelled and he hates it. But he is repelled by and hates what was done. Not you."

"Not me," Galyne repeated slowly. "Not me."

She looked toward Reaver's stall, and in the dim reach of the light she could see his head over the stall door, watching her and Nova, ears forward. She looked back, and the sorceress was walking away, silent and finished.

But her words remained. *You are what you do. You are not what has been done to you.*

Galyne traced the spear-scar. *You are what you do.*

"Survive," she said aloud. "Fight."

Galyne waited for Trainer Isabel early in the morning in the cobbled yard outside her quarters and office. All around her trainers, grooms, and tradespeople watched and went about their business and returned, curious, but Galyne ignored them all and waited. Eventually the stablemaster would come outside and see Galyne mounted on Nova without tack or harness, with two more unhaltered unicorns flanking on either side. And she would understand.

They waited, and people filtered through the yard in an endless stream of morning activity. Then Nova shifted beneath Galyne, and she tightened her seat. On either side of her the unicorns snorted or stirred restively. Galyne twisted a hand into Nova's mane and looked to each of them. "Easy," she called. "What is it?"

Reaver stamped and tossed his head. She followed the direction of his gaze and saw Rue.

He was staring at them all, disbelief and anger mingling in his expression. He had needed to ruin her, and he had not.

But he had angered those nearest her.

Reaver launched himself into the air with a furious warning buck and an angry squeal. Rue blanched and started backward, but he could never be fast enough.

"Reaver!" Galyne shouted.

But the unicorn was already in motion, pounding after Rue who turned and fled in frank terror. Onlookers shouted warnings or screamed as Reaver's head snaked out and seized the man's shoulder, lifting him and flinging him hard to the side. Rue flew flailing through the air and sprawled on the ground.

"Reaver, no!"

The unicorn hesitated, just long enough for Nova and Galyne to reach them. Nova's shoulder slammed into the other unicorn, knocking him aside. Galyne half-slid, half-fell to the ground to drag Rue away from them.

But Nova wheeled back and, pinning her ears to warn Reaver away, drove her horn down and forward.

"No!" Galyne threw herself against the mare's chest, trying to push her backward with her own inadequate weight.

Rue screamed in terror—but not in pain, because the tip of Nova's horn pressed the hollow above his collar bone and then stopped. Galyne looked down and back as she leaned against the unicorn.

Trainer Isabel had burst from her door and was already running toward them. Others were gathering tentatively around, trying to decide whether approaching would push Nova into the final stab.

"I'm sorry," whispered Rue hoarsely. His eyes never left Nova, did not so much as flick to Galyne. "I'm sorry."

"Step back," Galyne told Nova, pressing the mare's shoulder, looking away from the terrified man on the ground. "Step back."

Nova's ears flattened and she snorted her protest, but she took a long step backward and raised her head.

Rue might have survived if he had stayed still. One of the other trainers was already reaching toward him. But Rue pushed upright and rolled to his feet.

Reaver screamed his fury and thrust.

His tremendous power and Rue's own momentum pushed the horn deep, and Galyne saw the instant Rue died.

"Reaver!" she screamed.

The sea-foam mane rippled as the unicorn struck off the deadweight with a front hoof and threw his head. Snorting, he gave another indignant buck and then cantered across the yard, scattering spectators.

Two bystanders knelt beside the discarded Rue, checking for life, but Isabel turned her eyes on Galyne and Nova. Galyne stared back in dull horror. She clenched Nova's mane as if it were a line keeping her above water. She felt as if she should be crying—she wanted to be crying—but her body refused to cooperate. "I didn't mean…"

"I know," Isabel said. "We know."

"Trainer Isabel," called someone from beside Rue's corpse. He held up a piece from the spilled pool glinting around the body. "This is Scapian coin."

The words hardly penetrated Galyne's hearing. She stared after Reaver, who had come to stand at the far side of the courtyard where the other unicorns waited restlessly. "I should have stopped—"

"He's not fully trained," interrupted Isabel, "and you were holding Nova, and he was presented with the enemy who injured his trainer."

Galyne's breath caught.

Trainer Isabel looked at each of the unicorns, completely at liberty and unconstrained, and nodded once.

Galyne licked her lips and pushed the words from her tight throat. "I did not understand at first. Do you understand?"

Trainer Isabel smiled very faintly. "It is a truth with a terrible, terrible price. But it is still truth. You are what you do."

Galyne swallowed. "I train unicorns for war."

Isabel nodded. "You do."

RIDERS IN THE SKY
V.F. LeSann

Peregrine's hooves tore gouges out of the packed desert sand, sending up eddies of dust in their wake. Bending low to his neck, the Rider glanced over her shoulder. The ghost-storm roiled up behind them like a dark ocean wave, low and heavy in the sky. A rumble of thunder sent a bolt of fear through her bones. The storm would be on them before nightfall.

Peregrine's mind spoke into hers, tired but reassuring: *Calm. There will be shelter.*

For three days they'd thundered across the desert with neither rest nor drink, skirting ghost towns full of empty bandit-hives and rot. The sun-scorched land was a museum dedicated to the Fall; skeletons of electric cars long since scavenged and the burnt husks of solar-cycles littered the desolate landscape, artifacts of a time of peace, plenty, and technology.

They surged over the crest of a steep dune and Peregrine's plan revealed itself in the cracked valley below: a small settlement tucked in the shadows. Buildings surrounded by a circular stone wall topped with barbed wire coils offered a cold yet clear warning. She recoiled from the cross-tipped spires towering like sentries, threatening to pierce the clouds if they dared to sling too close.

Calm, Peregrine soothed again. *This place will do. It is very round, like an apple. I like it.*

She sighed. They belonged here even less than they belonged in the barren wastelands.

Before she could attempt to thwart Peregrine's stubborn horse logic, the storm growled and a crimson flash of lightning cracked over the desert like a whip. The sound worked its magic, turning the memory of old lashings into fresh blood. Pain scalded her back and the Rider wailed, the smell of burnt flesh stinging her nostrils.

Her hand shot to the searing heat at her shoulder. Gritting her teeth, she wiped her blood-sticky fingers on her shirt.

There was no divide between Rider and horse; what was hers was also his, including the wound that blistered across her spine. No further words were needed and they hustled down to the shadow of the village.

The wrought-iron gate stood open, yet was as unwelcoming as the spires that hailed the skies. She dismounted and led Peregrine in, his metal hooves striking sparks on the stone.

People milled about on the dirt streets, stealing glances that stabbed heavy judgement into the heart of her. *Stranger. Outsider.*

Do not fear, Peregrine spoke silently. *It is me they are looking at. I am a very handsome horse, you know.*

Smiling, she gave his neck a rub, running her hands through his smooth obsidian hair, doing her best to hide the fresh blood from his back. "C'mon, let's get a roof over our head."

Peregrine had led the way across the desert but the duty of shelter would fall squarely to her. Any knowledge she had was fragmented wisps of memory, floating without context like clouds in the sky.

She tried to focus: getting out of sight, a hot meal, a cold drink. Best as she recalled, taverns served as the tipsy hearts of these ragtag settlements. So she followed the sound of a guitar to a two-storey wooden building at the end of the main street. It was dominated on one side by a freshly painted church whose steeple stretched above the other roofs like it had something to prove. But the paint wasn't fooling her; she could still see where the old marquis used to light up the night's entertainment.

Behind them, the black tempest had risen above the dunes,

pressing closer. Steeling herself, she walked into the tavern like she belonged there and Peregrine followed, his hooves clattering noisily on the boards.

The guitar twanged into silence and a thick-shouldered brute stormed towards them, hands up like he was ready to push them right back across the desert.

Her hand slid to the pistol tucked inside her jacket, and she braced for a blow.

"You can't bring that rig in here, girl!" he exclaimed.

Confused, she glanced to her boots. She wasn't tracking any mud, best as she could tell.

"Your *horse!*" His voice cracked on a note of wild disbelief. A couple patrons snickered and a satin-clad blonde leaning against the bar laughed out loud. "I don't know who the hell you think you are but…"

The Rider took a mental cue from Peregrine and read the dirty label on a bottle of liquid amber that'd caught his eye. "Hennessy," she said, warily at first, testing the word. Then repeated it, as much to herself as to the barkeep. "My name's Hennessy."

The brute folded his arms. "I don't give a good goddamn what your name is—get out of my bar!"

Peregrine blew out a breath, hot on the back of her neck. Outside, the storm snarled, thunder and ghostly hoofbeats echoing through the valley.

"We just need a roof 'till the weather passes, that's all. We can pay."

The bartender's eyes flicked to the place where Peregrine's blood had begun to drip-drop in dark spatters on the floorboards. "We don't have any vacancies."

"Don't have any?" The bar was sparsely filled and the second level lined with numbered doors.

The mental link between horse and Rider buzzed with mutual anger—if anyone was going out in that storm, it was this man.

Together, they took a step forward.

The ashen-haired woman set her glass on the bar with a sharp clink, loud enough to send a ripple through the tension.

"Well now, let's not be too hasty, Sergei. Not all of us have enough coin in our pockets to be as fussy as you." She dipped a shoulder so her knit shawl slipped down, accenting the low cut on her dress, and dangled a key from her finger. "I've got a room if you've got coin, and are looking for something a little extra?"

Peregrine pressed his nose into her back. *Tell the shiny-dress woman yes. They're too close.*

A crack of thunder sealed the deal. "All right."

The barkeep shook his head. "No. Delia, no. I'm not selling her a room."

With a flap of her hand, the woman sashayed up to them, all eyes fixed on her. The blue shimmer of her dress mingled with black lace; she was strapped in so tight the Rider wondered if she could even draw a full breath.

The woman's ocean eyes slid from the Rider to Peregrine. "Stables are behind the bar. Get this handsome fella settled and then meet me upstairs. Room Six."

I'll be fine, Peregrine assured. *I'll be close.*

And you trust her 'cause she said you're pretty, the Rider mentally grumbled, earning a nicker of amusement. She mumbled her thanks to the woman, snatched the key from her like a lifeline, and turned to hustle to the stables before the storm hit.

The rain was relentless by the time Peregrine convinced her to leave and take her own shelter. The miasma of sulphur and brimstone hung in the air like a blight, choking and blinding anyone foolish enough to still be outside. She shoved her way past the barkeep as he boarded the door against the whipping wind and rain flooding the sandy streets.

His glare followed her up the stairs as she rounded the balcony to room number six. When she opened the door the soft scent of flowers and perfume caught her off guard and she stumbled, tangled in sensation.

Delia was seated at the vanity. She glanced back at the Rider through the mirror as the door closed. Her hair was loose now, ivory and sand coloured curls tumbling over her shoulders.

"Now I can't decide," she said, flicking a coat of red over her lips, "if you've got the biggest cojones I've ever seen, or if you're just plain stupid."

The Rider pressed her back against the door, tense and wary. "Maybe neither."

Delia pursed her lips. "No, I don't think so. Walking in here with a stallion as midnight black as the ones from the storms? That either takes balls or stupidity, sweetheart. In these parts, people show discretion."

She gave the Rider a slow studying glance in the mirror. "I've known women like you before. I'm not going to berate you with the usual questions. I don't care what wind blew you here. I've got no stock in secrets. But I protect me and mine, so the only thing I'm gonna ask is what business you've got in this town. And you'd best speak true."

"Shelter," she answered. "I'm only here for shelter."

Delia's look softened, and she spun around to regard the Rider directly, revealing the double-barrelled shotgun on her lap. She put it to the side and gestured to a bedside table which held a bottle and some bread. "Well then, Hennessy. That'll be forty coin for your share of food and drink, and the room I didn't sell you."

Without argument, the Rider handed over the money.

Delia wrapped a heavier cloak around her shoulders. "Believe it or not, I've known a few women in my day who named themselves from a bottle in a pinch. You're the first Hennessy though."

Hennessy tore into the food like a starved animal. She couldn't remember her last meal. The drink warmed her insides and washed the taste of dust from her throat. She could feel Peregrine sating his thirst with clean water as well.

The storm shook the tavern as it descended into the valley, drowning out most conversation between the women. Jovial whoops mingled with the wind and the distinct sound of iron hooves within the thunder. The hissing crack of a whip. Her shoulder ached fiercely.

The cacophony persisted for what seemed like hours and Delia eventually got to her feet, peering out through the boarded window.

"Should've been done by now," she murmured. "Clouds are dipping low. Looks like we're in the middle of the warpath."

Her voice trailed off as she peered closer, her eyes widening in shock, oblivious to the boards bowing near her face.

Hennessy leapt to her feet, pushing Delia to the ground as the wood splintered. Delia's scream was punctuated with another shout from within the tavern. She stayed crouched low, guiding Delia to the door as the storm whipped through the broken window.

"Delia?" someone bellowed, followed by the sound of snapping wood and another scream from a neighbouring room.

Hennessy kept Delia shielded as dusky wisps of cloud seeped into the room. She heaved the door open and launched them both onto the landing, slamming it closed behind them.

"We're all right, Sergei!" Delia yelled, finding her voice. "Damn it." She fumbled to tear the hem of her dress with shaking hands.

Instead, Hennessy pulled a handkerchief from her pocket and dabbed the blood dripping down the side of Delia's face.

"I thought I saw a boy in the storm. West Osmond." Delia winced at Hennessy's touch, and took over, pressing the cloth firmly against her temple. "You can't believe what you see. Sometimes the storm shows you things. Things to make you come out and get caught in it."

Hennessy steadied the other woman and hustled down the stairs. A prickle of fractured memories made Delia's suspicion feel true.

"I'll be fine," Delia assured. "We've got a bunker beneath the floor, but Sergei isn't going to let you in after how the two of you got off." Wind whipped through the exposed bar, slamming doors and shaking rafters. "There's a tunnel, under the last table on your right. It leads over to the church. Father Monaghan will let you in. He can't say no if you ask for sanctuary." She gave a wry smile. "Old custom, but useful for us shadowy women."

Delia quickly unfastened her cloak and tossed it to Hennessy before standing on her own strength.

"Take this and stay outta that storm, you hear?"

Hennessy clasped the cloak around her neck, running across the empty bar, and hauling chairs aside until she found the entrance to the tunnel. Slamming it closed above her, she fled into the earthy darkness.

Are you safe? Peregrine's panicked thoughts flooded her mind. *Has the wind blown you out to them? You are very small, with only two legs...*

I'm safe, she thought back. *Are you?*

She could feel relief wash over him. *Yes, but they are close. Looking. Hunting. I have convinced the other horses to stand around me, so we can shelter like a herd.*

Clever boy.

Hush now, they will sense us if we keep speaking.

The sound of heavy footfalls overhead froze her in place. She held her breath, hearing the jangle of spurs, and the clack of hooves. A flurry of dirt fell from the roof, followed by a guttural snarl as the patrol moved along.

Pressing her hands against the cool earthen walls, she crept as quickly as she could until a wooden doorway emerged from the darkness.

She stopped, catching her breath to ease her electric nerves. Fear boiled in her belly as she hesitantly touched the entrance. Maybe she'd be struck down the moment she stepped into the place of worship.

In a lull between gusts and the cries of the nightmare steeds, she heard it: the unmistakable sound of a sob. Not from ahead of her, but above.

Shit. She forced the door open, throwing her shoulder into it until something let go with a splintering sound. She barrelled into a dimly lit cellar, dread melting into determination.

"Excuse me, that was bolted closed." A boy dressed in black strode to meet her, a thin candle lighting his shocked face in flickers. "If you want entry, you knock. Perhaps a provincial concept, I know, but…miss? Are you listening?"

Hennessy pushed past, sending him stumbling into a small shelf of books. The cloth of his robe brushed her arm and she felt a sting of heat strong enough to burn: his clothes were blessed. Clenching her jaw, she started up the stairs.

"Sorry, kid. I need your priest. Right now."

The boy stomped after her. "And who the hell do you think you are? I'm not responsible for lodging every vagabond Sergei gets doe-eyes for."

Hennessy glanced back. "Did you just say hell?"

The boy put a hand on his hip, fingers drumming. "*That's* the part you listened to? Congratulations, you've found the priest. And if 'hell' shocked you, just wait until I tell you to scamper back to wherever the fuck you came from."

"You're Father Monaghan? Oh, come on…"

The boy had some height on him, but it only made him gangly without the muscle of a grown man. Trimmed roan hair, without a wisp of beard, the kid didn't look more than fourteen. Her eyes fell to the dusty white sash at his neck and she groaned.

"I don't dress like this for the sake of fashion," he answered crisply. "And I'm going to ask you *again*…"

Hennessy dragged her hand through her hair. "Sanctuary, alright? I'm asking for sanctuary." She jogged up the rest of the stairs. "And if you're the priest, we've got work to do."

"Sanctuary doesn't mean you own the place! Where do you think you're going?" He scampered after her. "There are demons up there."

She spun and stared him down. "I need sanctuary, but not near as bad as you need me right now. There's a kid caught outside."

The priest hesitated then reached past her and unlocked the trapdoor.

"You'll die out there." He trailed her past a modest altar and down the aisle of the church.

Religious symbols lined the alabaster walls, carved into every board, dusted in black charcoal: crucifixes, Celtic crosses, stars of David, runes, sigils, evocations, and hundreds more. The holy equivalent of 'armed to the teeth.' It made her skin itch just looking at them.

"I'd bet neither of us is gonna leave a kid to those starving wolves." She tightened Delia's cloak, securing the hood to shield her face. "Considering you're about twelve, and think you're dealing with demons, I'll nominate myself for the job."

I need a favour, big guy, she thought to Peregrine, smiling as he acknowledged her intention, riffling through her thoughts on the wave of their connection. "Take off your robe," she ordered the priest.

The boy's eyes bugged and he clutched the front of his garment like a maiden about to be ravished.

She rolled her eyes. "I need your robe, not your virtue."

The child is near some crates. Peregrine sent her the image: a barren corner with heavy metal boxes toppled to the side. The boy was tucked between them trembling, his hands balled at his mouth.

I know this could ruin everything for us...

If they find him, they will destroy him. He is too small to be a rider. His horse would be a pony. Peregrine sent her the full force of his

101

determination.

She nodded. Their minds were made up, but damn, if her belly didn't twist. The priest was down to jeans and a tee-shirt, fussily folding his robe. "Give it here. When I say, open the door, then shut it quick behind me. I'll come back with the kid, or not at all."

Father Monaghan handed the garment to her. She winced, her skin blistering under the weight of the blessed cloth.

Now, Peregrine urged. *Run now.*

"Open the door and wish me luck," she said with a grin.

Father Monaghan hauled open the door and whatever he said—luck or good riddance—got swallowed up by the storm as she tumbled out into the boiling darkness.

She flung the robe into the churning gale. It billowed and flared like the Devil's own bat and gunshots cracked through the clouds. The posse rushed towards the bait like ragged shadows. Keeping low, she sprinted in the opposite direction.

A whip of fire snapped from the iron gate and her knees turned to dry sand.

The large one rides tonight. Peregrine's thoughts prickled with fear.

She sent him all the courage she could muster, and hastened her pace.

The boy was right where Peregrine said he'd be, audibly whimpering. How the riders hadn't found him yet baffled her.

They weren't looking for him, Peregrine reminded.

The child cowered in the darkness, scampering backwards.

"You don't know me," she whispered, "but I know you, West Osmond. Father Monaghan sent me to get you safe."

He gave a small nod, and Hennessy scooped him up in one arm. Crouching in the shadows, she waited, feeling Peregrine's hesitation.

The large one has come beyond the gate to look at the black dress you threw. His back will be to you, but you must be swift.

Neither of them spoke their fears, aligning their breath and heartbeat. When it was time to run, she knew it.

She sprinted for the church and muscle-memory took over, her body recalling something she'd forgotten. Moving like a ghost, she blurred from shadow to shadow. Her blood burned like fire, driving her on faster than ever, until they reached the church.

The door was flung open from within and she tossed the boy inside, as light flashed behind her.

Dodge! Peregrine wailed.

She hit the dirt as the whip cracked above her. A tendril of fire forked down like a snake's tongue to lick her from forearm to shoulder, sending sparks spiralling like fireflies. She clutched the dirt, gasping, as the scourge zipped back, recoiling for another strike.

"Got us a filly out in the open, boys." The voice boomed through the storm. Her soul shook, pulling towards the sound.

She heard the whip release again and pressed her face down as hands tightened on her cloak. She slid through the dirt...forward, not back...and then kicked frantically trying to scramble inside. The stone floor was shockingly cold against her burnt hands.

The slam of the rune-etched door echoed through the church. Someone hauled her to her feet, but her mind reeled with more lashings: memories of hungry flame shifted into fresh wounds, and she stumbled. Thin arms caught her and the priest blurred in and out of focus while the church quaked around them.

The last thing she saw was West Osmond on his feet, little legs pumping as he ran for the cellar door.

The rush of warm air near her ear jolted her from a fever dream. Breath lodged in her throat, and she thrashed in panic, soreness bursting through her stiff muscles.

The soft velvet of a horse's muzzle pressed against her cheek.

"Peregrine," she breathed, sagging with relief.

Her vision adjusted to the pale glow; she was back in the church's underground chamber. A single candelabra cast inky shadows over the congested bookshelves. Father Monaghan sat at a small table, edgy and watchful.

Hennessy pulled her arm to her chest, finding her hand wrapped in bandages, instead of the shackles she'd half-expected.

"You said they weren't demons."

She propped herself on her elbows with a groan. "Yep. That'd be on account of them not being demons."

Father Monaghan rinsed a bloody cloth in a bucket of water. "I was taught they were demons..." He broke off with a pleading look. "Priest Yano wasn't able to finish my training before she..."

"They're damned souls," she offered. "Demons are wild. The damned herd demons—not the other way around."

"Of course. They're damned," the boy whispered.

Silence settled and she ran her hands through Peregrine's soft hair, feeling the tingle of the ointments as they nursed her wounds.

The cellar door creaked open and Delia descended the concrete stairs into the chamber, a plate in each hand. Her face had some scratches, but she looked heartened, dressed in her silks, her curls all pinned to her head. She passed a plate to the priest and set the other down on Hennessy's cot.

"You've got to be starving." Her eyes lit on Peregrine as she pulled a red apple from her pouch. "I hear horses like the red ones."

Peregrine gave an approving snort. *I like her!*

"Me too," Hennessy replied quietly.

Delia tossed the apple to Peregrine and made a space for herself on the cot.

"Any word from the masses?" Father Monaghan asked between bites. "Aside from the usual accusations of madness, of course."

Delia pulled an amber bottle from her bag. "People are scared, Sebi. But no pitchforks or torches yet." She took a drink before handing the bottle to Hennessy.

"Don't priests lead the witch-hunts?" she asked, enjoying the warm sensation of liquor on her tongue.

Delia chuckled. "Some priests operate on a 'burn first, ask questions later' method. Sebi dances to a different drum. He's bought you time, if nothing else."

Hennessy offered Father Monaghan the bottle. "Well then. Much obliged."

He took the bottle and tipped it back with practiced ease. "One does not squander an offer, be it of asylum or wine." The priest took another drink, studying her. "You're one of the riders from the storm, aren't you?"

"We were." Hennessy reached for the bottle.

He nodded, handing it over. "And what happened last night...that was because of you."

Peregrine grunted, scuffing his hoof hard enough to kick up sparks.

"The part where we saved that kid's life?" Hennessy snorted. "Yeah, that was us."

Father Monaghan shook his head. "I meant no insult. We've never had them strike directly before. Terrorizing, yes, but..."

He's trying to ask if they will be back for us, Peregrine clarified.

"They're on the hunt. That's what they're made for." She sighed, putting a hand on Peregrine's nape. "Search and seizure. Rogue demons, the fallen, whatever they're told to pursue. So yeah, they'll be back like a lynch-mob."

The priest chewed his knuckle, frowning. "But if they get you and your horse, that will end their quarrel with our town?"

Delia scowled. "Not an option!"

"Not likely. They've got your scent now. Besides, Peregrine and me don't wanna be riders no more."

A hazy image surfaced of the times between the rides. Long tables laden with rotting meat, drink that didn't quench thirst, and huge billowing fires. Debates on Odin versus Yahweh, pantheons or a high god. Fantasies of second chances. Memories of loves lost. Regrets.

"It's not the same for everyone," she said quietly. "Sure, some were malicious bastards making deals in the dark, but some were just hollowed out shells of people, not livin' while they were alive. And some were just the luck of the draw. Like the kid almost was."

A sharp knock made them jump. Sergei stuck his head through the broken wooden door. "Trouble, Sebastian. The clouds rolling in. Black as hell with fire all through them."

"Get everyone inside, tell them to batten down again," Father Monaghan said, calm as quiet water. "I'm praying on the matter."

Sergei shot Hennessy a glare before swinging back into the tunnel. Delia took another drink. "Praying on it? You have a plan."

He offered a half-smile. "Retribution. The city, not the concept. A broken-off rider could mean salvation. They can hold off the storm at Retribution and distribute the information to other cities. Give us a fighting chance."

But this village will die, Hennessy thought. *That's not a plan. It's a death sentence.*

The boy-priest thinks more lives will be saved if we leave them to die here.

Delia, pale and grim, straightened Hennessy's collar and fussed with her bandages. "You stay ahead of them."

"But…"

"Sebi will get you out of town."

Delia hauled her in with a tight, unexpected hug that ended Hennessy's protest.

"What you did for that boy, we ain't gonna forget. You give us something to believe in." When she pulled back, her eyes were shining but the set of her mouth was grim determination. "Ride like hell. And don't look back."

They rode with speed they hadn't matched in a lifetime. It'd be a five-day ride to Retribution, with thunder at their heels and the villagers' lives heavy on their shoulders.

Father Monaghan had stolen a precious moment to speak with her before they left. He'd been silent and pensive, but at the gate, the words tumbled out.

"My heart needs to know about the storm's purpose, Hennessy."

She studied him, feeling Peregrine weigh his sincerity and find him worthy. The more time she spent with him and Delia, the more the fog surrounding her mind lifted. She and Peregrine were coming back to themselves.

"Before the Fall, times were good for the posse," she told him. "We had a purpose. Saw the sunrise sometimes. I wasn't askin' for much in my penance. But afterwards, everything went to shit. We had no purpose, no one to keep our reins tight. We started doing what we *could* do. We're supposed to be empty, but now we're looking for a way to feed that hunger. And it's makin' us crazy."

Peregrine rubbed his head against her leg. *So we left.*

"So we left," she echoed, holding back a torrent of sadness and heartache. "The Fall wasn't some apocalypse rained down to restore faith. The gods didn't open the doors to let hell loose; they just left. Whoever was guarding those doors isn't watching the locks no more. And the storm ain't gonna end until someone mans those empty thrones, locks those gates, and gives these things something to answer to. You see angels fallin' from the sky since no one's tellin' them to fly."

Father Monaghan grimaced in disbelief. "Priest Yano always believed it was faith that worked, not the deity."

Hennessy nodded, speaking Peregrine's thoughts. "The damned brought their faiths with them."

The priest's smile turned pained. "I believed her research. I *saw* a rider dissipate at the sight of an ankh."

The fact that Father Monaghan would die knowing the truth wasn't even a cold comfort.

The hurt was a fresh wound at her heart even after an hour riding. They were high on the edge of a dune, free from the suffocating sulphur from the storm, when Peregrine stopped.

With shared distress, they turned, looking back into the valley.

The clouds looked like a burning tornado in the wasteland, circling the town. Fire flashed, casting passionate silhouettes, and Hennessy's breath caught.

"We can't do this," she said, watching fire ensnare the clouds.

We cannot, he agreed. *They will be dead or damned before the sun sinks.*

"We have to go back."

Peregrine tossed his mane, catching the hues of sunset. *Guilt forged our shackles. Because we did nothing, someone died. And inside, we wanted to die too.*

"We're not that person anymore. We have a choice, and I choose to die with them."

Peregrine shook his head, reins jangling. *We won't hide again.* She felt his muscles tense and braced for his explosion into a gallop.

"Being damned ain't so bad," she said, pressing herself to his back, the wind tearing at her.

We have vantage and power, Peregrine offered. *And faith.*

"In each other!" she yelled, letting out a whoop as he took a shortcut across a gorge, leaping right across it.

Hanging onto his tangled mane, she smiled, feeling the strength return to her, the blood blazing in her veins.

As he hit the peak of his speed, fire streamed back from his eyes and nostrils, grazing her face. Sparks burst up from his hooves like a kicked hornet's nest, burrowing into her clothes, her hair, catching in Peregrine's mane.

When they both began to burn, something in the rider who named herself Hennessy sang out with wild joy.

They tore across the desert like a comet, burning a trail behind them and when they hit the miasma of the storm, it ignited around them.

The crackling clouds encircled the village like a blanket. The spires hung low, bent and deformed, and Peregrine slowed.

"That's new," she murmured, running her fingers through the dancing flames. His ink-black hide was now a shifting pattern like the coals at the heart of a blistering fire. The veins on her hands shone with light and she felt horribly, painfully, exquisitely alive.

I like it, Peregrine decided, snorting white flame. *I am magnificent in every colour.*

She smiled. "Let's find our friends."

The church loomed at the end of the main street, gnarled as though something had been pulled from deep within and bust forth from its belly.

Figures of shadow moved within a billow of black clouds that swirled through the town. The shapes of men and galloping horses, swells of flame and bursts wild laughter cut like a sharpened blade.

She kept her hand on her gun as Peregrine moved towards the mass.

When they reached the end of the road, the boiling shades solidified, their bodies a wall between her and the desecrated church. Fire swirled from their hands, forming into blades and other weapons.

The sea of damned parted and she froze, bracing for what came. She felt the heat rise as he moved through the crowd, her soul pulling toward him as it was meant to: follow the commander. *Follow Vayne.*

Peregrine shied beneath her, whinnying.

"Steady," she pleaded, her voice shaking.

The final layer of damned moved aside like good soldiers, and the boss gave her a gold-toothed grin, winding his fiery whip in his hands.

"Hello, darlin'," he said. "I was beginning to think you were avoidin' me and the crew." He glanced back and a delayed chuckle rose from the crowd. A massive steed appeared behind him, at least three hands higher than Peregrine, snorting black smoke.

"Nasty rumours goin' round. Talk of deserters. Brings out the beasts in us, you know." He rolled his neck, his powerful stare fixed on her.

Hennessy wanted to speak, but words wouldn't come. Peregrine's dread churned in her gut and the newfound fire around them wavered, suddenly as fragile as one of Father Monaghan's candles.

Vayne beckoned for her to join him. "Come here, sweetheart. Look at what you done."

Every part of her obeyed his command. She slid from Peregrine's back, taking his bridle in a numb hand, and followed. The damned closed in behind them.

Vayne pointed to the town's square and the black fog ebbed to reveal a wild bonfire. Father Monaghan was on his knees, bare, bloodied, and bound by a yoke. More townsfolk were shackled nearby, some sobbing and shaking with veins black as midnight—damnation perverting their souls. Others had the life torn from them, their faces warped in horror.

"Seems we can't damn a priest, but we can escort them out real slow." Vayne chuckled. He smoothed his hair ruefully. "Little shit puts up a mean fight, all kickin' and hair-pullin'."

Vayne's words pulled her from her haze and she stopped, reaching for Peregrine's mind, tearing him from the compulsion.

"You made me angry, sweetheart." Vayne removed his hat and fidgeted with the brim. "I thought we meant something to you. Now I've gotta remind you who you answer to."

He gestured and shackles of flame ignited on her wrists, links forming into a fiery chain that wound around his fist. Peregrine reared, letting out a panicked whinny.

She screamed as he yanked her to her knees, dragging her through the dirt, and lifting her to face him. "You got a lot of guts coming back here, after you betrayed us."

"I betrayed you?" she choked, teeth clenched. "It was you who betrayed what we were. The second they let our reins loose, you went for broke. Not all of us were pieces of shit when we were alive."

Growling, he flung her through the blaze, and everything was fire until she slid to a stop in the dirt. The cord on her wrists snapped tight, jerking her back towards the flames. Staggering to her feet she ran with the tension, jumping to burst through the inferno, smashing into Vayne and driving him to the ground.

The chain dissipated into smoke and she stood, digging her boots into the sand. Whispers erupted, silenced as the boss got to his feet.

A shimmer of blue satin snagged on the edge of the bonfire's metal pit caught her eye. Cold horror coiled in her belly. And like a match set to gunpowder, her fear burst into rage.

His whip untangled at his side and he scoffed. "That's what's gonna set you off? No need to worry, darlin'. We relieved her of that dress so the rest didn't get torn." He cracked the whip and fire lashed towards her.

Hennessy yelled, and Peregrine reared, but no pain came. There was shock written plain on Vayne's face. The flames had returned, bursting from her skin, and the coils of his whip fell broken, sputtering to limp curls of ash at her feet. Her skin blazed with the heat of her anger.

"Damn you, this isn't what we are!" she snarled, feeling Peregrine's strong body behind her, supporting her. "You tainted our purpose. Sending us to slaughter and terrorize whoever you saw fit, but we're not your trained dogs. We're not *yours*."

The damned shifted, not like a storm, but like a group of bodies. Murmurs rose, silenced by the crack of a shortened whip snapping overhead.

"You're gonna shut your mouth," Vayne growled, striding forward.

"You sold your soul," she spat, her fists clenched. "You're the one that's not one of us." Her eyes flickered to Father Monaghan, crouched on the ground with wounds as deep as bone. His eyes met hers, helpless and pleading.

Vayne's eyes glowed with rage, but he stopped when Peregrine reared again, fire flaring off him. Spinning, she swung herself back into the saddle, horse and rider united once more. The voices of the damned rose: a hum of uncertainty, a reminder of choice.

"Peregrine and I are damned, but we're not monsters." She spun with Peregrine, addressing the other damned souls, knowing that Peregrine had Vayne fixed with his eagle stare. "We don't have to be what he wants. Now that our chains are gone, we get the choice of the type of souls we want to be. We don't have to be cruel."

Another group moved in from the darkness, and Hennessy tensed. Ten more riders and mounts came into view, with Delia at their lead, clothed in a black jacket and riding pants. She levelled a shotgun at Vayne, her expression fierce. "Lady's right. Y'all have a choice. Not all of you are monsters. Your time's done."

This time, the voices were audible. *We're done.* The cloud began to thin—not like folks backing off, but like folks disappearing. Smokey forms spiralled into the night while others solidified and took back their human bodies.

Peregrine trotted over to Father Monaghan and Hennessy reached down to grab the yolk with a glowing hand. The wood charred and splintered, fracturing until he was able to shake it off.

"Stop!" Vayne bellowed. "You pathetic, mewlin' little bastards, *stop!*" He raised his whip—or at least the handle of it. The rest had dissolved into ash.

"They ain't got faith in you," Hennessy told him. "You're not their boss anymore."

"You," Father Monaghan growled, levelling a glare at Vayne, "aren't wanted here." Reaching up, he moved his white-knuckled fist into the light, revealing a clump of bloodied hair, black like Vayne's. *Little shit puts up a mean fight, all kickin' and hair-pullin'...* Lighting it on Peregrine's fire he circled the stream of smoke in the air. "Vayne, I banish you. Now, get the hell out of my town!"

Vayne howled, his form sputtering, crackling, and then vanishing entirely. His steed screamed its rage, torn away with him.

Hennessy slid down out of her saddle and draped her jacket around the priest, scared to ask him what faith had fuelled that move.

Peregrine thought nervously, *Perhaps he was angry about the nice church?*

All around them, the damned wobbled on legs long since forgotten. Mounts neighed and pranced nervously at the sudden shock of being *alive*. Some slunk away into the night, but not so many as she would've guessed.

Delia slid up beside Hennessy. "I always knew you were something."

Hennessy smiled, taking a deep breath. "Listen up," she yelled to the new posse, and Peregrine let out a haunting whinny. "This here's Father Monaghan. As far as you're concerned, he's your boss now."

Father Monaghan stared at her wide-eyed.

She pointed to the townsfolk. "Now help them, and clean up this mess."

Father Monaghan coughed. "This isn't done. I banished him, not destroyed him. I…"

"Easy, Sebi." Delia steadied him and gave Hennessy a pleading look. "What do we do now?"

Peregrine whinnied. *There are more damned. Demons. Even the angels. They'll need us.*

Hennessy smiled, drawing herself up. "So now we start livin'. One day at a time."

ABOVE THE SILVER SKY

Dan Koboldt

I turned fifteen on the day the rain stopped falling in the vale. My father had taken me up to the mushroom field, where thousands of colorful fungi basked in the gentle mist that drifted down from the silver sky. They dotted every ridge, white-caps and speckle-spreads, ruby tops, greenbulbs. All living in gentle symbiosis with the moss that coated the old bones of the valley's northern edge.

"How do so many grow in one place?" I asked.

My father's lips curved into his clever little half-smile. "You'd have to ask the fairies that."

"I've never seen any fairies here."

"Maybe you're not looking hard enough."

I crossed my arms and *harrrumphed* at him. Father loved to stoke my curiosity, to send me on endless searches for nonexistent faerie creatures in our little valley. Nothing that lived here on its own had true magic, not the people or the dogs or the endless flora. Only the horses did, and he wanted me to have no part of those. That's why we visited the mushroom field in the north end of our vale, not the southern prairie where the four-legged beasts dipped out of the sky to graze on the long grasses.

"What do you want for your birthday, Neshka?" Father asked.

There was nothing I truly needed. The rain that fed our valley gave us grain and berries and dew squash. We had sheep and hogs for meat, goats for milk. Bees for honey, and a never-ending stream of cool clean water. But mostly, we lived on the mushrooms. Soon my father would begin to teach me the arts of mushroom-tending, and one day I'd take over for him. I watched a trickle of rainwater as it meandered down a stepladder of red-and-white toadstools, each one just shorter than the next, and told myself it would not be so bad. But my lips betrayed my heart to him, and I said, "I want to see the horses."

"Neshka," my father said, in his sternest voice. "You know better than to ask for that."

"Please, father? I only want to look."

"That's exactly what your mother said. She only wanted to look, and then the horses took her away from us. Is that what you want? To leave?"

"Of course not." My voice sounded as small as I felt.

"Good."

A pool of vague sadness welled up in me, for I'd meant to fight harder to see the horses. He would say no, then I'd throw a fit, and we'd meet somewhere in the middle. Maybe that was creeping up to the edge of the prairie-lands to watch them from a distance. Maybe it was simply hearing the story once more about my mother and the time she rode one. But the hurt in his voice took me aback, and his accusation stilled the arguments upon my lips.

Not that it mattered anyway, because at that moment, the rain stopped.

The gentle patter of raindrops faded into silence, a numbness against my ears. The trickle of water on those red-and-white toadstools slowed, then died. My father and I looked at each other, then up at the silver sky in askance.

"Has this ever happened before?" I asked.

He frowned up at the sky. "No."

"What does it mean?"

"I don't know, Neshka." He crouched to inspect a fragile fan-top as it curled inward, barricading itself against the sudden lack of precipitation. Other mushrooms followed suit, offering a collective sigh as they tucked their beautiful colors away to preserve them. His jaw tightened.

"Maybe we should…check the prairie." I kept my eyes on my boots, afraid that they might give away my intent.

"Why would we do that?"

"To see if the rain has stopped there, too."

His jaw tightened even more, but he gave a sharp nod. "We'll have a quick look. As long as you promise not to go near the horses."

"I promise!" I said, a bit too quickly.

He turned his frown on me, stitching his eyebrows together.

"What? I promise." I said.

"Stay close to me."

We ran along the narrow, rocky trail that bordered the rim of the valley on the west-hand side. Little curls of smoke drifted up from the cluster of frond-roof cottages below. A mass of villagers milled about the small green in the center of the houses, all of them looking up. The rain had stopped there, too. That said something about what we'd probably find at the prairie, but I clamped my mouth shut against this inconvenient probability. I took two steps for each of my father's, but I kept pace with ease. Barely breathing hard. Running up here on the valley's rim was the closest I got to freedom.

The rock path widened. Little green tufts of grass appeared underfoot. They thickened and joined together, forming a great mat of deep green tufted grasses. We halted at the end of the path and spread out our arms, searching for moisture in the air. Nothing. The rain was gone. The prairie lay absolutely still. No breeze whispered across the tops of the grasses. Normally they reached skyward to embrace the falling moisture. Now they drooped downward in rainless despair.

My father spoke in a hushed but fervent tone. "How can this be?"

I felt something then, a stirring in the air. Not rain, but a fey thrumming of anticipation. Ripples formed on the silver-liquid sky overhead. Then they burst through it. Five, six, eight horses. They tossed their heads, their manes drifting smoke-like in the sudden breeze that carried them gently downward. My breath caught as I watched them glide through the air. Their hooves glittered in the pale sunlight. They landed light as feathers, and set about grazing on the downtrodden grasses. All but one, the horse with the bone-white band across her forehead. She raised her head and looked at me. Our eyes met, both of us unblinking. My heart thudded in my chest. I took one step toward her.

"That's far enough," my father said.

The moment was gone anyway. The white-banded horse turned a quarter away, and wandered farther off into the prairie.

"What will happen to them, without the rain?" I asked.

"Forget the horses."

"But they'll be all right, won't they?" I pressed.

"They can fly somewhere else to graze."

He didn't say the rest, but I figured it out on my own. We and the other villagers couldn't fly away to another place where the rain still fell. The silver dome encasing our little valley kept us sealed in, like the cap on a butter churn. Our sky was broken, but we could not leave.

We climbed down to the valley floor, where a growing unease settled over the village. Passersby asked my father about the mushroom field, and the prairie. Some even asked about the horses. But he had no answers for them, and that did little to sway the rising tide of panic.

"Neshka, go to your grandmother's house," he told me.

I groaned, because grandmother's musty cottage was my least favorite place in the village. Including the hog enclosures. I sulked as long as I could, but could feel his eyes on me all the way to her door. I knocked three times and let myself in. Stifling heat washed over me. She always had a roaring fire in the tiny hearth, despite the fact that the temperature in our little valley never wavered. It's like she felt a cold that others didn't, and chased it away with their sweat.

"Who is it?" Her voice sounded like the crumpling of old parchment. She sat in her wide chair-hammock by the fire, so close that it was probably burning her. Not a drop of sweat glistened on her wrinkled forehead.

"It's Neshka, grandmother," I said.

"What's happening?"

"The rain stopped."

"Where?"

I shrugged. "Everywhere. The mushroom fields, the village. Even the prairie."

She grunted and returned to her endless hidework. She was forever working little bits of goat-hide in her chair, twisting them into complicated knots or sewing them onto slightly larger pieces of hide. My requests for sheaths and belts and a leather satchel had gone unanswered, but she still worked the hide.

"Father says this hasn't happened before."

"What?"

"The rain stopping. Father says it's never happened."

"He wouldn't remember," she said.

"So it has happened?" I settled into the little cot opposite her chair and scooted it away from the roaring hearth. It still had me sweating from head to heel, though.

"The rain's always changing. Sometimes I think we're wrong to call it rain, anyway."

I smiled at her old-woman foolery. "What else would we call it?"

"Dribs and drabs. Lost water. Leakings from the other place."

"What other place?"

"The place where the horses go."

I gasped softly, because she'd mentioned the horses. Father had told her on multiple occasions never to speak of them. I knew I should be careful with what I said next. Careful enough to keep her talking. "They came today."

"How many?"

I brought up the picture in my head again, of their silvery forms drifting down from the sky. "Eight."

She muttered under her breath and shook her head. "Fewer every time. Soon there won't be any coming down to graze. Can't say I blame them. We started ignoring them, so they did the same to us."

"I don't ignore them," I protested.

She scoffed and waved me off. "You're just a girl."

"Well, one of them looked at me."

"Yeah?" She cackled. "When's the wedding?"

"I'm serious. She has a white band across her forehead, and we looked at each other for a long while. I think she'd have let me approach her, but…"

"But your father was there."

I sighed. "Exactly."

"He's looking out for his future mushroom-tender." She reached out and felt around for another loop of goat-hide that lay drying by the hearth. I nudged it in front of her questing fingers. She found it, and wrapped the end around her current tangle of hide-work. Her fingers moved with a nimble urgency that I'd not noticed before.

"Will we have mushrooms to tend, if it never rains again?" I asked.

"Probably not."

"I just wish I could go with them. And see the other side of the sky that they see."

"You'll have to do a little more than make eyes at one, for that to happen."

A shadow loomed in the doorway. "Neshka?" my father called.

"I'm here."

"Gather everyone you can and bring them to the mushroom field. Tell them to bring sacks or pails. Anything they've got."

"Why? What's happening?"

"The mushrooms are shriveling up in the dry air. We need to

harvest as many as we can." He ducked away and pounded on the door of the next little cottage. "Need you in the mushroom field!"

I stood and made to follow him. My grandmother's caught me around the wrist. "Ow!" She'd grabbed me like a cat catching a mouse, and as if she could see far better than she let on. "Grandmother!"

"Now's your chance!" she whispered. "Everyone's going to the mushroom field."

"Chance for what?"

"To ride that horse."

"Father said he needed me," I said.

"You want to pick dying mushrooms, or you want to actually do something that matters?" she asked.

My heart leaped at the thought of a moment alone with the horses, but a cold uncertainty crept up into my stomach. "But I don't know how to ride them."

She shoved the jumble of goat-hide into my hands. "You use this."

"Your sewing project? How is this going to help me?"

Her hands found mine, and slid them to a loop of hide at one end. "Behind the ears." She moved them down to another loop. "For the brow." My fingers slid down two flat pieces of leather to a short bar. The metal was cold. "Between the teeth." Then she wrapped my fingers around the long, braided ropes of hide she'd tied to either side of the metal. "In your hands."

"What is this thing?" I whispered.

"A bridle." She brought my hand to her lips and kissed it, then pressed it against her cheek. "Now, *go*."

I ran up the switchback-path that climbed the side of the valley rim, clutching grandmother's ridiculous goat-hide thing to my chest. Distant shouts and the odd wail of despair drifted to my ears from the right, where most of the village had gathered to save what they could from the mushroom field. They formed a human chain, passing fungus hand-to-hand down the slope to the dark shelter of the water-shed in the village. There were gaps in the line yet. I should join them and help out, like my father said. If the mushrooms were drying up, every second mattered.

But if the mushrooms were drying up, so were the grasses in the prairie. Once they were gone, so were the horses. "This is foolishness," I told myself. Madness, that's what it was. But my heart and my boots carried me to the prairie anyway.

It was dying, too. A band of dull yellow encircled the sea of emerald grass. The stalks in the outer-most plants had become dry and stiff; they crunched beneath my boots. The sound of it made me shudder. I pushed ahead into the still-soft greenery, towards the silver horses that grazed in the center of the field. They walked without their usual grace, stamping their feet. Snapping at one another. Eating so fast that sparks flew from their mouths. They *knew*.

Only one of them acknowledged my approach, the mare with the white band across her brow. She lifted her head and looked at me, then turned quartering-to. I forced my feet into motion. One in front of the other. The other horses took notice and moved away. Not entirely fearful but untrusting of my intent. No one had come this close before, not since my father took over the mushroom field. I crept within arm's reach, the bridle still clutched against my side. I'd never realized how *big* they were. Her midsection was thicker around than our oldest tree. My head barely came up to her shoulder.

"Hello," I said.

Her ears quivered and turned toward me.

"I'm Neshka."

I reached toward her, but too quickly. She snorted and lurched away. I stumbled back, caught my heel in the grass, and fell on my rear. It didn't hurt, not really, but the shock jolted me out of my dreamlike state. The silver mare loomed over me like a great shining boulder. She could trample me in an instant, if she wanted. She hadn't run, though, and I took that for a good sign. I clambered to my feet and reached out with an open palm. More timidly this time, and with a trembling arm that revealed my fear. She eyed it dubiously for a moment. Then she leaned down and put her head beneath my fingertips. Her head was cold as spring water, and the touch sent a tingling chill up my arm. I bit my lip against the gasp that wanted to escape me.

She took half a step forward, and lowered her head a little. I figured that was as good of permission as I'd ever get. I stepped up to slip the top loop over her head, but she shied away again.

"It's all right," I said.

She eyed me distrustfully, and snorted. Never going to happen. Now that I looked at it, the bridle seemed far too small to fit over her head in any case. Maybe Grandmother hadn't realized how *big* they were. Or maybe she'd given me the thing simply to get me up here. To put me face-to face with these magical creatures.

It would be just like her.

I tucked it into my belt and walked to the mare's midsection, keeping my hand on her side so she could track me. That's where my plan fell apart. I could barely reach the top of her back, much less pull myself up on it. I tried anyway. I jumped and threw my arms across her, but my hands slid back across her smooth silvery coat. I tried it twice and failed miserably. She snorted and stamped, growing impatient with me.

"Neshka!"

My heart sank. My father strode across the dying plains-grass. It was now or never. I jumped as high as I could and slung my arms over her back. Miracle of miracles, I held on. I tried to scramble up her side but couldn't pull myself. I wasn't strong enough. Then my hands started to lose their grip. I whimpered, and plunked back to the spongy ground. Father's strong arms grabbed me around my waist.

"No! Let me go!" I shouted. I flailed at him, but not enough to keep him from picking me up.

My world tilted. Tears blurred my vision. Then I felt something firm and cold beneath me, and a tingling ran up my back. My father's hands released their grip on me.

He'd put me up on the mare's back.

I sat there with my eyebrows up and my mouth hanging down, not daring to move. I thought maybe he'd eaten one of the silver-and-black mushrooms by mistake.

"The mushroom fields are dying," he said. "We'll be lucky if we can last a month on what we saved."

"I'm sorry, father. I just—I just wanted to see."

"I know, Neshka. You've got adventure in your blood. And they chose you, just as I feared they would."

"Who chose me?"

"The horses. Every now and again, they choose someone to ride them. I worried that this time it'd be you."

"But, why?"

He chuckled, but there was no humor in it. "I was in a pose like this twelve years ago, in this very spot. But it was your mother on the horse, asking to leave." His eyes grew distant. "You were little more than a babe, and I knew so little of children. I begged her not to go. For your sake, if not for mine."

"And you're telling me this *now*?"

"I worried if you knew, you'd let them choose you." He gave me his sad smile. "Now I realize that was meant to happen all along."

"Come with me," I said. "I'm sure she's strong enough to take the both of us." I patted her silvery back, marveling at the beauty of it. "Aren't you, girl?"

But he was already shaking his head. "The horses only ever take one. Besides, I'm needed here." He untied the goat-skin pouch from his belt. It bulged with lumpy shapes, and I glimpsed the rainbow-colored hues of my favorite mushrooms inside. "Take these. They'll keep for a little while, yet."

One of the silver horses made a long high-pitched keening sound. They lifted their heads, looking skyward. One by one, they heaved in a deep breath, and lifted up from the ground. The mare shifted beneath me, large and ponderous and impatient.

"I'll come back," I said. "Once I figure out how to fix the rain, I'll come back."

"It may not be something you can fix. If that's the case, you must keep going. Find some other place to live. A place with shelter, and food. And a sky that isn't broken."

He squeezed my hands in a gentle caress. A sob escaped my throat, and I threw myself over to embrace him. I'd have tumbled right back off the mare, if he hadn't caught me. He squeezed me tight against his cheek, which was damp despite the lack of rain. Then the mare lurched forward. She was leaving, with or without me.

Father pushed me back onto her and tangled my hands in her mane. "Go, Neshka. Go!"

I'd just found my balance again when the mare launched herself from the ground. My stomach shot up into my throat. I cast a frantic look up back over at my father, who stood with hunched shoulders in our dwindling shadow. I nearly fell off again, craning my neck to watch him. I straightened and tried to get my bearings. The other horses danced in circles in the air above us, gliding back-and-forth as they drifted ever upward. They reached the silver end of the sky and disappeared into it, like fish slipping back into their watery homes. The valley grew distant and nauseatingly small below.

I looked up again in time for the sky to swallow us.

The silver threshold held me in a dark, icy grip for three heartbeats that felt like an eternity. Then daylight bloomed on my face, and a wave of sweltering air enveloped me. We stood in a mirror-pool in a desolate muddy plain. Broken trees bordered the wide basin all around us. Not a speck of greenery colored the landscape. The sky was the color of cobwebs. The air smelled of rotting wood.

The other horses trotted to the slippery bank and clambered up it. They did not fly here, and I got the feeling that perhaps they could not. The air felt thick and heavy, like an oppressive blanket that pressed us to the ground. My mare began to follow. I gave an experimental little tug on her mane. She faltered mid-step, but pressed on. I pulled harder. She halted so fast I nearly flew over her head. Ripples flowed out from her hooves on the smooth silver ground, like tiny wrinkles on an old mirror.

An image began to take shape in my mind...water pooling here on the silver floor, flowing across it. Seeping through ever so slowly, to fall like rain on the tiny valley below. It all fit, or would have, if the basin weren't bone dry. I touched the side of her neck with my fingertips in a gentle request. She turned in a slow circle, while I took stock of the muddy shoreline. It rose up like a dark brown wall, ten paces high and unbroken entirely around the rim. Well, *almost* entirely. There was a gap in that dark line to our left, away from the direction the horses had gone. I steered my silver toward it and she moved forward. She knew my desire, almost before I made it plain to her.

The gap seemed impossibly far away. I urged her to go faster. First by thinking it, then by pressing my heels into her sides. She sped to a trot that jounced me up and down. Then a faster clip that nearly sent me tumbling off. I clenched my hands around her mane. Its familiar softness took my fear away. I leaned low against her, and pressed her sides again.

She leaped forward, front and hind legs moving together, eating up the ground in great strides. It was somehow easier to hold on, to press my body against hers and flow with the bounding movement. The landscape became a blur. There was only me and the mare's muscular back and the sparks flying from beneath her hooves.

We neared the edge, and sat up straight. She slowed to a trot, and I felt an odd pang of sadness that the air no longer rushed past my face. The gap grew before us. It was twice as wide as the mare was long. Steep on both sides, and covered in dried, cracked mud. But this was the kind of mud that knew water, and grew parched when that water was gone. A streambed. The mare hesitated, but I nudged her forward again with my heels. The clip-clop of hooves caught my ears. The other silver horses had followed us around the rim. They whickered at us, tossing their heads, prancing with a nervousness I knew I shouldn't ignore. Still, I pushed my mare onward, around a sharp curve in the streambed. We nearly rode right into the obstruction but she came to a halt as it rose up over us. One of the broken trees had fallen over across the stream, catching bits and pieces of debris until the entire thing was dammed. Only a trickle of water made it through, dribbling down the broken tree's branches to pool in the hollow beneath it.

"Steady, girl," I whispered, and pressed in with a knee to turn her alongside it. That was easier than using my hands, and she responded just as well. I grabbed a broken bough and tried pulling it free. The tree shuddered, but didn't move. I could feel the pressure on it, the force of the water waiting on the other side. *Our* water.

One of the horses whinnied. They looked over their shoulders at something I couldn't see. A breeze picked up, a horrible foul-smelling breeze, from the direction they were looking in. I slid down to the ground. My boots squished in the mud at the base of the dam. I tried pulling the tree loose again, but couldn't move it enough. Too little again. Too *weak* again.

There was a leathery vine wrapped around the trunk, the kind that grew up the sides of trees like heavy ropes. This one was thicker than my arm, and a length of it had come loose to lie in the puddle on the ground. I lifted it, tested the strength. It might do.

I scrambled up the dam enough to climb onto my mare's back again, with the vine tucked under my arm. There was enough to drape it around her neck, against her chest. I used Grandmother's bridle to lash it back together. Then I turned her away from the dam with a touch and a whisper. I pressed my heels into her sides. She took two steps. The vine went tight against her chest, and she hesitated.

"It's all right," I said, willing her onward.

The other silver horses would not wait. They turned and fled, thundering around the broken trees along the muddy bank. Mud flew from their hooves. The foul wind rose up and chased after them.

"Come on!" I shouted. Maybe a bit loud. It startled the mare, and she surged forward. The dead tree shuddered and groaned behind us. Then came a deafening *crack*, and it gave way. A torrent of water twice our height swept toward us down the streambed.

She bolted, scrambling up the sides of the streambed, nearly tossing me off while the water pounded down behind us, snapping at her feet. Five paces up, then ten. The mud-bank leveled off as we reached the top. She halted there, sides heaving, long enough for me to look back and watch the rush of water surge into the streambed and then flatten out to fill the basin. The broken tree had floated out on the initial surge and settled somewhere near the torrent. Far enough, I thought, that it wouldn't jam things up again.

The foul wind grew, and a distant roar rose up behind us. We dared not linger here. Yet as I turned to see where the other horses had gone, I saw that another basin lay on the other side of the mud bank from ours. This one was wider and more rounded than the roof that covered my little vale. The silver horses churned their way to its middle and dove, disappearing below the surface to some other fantastic world. Beyond that was another bank, and another basin, the water glistening under the faint light of the cobweb-sky.

I looked back to the basin with the broken tree, the one that formed the roof of my snug little valley. I pictured my father and the others raising their faces as the first drops of new rain fell. With one press of my knees, I could dip down and share that moment of joy with them. Help my father rebuild the mushroom field. Live the quiet life he'd hoped to give me.

Yet there was no way to know if the silver horses would return, since they'd watched the grass die. And they were my only escape.

I missed my father already, but he was right. I had the blood of the adventurer in me. I turned my mare back to where the other horses had gone. I touched my heels to her sides. She leaped forward, to where other worlds awaited us.

A Mother Unicorn's Advice to Her Daughter

J.J. Roth

Hide in plain sight. Let the dappled light through the forest canopy color your whiteness with camouflaging shadow. Let stillness be your friend when the hunter's horn or adventurer's voice carries through the vegetal quiet.

Breathe without sound. Depend on secrecy and stealth.

Once you are sighted, the hunt begins. Once the hunt begins, you are vulnerable.

Be generous, but circumspect, with your gifts. Dip your horn in struggling streams when no one is looking. Draw its healing point along the withered bodies of sick ferrets and ailing fawns. Lay its curative spiral against the breasts of lost, unconscious humans, but stay out of their healthy fellows' sight.

Cover your tracks as you leave. If caught, you're more likely to be destroyed than loved.

This constant hiding may make you feel unreal.

This is normal.

Seek the company of your own kind. They are stronger than they look.

Never let anyone tell you you're only a legend. Those who say such things feel helpless in their own lives, threatened by those who are different. They're the problem, not you. If you believe in yourself, that's half the battle won.

Never trust a virgin. And for the sake of all that is holy, never lay your head in a virgin's lap. You may be caught and butchered, your horn ground to dust and sold as a remedy by glorified carnival barkers.

This last warning may not be literally true—but it's good advice, anyway. Most likely, some bored pre-Freudian made up the whole thing.

But you never know.

When you're generous, helpful, and put others first, there are those who will take advantage.

Don't shave your chin whiskers or bemoan your lion's tail.

Don't expect rainbows to shoot out of your ass, tinkly music to play as your life's soundtrack, or sparkles to spray like pixie dust when you shake your mane.

These don't define unicornness. The sooner you internalize this and believe it, the more likely you are to avoid depression or an eating disorder.

Always remember: you are immortal, unless slain.

When in doubt, run like hell.

LADIES DAY

Susan MacGregor

"Just so you know, I'm placing two hundred crowns on your Dainty Dancer tomorrow."

Lord Henry Dinglecrumb loomed over Sissy, making her colour prettily. Sissy always coloured prettily. Me, he ignored entirely. "I pray she won't let me down." He punctuated this last statement with a bold wink.

Sissy lifted her chin defiantly. Under that false show of pride, I knew she was delighted. She had been angling to capture Lord Henry's attention ever since the opening of the Season, and though it was just May, she had already succeeded brilliantly. As long as Dainty Dancer won the Gold Cup on Ladies Day, Lord Henry's marriage proposal was sure to follow.

"If you have any doubts, perhaps you should focus your attentions elsewhere." Sissy dismissed him, glancing over the ball crowd as if seeking a less boring man.

With at least two hundred of Society's best in attendance, there were many who would approach her at even the slightest indication of interest. She was Lord Sutherland's only child, an heiress to a large fortune, with an impressive magical lineage to boot. She was also the classic English beauty—blonde, with fair skin and rosy cheeks. As for myself, I am dark-haired and a bit too tall for current tastes, her unmarried first cousin. I envied Sissy, but I knew my place and was resigned to it, always the spinster, yet content to remain her closest friend.

Lord Henry burst out laughing as if she had made the funniest jest, missing her with an overabundance of spittle and spraying me instead. I gritted my teeth and strove not to dab at my face. Sissy smiled coolly, pretending not to notice. His laugh reminded me of a braying donkey, and not the English kind, but something of lower quality—American or Spanish, perhaps.

"Oooh! Spirited! I like that," Lord Henry leaned in closer, probably to peek down her bodice. He smelled faintly of cigars and gin. Other than his devastatingly good looks and his father's fortune (although there *had* been rumours suggesting it was no longer as substantial as it was), I don't know what Sissy saw in him.

Someone cleared his throat behind us. Lord Henry spun about, causing his dark forelock to swing rakishly over his brow. I wondered how often he had practiced that move. Behind him, a tall, be-speckled young man of about thirty stood, his stance as awkward as a school boy's and his expression earnest.

"Charley, old boy!" Henry crowed. "There you are! I thought I'd lost you to those boring old tomes in the library!"

"Uh, no. I was just checking Sir Robert's collection. He had mentioned one of his texts displayed some unusual hieroglyphics…"

Henry grabbed him about the shoulders and swung him about. "Don't be dull, old man. You'll put us to sleep. Ladies, might I introduce to you Mr. Charles Cavendish?" We bobbed Charles a polite curtsy, which seemed to make him mildly embarrassed. Henry blithely carried on. "Charley, here, has been studying ancient Egyptian magic—curses and that sort of trash. His area is world mythologies. When he's not dusting off the shelves at the Ashmolean, he's slumming about Africa and Europe. Bit of a blue stocking, our Charley. We were chums at Eton."

Charles turned a darker shade of red. Henry had insulted him, calling him an old maid and an intellectual—hardly proper in mixed company. The Ashmolean was the University of Oxford's museum of art and antiquities. If Charles attended there, he studied with an exalted group of minds, indeed. I bristled, having been called a blue stocking, myself. I decided right then and there that I'd had enough of Lord Henry *Dinglebits*. Yes, I know, a childish bit of name-calling, but sometimes, one can't help oneself.

"How do you do?" I asked, ignoring Henry. Sissy parroted my inquiry. "Yes, Mr. Cavendish, how *do* you do?"

"I...ah, reasonably well, for the most part. Are...are you ladies enjoying the ball?" He was so nervous, perspiration dotted his brow. Truth be told, I find that kind of male response much more appealing than Henry's *braggadocio*. There is something honest and straightforward about it. I studied Charles more closely. Beneath the spectacles lay a reasonably handsome face, if rather serious in mien.

"Indeed." Sissy smiled at him winningly. Sissy always picked the weakest member of any male group upon whom to unleash the full force of her charm. A ploy to make Henry think he trod on unsteady ground. As for Charles, his mouth fell open in astonishment. Sissy's talent is nothing to sneer at. Her ability to enhance appearance, strength, wealth, or whatever she wishes, runs through her family's blood-line like gold through a California river. Similar types of power are wielded by all the noble families in Europe. As for my own meagre talent, it's of a duller sort—a pathological tendency to see the truth. Visions assail me, most unexpectedly.

"I've put two hundred *quid* on her horse," Henry informed Charles. "Why don't you ante up too, old man?"

If it were possible to die by degrees of mortification, Charles did. I didn't need a vision to tell me he didn't own that kind of largesse. As for Sissy, her expression turned sour. Either she didn't like Henry's use of common slang, or she sympathized with Charles' plight. I suspected the former, but that was unkind of me.

"Butter upon bacon! Look who's arrived!" Sparing Charles from answering and falling into slang herself, Sissy turned her back on the main door leading into the ballroom. "No, don't look!" she hissed, as we all glanced past her to where she had been staring. A tall, pale goddess stood there. She was dressed in the latest Mariano Fortuny from Paris, a tightly pleated blue gown edged with beading from shoulder to hem. A blonde officer waited on her in attendance. His gold buttoned uniform was weighted down with so much braid, it doubled his shoulders in size.

Despite her own Paul Poiret creation, I sensed Sissy was envious. As for my own dress, my last year's Worth was hardly worth mentioning.

"What are *they* doing here?" For some reason, Henry was also put out.

"Perhaps she grew bored of Monte Carlo. Or maybe they threw her out. One can hope," Sissy replied tartly.

"Who is she?" Behind his spectacles, Charles' eyes were round with curiosity.

"*That* is Her Grace, the Duchess Ragnhild of Norway." Sissy spat the name as if it were a lemon pit. "We were at finishing school together in Geneva. Much good it did her. Despite her blue blood, she's the worst sort ever! A cheat and a...a...trickster!" She was gripping her fan so tightly, I thought she might break it.

Years past, Sissy had confided in me about the unfortunate 'bare bottom' affair she had suffered, a practical joke orchestrated by the duchess involving lost bloomers, a cruel trip over an extended boot, and a rosy exposure for all in her vicinity to see. It was still sniggered about in certain Swiss quarters.

The duchess surveyed the room and brightened, seeing us there.

"Oh please God, preserve me! She's coming over!" Sissy was so tense, I thought she might crumble to dust at any moment.

"Ceeceeleeyah, is dat eeyou?" Ragnhild's voice was weirdly musical, singing as much as speaking her words. She reminded one of the Valkyries from a Wagnerian opera.

Sissy spun about, a dazzling smile upon her face. "Raggie! What joy! What brings *you* to the shores of our little Empire?"

I could feel the waves of her charisma as they crashed against

Ragnhild and the rest of us, a bulwark the duchess would find hard to breach. Henry seemed at a loss for words beneath such splendour. Charles looked ill. As for Ragnhild's escort, his jaw dropped as if beholding the Artic sun for the first time ever. Sissy noticed his reaction. It steadied her.

Ragnhild quirked her pale blonde head to one side. "I un'erstand eeyou have a leetle ponyee entered in de Gold Cup tomorrow, ya?" she warbled, unaffected by Sissy's display. "So do I! 'is name ees Golden Toof."

"Golden Toof?" It was such a ridiculous name, I couldn't help but repeat it.

"Ya, dat's right." Ragnhild looked as if she couldn't decide whether or not I had intended insult. "Toof."

"Tooth," her bulky chaperone corrected.

A look of annoyance flashed across her face. "Dat's wot I said, Bjarn. Toof." She turned back to us. "'e actually has a diff-er-ent name in our Noher-waay, but it is tooo hard for you Englishers to say."

"How charming." I didn't bother to hide my sarcasm.

"Ya. Eet is. And he weel win de Gold Cup tomorrow too, dat's for sure." She cast me an icy glare before turning to Charles. "You look like de smart one in dis group, Mister Spec-ta-cles. Why don' you place a bet on hiim? You weel win lots of money if you doo."

"I say!" Charles stepped back. Only the lower orders spoke of money, Henry notwithstanding.

"Or not. Iss your choice." Ragnhild turned to Sissy. "Goodbye until tomorrow, Cee-cee Pink Cheeeks. Let us talk off old times. Come, Bjarn. We musst ceercul-late." He bowed stiffly as she led him away.

Sissy was too outraged to speak. We eyed her in uncomfortable silence.

"Well I, for one, don't think that old nag of hers will be worth a fig!" Henry said stoutly. "Dainty Dancer will be a veritable Pegasus in comparison! What does Norway know of horses? Not a jot!" He reached for a silver flask from inside his suit pocket. My talent for sensing the truth flared. He was trying to placate Sissy, but deep down, he was worried he had bet on the wrong horse.

"We shall see who bests whom," replied Sissy rallying. She tilted her nose into the air then snapped open her fan to flutter it.

Something about her self-assuredness bothered me. It was a presentiment perhaps, or the premonition of a premonition. I've had such sensations before—they rarely foretell anything good. I didn't like it one bit.

Charles spoke up. "There is something odd in all this." An understatement, if I had ever heard one. "She has a taint about her that isn't...natural. Or perhaps 'taint' isn't the right word." His brow wrinkled. "A glamour? An aura? It feels old. Maybe something even beyond that."

I straightened. Was it possible I had finally met a man who had a similar talent to my own?

"Punch?" Henry pointed at the punch bowl, as if that were the answer to everything.

"I think not." Sissy dismissed his offer. "It's time Cassandra and I retired for the evening." She looked at me pointedly. "Come, Cass. We should go."

My heart sank. Why would she insist upon leaving, just as things were becoming interesting? More to the point, when I was finding *Charles* interesting?

"But the ball's only just begun!" Henry was frowning moodily. "The music's about to start...what about that dance you promised me?"

"I'm sorry Henry, but you'll have to find another partner for the quadrille. This evening has upset me terribly, and I must prepare for tomorrow." Sissy drew in a deep breath.

"Prepare? What is there to do?" Henry refused to be put off. "Your filly is running the race, dear girl, not you!"

"Nevertheless, I cannot stay." She swept away, her head held high and her nose in the air, towing me in her wake as only Sissy can do.

The next day found us both in better spirits. We had parted to our own suites at her father's estate the night before, but as I readied for bed, I was quite sure Sissy had not retired to hers. It was frustrating not knowing. My talent is unpredictable. The visions that bring clarity never come as I wish, so I had no idea what she was doing but I had a niggling suspicion she had roused the grooms so she might spend more time with Dainty Dancer. The horse is a beautiful bay, gentle yet spirited when there is need. Her timing on the home track had been good and she had an excellent chance of placing in the Gold Cup, although I doubted she would take first place. Surely, Sissy couldn't expect it, but the encounter with the duchess had upset her.

In any event, we dressed for the occasion, it being Ladies Day and the third of the running of the Ascot. And I must say, despite all the clever hats and beautiful day dresses that were on display, I do believe Sissy and I outshone them all. She wore a stunning creation of cream and aqua silk. Her Merry Widow's hat was festooned with ostrich feathers and ballerinas dancing about the brim in matching tutus—appropriate considering she was Dainty Dancer's owner. I, who had scrimped for the event, was even more ornate than my dear friend. I had purchased a deep yellow Poiret in the latest style: a lampshade skirt with matching tunic in gold and black. My *chapeau* spouted pyramids and a large crouching Sphinx. Initially, I worried that the cat looked as if it were attacking my hair, but Monsieur Poiret assured me I resembled a high priestess of ancient times. I allowed myself to be convinced. I also secretly hoped, with his interest in Egypt and hieroglyphics, I would run into Charles Cavendish.

I wasn't to be disappointed. Both Charles and Henry found us in the Royal Enclosure, having been issued invitations to attend by Lord

Churchill, as had we. I thought Charles looked very handsome in his top hat and grey morning suit.

"My dear Sissy!" Henry enthused, catching sight of her. "You look the jammiest bit of jam!" He caught her by her gloved hands. "Why, you're positively glowing! Isn't she *glowing*, Charley?"

Charles swallowed and tipped his hat. "Why yes, you do look very fine, Lady Sis…Lady Cecelia." He turned to me and his eyes widened in surprise. "And you too, Miss Cassandra! What an astonishing hat! My goodness!" He peered more closely at my Sphinx, adjusting a monocle. "Is that a small priest you having standing between your cat's paws?"

"It is." I smiled, glad he had noticed. I had asked Monsieur Poiret to add it, so it might draw the eye and not suggest the Sphinx was about to bite off my head.

Charles stepped back to take in my entire outfit. "And the glyphs about your tunic…!" For a moment he lapsed into silence, then read aloud the inscription there. "'There is no one who deceives who is not deceived, no one who does wrong who prospers at great length.' How amazing!" He met my eyes. "You *do* know that saying is from the Ankhsheshonq papyrus held in the British Museum?' Behind the monocle, an eye brow lifted inquiringly.

I couldn't help but stifle the tiniest bit of indignation. Did he think I was such a slave to fashion that I would buy such a thing without knowing what the words actually meant? I had Monsieur Poiret stitch them there. I felt a slight headache forming behind one temple.

"Oh, dear. I've put my foot in it. You must forgive me." He lifted his palms in supplication. "Of course you know. How very clever of you, Miss Cassandra. I had no idea we had…so much in common."

Sissy's expression was smug. "That inscription holds the secret to our Cassandra, actually. Polite company prevents me from telling you what it is." She smirked, toying with him while I blushed an unholy pink.

"I love puzzles." Charles regarded me with even greater interest.

Unfortunately, what had started as a dull throb behind my eyes was turning into a full-blown truth attack. I clutched my head.

"Are you all right, Miss…Cassandra?" Concern in Charles' voice.

Suddenly, the Royal Enclosure with all its racing enthusiasts disappeared. I found myself standing in Sissy's barn at the estate in Windsor, watching her stroke Dainty Dancer across her long, ruddy neck. Sissy was murmuring something. *Faster and better*, she crooned. *Faster and better*. I saw a bright flash arise from her. It ballooned and enveloped Dainty Dancer. The mare pulled up her head, snorted, and then pawed the straw as if she needed to run. Sissy gave a short, nasty laugh. "That'll show you, Duchess Potty-Mouth. My Dancer will leave your silly 'Toof' choking on his tongue. See if she doesn't."

The world reasserted itself and I came to. I hadn't collapsed entirely—I was still on my feet—but Charles Cavendish was clasping me in his arms. I took a deep shuddering breath. The air smelled of *sal volatile*. Sissy waved a small vial of it before my nose.

"Are you quite all right, Miss Cassandra?" Charles released me slowly. "I believe you fainted."

"I am quite myself now, Mr. Cavendish," I told him, but I was anything but. "Thank you for your assistance." I smoothed down my skirt and glared at Sissy.

She met my stare complacently. She knew I knew what she had done, using her ability to strengthen Dainty Dancer. It didn't matter what the duchess had done to her in the past, or how much Sissy wanted to triumph over her now. She was cheating. It was wrong.

Worse, *I* would be blamed for it. I was always Sissy's scapegoat. Her father, Lord Sutherland, would demand to know why I hadn't stopped her from doing such a thing. What good was I as a companion if I didn't intercede, stop his daughter from causing a scandal, which in turn, would reflect badly on him? One did not commit fraud at the Gold Cup. It was unpatriotic—a crime against King and Country.

I took an unsteady step and clutched her. "Undo what you did," I said through gritted teeth.

"What?" She looked at me all blue-eyed and innocent, as guileless as a daisy.

"You know very well!" I dropped my voice even more, so the men wouldn't hear. "Sissy, this will lead to scandal. I saw what you did, and I have this terrible feeling you will not get away with it! Something more is about to happen. I am certain of it!"

As the things I see of the past are apt to grow worse, so too did this moment. "Dere you all are!" Duchess Ragnhild approached us, with Bjarn, her escort, in tow. She wore a fuchsia and black day gown, draped in what looked to be miles and miles of rosy tulle. A flock of pink flamingos rose from her brow. She looked simply ridiculous—like the god Zeus giving birth to avian Athenas. She eyed my Sphinx as if thinking the same thing. "I wass looking for all off you, soo wee might waatch de race to-geth-er!" She smirked at Sissy. "Care to make a way-ger on your lit-tle poneey, Sissy, *elskling?*"

Sissy rose to the challenge, heedless of me pinching her arm. "Name your bet!"

"Sissy, no!" I protested.

"How about one dousand Kroner? Eefen more, iff you like. What is dat in Englisher pounds, Bjarn?" She turned back to us in an aside. "He is sooo much better at money dan me. Dat iss why my father, the king, keeps him a-rount."

Lord Churchill's voice rang out. Looking the picture of dignity in his top hat and grey morning suit, he had climbed upon a small platform and was shouting into a megaphone. "Ladies and gentlemen! There has been a small change in the pre-race proceedings. Last year, as you may recall, there were some unfortunate triflings going on! To ensure a fair race, we have invited an expert to examine all of today's mounts and ensure none have been altered in any way…"

I glanced at Sissy, feeling sick. The worst was about to happen. It didn't make me feel any better to see she had turned white.

"Fix it! Now!" I urged.

She stared at me with a stricken expression and clutched my hands. "Oh, Cass, I can't! Once the magic's done, I can't undo it!"

If she suspected where our fates lay, I wondered if she knew mine would be worse than hers. I would be blamed for *her* wrong-doing. Lord Sutherland wouldn't allow scandal to alight upon his daughter for long. There is an old oriental custom of establishing a tank of koi with eight gold fish and one black. The black is meant to capture all of the family's bad luck. I was Sissy's dark fish.

"Whaat iss he saying?" The duchess's voice rose. "Whaat is going on?" Her flamingoes bobbed this way and that, as if pecking in a pique at Lord Churchill.

"Are you all right, Sissy darling?" Henry asked, all concerned, although I suspected he was more worried about his potential loss of funds. As he leaned past me, I caught a whiff of gin.

"They haf changed the requirements, your Grace," Bjarn informed his duchess. "Dere waas a tam-per-ing last ye-ear—"

Her voice rose to a shriek. "Wheen did they do that? I waasn't here! Why did you not tell meee?" She actually struck him on the shoulder. She was beside her pink and black self. Her flamingoes looked as if they were about to take flight.

"And so, it is my pleasure to introduce Lecturer Charles Cavendish of Oxford to these proceedings," Lord Churchill continued. "As well as being a noted don of that great institution, he is also one of the Empire's leading authorities on myth and magic. Once he has made his assessments, the race shall proceed."

I looked at Charles in growing terror. *He* was the expert? *And* a don? Why hadn't Henry introduced him as such? But then, Henry was such a prat!

"I do beg your pardon," Charles said to me, touching the brim of his hat apologetically. Behind his monocle, something flashed in those sombre grey eyes and then he turned and walked away. Had he heard me warn Sissy about the coming scandal? That I had insisted she change whatever she had done? Or would he think me guilty by association?

Suddenly, the inscription embroidered on my tunic felt like a sham. So much for representing the truth and benefiting from it. Perhaps it didn't matter what Charles thought of me. If he was as good as Lord Churchill claimed, Sissy would be exposed and I would be blamed. If Lord Sutherland was angry enough about it, he might even insist I leave the estate, never to return to Sissy's side.

Oh, the unfairness of it all! Why?

The crowd shifted uncomfortably as we awaited Charles' verdict. I noticed that Her Grace, the Duchess of Norway, and her blonde giant had left in a hurry. Sissy clutched me by the hands, her eyes squeezed shut as if she might avoid our terrible fate. Or perhaps it had finally dawned on her that my future lay in worse tatters than hers. Henry sidled from foot to foot, not even bothering to hide his flask. He kept drinking, as if needing to steady his nerves.

"I say, what's the hold-up?" he demanded abruptly to no one in particular. "Most peculiar! *And* inconvenient!" He looked to those in our vicinity for support.

Sissy exploded. "Oh, Henry, *do shut up!*"

He gaped at her and his mouth fell open in astonishment. Before he could say anything more, the crowd parted as Charles pressed his way to us, his expression grave.

Sissy wilted beside me. I met Charles' gaze dully.

Lord Churchill mounted his platform once again. "There has been *one* minor change in the race line-up," he informed the crowd. Sissy lifted her head, her eyes infused with fear. "Her Grace, the Duchess of Norway's *Golden Tooth* has been removed, having unfortunately gone lame."

The crowd oohed in surprise and mock sympathy. My heart beat wildly. One change? What was this? "Her Grace offers apologies to all who might have placed bets on her mount," Lord Churchill continued. "Her steed has been replaced with Lord Truscott's *Trafalgar's Victory*. The race will proceed in one quarter of an hour, assuming spectators wish to change their bets or make additional ones in the meantime."

He stepped from his stoop and nodded in Charles' direction. Charles tipped his hat and remained beside me, as silent as my Sphinx.

I stared at him, burning with questions, but dared not ask them of him. What did it all mean? Was I not to become Sissy's sacrificial lamb? Perhaps Charles would divulge what he had determined when the moment was convenient. He gave Sissy a look I could only take as reproach. Her lips trembled and her eyes filled with tears. I do believe it was the only time I have ever seen her so full of remorse. Even the ballerinas on her hat were drooping as if in a drunken parody of a Degas. Her contrition seemed to satisfy Charles, and his severity lost its edge. He glanced at me and smiled blandly. My ankles threatened to collapse. I felt as if the sun had come out from behind a cloud.

He had to have discovered Sissy's tampering with Dainty Dancer, but for some reason, he had refrained from exposing her. I doubted if he knew what his clemency also meant for me. Dainty Dancer hadn't been struck from the roster; she was still in the race. As for the duchess and her Golden 'Toof—the sudden departure of both duchess and horse remained a mystery, something the crowd whispered about.

The herald announced the start of the race. As one, we all moved to the rail. The horses pranced at the gate, ready to run. The crowd held its collective breath, binoculars at the steady, postures tense. And then, the gates were opened and the horses were off.

They rounded the first curve, then thundered past us, hooves digging and sod flying. I felt as if my breath were snatched away in that charge. Sissy, caught up in the race and quick to forget her own wrong-doing, urged Dainty Dancer on. I remained mute, still dazed by how close my own ruination had come.

In the end, the last minute substitution, Lord Truscott's *Trafalgar's Victory*, came in first. Some American's horse, with the ridiculous name of *Scarlet Garters*, came in second. No one was more pleased than Sissy, when her *Dainty Dancer* came in third.

"Damn!" Henry swung a fist at the sky. Lord Truscott glared at him as those ladies nearby gasped at his profanity. "I wasted good money on your Dancer to place first!" He frowned at Sissy as if the loss were all her fault.

Sissy lifted her chin. "Then pray, do not waste any more of your precious money on me a moment longer." She turned her back on him in the perfect snub. I could see she was still shaken by her close call with scandal, but Henry's rudeness was not to be endured.

"Dainty Dancer ran a good race," Charles said, speaking up and surprising us all. "She earned her third *fair and square*."

"What do you know about horses, old bean?" Henry demanded, still out of sorts.

"Far more than you might expect, *old bean*," Charles countered, which for some reason, made me rather proud.

"Sissy, my girl! Well done!" boomed a deep baritone. Lord Sutherland, Sissy's father, approached us like a battleship in full regalia on Empire Day. "You've won your *papa* a pretty purse! Good for you. I expected nothing less!"

"How so, Father? Dainty Dancer didn't win—"

"And I didn't wager she would. I bet on her to *show*." He caught Sissy in the crook of his arm. "It doesn't take a genius to know how to manage the odds. Come along now, and help your papa collect his prize money—which was never in any doubt!" He cast a scathing look at Henry. "You still here, Dinglecrumb? I could have sworn you were dismissed."

Henry's nostrils flared. He tossed his hair, turned on his heel, and stomped off. One did not argue with Lord Sutherland.

Which left me alone with Charles.

"Would you like a glass of champagne?" Charles asked abruptly. I nodded, and he steered me away from the crowd to hail a waiter with a tray. I took a sip of the said *apéritif*, thankful for the bubbles. Under normal circumstances, they would stimulate, but this time, they soothed.

"Why did you—?"

"I suppose you're wondering—"

We both began talking at the same time. I paused, as Charles grinned. Once again, I was struck with how handsome he was. Such a shame, really. Oxford's gain was my loss. Dons tended not to marry, although since the late 1870s, there had been exceptions.

"Please, do continue," I offered.

"I expect you want to know about Dainty Dancer."

"Indeed. And Golden 'Toof' as well," I added.

"Of course. Well, it's quite simple, really. Henry mentioned my area of expertise was ancient curses?"

I nodded.

"That's not *quite* the extent of it. My study encompasses all areas of magical 'extensions' if you will. That means any kind of magic that has been added onto something. Curses, glamouries, enhancements, and what-have-you. It took me no time at all to see—" he dropped his voice, "that Lady Cecilia had enhanced Dainty Dancer's ability to run. When I went to check the mare in the stable, she was glowing like a small sun. All *I* did was to take the enhancement off. So Dainty Dancer ran a fair race and won her third."

"That was a very gallant thing for you to do."

"Oh, I don't know about that. I could have let the chips fall where they may, but I overheard the two of you. The fact that Sissy *couldn't* undo the enhancement but wanted to, was what tipped the balance for me. She wasn't able to, but I could. So I did."

"That was most kind. You have no idea what a relief that is for me."

He pinked beneath my praise. "As for Golden Tooth..." He changed the subject and his lips twitched in a smirk.

"Yes?"

He leaned in quite close, his grey eyes dancing. "Golden Tooth *isn't* a horse at all."

I stared up at him in amazement. "He isn't?"

"Indeed, not."

"What is he then?"

He considered me carefully, and I had the oddest feeling I was being tested. "Have you ever heard of *Tanngrisnir*? It's Old Norse and translates to Tooth Barer."

I searched my memory. Out of interest, I had read the Prose Edda a year ago. *Tanngrisnir* was the name of one of Thor's goats. It, and *Tanngnjóstr*, or Tooth Grinder, pulled the god's war chariot. Every night, Thor sacrificed his beasts, only to have them come back to life in the morning. The duchess had said we 'Englishers' wouldn't be able to pronounce her horse's name. I choked on my amazement. "Golden Tooth is a *goat*?"

"Yes! Well done!" He seemed pleased I should know that.

I was flattered by his enthusiasm, but I hid it, not wanting to look like a school girl. "So the excuse that Golden Tooth had gone lame was only a fiction," I replied.

"Actually, no. The goat really *was* lame, just like in the tale. A peasant boy eats the marrow from one of the goat's leg bones, which made it lame. Even so, it still runs bloody fast. Which was what the duchess was counting upon." He coloured, realizing he had sworn in my presence.

I ignored it. "No wonder she left in such a hurry!" I laughed, unable to help myself. I suppose the sudden release from impending doom also affected me. "To be associated with a *goat*! How banal! The cheating was bad enough." I glanced back at him. "You didn't expose her."

"No. One does not expose a duchess, even if she *is* Norwegian."

We shared another chuckle—really, the most enjoyable joke I had heard in a long time. Whereupon, I felt an immediate regret. There were so few men I found attractive, and this one, being a don and married to his work, was unavailable. The waiter came by and raised a snooty eyebrow—a silent query as to whether we might like seconds of the champs. Charles reached for a glass, but I waved the man off. "I suppose I should go find Sissy," I said regretfully. There was no point in pining for someone who would never be. Best to nip this attraction in the bud. And if I had anything more to drink, I would say too much.

"Cassandra," Charles said quickly, dropping the 'miss' in a very familiar way, and yet, in a manner I desired. "I wonder if I might call upon you tomorrow?"

I stared at him. "But I thought..."

"Oh, I see. You already have prior engagements." He was so quick to dismiss himself, to think I might not want to entertain him.

"It isn't that," I replied quickly. "It's just—" How very awkward. How does one explain to a man how much one *would* like to see him, but it's impossible because he will never marry? It reeks of desperation.

"I misunderstood. You're so lovely and clever, you must already have an understanding with some lucky gentleman."

He thought I was lovely! And smart! "No! I—" and suddenly the grey overwhelmed me. I saw myself *and* Charles, working quite happily together on a dig in Egypt. We were waist deep in a square hole that had been sectioned off, and there were children—a boy and a girl of about five and six, sitting on the edge of the dig and kicking up the dirt with their plump little legs. *Mummy, I'm thirsty*, the little girl whined. *And Wills has found a scarab. I want one, too!*

Daddy has something even better for you, my darling, Charles told her.

What?

How about a nice lemon ice?

Oh, pooh! We had that yesterday.

As I came to, I found myself once again in his arms. I had fainted quite completely this time. This hadn't been a terrible premonition as most were, but a wonderful one! Had he experienced the vision, too? His eyes were round—I wasn't sure whether this was due to surprise or horror. Sweet heaven, what must he think? "I'm all right." I pushed him aside.

"So…you *are* free for me to visit tomorrow?" he pressed.

Destiny is a funny thing. There is a point, very early on, where you *can* alter its course, despite what a vision of the future shows you. I didn't want to change a thing.

I took a deep breath, still feeling a bit dizzy from it all. "I suppose I must be."

Which was a most delightful outcome to the day, all things considered. Sissy had avoided scandal, Dainty Dancer had earned a third place, but the real winner of Ladies Day was me! Who could have foreseen it? I felt as if a wreath of flowers had been dropped about my neck and I had won the King's Cup.

"Champs?" Charles waved the waiter back over, sensing I had changed my mind about seconds.

"Absolutely." I was floating with excitement. Charles looked as if he were drifting about the aether, too.

I swear, I heard a goat bleat as we clinked glasses and toasted one another.

THE BOYS FROM WITLESS BAY
Pat Flewwelling

Jimmie and I, well, we used to get in all sort of trouble down in Halifax when we were away at the university. The only way you were safe from his pranks was by holding his beer for him.

Like that time we tied up Berton Blake the night he got drunk and started pawin' on my girl Millie while I was away to home one week. Soon as I had come back, we took him out for a good night's drinking, and once he was about half-cut, we left him down on Barrington wearing a tutu and bra filled with about three bags of sparkles—you know the kind you get at what's-it, Michael's? Anyways, he comes to in the middle of Friday morning traffic, and he sees what 'e's wearing, he screams blue bloody murder, and rips the two cups apart like he's Hulk Hogan—sparkles everywhere, like friggin' fireworks from his man-titties. I handy 'bout died dat day, laughing so hard. Berton never laid another hand on Millie, but he sure laid a few on Jimmie and me.

Jimmie, he's an engineer now, and I'm a financial advisor. That means he thinks up the pranks, and I'm the b'y who pays for it all. Five times now, I've had to cough up Jimmie's bail, and it was worth every penny.

So you'd think I'd have known better than to go out to his house, middle of October, dark as Satan's arse, raining so hard you can't tell sea from shore—the same night I'd forgotten it was Millie's birthday—when he calls me up all out of breath and begs my help.

"What's wrong for ya, b'y?" I ask.

"You remember Buddywhatshisname?" he pants.

"Oh, sure! Him! The one with the face and a couple of arms."

"George MacCrae!" The name rings a dim bell from our boyhood days.

"He the one with the growth over his eye?" I ask.

"No."

"The one who married his own sister by accident?"

"No."

"The one—"

"The b'y who disappeared in '82, suspected drowned in Dunker's Pond."

"Oh, him," I shout, and Millie turns up the TV. On the maps, it's Dunkirk Pond, but it's so deep and deadly that it's been called Dunker's since long before Georgie took his final dip. There'd been a hell of a hue and cry when he went missing. Nobody could ever explain why the ten-year-old had walked off in the middle of the stormy night, leaving one shoe on the banks of Dunker's Pond, and the other under his bed.

"What about 'im?" I ask.

"I think I know what got 'im."

"What?"

"Come over, and I'll explain when you're here."

I laugh at that and lean into the phone with my hand around my mouth to tell him I've already got a pan-shaped face, thanks to me forgetting it was Millie's birthday.

"Tell her you left her present here!" Jimmie says.

"I'm not coming over in falling weather like this just to hear another ghost tale about Georgie Frigging MacCrae!"

"No ghosts," he says. "People. And they're at it again."

"Well, call up the cops!"

"They're already on the job, and they're lookin' every way but directly under their noses."

"You're cracked, b'y. Remember the time in '86 when you called the police because you thought you saw a green horse on Cemetery Road? Or that time in '88, when you thought old Mrs. Pettigrew was skinny-dipping in—"

"Paulie, all you've got to do is bring your GoPro and a flashlight, and I'll do all the rest."

"The rest of what? Gettin' us drowned alongside Georgie?"

He sighs and says, "All's we gotta do is show the cops a sign I'm not off my rocker this time. I know what I saw, Paulie, and so do they."

I wasn't convinced, but there was something unnaturally serious in his tone.

"We won't need to go near the water," he promises. "And all's we've gotta do is take pictures."

"It's a Tuesday night! I've got work in the morning."

"It's already stopped raining, though. And what else would you be doin' at seven thirty?"

I look out the window to see whitecaps rolling up the bay. White horses, they used to call 'em. Weather aside, I've now got a choice between misadventure and missus pissed-off.

Jimmie knows my silences too well. He laughs his triumph.

I groan and say, "All right. Stay where you're to, 'til I comes where you're at." He tells me he'll see me in half an hour.

So, against my own sense of self-preservation, I sneak out the door, jump into my car, and drive from Goulds down the coast to his place in our old hometown of Witless Bay.

Before I can knock, Jimmie opens the door a crack and slithers out to meet me. "Got all the kids in bed and Janey's off to church bingo," he whispers as he closes the door. "Let's go."

"Where?"

Half a-giggle, he says, "Get in the truck, I'll explain on the way."

He's got his truck with the four-wheeler already in the back, and I know I ought to get back in my own car with roses in one hand and whiskey in the other. But he's got that friggin' giggle that tells me somebody's about to burst his titty-sprinkles on Barrington Street, and I'm aboard before you can fart. I know this is the night I'm bound to die, but at least this way I'll die on friendly terms.

"Does your GoPro shoot in the dark?" he asks.

I take it out of the case and take a look. I haven't used it since the last time I went diving. It still smells like sea water. "It shot pretty good in Conception Bay…"

"So it's waterproof, too," Jimmie says, as if checking it off his mental list.

"I'm not goin' in any water," I tell him.

Jimmie points at the sky and tells me he expects more weather, that's all. I expect he means I'm goin' in the water.

"So what's all this about," I ask him. "Somebody else's gone missing?"

Jimmie glances at me, then he makes a turn on to Gull Pond Road. "So it hasn't got to the news, then."

I shrug at him as we pass between houses and driveways, each throwing yellow and orange light on the late-autumn lawns.

"You remember those guys that used to come into Mudder's Donuts and sit by themselves with all their equipment and papers, and never talk to anybody?" Jimmie asks.

"Sure," I answer. "Ecobay Corporation. The ones with the big black bus. Trailer. Whatever." I remember it: big copper letters and a sharp line under it, the full length of the truck. Always reminded me of some '80s science fiction TV show.

"You ever notice that as soon as Georgie was found missing they up and left? Stuck around for six months, and then alluva sudden, gone?"

I give him a dull look. "Ecobay is a consultancy. All above board. I know, because one of the VPs is a client of mine."

"You know what they consult in?"

"Mineralogical surveys," I say. "What're you asking me for? You're the geological engineer!"

He shows me a toothy, angry grin. "Waste disposal. Of the toxic variety."

I snort.

"Illegal toxic waste disposal," he insists.

"That's what you're going on about?" I ask.

As we wind our way down Gull Pond Road into darkness, he says, "They're back. For the last three weeks, I've seen them driving every day, up and down Gull Pond Road. First time in ten years, and people go missing again?"

This is news to me. I get gooseflesh. "You think Ecobay is making people disappear?"

He shrugs one shoulder. "I think something is happening up Gull Pond Road, and I think Ecobay's got something to do with it, sure. And if they're making people disappear, I don't want them to catch me midday."

"What people?" I ask.

"My neighbour John, he was the first. Disappeared Friday night. And up the road there, a little girl named Emmie—seven years old, left a shoe behind at the foot of her bed. Just Sunday night. Everybody knows about it, but official word's not gone past Witless Bay. Explain that."

I shake my head. "This is bad."

"I know."

"I mean, it's a bad idea. Turn around, let's call the cops."

His foot eases up on the accelerator, only because the turn is tight. He doesn't stop until we're on the far side of Little Country Pond, where we see his headlights reflected in the brakes of a parked tractor trailer.

"It's none of our business," I tell him. "What if they're only doin' their job?"

"In the middle of the night?" He points up. "In this?" The rain's not so bad now, but he's made his point. "What if that big truck is full of nuclear waste?" I give him another dull look. "Or something poisonous. Mercury, maybe."

"And dump it here? Who in God's green Earth would come all the way out to the middle of nowhere and…" The more I talk, the more I realize he might be onto something. Small towns are easy to buy off. "You think somebody caught them dumping the stuff, and Ecobay disappeared them along with the waste?"

For the first time in ages, I see Jimmie with a straight face. "If we get honest-to-Jesus proof what's going on here, then we can ask for help from outside Newfoundland."

I can't say this is a better way to spend my wife's forgotten birthday, but maybe I can keep Jimmie outta trouble for once. Or at least know where to look for his corpse.

Some distance ahead, we pull off to the side of the road, and unload the four-wheeler. He gives me a helmet. At least nobody'll see my face. We board the four-wheeler and backtrack along the snowmobile path toward the creek between Little Country Pond and Larry Neals Pond. It doesn't take long before we spot some tracks. He stops the four-wheeler, and I get off to take a closer look with the flashlight. He takes off his helmet to hear me better. "And?"

I don't have to answer, and we've got to move. We see the trees light up yellow, long before we hear the motor. Jimmie shuts off his engine and the lights, puts the four-wheeler into neutral, and we shove it off the track and around a big rock, where we hunch down and hide. Another heavy-duty off-roader comes peeling down the track, hauling an empty low-bed trailer that bounces left and right behind them. One of the riders keeps looking over his shoulder like the devil's on his heels.

In their haste, they don't see an axle-snapping dip in the path. They both go ass-over-teapot, clean over the handlebars. But does that stop them? The first one gets to his feet and runs so fast he's punching his chin with his knees. Then the other one gets up, breathing so loud it sounds like somebody's sawing trees, and then he starts to cry. A second later, he's flinging himself up the path after his buddy.

Jimmie has his head on a swivel, like he doesn't know if it'd be more fun to chase down Ecobay or go deeper into the dark and find out what they'd done. Finally, after we hear their big old diesel engine whinny, he makes up his mind and grabs me by the jacket front. "Come on."

"At least Millie would have the decency to kill me in the comfort of me own home!" I whine as I put my helmet back on.

We drive slow for probably twenty minutes. There's nothing out here but rocks, moss, bog, trees, and trail. It's not even ten o'clock, it's cold, and I'm tired. I tap Jimmie on the shoulder and tell him to turn around, but he doesn't. He keeps following the trail.

Suddenly, he points ahead. I don't see what he sees.

"The water," he shouts over the engine.

"I'm not going in!"

"See?" He stops the ATV and turns off the motor. "Dunker's Pond. Last known address of Georgie MacCrae's left shoe."

Ecobay has left behind four pallets of unmarked metal canisters. I see evidence that something heavy has been dragged into the water. Jimmie tells me to start filming while he brings the ATV up closer, to shine a brighter light.

I creep a bit closer to the water's edge, where the weeds are broken down. The funk of the bank makes my nose wrinkle. It smells like mold, rotting pork, and dead fish. All the tracks here are jumbled. I see the curve of a lot of wide heels.

And then I realize these shoes have no treads, and they're shaped like the leaves of a water lily.

That's when I see the gouges in the mud, the kind your fingers make when you're being dragged arse foremost to your death.

At this point, I am shitbaked and ready to outrun the Ecobay truck all the way back to Witless Bay—a better name for our port-of-call they never found! I dash over to tell Jimmie what I seen, and there he is, standing ankle deep in water, staring straight down with his gob open and his eyes half-shut. I run at him and plow him down to earth with a big splash for both of us. He's yelling at me, and I'm rolling him over mud like he's on fire until we're twenty yards uphill of the nearest puddle. He finds his traction and shoves me back.

"What's wrong wit' you, b'y?" he demands, and all of a sudden, I can't remember. I only remember being scared hairless of something I seen in the mud.

"Somebody's been dragged into the water." I haul him over, careful to keep my hands on him in case one or t'other of us get pulled in.

There's no sign of the lily-pad shaped prints. Only shoe prints and the finger-drag marks.

Jimmie holds me out at arm's length and stares at me. When he's unsatisfied, he takes the flashlight from me and shines it in my face. "This is big," he says. I can't see him—I can't see anything but orange neon squiggly marks burned into my eyes—but his voice is grinning. "Come on." As we run floundering to his four-wheeler, he says, "I'll bet that's where John went in!"

I switch off the GoPro and say, "I don't think so."

"Why not?"

"Because it's been pissing down for twenty hours straight. No way John's tracks would still be here, if 'e went missing on Friday night."

He turns in the driver's seat to look over his shoulder at me. I can't read his expression, but I can read his body language. He's as alert as a hunting dog on a duck fart. He puts on his helmet, and so do I.

We don't say another word until the off-roader is loaded and we're back inside the nice warm cab of his truck. We stare bug-eyed at the windshield for a while, until he turns to me.

"We need to find out who else has gone missing from town," he says. "Before those Ecobay b'ys get too far. That's why they run off so fast. Dump and run before anybody knows they're gone from town!"

"No, b'y. They weren't scared for their secrecy. They were running for their lives."

"You're right… Only two men came out, but how many went in?"

We drive back in silence, covered in stiffening mud, dutch-ovened in our own worry. By the time we're back in his driveway, the rain has stopped and a fog has rolled in. That's when we both get a case of smarts and call the cops to tell them what we seen. I upload a copy of the video to his computer and beat it home to Goulds, where my wife is keeping our bed company, and where a sleeping bag has been laid out on the couch for my personal convenience.

I dreamed all night about being chased by the Swamp Thing. I cancel my first meeting of the day, so I can call up Jimmie and find out what the police are going to do.

I get his wife, instead. She gives me the gears for letting Jimmie slip out at night with all of her kids at home alone. It takes a lot of cooing before I can get an answer out of her: Jimmie left for work strangely early. She knows, because she heard him turning on the kitchen radio at 4:00 a.m., when he's never done so before. When I hang up with her, I see a voicemail waiting. It's my own missus, advertising a local hotel that specializes in rooms for one.

I try calling Jimmie again around noon, but this time nobody's home.

I mean to try again when school is out, but I get caught up in a conference call that goes into double-overtime. Once I finish, the receptionist hands me a lengthy note. I've had two urgent calls come in. One was from Millie. The other was from the cops—a Sergeant Francis Noseworthy of the Royal Newfoundland Constabulary.

I don't know who to call first, but I do know it's got something to do with Jimmie. I call up the missus. She tells me about how Jimmie's wife Laney called her up in a panic, because she'd found one of Jimmie's shoes on the driveway. Millie understands the significance of this, and she asks what she can do to help. I don't know yet. So I call up Sergeant Noseworthy next. He tells me to meet him in Witless Bay and answer questions about last night. I can't shake the feeling that he wants to give me a brand new pair of chrome-plated bracelets.

I do what I can to get through the rest of my work day, and then I get in my car.

I pull off into Mudder's Donuts, because I'm going to need a last meal. While I wait at the counter for my donut, I hear an old familiar voice. I turn on my stool and see Mrs. Pettigrew. She's as ancient now as she was when she was our grade three teacher, back in '82. She's got her hands on her walker, but she's still seated. Her eyes are wide and bright, but she's not looking at me. She's not looking at anything. She's flushed. "Did you hear it?"

"Hear what?"

"Last night," she warbles, "under the rain and over the waves…"

I don't remember Mrs. Pettigrew waxing so poetical before. All I remember was a lot of "Paul, don't eat that" and "Paul, don't put that in your nose."

"Hear what?" I ask again.

She says, in a wondering, musical, but cracking voice, "The white horse rolled ashore, so many years ago…the night of the perfect storm…" Her eyes flare open a little wider, and she whispers, "John heard it too… And Georgie…"

I quit my stool and sit in her booth. "Mrs. Pettigrew—what do you know about Georgie's disappearance?"

She smiles, showing me teeth the colours of Indian corn. "I could never catch up. I'd always get turned around, somewhere between Little Country and Dunker's Pond... Following the music, leading me around and around until I was back on the road, far away..."

"The music?" I ask. I remember Laney telling me she'd heard Jimmie playing music downstairs around 4:00 a.m. "Mrs. Pettigrew—"

"But the boy," she whispers hoarsely, "he stuck to it like glue..."

"Missus—"

The bell jangles over the front door, and that's the end of that goosebumply conversation. The police have found me.

At a borrowed room in the town hall, I tell Sergeant Noseworthy and three scowling members of the RNC everything I know. I give 'em my GoPro and its storage card. They take plenty of careful notes, too, comparing them against stills from my camera, double-checking spelling and times. They seem real interested about the canisters and the guys who left 'em behind.

They ask me a lot about our boy's night out, too. I hold nothing back. They ask me if we'd been drinking, or fighting, or smoking up. They ask me about what happened when he came home—Laney gave him a hotter reception than Millie gave me, what with hell hathing no fury, etc., etc.

After forty minutes, they let me go, hinting that if I ever wandered back to Dunker's Pond, I might scare off Ecobay and undermine the investigation. Worse, I might get myself arrested for tampering with evidence, and Sergeant F. Noseworthy looks greedy to fill up the St. John's jail with the likes of Jimmie and me. I leave, feeling like a traitor, a suspect, and a real scut boob all in one.

I'm halfway out the door when I realize I forgot to ask if I could at least join the search party, so I go back inside. Before I open my mouth, I see Noseworthy and his cops ripping off their notes and dropping them into a box marked Shredding. There'll be no investigation, and probably no search party, either.

This pisses me off. Jimmie's only one of three people gone missing this week, and those are the ones I know about. I hear one of the cops say they're going to call in the Army to help drain Dunker's Pond so they can get at all the bodies.

Still haven't got my GoPro back, yet, either. Bastards.

Now, I know there's only one way Jimmie's gonna get found alive, and that'll be by me opening my eyes and taking a walk. I exit the station like a business man, and as soon as I'm around the corner, I gallop off to my car, drive back to Mudder's Donuts, and find that Mrs. Pettigrew has already ambled off to nobody knew where, never to be seen again.

I don't know what else to do. I call up Millie and apologize. I tell her everything, and she doesn't interrupt. At the end, she asks if I want to come home. I tell her I do, but not until I know what the cops are going to do about Jimmie. She tells me she'll come down and wait for me at Laney's house. I tells her I loves her. She tells me I'm an ass, but in the best kind of way.

I get into the car, drive up Gull Pond Road, and park on the culvert. There's no signs to say "police investigation" or whatever, and no sign of search parties. I don't see Jimmie's truck nor any fresh ATV tracks. I spend the last shades of daylight looking for the boy, but not a sign. I go back to where I started from, grab my flashlight, and get out again.

It's unseasonable warm now, and as I'm walking through the woods, I look up and see that the sun's setting in the east. I stop and look behind me, and I see that the sun's also setting in the west. That one's a normal reddish colour—Sailor's Delight—and in the east, the sunset's an ungodly greenish colour—Sailor's Incontinence.

I think maybe Jimmie's on to something with his conspiracy theory about nuclear waste.

My feet start to turn back, but then I remember Jimmie saying it was people involved. I figure it's just construction lights shining through the swamp gasses, so I shush up my feet and soldier on.

I get past the banks of Little Country Pond, and about ten minutes later, the green glow's brighter than the sunset behind me, and the air takes on a funk you can taste and feel. That's when I hear the radio, and all my hair stands up.

"Jimmie?" I call out.

It sounds like a man singing over a crackling a.m. radio down there by the banks of Dunker's Pond. I hear rustling, too. That's when I stop and tie double-bows in my runners, just in case.

I stand up again, and I come to the spot where the canisters were left behind. In some spots, my sneakers make loose farty noises when I gotta pull them out of the mud. Dunker's Pond overflowed with all the rain.

Out of the corner of my eye, I see motion on the far bank. At first I think it's one of them guys from Ecobay all dressed in green, but then it moves the upper part of its body. I blink, and I rub at my eyes, and I squint, and I look again. I figure it's gotta be a horse escaped from somebody's farm, but it looks mighty sick and sad.

And then the horse turns and comes towards me, through the green fog. I hear splashing noises like when my mudder used to slap the water out of my wet jeans before hanging them on the line, and I see that horse is *walking across the damn pond.*

A more sensible man would have turned and put those double-knots to use, but I was out of my senses, so I just stood watching this horse come toward me, thinking about the Swamp Thing and the Toxic Avenger, and about how my face was gonna melt off like that guy in the original RoboCop movie.

This horse is so big I could run under him without ducking. His mane clings like watery green tar on both sides of his head and neck. As he gets closer to the bank, the weeds bend away to make room for him. All around him, seaweed waves from his viridian flanks like he's dragging it through a tide. His hoofs are as big as garbage pail lids, and green as algae, and when he snorts, ropes of snotty pond scum come out of his nostrils.

It takes me a while, but I realize now the a.m. radio is coming from the horse, the same four notes, over and over again, humming like wind in the rigging. The closer he gets, the louder and harsher the noise, like a gale coming to shore.

"Now, now hold on there, Nelly," I hear myself say. The horse keeps coming toward me. "I'm only here for my buddy Jimmie." The horse stops singing and stares at me out of one big bleedin' eye, making a noise like he's drowning in his own phlegm. I hold up my hands and try to think of soothing things to say, but all I've got is "Sweet Jayses, Mary, and Joseph!" The horse gnashes his teeth—and not them square kind of teeth you expect to see, but a mouthful of knives and a couple of tusks—and even though I got smart earlier and took a good piddle, still a little squirted out of me. I know toxic waste can do weird things to a lotta animals, but fangs on a horse and wavy seaweed tentacles are beyond the pale. I smirk like a fool. "Jimmie," I say. "Short wiry fella with a nervous giggle."

The horse blows at me, and damned if he doesn't toss his head up and down like Mr. Ed. His mane slaps against his neck.

"I'm just here to take him home," I say. I avoid eye contact, because I don't want this seahorse to drag me to the bottom and drown me, like I suspect he did with Georgie and John and Emmie and Jimmie, and maybe some of them Ecobay guys. "This your pond?"

The horse turns his head and looks along his flank at the pond behind us. The water's more radiant than ever, as if there's a whole city under there.

I clear my throat and try not to think about me having a conversation with a demon horse on the banks of a glowing pond. "Been here long?"

The horse raises his head and stomps a hoof. I half-expect him to start counting out the years, but nope, that was it, just the one stomp.

I hear his drowning, growling noise again. He squints at me, impatient.

"You must be a bit pissed off about all this garbage in your swamp, b'y..."

The horse whinnies angrily, and I apologize right quick with hands and words.

"Pond," I say, "pond, I meant to say pond. It's a pretty one."

He whickers.

"My Jimmie, he..." I point to the pond, because that's the only place I expect him to be. "He was trying to get people out here to show 'em what's been dumped here, because nobody believes him. No—people believe him, but they've been bought off and won't do anything. I don't know if it's because the police're afraid of you or afraid of Ecobay, but Jimmie wasn't afraid enough. Honest to God, he just wanted to help."

The horse wheezes and listens.

"Is he in there?" I ask. "Did you take him?"

Another big, splashy nod.

"Well...could I..." I rub the back of my neck. I have to keep talking, or the crazy will set in. "Could I get him back?"

He squints his flaming green eyes at me.

"Did you eat him?" I hear myself ask.

The horse blows and shakes his head and neck.

"Oh, well that's a comfort," I say. "You took him because you're pissed off about what's happening? You took all of 'em?"

Another nod.

"Including the Ecobay folk?"

Another nod.

"Oh, well, *them* you can keep," I say.

The horse whinnies.

"Listen," I say. "Those people down there, my people, my folks, they've got families, and friends. Jimmie, he's got five kids, he does! He's a geological engineer, goes out to find safe places to store waste, to prevent just this from happening. But if you keep him all to yourself..." I wave indistinctly in the direction of His Highness the Whinnying Bog. "Who knows what else creatures like you may have to suffer if he's not out and helping save them?"

The seaweed sags all around him.

"You want to keep people out of here, don't you?" I ask. "You don't want people to know what you are, or you'll have every man, woman, and dog out here with their cameras. You ever hear of Nessie?"

The horse gives an angry scream.

"Yeah," I say. "They wanna drain your swa—your pond, so's they can find the people you took."

Another angry scream, and he paws the dirt like he's going to charge me, bull-like.

"Well," I rush to say, tamping down the nervous air between us with my hands, "well, Jimmie...now, maybe he can do something. He's smart, and he's a..." The idea comes to mind at the same time it comes out my mouth. "He's a prankster. Take me to him, and I'll tell him what he's got to do."

Before I can give it a second thought, seaweed lashes around my wrists, and I'm hoisted up over the horse's head. Next thing I know, I'm sitting backwards on this truck-sized horse, my hands sinking into its hide like it's made of molasses, and I can't let go. My jeans get sucked in, too, before he's even turned around. My inner thighs fuse to the sides of the horse, and I'm on for the ride of my life. Two bounds, and we leap into the air. I gasp—a good thing, too—and we break through the surface of the pond without a sound. Night turns into day, as phosphorescent beams of light filter through the blackest, coldest, oiliest water I ever been in.

I'm already out of breath. He kicks his lily-pad hooves and Clydesdale legs, while his green tail floats like beautiful streamers behind us. I hang onto my breath as long as we can, but the pressure increases, squeezing out the air I've got. Down we go farther, until my ears crackle and air burbles out from my nose. One hand comes free, and I use it to squeeze my nostrils shut, because I know I need to hang onto this air. My jacket and clothes float around me, and my hair waves all over, with bubbles trickling up my neck and over my scalp. My other hand comes free, then my legs. We settle to the bottom of the bright pond, and he bucks me off.

Instead of crashing hard, I kinda float and bump to the silt. But I've gotta breathe. I can't hang on much longer. Glow be damned, the world is going dark.

I feel something touch me on the shoulder. I look up, and there's a balding old skipper in red plaid, suspenders, and fishing boots. I watch as his mouth makes words into an ever-growing bubble, at first as big as a gumball, then as big as his head, then as big as my chest. He chews off the bubble and lets it float toward me. I close my eyes as the filmy skin passes over me.

"Breathe," I hear in my ears. Water trickles down my body, so I open my eyes and see that I'm inside the bubble. I breathe, smelling dulse and dead fish. "You're in the kelpie's pasture," I hear the man saying, though his mouth has stopped moving. "You're safe, for now." Everything looks warped outside the bubble's skin.

By God, I wish I had my GoPro.

The bottom of the pond is a glimmering meadow of sea grass as far as the eye can see, and everywhere, I see sluggish figures of men and women working the field. Off to one side is a stable, where the horse wanders, all a-shimmer. A boy and girl are waiting with a pail, out of which the horse eats. Closer by my foot, there's a pile of dead old men in Ecobay uniforms. One of them rolls toward me, and I use up good air, screeching.

I'm full to the gills with questions and exclamations. I turn to my bubble-blower to see he's at it again. A second speech bubble merges with the first.

"Why has he brought you here? Why has he let you live?" ask the words in my air.

"Who are you?" I ask instead. He doesn't look like Jimmie, or like anyone else I know. I wonder if this is his neighbour John. "Where's Jimmie?"

The man in plaid gestures for me to follow. I bob along behind him like a guinea pig in one of those plastic globes. When I brush too close to a rocky outcrop, water leaks in, and I jump aside. The bubble seals up again, but it's smaller, and my escaping air rocks skyward.

He leads me to the far end of the pasture where black sludge has been drizzled all over a field of glowing mushrooms. There's Jimmie, with shovel and bucket, working alongside a few other men. His skin is waxy, and he moves like he's sleepwalking.

"Jimmie," I shout at him.

He looks up from his work, eyes smouldering green. He gesticulates happily and makes word-bubbles like his lumberjack buddy, so it takes a second or two for me to hear what he's said. Bubble after bubble merges with my cocoon, and he gives me the whole story: how he heard the music, how he couldn't help but walk outside, and how he saw a little boy walking toward a green horse standing in the middle of Cemetery Road. Next thing he knew, he was stuck fast to the horse, riding side-saddle behind the little boy.

"And I found Georgie," he says. He points to the old skipper, who inclines his head in a sad but friendly way. I'd been expecting the same skinny boy he'd been when he disappeared, but seems he's aged at the same pace as Jimmie and me. "He's been here cleaning up the mess since '82."

"And who are they?" I ask, pointing to the other sluggish men with skeletal faces and shining, blind eyes.

"Ecobay technicians who came in second place at the Dunker's Pond fifty yard dash," Jimmie says. "Some of 'em's been here since 1942!" He points to the pile of dead men.

"Why do they keep coming back, then?" I ask.

Jimmie explains that they came a few times to dump their crap in Dunker's Pond, thinking nobody'd ever find out. The last time was in '82. After that, every ten years or so, Ecobay would send in investigators to see what happened to the first guys who never came back. One or two would get nabbed by the kelpie—that horse-plant-demon thing—and the rest would come home with a story no one would believe. They came back this year to start dumping again.

My air is getting stale, so I tell him my plan. The horse—the kelpie—comes over to eavesdrop with ears pricked forward. Jimmie explains to him my plan in greater detail, pointing to this person and that. The kelpie cocks his head and considers.

Then the horse comes over, nips my bubble and bursts it. I shoot straight up on out of there, and I don't look down until my head's in the open air. I don't care how much it smells like a latrine, that is the sweetest air a man could breathe. I swim ashore and slither through the mud and weeds before I turn around and see Jimmie right there behind me, pulling one of the Ecobay guys along for the ride. We're so out of breath that we have to sit on the bank for a bit, swiping slime from our eyes.

Jimmie's eyes are still green, and though they don't glow, he looks a bit mad in the head.

"Right," Jimmie says with a grin. "Let's take him to the police."

I cough and say, "I gotta make a couple of calls before we go."

Back at the Town Hall, our dampish hostage raves for a good ten minutes about a ghost horse and an underwater kingdom. Sergeant Noseworthy and his cops listen hard and take notes while they lean over the box marked Shredding.

Jimmie interrupts the Ecobay guy, because we're losing our audience. "You remember in '09 when you caught me sitting naked in the big donut on top of Mudder's Donuts?" he asks the assembled cops. "And that time in 2010 when you arrested me for filling up Jack Falls' car with fish heads and seawater, out of spite for him beating up his wife?"

I've got an account with ten thousand earmarked for the next time Jimmie gets arrested.

"And back in '06, that time when I made Janice Bejanice think the whole town was overrun with zombies, and we had to put her in hospital for a month— ?"

The cops are getting impatient, so I break in and say, "He made a ghost horse out of an oil barrel, seaweed, and that stuff in glow sticks. This one—" the babbling technician "—got so scared he ran right into the water and knocked himself out and had a bad dream."

"Why?" one of the cops asks me. "Why the prank?"

"To scare these guys off and stop 'em from dumping all that poison in our water," I say. "Since you boys weren't doing such a hot job of it." They don't look convinced.

"Got a better story to give the newspapers?" Jimmie asks. The Ecobay guy is still yammering on, clutching at his skin and hair. When he finds a bit of seaweed, he screams.

"What newspapers?" Noseworthy asks. He has to yell until Jimmie can clap a hand over Ecobuddy's hollering mouth.

"The ones I just called," I say. "Should be here in about an hour."

"You could tell 'em how Ecobay paid, legally but secretly, for the right to dump toxins in our water," Jimmie suggests. "Or you could tell 'em that three people went missing this week, and you didn't tell anybody—especially the press. Or..." His eyes flash radioactive green when he grins. "You could tell 'em there's a people-eating sea monster in Dunker's Pond."

While he talks, I "accidentally" bump against the shredding box, and the top unlatches as it falls over. "Oh, lookie dat," I say, "all of them witness statements. Jimmy-b'y, think I'll find receipts at the bottom of this? Y'know, for all the kickbacks they've been paid?"

Noseworthy moves to grab me by the collar.

"No, I've got a better idea," Jimmie says, grabbing the Ecobay fellow by the arm. "Let's go tell the kelpie that it was the cops who let you Ecobay folks come in and ruin his pond."

The Ecobay technician screams and tries to climb up the nearest cop to get away from the invisible kelpie. "It tried to eat me!" he screams. "Underwater!"

"What do you want?" Noseworthy demands. "Do you want to cause a panic?"

Jimmie says, "The kelpie only wants to protect his home. He only takes us when he's mad about Ecobay." He gives the whimpering technician a shake. "Keep them out of Witless Bay, do your job, and we'll never hear from the kelpie again." He thrusts the technician toward Noseworthy.

"We could just kill it," says one of the other cops.

"Georgie tells me you been trying to do that for seventy-five years," Jimmie says. "And I saw a few bodies in uniform at the bottom of that pond."

Grown men go pale.

"And what do we tell them about the missing people?" Noseworthy asks.

"Which ones?" Jimmie asks. He turns, and we see four people walk into the station, all of them with bright green eyes like Jimmie. They're wet, tired, hungry, but unharmed, and seeing the world in a new light. "Who, those ones?"

Two more people come in. Laney goes to Jimmie and falls into his arms. Millie sidles up to me and checks me over.

Noseworthy looks from Jimmie to me, asking, "What about the missing Ecobay people?"

"They stay until the pond is all cleaned up," Jimmie says. "That was the bargain to get our people back."

"And how are we supposed to explain where they've been all this time?" Noseworthy bleats.

"We could tell the truth," Jimmie says. "But we keep it amongst ourselves. Anybody from away won't believe a word we say, and that's good enough for me. Just another Newfie ghost story out of Witless Bay."

THE HORSE WITCH
Angela Rega

Like a big sugar cake of lights, the carousel unraveled the dark with each rotation. The brightly lit horses and their candy-colored saddles looked out of place in the yellowed paddocks of Coorooma. Wendy watched, perched on the fence, her chin on her hands and her bare feet curled around the bottom rail. Small for her thirteen years, she looked like a little bird resting.

The horses were frozen, it seemed, somewhere between a canter and gallop, some had their long necks arched, others, their necks lowered as if indicating a joyousness that real horses show when they are free. A paradox, Wendy thought, since the poor creatures were all impaled on poles that circulated on cranks. Still, she thought, against the ebony of the night sky clean of stars, they lit up Coorooma like a big Christmas tree.

Soon they might be the only horses of Cooroma, more alive than the wild brumbies that ran free on the land here. "All to be mustered for shooting," her father had said to her as he took off his oilskins that evening and threw a fish in the pan for their dinner. She didn't answer him. She had learnt long ago not to reveal things she loved, lest they be destroyed. She kept the photos of her absent mother in a gift-wrapped shoebox under her bed, and now, a tuft of her wild brumby's tail, too.

"Want a ride?"

Wendy lifted her chin off her hands and looked up at the woman operating the carousel. She was a thin elderly lady wearing an old top hat and a long grey plait slung over her right shoulder and hung long to her waist. If Wendy had a grandmother, she would have liked her to be a bit like this lady, particularly because her gumboots were a bright purple and in the end of her long plait, she wore what looked to be magpie feathers.

Wendy tucked her right hand inside her pocket. All she had was a burnt out cigarette stub she'd been using to practice smoking with Elouise behind the bushes at school. "I don't have money," she said.

"I'll give you a free ride," the woman answered and she smiled.

Wendy stepped off the fence. "Nobody round here gives anybody anything for free—except Lillian Jones who gives people pumpkins in autumn, but that's because she's supposedly Coorooma's very own fairy godmother."

"A fairy godmother in Coorooma? Do you believe in magic?"

Wendy shrugged. "I don't believe in fairies and I've never liked pumpkin." She wasn't even sure if she liked Lillian. Her father did, though. He liked Lillian very much. She was over at their place a lot these days.

Wendy eyed the empty carousel as the music and the movement slowed and came to a complete halt. Now she was hesitant to step forward. No other children in the town were here. Normally, they would flock like flies to cow pies at anything new in town.

"So where's the rest of the carnival?" Wendy asked.

"I'm a one women show," the woman said. "A carousel but no carnival." She opened the gate and gave Wendy a horsey grin that revealed very large teeth. "Come on in."

Wendy walked in and put out her hand. It felt right to introduce herself since not many new people came to Coorooma. "I'm Wendy," she said.

"Devon." The woman answered. Wendy noticed how warm her hand was, then bee-lined for the silvery grey horse whose reins were long and hung in loops down his neck.

"You like that one?"

"Yup." He reminded her of the brumby that she had befriended down near the edge of Wallory Creek. It was a silvery grey with dappled hind legs and had come to her on the first day she had sat alone at the creek and cried about missing her mother. It was his tuft of tail that now sat in her shoe box. She was surprised at how much hair he shed. She wished she could groom him but brumbies are wild and she was sure a brush would have made him skitter off. He was her secret. She fed him carrots and sometimes sugar cubes, even though she knew it wasn't good for him. A treat was good for the soul, though, her mother used to say. That made a bit of sugar okay.

The music began and after a quick jolt the carousel started. Wendy was the only one on it, besides Devon who turned the handle in the center of the platform. As she rode, up and down, round and round, the carousel horse started warming between her thighs and soon Wendy felt the pelt of a living, breathing horse beneath her. She opened her eyes. Nope. These horses weren't real. They were carousel horses. She clung on and closed her eyes and then she was riding, out across an open field with the wind blowing past cheeks whipping her hair out of her eyes.

The carousel slowed and the music faded to a whisper; Wendy opened her eyes. She was back on the merry-go-round horse and back in the small town of Coorooma.

"You enjoy that?" Devon smiled and Wendy noticed sweat glistened from her forehead.

"Yeah. That was cool." She was confused at the feelings that washed through her. A combination of embarrassment and shame, excitement and adventure.

"Feel free to come again."

"How long you here for?" Wendy hoped she would be here a while. She wanted to ride the carousel again.

"As long as I need to be."

"I wish I was only here for a while."

"Everything is temporary, Wendy."

"Doesn't feel like it." Wendy clung to the horse's neck. Her eyes started to well. Carooma's stark landscape of flat yellow lands reflected the loneliness she felt since her mother left. She wiped her right sleeve under each eye and raised her tongue to the roof of her mouth. Her mother had told her that was how one stopped themselves from crying in public. She'd had to do it a lot these days.

"Maybe see you tomorrow, kiddo."

"Maybe."

Wendy slid off the horse. The carousel experience left her elated and emotional at the same time. She'd really felt like she was on a real horse but of course that wasn't true. Just like Lillian Jones wasn't a real fairy godmother just because she grew pumpkins.

She walked home and stood out the front. Should she go in? Through the window she saw her father slouched on the couch mesmerized by the television and smoking a cigarette. Good. Lillian wasn't there. She walked down the side lane past the house to the shed.

She undid the latch for the shed door and went inside. The bags of carrots were there. Her father had never asked her why she kept so many but then, he gave Wendy a lot of freedom. "Provided you ain't up to no mischief, won't hurt you to climb rocks and trees," was all he said. She slung a bag of carrots over her shoulder and walked across the back paddock. She separated the two lines of wire that made up the fence and slipped through. She walked up the small hill, over the boulders marked with the graffiti of lost loves and through the bushes. Then down towards the sandy soil that led to the pebbles and the creek.

She whistled and waited.

She heard the splish splash of horse's hooves walking through the shallow waters before he appeared. It was the silver brumby. He sauntered towards her, his head down for her to stroke his long neck. He was getting used to her.

"Hello," she cooed in his ear.

The horse muffled a snort and nuzzled his velvet nose into the bend between her neck and shoulder. Wendy giggled at how it tickled her.

"Okay. You want your treat, right?"

She opened the bag of carrots and let the horse break the first carrot in two with one bite.

"Soon there'll be culling, Dad says." The horse munched on the carrots and blinked. Wendy noticed for the first time how long his eyelashes were. She didn't want Silver to be culled. From 6,000 to 600 her father had said when he was telling Clive. Old Clive was all for it. Destroying the soil he'd said and Wendy's Dad changed the subject. Clive was known for his foul temper when people disagreed with him.

The town hall was cold and the floorboards coated in the fine dust of time caked onto them no matter how much they were mopped.

"It's always ten degrees colder in here than outdoors," her father said to her as he put his beanie on her head pulling it down past her eyebrows.

"Thanks." She pulled it back up to see. The town hall was crowded. There were folk that weren't even from Coorooma but from towns around the valley. All had made it their business to attend the meeting. Tension iced the already cold air and Wendy could see it in the way men stomped their feet and the women wedged their hands in their pockets as far as they could for warmth. The Mayor stood behind the lectern and cleared his throat.

"We're here tonight to discuss the proposal the Government has planned to cull the current population of Coorooma's National Park of Brumbies from six thousand to six hundred."

Silence. Then murmurs began.

"The brumbies have been here for a hundred and fifty years!" Lillian Jones shouted out. "They're part of the landscape!"

"The brumbies are destroying the natural habitat! They're destroying the moss! There's over six thousand!" Wendy recognized

Clive's brittled voice.

"Six thousand, huh? Where did you get them facts?" Lillian asked. Wendy noticed she stood on tiptoes when she raised her voice. "They're part of our history! Think of the wartime heritage of these horses!"

"Why don't you just keep to your pumpkins?"

And then there was uproar. Wendy put her hands on her ears. She didn't want to hear of the culling.

"Why not take them and break them in? Give them to children as pets? Or for Horse Riders Groups and to muster cattle?" It was Ms. Nguyen, but she was the newest member of Carooma so nobody was listening. Wendy thought of her brumby's long eyelashes. She poked her father's arm. Her father ignored her, listening to Clive yelling about do-gooders and that they didn't belong here. She poked her father's arm again.

"Can I go home?"

"Sorry kiddo, sure. Straight home, okay? Things could get a bit heated up tonight. People might go out and shoot brumbies. You know what I'm saying? Silly folk that take an idea and ride it like a rodeo."

She knew he meant Clive. "Can't I just..."

"Straight home."

Wendy didn't look her father in the eye. He had always trusted her to do the right thing but the brumby was more important. She had asked him many times if he would help catch a wild brumby and break it in for riding but her father said no. She'd said it without saying there was any special horse. That was still her secret. Like the way she constantly thought about her mother since she'd left.

"They belong here to roam free," was all he had said. *Like my mother*, she'd felt like answering but she didn't say anything.

She left the hall and made her way to Werrily Creek. When she passed the high street, Devon was there, just like she said she would be, with the carousel revolving to the sound of slow organ music.

Nobody was on it. Wendy looked at the horses. Tonight they weren't adorned with their candy-colored saddles but were bare back and without reins. They looked like a herd she'd seen once at Werrily Creek.

Devon waved at her but Wendy pretended she didn't see her—she wanted to see her brumby. The real thing. Not a wooden horse. When she looked at the carousel again it seemed the horses were real, some, their necks down as if grazing and others shaking their manes and flicking their tails. She slapped the side of her head and kept on walking.

The horse came without her whistling. She put her fingers through his mane and rubbed her face against his neck. He knew her. She knew him. Friends. They were friends.

Wendy took out her treats from her pocket: some sugar cubes and half a carrot. He ate from her hand and she felt the velvet texture of his muzzle and scratched him under the groove of his chin. She sat down by the creek and the horse stood next to her, grazing quietly, occasionally flicking his tail. They were like this for some time and Wendy thought she would doze off when suddenly, he lifted his head and perked his ears. He stumbled backwards, then turned and ran through the creek in the direction he'd come from with a soft whinny.

Wendy turned to see Clive. His eyes narrowed and tobacco and gin smell stronger than she'd remembered. On his head he wore his prized possession, a hat made out of the fur of a feral cat. She stepped backwards.

"What are you doing here?"

"I've seen you, here with that horse."

She didn't answer. He was staring at her, without blinking. His mouth wide open in a grin.

"That your horse?"

"What horse?"

He laughed. "The silver you were with."

"There's six thousand, remember? Could be one of many."

"Liar."

Wendy shrugged.

"Scared, aren't you?"

She felt him staring at her bare legs and was compelled to run. She did. A large stone hit her hard on her right shoulder and then she heard laughter. Wendy kept running. She didn't turn around.

"Next time it'll be a bullet in your back. Stay away from the brumbies, or they'll shoot you, too," Clive yelled.

Wendy ran up the hill. Her ankle gave way over a loose rock but still she didn't stop.

When she came past the carousel the lights were switched off and Devon was unrolling the canvas awnings.

"Rain coming in this evening," she called to Wendy but Wendy couldn't answer. She was short of breath and her chest was heaving.

"Who you running from?"

Wendy kept panting and rubbed at her sore ankle. She wouldn't tell her father let alone a stranger.

"You can talk to me, if you like."

Wendy thudded to the floor. Her ankle ached and she needed to catch her breath. She looked up and noticed the last canvas awning had been rolled down. A pang of disappointment stabbed at her.

"You moving on?" she asked.

"Not just yet, but soon. Smells like a storm is coming, don't want my horses to get wet," she said and tossed her neck forward and back so that her long plait flew over her shoulder and rested on her back. "You'd best go home but I'll see you tomorrow. I promise."

Devon smiled at her so that the wrinkles on her face seemed to stretch behind her ears. Wendy smiled back. She liked Devon. A lot. And she knew that Devon liked her, too.

"Good night," Wendy said. And hobbled home, even though she was out of breath. There was something unusual about the scent of the night air and she wanted to get home before her father did.

The light was on. Her father was already home. She stood nervously at the front door before pulling the screen open as quietly as she could.

"I'm in the kitchen, Wendy," her father called out.

It was now or never. She was going to get into trouble and there was no avoiding it. She pushed the kitchen door open and there sat her father, sharing a woodbine with Lillian, a tureen of pumpkin soup in front of her on the table.

"Where did you go?"

Wendy bit her lip. The more people knew her secret—besides Clive—the greater the chance of her silver being killed. Then she remembered Devon, rolling down the canvases.

She sat on the wooden chair nearest the table, where her mother used to sit. She had never sat in it since she'd left, that would be two years now.

Everything she loved ran away.

She rubbed her sore ankle. Then she was crying and telling her father and Lillian what had happened at Werrily Creek.

The gunshots came at 1 AM. Wendy woke and sat upright in bed. She put her jeans over her pajama bottoms and her big black jumper and headed to the kitchen. The light was on. Her father was already up. He was sitting on her mother's chair in the kitchen leaning forward to lace his boots.

"You're staying here," he said firmly. "There are guns out there."

Wendy stared at her father. She thought of the brumbies and Clive and Devon and Lillian and her pumpkin soup.

"I'm coming with you."

"You can't."

He got up and locked the door behind him. "I've locked you in," he called out. "It's for your own good, Wendy. Things are dangerous here tonight."

Wendy bit her lip and swore under her breath at her father. Her cheeks grew hot and she felt a bit of vertigo. She had to get out. She went to the bathroom and found the bandages. She wrapped her ankle, securing it tight and put her socks and sneakers on. Then went back to the kitchen.

The window. She would get out of the window. She climbed up onto the sink and stood on her knees as she pushed the stiff window open. There was enough of an opening for her to squeeze out of even though she knew that she would have bruised ribs next day. She landed on her side in the bushes, jumped up to stand and brushed herself off. Wendy hobbled down the dirt road toward the center of the town.

The carousel was covered from the awnings to the floor in hanging canvas pegged down as if a tent. It seemed lifeless but light cracked through the curtains of Devon's caravan windows. Wendy decided not to knock.

Instead she hobbled, walked, and jogged down to Werrily Creek. The wind whipped her cheeks. The storm that Devon had predicted hadn't quite come...but it threatened to. She pushed her way through the bracken before the sandy beds at the creek.

Clive stood, his right hand cuffed around Wendy's dad's collar. In his left hand, he held a rifle. "Dad!" Wendy screamed.

At the sound of Wendy's voice, Clive let go of her dad and stepped back. For a few moments, they stood in a suspended silence except for the gentle rippling of the creek water against rock. Then Clive took a step towards Wendy, his face blotched.

"You shouldn't be here, girl," he said.

"Yes I should." She stood straighter, angry not scared.

"I told you to stay home!" Her father yelled. "Go!"

"I won't. Until he does!" She pointed at Clive brandishing the gun as if it was a sword, his finger on the trigger.

"I shot your horse!" Clive called out laughing.

Wendy ran towards him; her hands went numb. She grabbed his hair on either side of his head and pulled.

"You little cow!"

"Wendy!"

Then her father was running towards her.

A shot fired. Wendy threw herself onto the ground, skidding on her stomach across the edge of the creek. Had Clive shot her father? She clenched her teeth, too scared to open her eyes.

Then there was another shot from behind them all. It surprised Wendy into action—she scrambled to her feet and looked for a bush to hide behind. Who had fired the second shot? Wendy saw the purple gum boots first, then trousers and the bottom of a long silver plait.

"Devon?" Wendy asked, incredulous.

"Put your gun down or I'll shoot you square in the balls. I have excellent aim."

Clive dropped the gun and put his hands up in the air.

"Get outta of here."

As Clive scrambled away she walked through the edges of the creek and put her hand on Wendy's back.

"You okay, kid?"

"Yeah."

"Who are you?" Wendy's dad asked.

"Devon. Carousel owner. Horse tamer of sorts."

"The carousel in town is yours then," he said.

"That's right."

She offered Wendy a hand and she took it. Wendy's stomach and thighs were drenched from the creek, her ankle ached, and she was shivering from the cold. She put her arms around Devon's waist and then she was hugging her tight. In that hug there was the smell of wet grass and horse hay, and the warm soft textures of Devon's jumper.

Wendy took her hand and let her walk her home.

The next morning was unusual for its silence. No birds sang and the sound of cars rambling down the town's one road was absent.

Wendy sat up from her bed and looked out her bedroom window. She couldn't believe that people would want to harm horses that had done nothing but been alive. The brumbies had been part of the landscape for over one hundred and fifty years. They had even been used as war horses during both world wars.

When she got out of bed and went to the kitchen, she found Lillian at the stove frying pumpkins with cinnamon for breakfast. Had she stayed the night? She had never done that before. But here she was with her father's dressing gown on. A place had been set for Wendy, complete with sliced bread and a small knob of butter on a white plate.

"Good morning, Wendy. Fancy a pumpkin fry up?"

Wendy didn't want to answer.

"You slept here last night with Dad?"

"Yes." She handed Wendy a slice of thickly buttered bread like a peace offering.

"I'm not hungry."

Lillian put the toast onto the plate she had set for Wendy and turned back to the stove, flipping the slices of sizzling pumpkin. "Clive was arrested last night and your father's called an early meeting to suggest methods to keep the population down that don't involve killing."

Wendy played with her bread on the plate. "Were many brumbies shot last night?"

"Clive killed a few, yes." Lillian didn't look at Wendy as she put the hot pieces of pumpkin into a serving dish.

Wendy poked at the butter on the toast with her index finger. She didn't look up.

"Are you going to be sleeping here from now on?"

"Sometimes."

"I want to visit Devon."

"The carousel lady? Sure, but eat your toast. I'll take care of this and then I'll be off. Your father asked me to be here when you got up on account of last night and all."

Wendy shrugged. "See ya."

When Wendy got there, the carousel had been packed up. The sun shone on Devon as she walked towards her station wagon and Wendy thought her shadow looked centaur-like for the briefest of moments.

"You leaving?"

"I must." Devon stopped and smiled at Wendy. It was a restrained smile.

"You coming back?"

"If I need to."

"Brumbies were shot last night."

"Yes, unfortunately," Devon said.

Wendy noticed the carousel horses stood on their poles, side by side. There seemed to be more than should have fit on the carousel.

"Can't you stay?"

"It's kind of urgent. Why I have to leave."

"Where did you get them those extra carousel horses?"

"That's my hobby, I collect 'em…" She unlocked the trolley that pulled the carousel.

When Wendy looked again, Devon's silhouette once again looked like a centaur. Her body was elongated like a horse but her torso was human and the long plait's shadow seemed to flick on it's own as if shooing away flies. Devon noticed Wendy's gaze at her shadow and flicked her head back, the shadow transmogrified again to a woman with a long plait.

"Take care of yourself, kiddo. Remember everything goes round and round, what's gone comes back, what's old is new and all that."

"You too, Devon."

Wendy stepped forward and put her arms around her. She smelled like horse hair and fresh lawn. "I hope I see you again."

"You will."

Wendy turned and left. She wanted to ask Devon if she knew which of the horses were shot, if her silver brumby had been but she knew it was best not to ask.

When she walked back home she found her father and Lillian sitting on the verandah together, mugs of coffee in their hands. She pretended she didn't see them and walked through the lane on the street parallel to theirs so they wouldn't see her.

Back to Werrily Creek. But the caution ribbons of yellow and black were up and Coorooma's one police car was there with the hazard lights flashing so Wendy knew best not to go forward.

She walked back home and found her father and Lillian had their arms around each other. Like children doing the wrong thing, they moved apart but Wendy shook her head.

"It's fine with me." Her father patted for her to join them and Wendy sat between them. They sat together on the verandah in silence for a long time.

Wendy went back to Werrily Creek two days after that. She'd returned each afternoon after in the hope the silver brumby would return, but he never did. At first she'd cried and asked the people of the town if they knew the colours of the brumbies that were shot but nobody knew and Clive would have never told her the truth.

One day a hand written envelope addressed to "Wendy who doesn't believe in fairies" was in the letterbox. When she opened it there was a photo of a carousel. The horses were unadorned with no saddles or reins. Nor were they attached to the carousel with poles. They looked like wild horses and in the front, breaking into a canter, was a silver brumby. *Her* silver brumby.

"Believe. Love, Devon," was scrawled in messy writing on the back.

Wendy did.

ELI THE HIDEOUS HORSE BOY

Michael Leonberger

Taryn escaped from home whenever she could, dashing through crooked neighborhood streets lined with shuddering houses, leaning almost together in a show of support. She'd dart past the woods and the shopping centers, all fetid litter and glittering candy huts and boarded-up windows, before emerging on the sloping hills beyond. There she'd lounge on green grass nearly untouched, cut through with the dull gray arteries of water drainage units, unfit for urban development. She'd lay with a book open, shoes and socks kicked to the side, stretching toes through blades of grass and imagining that she was someone she was not, somewhere she was not. Someone brave and inquisitive and capable of great adventures, in a town that was not this one. This synthetic scoop, where most of her adventures came from television, where most of the local culture was provided by corporate supermarkets, and all the memories she'd developed in their parking lots with her friends weren't as unique as she thought. Just adolescent discoveries in the glow of artificial street lamps, by the metallic cattle of shopping carts and old cars, surrounded by the trash of old receipts and plastic bags blowing across the blacktop like tumbleweeds.

When they were especially adventurous they'd take their indiscretions to the woods, and there was a sort of untouched magic there, if you stepped over the crushed fast food bags and French fry containers that sprouted like garish, greasy mushrooms. She'd had her first sexual experience there with a boy whose clammy hands had made it beneath her shirt and down her pants, and it was so genuinely exciting and made her feel so much a complete person that she had to imagine his beautiful face hadn't been lit up by a gas station sign. That she hadn't peeled away a straw wrapper from the sweat of her naked back when they'd finished. That she hadn't pulled her underwear back over her feet with the smell of gasoline as thick and sweet in her nose as his sweat and the subtle humming green smells of the woods underneath.

He'd joined the army afterwards because he hadn't known what else to do. Having sex with her hadn't made him feel as much like a man as he'd needed, she thought. She resented herself, maybe. Thought those things bitterly at his funeral, after he'd taken a bullet to the head. Thought him heroic and beautiful and remembered his silly smile and blamed herself, yes, for not being reason enough for him to stay.

Not that she'd been in love. In love with the soft sinew of his body, maybe. The muscles that rippled beneath, the way the sweat coated him, made him bestial, even. The glorious scribble on his face when he'd buck and finish, and he was too embarrassed for her to look. But even the darkness wasn't safe from the electric glow of the florescence and she could see the sweat gleam up in the woods in neon that clung to every inch of him like plastic wrap.

She'd think of him and feel the flutter in her stomach, lightheaded and out of breath and then remember he was dead and the colors in her memory would fade and her lust would dry.

He had been stardust and now burned far away in a skyline where the stars couldn't make it past the electric pollution anyway.

His sensitivity and thoughtfulness had been unique to the boys she knew in town, blunted by the men in his life who hadn't any use for that. Who'd snipped off those bits, and sent him perforated to a pinewood box.

She missed him and hated them and found herself on the top of the green hills, feeling widowed but young and finding mirror versions of herself in the stories she'd read. Even the stories she'd write, that she didn't show anyone, naked and panting as they were. She worked at a diner on the weekends and shelved books at the library weekdays, and figured if she saved enough she'd make it to college, and maybe then, if she kept her wings relatively muscular, she could learn to fly.

Derrel Johnson had fallen in love with Taryn's quiet eyes, the plump purse of her lips, her flowing, thick coils of charcoal hair and the idea that she'd never had sex in the woods, that she didn't know what that was at all.

He saw her and wanted her and thought she'd be a good thing to fill in the negative space of photographs in his life. She dressed politely at the diner and he'd try and pinch her backside and act like he hadn't, while his friends laughed and snickered and he figured she liked it.

He pretended to browse for books at the library, where she wore skirts and sometimes kicked off her shoes, and he'd ogle her transparently from above books that he'd sometimes read upside down, which was a little joke to him. Her face alive with discomfort, and he liked that, too. Figured she couldn't look bad. Figured her discomfort was like a growing pain, the last part before she learned to lust for him, before she entered the world of adults and sex, and what was there not to lust for?

He had a perfect sculpt. A scar on his right temple from when his younger brother had swung a shovel at him, but the hair had grown back okay over it. It hid the damaged part where the seed for violence had grown in his brain. He had a strong nose and a powerful neck and shoulders. A little too much beer had created a community center in his gut, but he looked in the mirror and saw power there, too, especially when he sucked it up, and what did women care, anyway? Men weren't attractive besides, and women weren't visually engaged. That's how his mom had ended up with his ogre of a father. She'd left, of course, eventually, because she'd been a monster, too, underneath a charming exterior.

He pitied his old man but thought he was a little bit of a sap for allowing her to go in the first place. The old man had taken those frustrations out on him, with his fists, when he'd been too small to fight back. Only now he was bigger, and he'd have a lovely girl in his life soon enough, and then the old man would have to admit, somewhere in the crumbling mania of his aging mind, that his son was superior.

He saw Taryn lastly at church, in a powder blue skirt that he figured was too short, that showed her pretty knee caps too plainly, that he wouldn't let her wear when she was his, but that was somewhere in the future, and so he soaked her up now. She volunteered to give out food to sick older women, with oxygen tubes coiling out of their noses like awful snakes, and he figured time was not on her side. Someday she'd look like that, too.

He hoped they'd made a pile of children before then.

Boys stared. Even those adequate at conversation, polite enough to maintain eye contact and crack a joke until Taryn walked away. But if she looked back at the right moment, she'd catch them looking.

With Derrel, it was worse. There was a meanness there, a possessiveness, and he didn't ever talk to her in real life. Just looked. Tried to touch her. Spoke about her loudly and showered her with vulgarities if he was drunk. How good she looked, how much he wanted her, always with the smug air of someone waiting. She'd catch him waiting in places she didn't expect, outside of her house at night, or in the library when she was working, with that piercing, childish meanness in his small eyes, and she did her best to avoid him.

He'd taken to sitting at the diner for hours, just so he could pinch her.

She'd told him off but he figured she was joking. Most people did, actually. He was attractive. Athletic. Going nowhere, but in this town that didn't count against you, so people didn't understand maybe why she wouldn't just take what was given to her.

Well, she wouldn't. Not from him or anyone else. She had her own designs on life, and he wasn't anywhere near being a part of her plan.

The only thing they had in common would have repulsed him, and she let it warm her heart on cold nights when she'd look out her window and catch his brake lights peeling away, down the road, curving with drunk imprecision.

She'd wonder how long he'd been outside her home, drinking in his car, thinking about her, and to prevent herself from screaming she'd think about her secret.

The sideshow girl.

The one in the traveling carnival that had set up their tents outside town, by the old mine. If you were standing at the top of those green, sloping hills, you could see their lights, dotting the horizon like Christmas colored cigarette butts twinkling in the dark. The sounds of crashing metal and hushed screams carried along the breeze at night.

At the carnival the world didn't seem so small, so mean, and failed dreams didn't seem so gutting.

Kids climbed in their cars and headed towards those pied piper lights, to ride the bone-rattling machines, pile-driving along rickety tracks through clouds of grease and hot butter. The show tents surrounded the rides in candy-cane stripes faded the color of nicotine, and inside one of those tents was Carlotta.

Her hair waxy red, the soft muscles of her tan and sturdy body accentuated by the burlesque corset and hole-punched fishnets she'd wear. Her eyeliner was perfect, peeling her wide eyes with carefully paralleled streaks, underscoring her sly wisdom—like she would teach you things, but only if you began by getting comfortable with the idea that she was superior to you, that you were only an amusement to her.

The sideshow girl's eyes spoke of power.

And Taryn wanted to be seen in those eyes.

She wanted, she supposed, to break a little in those eyes, wanted Carlotta to instruct her in things she couldn't learn from anyone else in this town.

She'd heard the boys talking about it. Derrel in particular. How, if you paid her a pile of cash, she'd teach you things, in the smoky darkness of her tent.

Things Taryn certainly hadn't learned in the woods with her previous lover, as good as he'd been.

And he was dead now, and she was stuck here, so she figured it didn't much matter how she learned anything, besides.

So she waited around after the show, after Carlotta had attached ribbed metal cones over her breasts and caressed them with a buzz saw until yellow sparks leapt off the stage. Taryn tingled all over watching her. The command she had over her audience. The sly mystery in her eyes, and the efficient sensuality of her body.

Once the show was over and everyone had piled out Taryn approached her, trembling all over, sweat pooling on her scalp beneath her hair.

Carlotta had thrown a cream silk robe on and was lighting a cigarette beside a ladder made of blades she'd climbed up moments earlier. Her eyes flicked up and she smiled.

"Hi," Taryn said, curling her fingers in the air in an embarrassed school girl wave. Then: "You're amazing."

"Thank you," Carlotta said. Her eyes belonged to a cat goddess, her grin too. She was tall, even without heels, taller than Taryn had been prepared for. She could see the thick smear of her foundation up close. The beads of sweat that couldn't break through it.

"Um...I was just wondering..." Taryn started. She had the cash in her right hand and was fidgeting with it. Carlotta's eyes dropped to it and her grin grew a little wider.

"What are you thinking about, honey?"

"There are things I'd like to learn," Taryn stammered.

"There are things I'd like to teach," she said, stepping forward, looping one finger beneath the strap of the white tank top Taryn was wearing and pulling it down her shoulder. "This'll be fun. Usually it's only boys. Slobbering hard-ons. This should be more sophisticated. But..." And she stopped for a moment, stepping backwards, finishing her cigarette and crushing the butt beneath her toes. "I'm going to need to see your ID."

Taryn swallowed and fished it out of her drawstring bag, hands trembling, almost dropping it as she passed it along to Carlotta.

"Nineteen. You're Eli's age. Down to the month."

"Eli?" Taryn asked.

"Oh," Carlotta said, clearing her throat. "The Horse Boy." Behind her, a fan rotated lazily, murmuring electric. Taryn caught onto its rhythm and it calmed her. So did this small talk, and she allowed it go on so she didn't collapse into a jittery heap of desperate nerves.

"I don't know who that is."

"Sure you do. That's why you kids come, at least when you're younger. I am more popular with a slightly older crowd," she said, smiling. "I only bring him up because of your birthdate, but also that." She nodded towards the dog-eared paperbacks climbing out of her bag. Steamy southern gothic pulps. "Strange kind of girl brings books to a carnival. Then wants to pay the sideshow performer for sex."

Taryn blushed somewhat defiantly. The truth was complex, but she didn't feel too strongly the need to defend herself. Part of this whole thing was about being broken down, she figured. At least that's what the boys had said.

"Doesn't matter to me," Carlotta said. "You're looking for a thrill, then I can provide. Just don't let him see you with those, if you go to his tent. He'll talk your ear off."

"Eli the Horse Boy?"

She nodded. "We all thought he was dumb as a stack of bricks, until one of your local boys hit him hard enough. Unlocked his jaw a little, we figure. One way to fix up that mass of cartilage he calls a face. Cheaper than surgery besides, and now you can't get him to shut up. It was a little easier, to be honest, when we thought he was stupid."

Taryn stopped shaking, and something cold ran through her, putting out the flames at the tips of her nerves. "You call him the Horse Boy?"

Then Carlotta rolled backwards on her heel, a confused look on her face. "Yes. The Hideous Horse Boy. It doesn't matter, just when people come around here with extra cash, it's for one of two things."

"People spend the night with the Horse Boy?" Taryn asked.

"You could call it that," Carlotta said, but her face was a frown now, and whatever chemistry had connected the two of them was starting to evaporate. "Hey, I'm just making chit chat. It doesn't matter. There's a bed in the back, and that cold money isn't getting any warmer in your hand..."

Taryn looked at her, but folded the money back up. "I think I have to go," she heard herself say.

"Oh, come now," Carlotta said. "Don't be shy. You're young. You've still got the baby fat in your cheeks. There are things I can do to your soft little body that you can't imagine..."

But it had passed, and she couldn't get the idea out of her head: someone being hit hard enough that their bones finally slid together correctly. That they could finally speak. And this was somehow amusing to Carlotta.

"Another time," Taryn said, walking backwards towards the tent's entrance.

"You know where to find me," Carlotta said, firing up another cigarette and watching the girl leave.

The cool summer night took to her sweat when she stepped out, and she felt something rotten in her stomach that she wasn't sure what to do with, only that she was a little bit out of control, navigating through a nightmare, and somewhere in the center of it was a sad, unfortunate person who liked southern gothic and could only tell anyone after being hit hard enough.

The story went round and round in her head like an endless wash cycle and she turned with it, scanning the tents beyond the rides, themselves mechanical beasts who'd been buried beneath the Earth, but were just now climbing free, their great steam-powered fingers crawling with children.

And then she saw it: the Hideous Horse Boy.

One of several attractions advertised at the Freakshow tent. She'd never gone inside, never even considered it. Always thought it probably tacky and fake, and horribly insensitive, besides.

But here she was, slightly outside of herself anyway, and she found herself crossing the gravel fairgrounds towards the Freakshow tent.

She shelled out the money to the caramel-toothed barker, his face ruddy from the sun, his wrinkles perfectly filled with lines of dirt. He peeled back the entrance with a cane. It was hotter inside than in Carlotta's tent and smelled like hay and manure and something miserable. She made it through rooms bathed in different colored gels, all sea-weed greens and toilet-cleaner blues, which made her slightly sick. All around her animals with multiple heads and distorted fetuses floated in tubes of formaldehyde.

And then she was in a dark, quiet room, black as slate but with a soft cream light that came up gradually.

In the center, a large cage with the words "The Hideous Horse Boy" written loudly above it and a hunched body inside. His knees were pulled up to his chin and she couldn't see him entirely, but his silhouette was misshapen, and what she could see of his right foot was wrong. The toes had jammed together, only a nail or two growing across all of them, and she saw what the designers of the carnival wanted her to see: that it was a hoof.

Then the light was high enough that she could see one eye above his knee, the rest of his face bulky and obscured by shadow. He watched her sadly and she stepped towards him with a feeling that overwhelmed her, where nausea and outrage cohabitated.

"Is your name Eli?' she asked, kneeling before the bars of the cage. He blinked and slid backwards, and she caught more of his face. It was flat, the top of his mouth and his nose merged together and the left side of his skull was bulbous with small strands of brown hair growing out of it and down his face without any sort of pattern. But the right side was smooth and young and spoke to what his face might have looked like, beneath the mass of scars and cartilage Carlotta had spoken of.

Then Taryn felt that tightness in her guts explode and she hated herself just a bit for thinking about what his face might have looked like when he clearly *had* a face, for treading with trepidation on the other side of bars. For going along with it, whatever *it* was. She stood, dusting off her knees.

"Do you want to get out of here?" she said.

He tilted his head.

"What I mean is, this doesn't look like you're having any fun," she tried again. "Do they pay you well?"

Then she felt rude, as though she was being presumptuous. Maybe he loved this job, though she doubted it from his body language and the way Carlotta had spoken of him. Maybe this wasn't a job at all.

So she sat down again.

"I'm sorry, I don't mean to be like this," she said, combing her hair behind her ears. "I'm just…"

Terribly lonely, is what she wanted to say, but didn't.

Instead, she said, "I don't know who you are, and I heard you liked these books is all." She produced the books and looked at him eagerly.

He stared at them, and then moved his arms away from his face. She saw him in full, the bones piling together, the vertical drop they made, the way they carelessly accentuated features without bothering to resemble the way most people looked. He was one of the most interesting-looking people she'd ever met and he was looking at the books with sensitivity, and now an urgency, that she hadn't seen in a long time.

He smiled, his lips thick on one side and coiling upwards.

"You like them too?" he finally said quietly, and the timber of his voice shocked her. The words came out slow, with difficulty, but the sincerity there reflected what she saw in his eye.

"Oh, yes," she said, sliding down on her knees. "And you've read them?"

"Yes!"

"That's amazing, I don't know anyone who's reading these," she said. "Do you read a lot?"

He nodded and smiled and it unlocked something boyish and sweet in his features. There was an unevenness to everything, especially his smile, but the part that curled up was dashing, and the younger-looking eye was arched now, almost conspiratorially.

"All the time," he said. "When they get me books."

"You don't have, like, a library card?" she said.

He laughed. It was husky, metallic, and he said, "I've never been. They say I'd scare people."

He moved an arm and she could see that both of his legs were like that: hooved and arched dramatically. It was too dark for her to see everything, but she could tell he was shirtless, and blushed a little at the sight of his chest, hairless and tense with coiled muscles. Nothing wrong with that part of him at all.

She was staring, and did her best to look away.

"There's nothing wrong with you," she said. "Are these people your parents? Your family?"

"Something like that," he said.

"Well they should let you have some fun," she said. "Can we take a walk together or something?"

He shook his head. "No. It'll ruin the show."

"Okay. Well when the carnival shuts down, then."

He paused, then looked back at the books. "No. No I don't think so."

"Do they let you out of there?" she finally asked. "Because if they don't I'm going to call the police."

She smiled at that, but the look he reflected back at her was tense.

"Of course they let me out," he said, though he couldn't look at her. "This is just part of the act. Anyway, don't call the police."

The distant way he spoke made the tension rise up in her belly again.

"They don't let you out, do they?"

"Don't call the police," he said again.

She put her hands on the bars.

"They won't let you take a walk with me."

Then, there was a shuffling behind them. Someone else walking through the freakshow.

"You should go," he said quietly, then reached for her fingers with his right hand. His fingers were soft and delicate, and he squeezed her hand. "I'm fine. Really. This is all just for show, but I don't want to go out tonight. Okay?"

"Okay." More shuffling behind her, and she stood.

"But what books do you want me to bring?" she asked, and he blinked at her. "For when I come back. What books do you want?"

Then, without missing a beat: "Flannery O'Connor."

His smile was uneven and broken and somewhat sophisticated and she smiled, too.

"I'll be seeing you soon," she said, and left the tent.

Derrel was outside. Stumbling, plastic cup of beer frothing into the dust of the ground. He demanded to know what she'd been doing in there. What took her so long. She brushed past him and kept walking as he howled at her to stop.

She saw a policeman working security and understood something when Derrel called her a bitch and the officer only chuckled.

By the time Derrel stumbled home, his father had already begun his talk about the Horse Boy's mother. Derrel collected himself in the doorframe of the kitchen and ran a hand down his face. His father stopped his speech and gazed up at him, his grin folding upwards into a hideous wrinkled sneer above a grease brown wife beater that had once been white. A whisper of tangled silver hair clutched at his collar. "Derrel, so nice of you to join us," he drawled.

The old man sat before nine or ten young men, situated around a dinner table that hadn't known a woman or a child since Derrel's mother had left. Derrel's grown little brother sat front and center; a round, happy-looking head wreathed in peeling wallpaper that honestly advertised the nothingness that lived behind his eyes. He stared up at his drunk brother, giggled, then returned his attention to his father.

"The Horse Boy's mother was a magnificent beast," Dad said, fanning warped, knuckly hands before the boys. "Strong legs, like a horse, but the upper half was all woman." He pantomimed sloping breasts on his chest and some of the youngest men laughed. "She even had wings in the back. Great, terrific flappers, though I never saw her fly. Never saw anyone fly around this shit heap."

In the old days, Derrel thought, when Dad would give this speech, some young knucklehead would inevitably call bullshit, that there had never been a voluptuous horse woman at the carnival, and Dad would punch them so hard their teeth would rattle around, or ooze out in thick, molasses coils of blood.

Now no one questioned him. The Horse Woman had been real.

And she'd killed a child.

That was the secret.

So the men in town had chased her into that mine and pulled her wings off and cut off her legs and slit her throat and talking about it was the only thing that could get them excited anymore.

Derrel grimaced, collected himself, steadied his consciousness behind his eyes. He was too drunk, though Dad said it helped with the hunt. He wasn't wrong.

"What she did to that little child…" Derrel's father frowned, and when every wrinkle frowned with him, he looked truly tortured. A mask of guilt and horrified sadness that Derrel knew was only show, but the effect was impressive. "Pulled her fingernails out. Tore her hair and scalp right offa her head. Ate her, mostly. That little girl surely died screaming. So, in return, we took the horse woman's son. Tit for tat. Normal-looking baby who'd started developing his mother's…*eccentricities*. His baby feet were becoming baby hooves and little wings were starting to grow in the back. So we got rid of the wings. Broke his fingers and toes to make sure those eccentricities would never develop and beat his face that might have otherwise been beautiful. And now we do it every year, in honor of that little girl. We chase him through the mine. We hunt the Hideous Horse Boy."

All ritual. All hokem. But the young men were bowing their heads, seriously taking to the old man's challenge. To rise up. To serve in this ritual, to become men. The goose step was fraternal, and they took to it. Derrell took, too. To not was to admit something too terrible to contemplate—that there wasn't a point to anything around here. That all they had in this town was the yawning blackness.

"You all don't know how lucky you got it," he said. "Catching his bitch of a mother, now that was hard work. Man's work."

They also didn't know something Derrel knew: that the Horse Lady had never killed a child.

They'd stumbled upon that little girl in the basement of a man in town too decent to have done what the scars on her body suggested he did.

So they blamed it on the Horse Lady. And hunted her.

Now they got to hunt the Horse Boy. And so it went.

In the meantime, Derrel was hunting a lady all his own.

He had the gun in his car. He thought about Taryn, thought about how he had enough bullets to do them both, if it came to it—if the sun ever went well and truly down in this empty town and the yawning blackness got to be too much.

Until then, there was the hunt.

So he filed out of the kitchen with the other boys and went to work.

Taryn rooted around in the dark, moving delicately so as not to wake her parents. She found a flashlight under the kitchen sink and scanned a small hoarder's collection of used books until she found O'Connor. She smiled happily, grabbed the volume, and schlepped her way through the dark toward the carnival, where the lights had been put down. She felt their absence in the skyline, like the stars she knew were there, and took it on faith she was marching in the right direction.

She started at the hills, their greens newspaper gray at night, then followed the veins of roots on the outside of the woods, before finding that hard scrabble road that scarred the ground, the small petrified houses that lined the way. She followed blacktop until it was gravel, until the landscape rolled and they were near the old mine that the carnival's midway backed up against.

She slid into the freakshow tent undetected, and stood before his cage again.

She figured the show must have only just recently ended, as he was still in the cage.

At least, that is what she hoped.

He was standing, his back to her though the chiaroscuro of the dark created an effect that might have been misleading. It looked as though the corners of his back beneath his shoulders had little broken thumbs that wriggled in the dark, like the roots of mutilated wings. The thought made her dizzy—her eyes must have been playing tricks.

He stood up on his toes, his knees almost bent inwards at what must have been double joints. Legs wide, his exposed backside plump and lovely, strong and dovetailing into a back cut through with slashes of raised keloid. His nakedness startled her and she cleared her throat.

He spun around, made no grabs for modesty and smiled at her through the tortured landscape of his face.

Once more, the young man shone through his eye.

"I've got her," she said. "Flannery."

"Excellent," he said, pulled by excitement towards the bars. Then he paused, dipping his eye, and said, "I didn't know you were coming back tonight."

"I don't really know what I'm doing," she said dreamily, marching up to the bars. "You don't mind...?"

"No," he said.

"All right then. So how about that walk, like you promised."

"I can't..."

"But the show is over."

He bowed his head, delicate fingers curled around the bars, arms strong and unspooling from broad shoulders, the divots in his face emphasizing the concern in his eyes.

"What don't I understand?" she frowned, and that nervousness returned to her stomach.

"It's better for me to be in here. At least for tonight."

"What happens tonight?"

He parted his lips to speak, then swallowed whatever it was.

"I think it would be better if you came back tomorrow. I'll read this and we can talk about it then."

She tilted her head. "And if I don't? It's just...I feel like you're in trouble. That if I leave I won't see you tomorrow. Am I wrong?"

He nodded slowly, silently, then said quietly, "It's just this thing, you know."

"I don't."

"For being born. Something they say my mother did. So tonight, I have to pay. I don't mind it anymore, but I don't want you to be here when it happens."

"I don't know what you're talking about," Taryn said, tracing her fingers down a bar, feeling an apology bubble at her lips, when a rustling sound behind her snapped her out of her reverie.

"You need to hide," he said, the sudden clarity of his voice frightening. "*Now.*"

She folded herself into the shadows of the corner as a figure approached.

She recognized the tall elegance and even the smell of Carlotta, whose silhouette was an oil drop navigating wet shadow. She'd been drinking and swayed in the dark.

"Eli?" she whispered, her voice dry. Quiet. "Are you ready?"

"Yes."

The rattling of keys and the cage was open. He stepped out, hunched over to stand her height. Without the hunch, he would have towered over her.

She pulled his head gently towards her lips and kissed his forehead, her hands visibly trembling. "Remember to run for the promised lands," she said. "They just want a chase, they're not looking for a fight. Okay?"

"Okay," he whispered.

"Promise. For your mother."

"I promise."

All the while, the faint growl of diesel had been rising beyond the thin walls of the tent, like the bilious gurgle of demons, and rising above that was some kind of shouting. Hysterical, hyena cries. Taryn's eyes widened, as the hostile laughter became closer. Footsteps rattled the midway alleys outside and then they were in the room, young men in jeans and boots, the smell of liquor and sweat thick in the air. One ran a crowbar over the bars of the cage, while the other closed his grip over Eli's throat.

And then a third appeared in the doorframe, his belt wrapped around his fist, and when he raised it in the air Taryn screamed.

"Stop!"

Propelled by a nervous energy she didn't know what to do with. She rushed forward, and the first man let go of Eli's neck while the one in the door lowered his fist. He stepped forward, and the little bit of light in the room caught his face. The cruelty in his eyes. He tilted his head, his face a horror show of contempt.

"Taryn?" Derrel said slowly. "What are you doing in here?"

She stood defiant as he raked his eyes over her body. She'd left her sandals in the shadows behind her and now stood barefoot in a sundress that rode up her legs, dirt and dust drizzling her skin like sugar. His throat bobbed and he sighed a little.

"You won't touch me...but you'll spend the night with the *Horse Boy*?" he whispered. He didn't ask so much as declare, and she felt words forming at her lips when he pulled a gun from the back of his pants. Carlotta gasped and Taryn felt the words in her throat mutate into a scream.

Then he fired.

Flashbang.

Eli shoved Derrel's hand away, the bullet buried itself in the ceiling, and Derrel stumbled back.

One of the other boys rushed Eli, but he kicked him in the throat with his hooved foot and the boy fell to the ground, thick spittle sputtering from his lips, black with blood. The other boy only stared.

Then Eli was rushing toward Taryn, terrifically fast on powerful legs and scooping her into strong arms, his concerned eye finding hers in the dark as another slug ate the dirt by their feet.

Derrel watched the monster pick his girl up and bolt out of the tent. He squeezed the trigger but his vision was spinning and he could feel the sideshow girl's hand around his arm.

"You *monster*..." she was saying.

He threw her to the ground.

She sobbed. Bitter, wet tears slithered down her face and into the dirt, formulating spots of mud. He turned from her to his friends.

"This is as real as it gets," he said, reloading his gun. "This isn't like last year. He's got a victim, now. Just like his mother before him."

None of the boys questioned him. The one clutched his throat, his eyes pink and swollen in his head as though they were trying to dislodge themselves, as the other helped him to his feet.

"Just watch out for Taryn," he said. He couldn't bear it if someone else hurt her.

He couldn't believe he'd missed her in the first place.

They pounded through the grid of the midway, toward the mountains that huddled against the horizon in perpetual shame, ever since the mine inside its bowels had shut down.

"We're going in there?" Taryn asked, and Eli gently nodded, placing her on her feet. Shards of gravel in the cool grass bit at her soles.

He fidgeted. "It's where the hunt usually happens. Down in the mine." It huddled over them, the silhouette of a crouching giant whose interest in them had become perverse. The logo for the old Minotaur company was still emblazoned in the rock. Eli made a motion to enter through the giant's groin.

She grabbed his arm. "Why should we go in there?"

"Because I've learned it well. They used to catch me in there, but they rarely do anymore. I'm too quick, and the shadows are too dark. And there's a special spot I've found where they can't find me."

"The promised land?"

He smiled, that thick curl on the one side of his mouth.

Behind them, the sounds of motors increased, and they could see the trucks and cars whizzing through the midway, kicking up white clouds of dust backlit by the moon, boys hanging out the car windows like sneering demons, with guns and blades and pipes.

Eli looked from the commotion to Taryn, his hands tense at her arm.

"Why are they doing this?" she asked.

"They think my mother killed someone," he said.

She almost said, *Did she?* But it didn't matter.

She looked at the deformity of his face, his radiant otherness, his sensitive eyes. And she let him lead her into the mine.

Its cool darkness enveloped them. Behind them, the boys chattered and laughed, their sneers sailing by like invisible bullets, ricocheting in the dark.

Eli gripped her hand and at first she stumbled behind him, as they navigated sharp turns and into narrow passageways she couldn't see, until the rhythm of her body matched his, and she could anticipate turns, almost feeling them through the electric tingle of his finger pads.

Whether they were close, to the entrance or to this promised land, she had no idea, but the dark was more of a comfort than the flashes of light that would occasionally illuminate them.

The boys' flashlights. Firebombing the dark, and she was sure they couldn't find them, but when white light would flare up before her and catch her eyes, glaring off the scaffolding the miners had left behind, or the lip of an old elevator, gathering dust, her spine would stiffen and she'd press herself closer to Eli.

Then he pressed her flat against the wall, the artery in his arm throbbing against her chest. She heard him inhale sharply and figured she should hold her breath, and she did.

As they walked right past them, the boys didn't look like they were having fun anymore. They were red-faced and frustrated, and she could smell the sweat and the anxiety on them. The blood rattling in their throats, their bodies inches from her nose. And yet they couldn't see.

She looked at Eli, and could see his eye staring back at her.

A flashlight had caught his eye. Its pinpoint of light stained his iris and she could still see it in the dark long after the boys had passed.

Time passed with them, lost to the blackness, and that point of light seemed to multiply, until it was a whole constellation.

Centaurus, burning bright, always hidden by the smog in the sky.

But not tonight.

Tonight it blazed and she counted herself lucky that she'd ever been given the opportunity to see the stars at all.

"You ready to get out of here?" she finally whispered.

"I am," he whispered back. "But where will we go?"

"Anywhere," she said. Then he lifted her in his arms. Carried her through the dark, so quickly she felt as though he might have been galloping, that they might even have been flying together.

And though she knew it was impossible, she figured maybe they were.

Eventually, she could see light. Shafts of gray tinged with silver, perhaps by more stars usually buried in clouds, and when they emerged they found themselves at the side of a cliff that peered down over town.

She could see the way the water drainage units scarred the green grass of her favorite spot, and realized it was just as small as she'd always figured it was.

Yet the woods sprawled out farther than she'd imagined, and in the distance beyond the tree line, gray and shrouded in mist, was somewhere new. Somewhere she'd never been. A place she'd never thought possible.

"There," she said, pointing, jamming her toes into the hard ground beneath her.

"What's there?"

"Some place new. Some place that isn't here. You ready to take that walk with me now?"

He nodded and took her by the hand. Together they made their way towards that promise, buried slightly beyond the darkness on the edge of town.

DIFFERENT

Sandra Wickham

The last six years had given me a tough hide. Most of the stares, pointed fingers and whispers bounced like steel off a shield but my armour wasn't impenetrable. As we stood in line for our appearance before the unicorn, a girl close to Kyra's age pointed at her and asked her mother what was wrong with her. Her mother pulled her away from us, glaring. "Don't get too close, you might catch it." My fingers tightened around Kyra's. I held my tears and my tongue—it wouldn't do to make a scene in the middle of Unicorn City.

Kyra gazed up at me with her precious brown eyes and my heart bled. I knew she understood, knew it hurt her when people were cruel. They teased her because her eyes were slanted, or because her nose was tiny and her tongue often stuck out, or because she didn't walk and talk the way other kids did. Today, we were going to change all that. Today would be the end of Kyra being different.

There were those in our own village who mocked Kyra and not everyone had contributed to the offering gently bouncing from its leather strap against my heart. Bale and his two sons had tried to convince everyone it was a waste of coin. Days before leaving, I took Kyra to the centre of the village. She loved to watch people and wave to them. Unfortunately we ran into Bale and his sons, who started in on us about what a blemish Kyra was to the village. They yelled such horrible things at us, what they'd do to Kyra given the chance, it made me angry and frightened all at once. It strengthened my resolve to leave, to bring Kyra to the unicorn. I never wanted anyone to hurt her, ever. I snuck Kyra away in the deepest of night to prevent them from stopping us.

Unlike Bale and his sons, those who got to know Kyra, loved her. It was those people's generosity that made it possible for us to be here. People like old Clay, who'd brought us in his rickety wagon and waited now outside the city.

The line moved slowly. Our fellow devotees shuffled along, hope palpable in the air. It was obvious why some were here; a broken limb, blindness, infected wounds. Others didn't wear their hurt so visibly. Perhaps some of the women struggled with fertility, like I had. Kyra had been a blessing, then a challenge.

She was currently absorbed in the city, flinging her head from side to side to take it all in. The walls were painted a regal golden colour and a constant melody of voices, almost like singing, came from the alehouses, shops, smithies and tall homes people here lived in.

Banners bearing the unicorn horn insignia waving from windows high above enchanted Kyra and she stumbled a bit at her own exuberance, but I held her up by the hand and she got her feet under her again. Most kids her age had been running for ages but she'd only managed to walk a year ago. Her legs still wobbled, her feet planted awkwardly and she relied too much on me to hold her up.

Morning moved into afternoon faster than the line moved toward the unicorn. We ate, sang Kyra's favourite songs and I imagined what she'd be like after we visited the unicorn. I wanted the best life for Kyra and would do anything to give it to her.

Finally we made it to the steps lined with guards bearing spears twisted like the unicorn's horn. Kyra broke my grip and ran toward one of them, her legs flinging out to the sides like a newborn colt.

I raced after her. "Kyra, no!" My heart clenched with fear as the guard brought his spear down. A guard a step higher descended and stayed the spear arm.

"Hold," he said to the younger guard. I scooped Kyra up in my arms as she reached for the spears, their shine too much for her to resist. With a bow to the grey-haired guard who'd come to our rescue, I backed away into the line. Kyra's cries of complaint drew hushing sounds from around us. I held her close as we worked our way up the stairs. It would be our turn soon.

Priests clad in white robes, hands clasped within sleeves embroidered with the emblem of the unicorn stood at the entrance to the unicorn's grove. One ushered us forward. I helped Kyra up the last steps to the top. The priest examined my letter of admittance, crinkled from dried teardrops. He nodded to the other priests and they stepped aside from the steel plated wooden doors. The wait had allowed me to focus on keeping Kyra occupied but now we were about to see the unicorn, I could barely breathe. Would she help?

Two guards pulled open the doors and the rush of air smelled like home, of trees, luscious grass and moist, turned earth. This used to be a coliseum but was transformed into a self-contained grove with the aid of the unicorn's powers. The doors closed behind us and we were in a forest worthy of myth. Kyra pulled me along the dirt path lined by blossoming deep green undergrowth which wove through strong trees reaching to the open sky. The walls remained somewhere, but we couldn't see them. It would've been easy to forget they were there.

Nerves made my palms sweaty and Kyra's tiny hand slid out of mine. I ran after her, skidding to a stop at the sight of the unicorn. She stood in a grassy area at the end of the path, her fine white hair shining in the fading daylight. Her mane cascaded down her long neck like a waterfall, but it was her golden horn that held me transfixed. Kyra, however, didn't stop. She ran in her lopsided way, straight toward the unicorn.

"Kyra, stop! It will hurt," I yelled. Kyra ignored me and threw her arms around the unicorn's lowered neck.

Time slowed as my daughter's face buried into the unicorn's mane and I braced for the screams that didn't come. The mere touch of the unicorn should've had her skin burnt to blisters but Kyra only giggled.

"Kyra, come." I rushed forward to detach her.

"Leave her," the unicorn said, her voice beautiful and powerful. "Shall we sit, little one? It is not often I meet someone pure enough to hold me so." My soul filled with light at the kindness in her tone. While Kyra clung to her, the unicorn lowered herself, gently easing them both to the soft grass beneath.

Kyra laughed with pure delight and I felt the same giddiness rising inside of me. It was a moment of pure perfection. The unicorn lifted her head and met my eyes. For a moment I couldn't breathe, couldn't tell if my heart still beat. Those eyes held centuries of wisdom and a deep magic I could almost see but never understand.

"What do you wish of me?" she asked.

I reached under my shirt and pulled the satchel of coins from around my neck. "I have brought your offering." I pointed a shaky finger at Kyra. "My wish is for you to heal my daughter."

The unicorn studied me until I might have melted under her gaze and then nudged Kyra, who laughed again and clapped her hands.

"Your daughter does not need healing."

My heart fell heavy in my chest. "What do you mean?"

"There is nothing wrong with her."

"Nothing? Can you not see?" I flung both hands toward my daughter, begging the unicorn with my entire being. "She is not normal."

The unicorn's head bobbed up. "What is normal? Am I normal? I do not think so. Still, would I wish to be something else? Definitely not."

I faced the unicorn with the same ferocity I used too often to fight for my daughter. "All her life she has struggled, to eat, to walk, to talk. You think that is not worth healing?"

"She eats and walks and talks now, does she not?"

"But her life is so hard," I protested, falling to my knees, all my hopes and dreams for Kyra crashing away. "She does these things but not as well as others. Can't you see how hard it is for her? Please?"

"She is simply living in her own time."

I shook my head. "I wish things to be easy for her, like everyone else."

The unicorn let out a soft laugh. "You think life is easy for everyone else? You don't think other children have challenges? Other mothers suffer to see their children work through hardship? Your daughter does not need my help."

Her words were daggers to my heart, to my soul. "I want a better life for her. Many either mock her or ignore her, dismiss her as nothing—even her father abandoned us when he saw her. What will she do with her life?"

"What do you do?" the unicorn asked.

"I care for our elderly," I answered. "Clean, cook, do errands, help bathe them, whatever they will pay me for."

"Your daughter could not do this when she is older?"

"I want more for my daughter than what I have become."

"What you have become is the mother, teacher, and protector of this wonderful being. A most worthy existence. Your daughter will influence many people and do great things in her life."

Frustration and anger churned together inside of me. I pushed to my feet. "We waited for three years to come see you, travelled days to get here, stood out in that line all day and you refuse to help us?"

"I am sorry it was difficult to see me. Many people seek my help and it fills my days." She allowed Kyra to rub her neck, my daughter's hands clumsy but as gentle as she could be. "I am glad to have met you."

Something inside me snapped. Years of waiting, months of swallowing my pride as people brought us coins, days of travel and now a return trip with nothing to show for it. What would my people think when I came back and Kyra hadn't changed? What would Bale and his sons do? "You cannot do this to her. She isn't safe," I said, jaw tight.

"She has you," the unicorn replied.

"I am not enough," I yelled. The words of Bale and his sons splintered through my head. "There are those who would hurt her." Kyra flinched and I took a breath to calm myself. Stress already showed on her tiny face.

The unicorn bowed her head slightly. "She is strong. A survivor."

Anger flared hotter inside of me. "How can you refuse us?"

The unicorn lifted her head with a small snort. "I am a unicorn. I do as I choose. It was your choice to come to me, mine now to tell you she does not need me."

I kept my voice steady for Kyra's sake, though I wanted to scream at the unicorn. "Is it your choice to be kept here? Do you enjoy being locked within the city? You may have decided to be here to help people, but look around you. Have you forgotten walls hold you in? Priests and guards stand at the door? It's an illusion of free will. You're just a prisoner here, aren't you?"

"That is not true," the unicorn replied.

"No?" I shook the satchel at her. "What use do you have for coins, then?" I threw it on the ground.

Kyra hit her breaking point, burst into tears and reached for me. I scooped her up and as she wrapped her arms around my neck, pressing her cheek to mine, our tears melted together.

The unicorn got to her feet. "It is getting late. Stay here with me tonight, I'll have food and blankets brought to you. In the morning you can begin your journey home." Her hooves crunched along the path as she walked away.

Kyra still latched onto me, I fell to my knees and whispered, "We're going to be all right, my love. It'll be all right." I didn't believe it, but I repeated it until she calmed, pulled back to look at me, gave me a tiny pat on my cheek and then smiled. I smiled back, my heart shattered. I had failed her.

I woke with a tiny arm around my neck, a leg across my stomach and the smell of lilacs overwhelming my senses. The unicorn lay in the grass so close I could feel the heat from her body. Only Kyra's sleeping form kept me from jumping to my feet.

"You are safe," the unicorn reassured me.

As devastated as I was, her beauty and power overwhelmed me. "Please," I whispered, wrapping an arm around Kyra. "Can you not help us?"

The unicorn flicked her head and the grey-haired guard who had stayed his comrade's spear appeared. "Alkippe will accompany you to the edge of the city." She nudged Kyra with her nose and she threw her hands around the shining white head. "I wish you joy. Perhaps you will come visit me again. Or I will come visit you."

Two priests stepped forward. "The unicorn does not leave to see commoners."

The unicorn shook her head, mane raging and then settling. "Perhaps I should."

My heart a tumultuous disaster of sadness and failure, I held back tears as I clutched Kyra's hand and bowed to the unicorn. "And I wish for you, your freedom. No creature should live restricted, defined by others."

The unicorn bowed her head. "Good advice for your daughter, as well."

No reply came to me so I steered Kyra away. She waved at the unicorn and pouted as we left.

Clay's confused expression when he saw Kyra tore at my already shredded heart. I had no words, only shook my head at him. His face showed a moment of sadness but it was quickly replaced by a smile.

"Ready for a fun trip home?" he asked Kyra, who beamed back at him. He gave me a nod that held so much support it was hard for me to continue to meet his gaze. Would the others accept the unicorn's decision, as Clay seemed to? Could I?

We made our way slowly away from Unicorn City. The day went well, though my heart felt heavy and my mind spun with worry. Cray's wagon was a blessing, but was crowded with supplies from the city. I walked beside him when Kyra fell asleep.

"What do I do now?" I asked, so drained, so tired.

"Think on this," Clay said. "Is she happy?"

"Yes." I choked back tears.

"Is she loved?"

"Yes," I smiled, despite my anger. "So much. But that is why I want the best for her."

"Is she at peace?" he asked.

"Most times," I answered.

"Then all you need to do is love her." He smiled down at me and I remembered my words the unicorn had thrown back at me.

"No one should be defined by others," I whispered.

Kyra sat up in the wagon. Clay turned back to her. "The air is warm tonight. Should we camp?"

My daughter grinned. "Camp," she shouted and threw her hands up.

"I guess we camp," I told Clay. We found an area to stay and darkness fell over us as we set up for the night. The horse grazed as we ate beside the fire until the snaps of branches followed by footsteps made us all freeze.

Clay rose, taking out his hunting knife as I pulled Kyra to me.

"Who's there?" Clay called out. "Show yourselves."

I held Kyra tighter as my worst nightmare stomped out from between the trees. Bale and his two sons appeared in our circle of firelight, each holding a sword.

"What are you doing here?" I demanded.

Vaso, the younger of the brothers, always with the sharpest tongue, pointed his sword at Kyra. "You thought you freaks could just sneak away with our money?"

I shoved Kyra behind me. "It wasn't your money."

"Good as," his father said. "Taken from our people."

Clay moved forward, knife at the ready. "What do you want, Bale?"

My heart raced as his eyes settled on Kyra, peeking out from behind my legs. They could see she hadn't changed, they'd know we hadn't used our offering. "Here." I grabbed the bag of coin the unicorn had insisted I take back. I threw it to the ground near him. "Take it."

He glanced down his nose at the bag. "That's a start," he said.

"That money does not belong to you," Clay stepped forward again.

The older brother, Alon, slid toward Clay, sword pointed. "Back off, old man."

Clay shot me a sideways glance and I saw the decision cross his face. "Clay, don't," I tried.

"Your daughter," Bale spat at me, "is a curse on our village. You are not taking her back there."

My grieving heart turned to stone. "It's our home as much as yours."

"Wrong," he snapped back, pointing his sword at us. "That worthless thing doesn't deserve to live, least of all among normal folk."

"Unicorn," Kyra said, and lifted her head higher.

I nodded. "That's right, Kyra. The unicorn said she wasn't normal either." The memory of her presence gave me strength. "Leave us alone, Bale. We are going home."

He cleared his throat and his sons stepped to either side of him, swords ready. "We can't let you do that."

Clay took another step forward. "You've got no business here. Leave, now."

"You would defend them?" Alon demanded.

Clay was no fighter and we all knew it, but he nodded. Alon

started to laugh, but Clay rushed forward and slashed with his knife. Alon brushed off the attack and countered, his sword coming up and into Clay's gut. He exhaled like he'd been punched, went limp and collapsed to the ground. Alon's withdrew a sword covered in dark red blood.

Kyra screamed and I buried her face in my chest. "It's okay, my love," I lied, staring at Clay's motionless body.

Kyra's little hands gripped my neck. "Unicorn," she said again and I hushed her just as the unicorn ran through the trees behind Bale and his sons, her horn glowing golden as the sun. Alkippe stood by her side, spear at the ready.

"Step away from them. Now." The unicorn's voice rang through the night air and my soul leapt with hope.

"Boys." Bale's voice was low, overly controlled and determined. "The unicorn seems to have left the city with one old guard for protection. How much do you think they'd pay to have her back?"

"Dead or alive?" Vaso growled.

Bale smiled at his son. "I'm sure there's money in it either way."

My legs went limp. She was immortal but not invincible.

Bale, Alon and Vaso spread out slightly and advanced on the unicorn. Kyra broke free from my grasp. I screamed at her as she ran past Bale and wrapped her arms around one of the unicorn's front legs. "Hello again, little one," the unicorn said as though everything was fine, but it wasn't.

"Attack," Bale yelled at his sons and they charged. The unicorn pushed Kyra away from harm, reared and slashed at the men with her front hooves. The older brother Alon sidestepped and Alkippe mostly deflected his strike to her flank, but it still drew blood. The unicorn rose up, swung her head toward Alon and planted her horn into his chest.

Bale screamed with rage as his son sank to his knees. I grabbed a log from the fire, the end hot but bearable for me to handle. The unicorn backed up, pulling her horn back out and Bale raised his sword with both hands above her exposed neck. My daughter's horrified cries propelled me faster than I ever knew I could move and with both hands, I swung the fiery branch at Bale's midsection. He buckled and stumbled back which gave the unicorn time to face him full on. She reared again and I went to Kyra, the branch flames lighting her teary face.

"Mama." She reached for me and I threw the branch down to pick her up.

"You do not need to die," the unicorn said. I spun around to find her standing over Bale, one delicate hoof pressing on his chest. His sword lay on the ground out of reach. "Nor him."

Closer to the fire, Alkippe held his spear against Vaso's throat. Bale squirmed and grabbed the unicorn's leg with both hands, screamed and yanked them away. Even in the dim firelight I could see the red burns and bubbles where he'd touched her. He tried kicking his legs, but stopped as the unicorn leaned on him. "You will not return to the home of these ones," the unicorn said.

"It's our home!" Bale spat, writhing beneath her hoof.

The unicorn flicked her head up once then touched her horn to the side of his neck and he screamed as it burned a black, swirled marking into his skin.

Bale changed instantly. He became still and gave a nod. "We will not return," he wailed.

"Good." The unicorn lifted her hoof and Alkippe released Vaso. Bale and Vaso retrieved Alon's body and scurried back into the trees.

The unicorn went straight to Clay and touched his wound with her horn. He groaned and after a tense moment, to my utter joy, he sat up. He startled at the unicorn's closeness, then grasped his stomach, checking for a wound no longer there.

We gathered around the fire, Kyra clinging to me, Clay clinging to the blanket around him. Alkippe kept vigilant watch on the edge of camp, but I was sure no one else would bother us this night.

The unicorn's eyes shone sad in the flickering firelight. "I am sorry this has happened, but glad I found you."

"You left?" I asked.

She lifted her head a bit higher. "I wanted to know if you were right. If I was a prisoner."

"And?"

She snorted. "I was, but no longer. I had some help leaving." I looked at Alkippe and he gave a small bow.

I nodded understanding. "Thank you for helping us."

"You helped me to escape what I'd become. I thank you." She bowed her head slightly and my world flipped on its head. A unicorn had bowed to me.

"You may have your wish," she continued. "If you want your daughter to be like everyone else, I can do so."

What I thought would bring joy instead roused defensiveness. My grandest wish had been for my daughter to be like everyone else, but now I knew better.

"No," I shook my head. "You were right. My daughter is perfect as she is and I wouldn't want her any other way."

"What about others like Bale?" Clay asked, voice gruff, injecting a cold dose of reality into the dreamlike scene.

I took a deep breath and smiled down at my daughter. "It's not Kyra that needs to be different, it's the world that needs to change. I have to start making that happen for her. For now, she has me and others who will protect her."

"She does."

The unicorn lowered her head and Kyra wriggled from my arms. She wrapped her arms around the unicorn's neck. "Unicorn," she whispered.

"I would come with you, for a bit at least," the unicorn said. "If you would allow. It has been so long since I felt another's touch. Your daughter has captured my heart."

Tears flowed and I didn't fight them. "She has that way," I replied.

To Ride a Steel Horse

Stephanie A. Cain

The magic wouldn't leave Demy alone tonight. All the usual tricks—solving math theorems, reciting poetry, kickboxing—had failed. This close to Samhain, the human world and otherworld drew nearer to one another, the border between them thinning.

She leaned her forehead against the cool glass of the window, staring out into the darkness. It had rained earlier, and it was still windy, but she couldn't stand to be cooped up inside any longer.

She pulled on her leather jacket, went out to the garage, and gunned the Triumph Bonneville out of her drive. The cold air that hit her face smelled of wet leaves, bonfires, and harvest.

Highway Eighteen curved along the shore of Whiskey Lake between the trees on one side and the expensive lakeside houses on the other. She took a deep breath, enjoying the ache of the cold wind against her teeth. This was exactly what she'd needed—the sound of the Triumph's engine, the throb of power between her thighs, and the wind in her face to drown out the magic's seductive song. It took her back to her childhood, when she'd outrun her problems on the back of her horse Foxy. This was louder, more thought-drowning, but it had the same freedom.

Her mother would be ashamed of her but Demy had seen the magic take and take from her mother and grandmother, driving her sister Brenna away and barely giving anything back. Demy wasn't going to let it have her.

She opened up the throttle. She would ride past midnight, ride until dawn if she had to, just to silence the call.

She was halfway around the lake, approaching Bear's Roadhouse, when a *bang-clank* ripped through the sound of the engine. The bike shuddered and died.

Swearing, Demy managed to guide it to the side of the highway before it quit rolling altogether. A car she'd passed two miles back flew past, horn taunting her. She restrained herself from putting up a finger, closed her eyes, took a deep breath, and centered herself. "*Half a league, half a league, Half a league onward, All in the valley of Death Rode the six hundred—*"

The sharp blare of a horn broke off her recitation. A truck slowed to a crawl next to her, the passenger window cranked down.

"Need a hand, Demy?" called the driver, a burly guy who happened to be her neighbor—and the owner of the nearby roadhouse.

She grunted and shook her hair out of her face. "Just have my Moundbuilder waiting for me when I get there," she called back.

She could hear his laughter as he pulled ahead again.

The bike let her down occasionally, but she'd taken it as a challenge, an entirely non-magical hobby to keep her mind occupied. A lot of her skill she'd learned from Jack, who ran the bike garage next to the roadhouse. What Jack couldn't teach her, he fixed himself.

Demy pooched her lower lip out and blew her hair out of her face again. Another hundred feet and she'd be able to turn the bike over to Jack.

"Not this time." Jack King was a white-bearded guy of about seventy, with sinewy forearms and powerful shoulders. He was shaking his head. "It's dead, Demeter. Threw a rod. That's a whole engine rebuild. Don't throw good money after bad."

Demy blinked several times, staring at him. In six years, nothing had been too much for Jack to fix. She'd bought the used Triumph as an act of defiance in the face of turning twenty-five—her sister had laughed and called it a quarter-life crisis. That had been the only truly good thing about her twenty-sixth year. That had been the year the magic took her mother and sister both, but Demy had gotten through it because of the, well, zen of motorcycles.

"I'm sorry, D," Jack said, patting her shoulder. "Go next door and make Bear feed ya. I'll drop ya by home when I close up shop."

Demy shook her head. Jack was open until seven, and it was already past six. She didn't want to be stuck at home with five more hours to get past midnight—there was too much temptation there. As much as she'd refused to follow in the footsteps of her matriarchs, she hadn't been able to part with the various magical paraphernalia she had inherited. If she were home when the witching hour of Samhain hit...

"It's fine. I'll get Bear to take me home when he closes."

Jack's thick, white eyebrows shot up, but he smirked. "Raise a glass for me, too, then," he said. "Happy Halloween."

Demy trudged across the parking lot, her boot heels grating on the gravel. There were two dozen bikes parked outside the roadhouse, mixed with a few trucks from local non-bikers, because Bear made the best breaded tenderloin in north central Indiana.

She paused halfway across the parking lot and shoved her hands in her jeans pockets, tilting her head back to stare up at the stars that were beginning to appear. This bike had gotten her through the toughest years of her life. How was she supposed to just turn her back on it?

You could fix it, whispered a voice in the back of her head. *Magic can do anything.*

"Not anything," Demy snapped, her voice harsh. It hadn't brought her sister back. It hadn't kept her mother from dying.

The door to the roadhouse opened and a laughing couple came

outside, borne on a tide of southern rock music. Demy lowered her gaze, blinking away the tears in her eyes, and made herself go inside.

When Bear saw her, he set a plate next to the two glasses waiting for her at the bar. Demy couldn't keep from smiling. He knew her too well—the plate held a breaded tenderloin and a small mountain of fries. One glass was a shot of bourbon, and the other was her requested IPA from the local People's Brewing Company.

"How long's it going to take him?" Bear asked over the Black Crowes.

Demy's throat tightened. She shook her head and downed the shot before she answered. "It's dead," she whispered.

Bear leaned in, frowning. "What?"

Demy cleared her throat and repeated herself louder. "It's dead. He can't fix it."

Bear's face melted into a sympathetic expression. "Shit, Demy."

She nodded, unable to speak. Somehow, Bear's sympathy made it more real. He patted her hand and went down to the other end of the bar. Demy shoved a couple of fries in her mouth, grateful he wasn't going to try to cheer her up. She started on the tenderloin, hoping Bear—or his Halloween-costumed wait staff—would keep the drinks coming. After all, it wasn't like she was going to be driving herself home. She might as well mourn the bike properly.

"It's like watching my horse die all over again," Demy lamented. She was sprawled halfway across the bar, partly because the world was starting to do a slow roll and partly because she was just too sad to keep sitting up. "Did I ever tell you about that?"

"Maybe once or twice," Bear said, setting another glass of water in front of her. This was, Demy calculated, her third glass of water. She probably should have gone a little slower with the bourbon shots.

"Foxy. She was just the color of a fox, that bright russet color."

Demy rubbed her face. "She was such a good horse."

"Smart, too," Bear agreed.

Demy felt her face heat up. She'd told him this already tonight. She just couldn't get over how much it hurt to think about the bike.

"There are some things even magic can't fix," she said. "Magic can't make a horse live forever." She pinched the bridge of her nose, fighting the stinging in her eyes. "Can't make a person live forever, either."

"Nothing lives forever, Demy," Bear said, his voice gentle. The jukebox had quit playing twenty minutes ago, and since the roadhouse was empty except for the two of them, a zombie waitress, a kittenified waiter, and a self-absorbed couple in the corner, no one had started it up again. "We're not meant for it."

She sighed and shook her head. She knew he was right, but she was tired of losing people she loved. The bike's breakdown felt like another loss.

"I could make the bike live forever," she muttered.

"What's that?" Bear leaned in, a quizzical look on his face. Demy shook her head again, glad he hadn't heard.

"Nothing. I think I need some more fries, or you'll have to just leave me here to sleep in a booth."

Bear snorted and went to get another basket of fries.

As a horse-crazy girl, Demy had read every book about horses she could get her hands on. It didn't matter if they were famous race horses like Man O'War, fictional horses like the Black Stallion, or even mythical equine creatures like the Pegasus and hippogriffs. Despite the Dutch surname bequeathed them by an ancestor silly enough to get married, the Van Zant witches were Irish through and through, and Demy had grown up on stories of kelpies, each uisce, and pookas.

Demy had never known a Van Zant who wasn't crazy about animals, but they'd never gone in for familiars. Demy had always been a little wistful about that as a girl; she'd wanted a pony familiar that would follow her everywhere and be her faithful companion.

When she finished her fries, Demy drained her ale and stood up.

"You all right?" Bear called from the other end of the bar.

Demy just waved. She was fine. She just wanted to be under the stars again. She was getting twitchy in the stuffy bar.

Once she was out in the biting air, the parking lot dark except for a single security light, Demy's chest loosened a little. She took a deep breath, closing her eyes and feeling the air stretch into her lungs.

She missed Brenna. She missed having a family. Bear and Jack were great, but they weren't family. They weren't familiar. She'd talked to Bear about the magic, but she wasn't sure how much he believed. And she'd never even tried to tell Jack.

The wind slipped through her hair, tugging it out of the ponytail she'd tied at the nape of her neck. Demy shivered happily and unzipped her jacket. It was a windy, wild night, and she loved it. Leaves whispered in her ears and naked branches scraped against each other in a creaking secret language.

Demy?

She straightened, jerking her head around to search for the person who'd called her name, but the porch of the roadhouse was empty. Jack's garage was dark. No one stood in the parking lot but Demy herself.

Her heart started thumping in her chest. She had a sudden, visceral certainty that her sister was close, maybe watching her, maybe reaching out spiritually to her, but—

The wind swelled, skidding a raft of leaves across the gravel to swirl around Demy's feet, and the sense of Brenna's presence faded.

Demy lifted a hand to curl against the side of her neck, where her pulse still pounded. Then she realized she was looking at the Triumph, parked where she'd left it in front of the garage door.

She crossed the parking lot without letting herself think about what she was going to do. What she knew Brenna would do if she were here. When she reached the motorcycle, she rested her hand against the fuel tank.

"Live," she whispered. She closed her eyes against the swelling joy of magic in her blood, the pins and needles of long-unused talents blooming back to awareness. "*Live.*"

Her fingers shook against the gas tank. It had been so long since she'd channeled the magic, it bucked like an untamed horse, but Demy exerted her will. She visualized the thrown rod, the resulting hole in the cylinder. It was like a compound fracture, she told herself. She'd seen her mother use the magic for healing often enough. She ought to know how to heal this.

But magic was a living thing, and after being ignored for so long, it held a grudge. It twisted in Demy's grip, stinging her fingers and snapping away from her. The rod shot out of the engine and crashed into the cinderblock wall of the garage.

Demy swore. "You've been trying to get my attention," she snapped. "Well, you've got it. I give in. Quit fighting me."

She didn't have to give herself entirely to the magic, after all. She could coax it just enough to fix the bike, just enough to make it quit calling her out on the road to escape it.

She glared at the bike and stroked one hand down the gas tank to press her fingers lightly against the now-cold cylinder. "Come on, maybe magic can't make a horse or a person live forever, but it *can* make a bike run forever," she said.

Demy studied the bike, extending her senses to try to understand the failure in the engine, but ultimately sensing nothing except a broken rod and a hole.

She pulled up a diagram of the engine on her phone to try and recreate the broken pieces with magic and noticed the time—almost one. "Shit," Demy hissed. "Shit shit *shit!*" She'd missed midnight. She was so rusty with the talent, who knew if it would even work now?

Over the next hour, she tried everything she could think of, forcing her brain through mathematical gymnastics, trying to translate the logic behind the engine into magic. By one-fifty-three in the morning, she was sitting in the gravel cradling her head and trying not to admit defeat. Her eyes were stinging.

How would Brenna have done this? Her approach to magic had been fluid, almost musical, compared to Demy's. For every theory Demy had slogged through to reach a logical conclusion, Brenna had blithely accepted the magic without explanation.

Maybe Demy was making this too difficult.

She shook the tension out of her shoulders and folded her legs, resting her hands on her knees. She thought about Foxy, about the bright russet of her horse's hide, the curious quirk of Foxy's ears, the surprisingly smooth trot, the way Foxy always greeted Demy by snuffling at her shirt pocket for a peppermint.

Then she thought of something fiercer, a horse faster than the wind. She remembered the legend of the fíorláir, the true mare—the seventh filly born in a row to a single mare, the fíorláir could protect her rider from all harm and could never be stolen by the fairies. That would be a fine thing for a Van Zant witch, Demy thought, to have a fíorláir answer her call.

For just a moment, Demy thought she heard the snort and stamp of a horse. Then it was gone and she was left with only the wind blowing across the parking lot.

She sighed, her shoulders slumping. A moment later, something large sighed behind her. Demy froze and then straightened. She wasn't alone.

It wasn't Foxy—Foxy had been a mortal horse, and when her time was up, she'd passed beyond, to whatever afterlife of tall, sweet grass that awaited faithful steeds—but it was some sort of equine spirit. She felt its breath against the side of her neck, accompanied by the tang of salt water and seaweed.

Slowly, Demy lifted a hand, palm upward. "I don't have much to offer," she whispered. "Freedom and an open road. Warm stalls when they're wanted and a chance to run under the sun."

Gravel crunched behind her, but she didn't turn.

"I know it isn't much," she added. "Maybe I can relearn the things I've forgotten. If you would teach me." *Maybe,* she didn't say, *we can find my sister.*

Warm breath touched the back of her neck.

Would you bind me, mortal? said a voice in her mind. It was ancient and filled with the roar of ocean waves in November. Demy felt a shiver trickle down her back—she hadn't expected the each uisce to answer her call.

"Not bind," Demy said, thinking back again on the old stories. "Nor even tame like the hero Cú Chulainn. I would not ask you to fight any battles for me like the Liath Macha fought for him." Cú Chulainn, in Demy's opinion, had suffered from overwhelming entitlement.

Nor like Féchíne of Fore? If you use a holy name to command me, I will devour all but your liver, as I did him.

Demy almost opened her eyes as her breathing hitched. "The stories say Saint Féchíne freed you?" The stories also said the each uisce came out of the sea each November and glutted themselves on cattle.

There was no answer but a snort that sent shivers down Demy's spine.

"I revere the triune God, but I would never command in His name," Demy said after a moment. "I would not command at all. I ask. I invite."

You offer me a new life, inside that metal steed before you.

"For as long as you will accept it, each uisce," Demy agreed. The stories *also* said a tamed each uisce made the finest steed one could wish for. "But no longer than you wish to travel beside me. I do not bind."

There was silence between them for several heartbeats. Then the each uisce spoke again. *It is well you live so far inside this mass of land. If ever we journey together within scent of salt water, I will devour you as*

I did Féchíne, and I will feel no remorse.

"We are each as our nature makes us," Demy said. She felt the bitterness of the words as she said it. No matter how much she had tried to resist the magic, her nature made her a witch. Her sister had embraced it and paid the price. Demy had rejected it, and still paid the price. Whatever she did, the magic would have her.

But her statement, bitter as it was, seemed to strike some chord within the each uisce. For several heartbeats Demy felt only an approving silence, and then the spirit spoke.

Perhaps there is hope for wisdom in you yet. You can see no truth at all until you accept the truth of yourself.

Hooves crunched softly on the gravel, and Demy couldn't help opening her eyes, hoping to catch a glimpse of the spirit as it passed. But she heard the switch of a tail and a cloud of dust stung her face, making her eyes water.

While Demy was still wiping away the tears, the motorcycle engine roared to life.

I am Aenbharr of Manannán, and long have I sought a brave companion, the each uisce told her. *We shall ride together. It is long since I had a true adventure. When the magic calls, we shall answer.*

THE LAST RIDE OF HETTIE RICHTER
Cat McDonald

"Anse, get your rifle."

Hettie looked up from the table at her older brother, Hector, stern and broad-faced, his nose already starting to look like Pa's and the arsonist look in his eyes exactly the same. He didn't advance past the threshold, standing like an old tree in front of the door and blocking the light with his huge, dense body.

"Why?" Hettie set her mending down for the moment. "What's going on?"

"Word from the courthouse. Uncle Ed's gonna hang. Anse, get your rifle."

Hettie's twin brother Anderson, who didn't look a thing like Pa except that strangers always said he did, hurried out of his seat at the kitchen table. His rifle was, as always, hanging with the others by the door in case of trouble. Last time trouble had come to Richter Hollow, it had been Lee Stewart and his boys burning Big Geoff's house and shooting Pa Richter in the shoulder. The time before that it had been Uncle Ed shooting Jeb Stewart, and the time before that it had been the Stewart boys come hog-thieving.

"Anse, don't you dare," Hettie said, using the voice she'd learned from her mother. "You either, Hec. Ain't nothing but the noose in it for you."

"Well, where's old Lee Stewart on the gallows then? Uncle Ed was defending his own. Anse, hurry up."

Anderson looked back and forth between them for a moment,

wide-eyed.

"Anse, sit back down!"

"Hettie, he's right...can't just trust the county anymore. Anyway, I like Uncle Ed." Anderson was old enough to shave but didn't have to, his arms not too much thicker around than his rifle. Everyone said he'd grow up like Hector and Pa some day, but Hettie didn't see it. She and her twin brother still looked alike to her.

Hettie stood. "Anderson Richter don't you dare! What'll Ma say when they send you to the gallows?!"

"That we were men, Hettie." Hector took Anderson by the arm to guide him to the door, "Kind of men who stood for their own and can walk tall in Heaven."

"Hec, I wasn't talking to you, and you know damn well—"

Hector turned his back on her and left, opening the door to sunlight and humid forest air and the sound of the wind in the timbers overhead. Hettie shrieked after them again but the door shut on her protests.

For a second, she reached for her mending, her fingertips grazing coarse canvas and a tangle of thread and she bent as if to sit back down. At that tiny motion, that moment of contact, her stomach turned. She felt a fury spark to life and expand in her chest, putting pressure on her lungs and heart, and she clenched her teeth to stop it from coming out in a roar.

Instead of screaming, she threw her chair aside and ran outside into the sun and wind. She could hear the rattling of the horses' trappings out front, and ran toward the sound, teeth still clenched, heart still swollen with anger and panic, her own pulse pounding against the inside of her throat.

When Hettie made it off the porch, her footfalls light against the long-trampled earth in front of the Richter home, she saw four horses saddled and ready, and her twin brother halfway into his saddle. Hector was mounted already, as were their cousins Pat and One-Eye, their horses shifting and stepping and pawing, eager for whatever would happen next.

"Anderson, get—" she began to shriek. Her voice joined the wind in the leaves, and silenced a whole holler of birdsong.

It didn't silence the hoofbeats. Heedless of her screaming, her brother settled into his saddle and the four of them started off down the road together.

Hettie chased after them. At first, the running was easy, and she could hold the riders in her vision as solid earth flew by beneath her. Her breaths carried in the scent of the nearby creek, bloated with summer heat and rot, and thick, wet summer air coursed in and out of her.

But step by step, they drifted away from her. She bruised her feet on stones in the road, struggled to fill herself with air, wore her knees out, and still the riders drifted away. Hettie only managed to keep up with them—screaming until she had to choose between screaming and running—until the crossroads where her family's lane met the main road.

There, at last, hats and heads disappeared around a corner, shrouded by thick greenery. Without that fixed point in her vision to focus on, she collapsed. A pain leeched out of her knee to the rest of her leg, her ankle rolled under her, and she toppled to the ground, knees first, in a wheel-rut.

"Damn you," she whispered through the wreckage of her voice on heaving, desperate breaths. "Damn you both. Walk tall in heaven, my ass."

Dirt wedged its way under her fingernails as she tried to force herself back up, and brutal sunlight beat on her back. The rage that had drawn her out of the house still pressed on her insides, squeezed against her stomach. She fought for every breath, and coughed bitterly as her burning lungs failed each time.

She coughed and choked. The burning rose up inside her, past her heart, under her ribs, and into her throat as a huge, solid mass. Another cough brought something thick and warm up to touch the back of her throat. She gagged as it slithered out over her tongue and fell to the earth in front of her, a huge black-red fleshy lump about the size of an apple.

As she watched, it soaked into the ground at the crossroads. Spit and iron-tasting bile dripped over her teeth after it, and she sat there shaking for a few moments, confused and cold and slightly hollow. When she felt she had the strength again, she pushed herself back up to her feet and started to stumble back to her home and her abandoned chores.

In the back of her mind, she could still see those riders.

Hettie woke late the next day, her body heavy with aches and the streaming sunlight in the window heating her through. From her bed, she could see her mother in the kitchen setting aside fresh bacon and corn pone on a handkerchief.

Pa sat in his chair, not far away, a great silent mountain man like a half-animated willow tree, shaggy and knotted and distinguished through the gin blossoms burnt onto his cheeks and nose.

He looked down through the smoke of his corncob pipe, met her eye, and just about smiled.

"Heloise," he said, "there's work to be done. Lee Stewart and Robert Miller been shot."

"Where's Anse?" Her voice sounded like a stranger's, hoarse and foreign.

"He's safe. Ma's wrapping up some lunch for him and the other men."

"Oh." Hettie sat up in bed, and even in that little shift, she felt her knees and hips resist. Her left foot throbbed and her chest felt empty.

"I'm about to take it to them. Thought you might like to come."

She searched for the feeling she knew she was supposed to have, but couldn't find it. Had she thrown it up? A memory of anger lingered in her throat, and something like sadness tried to kindle in her eyes, but now, in the moment, she didn't feel anything. She'd dreamt of their flight deeper into the holler, of Hector's whoops of triumph startling the effervescent dream-birds from the trees, of Anderson weathering the congratulatory shoulder-claps of his brother and cousins.

"I think I'll stay, Pa."

"Well, all right. Ma will be wanting your help with the cooking, and when I get home I need you to come help me run the still. Best be up and moving."

"Sure." Hettie got up and staggered on weary knees to the counter where she kept her hairbrush.

He waited a moment there and finished smoking, occasionally looking down at her, across the room at her, into the kitchen at her, until he'd satisfied himself that she was going about her business and wasn't about to change her mind. Then, with a deep, dark sort of groan, he shoved himself up out of his chair and left, carrying Ma's bundle of food and a couple jars of homemade whiskey.

Her mother wrestled the ingredients for another batch of corn pone together in her one huge mixing bowl while Hettie started gathering the relics from the last batch off the counter to make way for her.

"Hettie," Ma finally said, and Hettie realized she could never really mimic that voice. "Stop worrying your Pa."

"Me?" Hettie felt an empty space where she knew her anger should have been.

"You have to learn to be one person, Hettie. Can't go on just being half of Anderson. Not while Pa's already worried he's gonna lose his boys to the noose."

"Yes, ma'am." Hettie could hear that dark space on the edge of her voice, however hard she tried to force it back down her throat. It swelled up until it overflowed into her arms, shaking between her finger-bones and deep in her wrists. She stood there, hands full of damp rags, shaking and trying to identify the swelling emptiness that crested in her while her vision went dark around the edges.

Her mother's voice came into focus out of the blur. "—nymore than Anderson can go on using your brain in place of his own! If he goes on and that fool Hector ain't…"

"Ma, please." Hettie couldn't really hear herself, but felt herself speaking in the dark.

The oven door slammed shut on the conversation, and Hettie snapped back to normal at the sound, jumping and landing back in her own skin, surrounded by a too-vivid kitchen. Seconds later, far off in the distance, the popping sound of a gun bounced in echoes through the forest not far away.

"Heloise, the shotgun!" Her mother shed her dish-towel in a blur of smeared apron, ran to the gun-rack and grabbed a rifle. In seconds, she was at the window, eye to the rifle with its stock buried somewhere in the sleeve of her dress. She took her free hand from the trigger just long enough to motion Hettie toward the guns with a flicking, dismissive gesture, then resumed her watch.

They stood like that, Hettie with her back to the wall next to the door and a loaded shotgun in her hands, and Ma Richter with her eyes and sights on the road, in complete silence.

"Reckon it's a hunter?" Hettie finally said when five minutes passed without a repeat of the shot.

"Whole county knows better'n to—Hettie! Get out there and help him!"

Even though she could hear the panic in her mother's voice, Hettie didn't feel it for herself. Still holding the shotgun in her steady right hand, she pushed the door open, and now she could hear the urgent braying of her father's old donkey.

Her father's cart was half-destroyed, stove in on one side and still smoking as if it had been lit afire while he still rode it. One of the wheels was missing, and its bare axle had scored a deep furrow in the dirt road. Pa clung to the driver's seat, doubled over, his face hidden under his broad-brimmed hat and his posture desperate.

And beyond him, the demon. She caught its eyes first, its bright orange eyes alive with the same enormous rage she used to know, or else she would have thought it was a horse.

It watched from the bend in the road near the old chestnut tree, a great black draught horse with a chest like a bull's and legs thicker than Hettie was. Grass and fallen leaves around its hooves withered, caught fire, and disappeared in embers like falling stars, and its mane and tail whirled in midair like black smoke. Just above those incandescent eyes, a tangle of black briars sprouted from its head, a magnificent set of antlers swept back until they seemed to join the endless Kentucky forest.

It made eye contact and watched her hurry to her father's side but when next she looked up, it was gone.

"Pa? What happened?"

He still held on to the reins in his lopsided cart as if it were in his power to control that donkey of his. Hettie took them from him and offered to support him in his dismount. As if it could sense someone smaller, weaker at the helm, the donkey made one final charge and snapped the last of its tethers, yanking the reins out of Hettie's hands and running to the barn.

As the cart lurched further over, Pa Richter accepted Hettie's hand and climbed down, even though his huge, shaking body was too heavy for her to support.

"You best...you best get indoors, Heloise," he said to her. "Ain't safe to be out on the roads."

"I'm real sorry, Aunt Patty," said Hettie's cousin, "I tried to get word to 'em, I did! But when I hit the crossroads, something came up on me!"

"What came up on you, Small Ellis?" Hettie's Ma poured some

more moonshine for him and cast a glance over at Pa, asleep in his bed in the common room. Hettie had been sitting there all day, trying not to meet her mother's gaze.

Hettie still didn't feel much. Sometimes, that catastrophic rage flickered through her mind like a ghost, come from nowhere and headed to nothing, sparking feelings that ricocheted off her understanding of the situation and set the back of her mind ablaze.

Word had come up from the town that Rob Miller had died of his bullet wound, making one of the boys a murderer. Lee Stewart still had a chance to pull through, but the doctors weren't optimistic. Ma had sent Small Ellis to their safe house with the message that the sheriff would be after them soon, and he had come back to the house, hat in hand.

"That Small Ellis I hear, Heloise?" Her father sat up, having evidently swallowed whatever emotion had him jerk awake from sleep.

"Yes."

"Bad news from the doctor?"

"No, same news. Still can't get anybody to the safe house."

He laid back down against the pillow, staring straight ahead at their ceiling for a couple moments. Hettie poured a cup of still-warm tea from the big earthen pot her mother had left nearby, and he sat up again to accept it.

"Have a drink."

"Don't make me." He laughed at the strong scent of Ma's special cure-all, and Hettie didn't envy his having to drink it. When she didn't laugh with him, though, he fell quiet and drank without protest, and gave his cup back to Hettie.

She'd been ordered to make sure he had two, so she poured another.

"Heloise, are you all right?"

"Are you all right, Pa?"

"Of course I ain't." He settled back into his bed once he'd drained the second cup of tea and given it back to her. Under the heavy brows and shaggy beard and unkempt hair, he looked at her the way Anderson did. Like he needed someone to hold him up. "Of course I ain't all right. My boys are in danger, and I can't get to them."

Hettie looked up at Small Ellis, a man well over six feet tall, circling his hands around the brim of his hat while her Ma lectured him. The sound of her mother's voice and the scent of that tea and the ache in her throat, where her feelings were supposed to be, suffocated her.

"...where's the safe house?"

"You ain't going, Heloise."

"Might be safer not to take the roads, and I know these hills. Besides...I want to get out." Hettie hated strategy meetings, the heads of the family gathered in close together late into the night with threatened gunsmoke hanging in the air. From the first time the sheriff's men had been to Richter Hollow looking for her kin, she'd hated it.

"Take the shotgun. You see anything, you turn and run back here. You and Hector, too much like your Ma for anybody's good."

Once he'd given the directions, she crept to the door and grabbed her shotgun, along with the bundle of food Small Ellis had left by the door after his failed delivery.

And outside the house, it was dark and it was quiet.

"Don't compare me to Hector," she said into the empty woods, now that she could be sure her father couldn't hear her, and started on her path, a little trampled road that led from the corner of the front porch to a deep hollow in the earth. Beside the house, the forest dropped down into a narrow overgrown valley completely invisible to the road, where Pa had taught the twins to hunt.

Here, the foliage closed over her head, the moon disappeared from view, and the problems in that smoky little farmhouse were scattered on the wind. Here, it was just Hettie and the earth.

Gunfire broke out farther down the trail. One shot, at first, a sharp cry of terror that echoed everywhere in seconds, but others soon followed. Two, three, five, seven shots.

Before she made it to the road, a dozen or so more shots had peppered the air, and now she could hear men shouting, unfamiliar voices screaming in the darkness. As she approached, she heard hooves and the cries of horses, and long before she could see what was going on, the smell of sulphur blanketed the woods and filled her little ravine like a wash-basin. When she broke through the trees, she knew to expect those live-coal amber eyes and that writhing mane of cataclysmic smoke.

It stood in the middle of the road, facing straight forward, completely still except that one of its ears turned to listen to her. Ahead of it, in the mud and the tangle of the roadside woods, a handful of men scrambled away, smeared in dirt and gunpowder, and it watched them until the sound of their flight disappeared into nothing. The sound of their panic triggered a wicked little spasm right next to her heart.

Then, while she clutched at the bark of a slender tree and tried to steady her breathing, it turned its massive neck to look at her. This close, she could see the smoky fluttering of its translucent mane and the tiny reddish leaves buried in the tangle of its briar antlers.

Her heart still twitching and trembling, she stepped out past that determined little tree, over its treacherous roots, and out of the curtain of leaves. The demon stood still until she was close enough to lay her hand, as tiny and pale as a crescent moon in a dark sky, against the side of its neck. Now she could see the deep, familiar red-black of its coat, and taste the memory of her bile, and remember the feelings she'd thrown up at the crossroads.

Somehow, some time since she'd learned to walk, she'd come to hate her family. One day, she had looked up at her big brother and wanted to kick him until he toppled, and the feeling hadn't faded no matter how often she'd smothered it. Her mother's voice made her want to scream. The tangled schemes of her father and uncles and cousins made her imagine burning the house to the ground.

It rested its broad, warm chin against her back while she stood there crying in the middle of the road and her tears sizzled into steam around her. No scent existed but the black sulfurous smoke of its mane, and it pulled Hettie deeper and deeper into her forgotten hatred.

"I hate this," she said out loud for the first time. "All of it. I hate it."

Its breath puffed across her back, ruffling the back of her dress, and in its voiceless whicker she heard the only comfort she'd ever needed. She couldn't fit her arms all the way around its neck; her discarded hate and fury were powerful. Enormous.

Strong enough to fight back.

She let go of its neck to wipe her tears. "I have to go find the boys."

It raised its head so she could duck under its chin and run back to the treeline where she'd left her package of food and whiskey. When she returned, she looked up at its back, slightly above her eye level, and realized she couldn't climb up on her own. So, with one hand carrying her package and the other resting against the demon's ribs, she walked along the old dirt road toward the safe house.

As they walked, the dried edges of the forest burst into flame by the roadside and vanished in embers, framing their journey in red light and smoke. Her hip brushed against its stomach from time to time, and its antlers snagged at the top of her hair, and the empty feeling in her chest had completely evaporated. They hadn't just met; they'd been reunited. They'd known each other since the first time she'd dreamed of shootouts and woke up angry. She couldn't hear the difference between her hoofbeats and its footfalls.

"You'll have to stay behind when we get there," Hettie said, and she saw by the flicking of its black ear that it heard and understood her. "They'll be frightened of us."

When they arrived at the safehouse, she left her anger at the gate to watch from the treeline as she advanced on what had once been a sturdy little hunting lodge. The forest had started, piece by piece, to eat it, and vines hung from the roof clear down to the porch. A quarter of someone's head watched her from the gray windowsill, and no other signs of life could be seen.

"It's just me, One-Eye. Lemme in."

The rest of her cousin's head emerged from the window and disappeared again. Then, old One-Eye opened the front door to let her in. He'd only been in the woods a day, but his clothes were filthy and his hair and beard had started sprouting off in all directions. He looked, like all the men in her family, more or less like Pa Richter, though One-Eye swept his bangs low over a black eye-patch he'd worn ever since a boyhood hunting accident.

"Anse, Hec, Pat, get up!" he hollered back into the house, and soon all four filthy shades staggered to the doorway to greet her. Hector glanced over her shoulder and, for a second, his expression went rigid.

Hettie climbed up the four ancient steps to the front porch. "Food and whiskey," she said, and held out the package. "And news."

"What kinda news, Hettie?" Hector finally returned his gaze to her when he took the bundle.

"Rob Miller's dead, and Lee Stewart may not last the night. It's murder." She could only get the words out if she imagined the feeling of the demon's breath on her shoulder, and only then if she avoided her twin brother's desperate gaze.

"Hettie, I heard gunshots. Are they hunting for us? What do we do?" Anderson pushed his way forward to stand directly in front of her, like a full-length mirror covered in forest grime and gunpowder, clutching at a rifle too big for him, eyes wide and wet now that her prediction had come true.

"Yep. 'Course they're hunting you. You idiots are killers now." Fear stung at her now that she was split in two; this half of her still wanted Anderson to survive. Even Hector.

"Why the shooting, Hettie?" Hector hauled Anderson back into the shadows so she didn't have to look at him anymore. "Is it a shootout? They come for Pa and the others?"

They weren't ready, and they had too much to worry about already. "No, everyone else is more or less safe. Might be hunters."

"What's Pa planning?"

"Pa's bedridden."

"That all you came to tell us?"

She permitted herself a glance at the reddish briars tucked into the forest beside the road, and the faint wisp of smoke only she knew to look for.

Before she turned around to get back to her stronger half, she heard voices. Hector must have heard them too; he disappeared into the cabin and re-materialized at the window, rifle at the ready. The rest of the men followed his lead and armed themselves.

"Give yourselves up!" Hettie recognized the voice of the sheriff; she'd sold him whiskey once or twice. He and the rest of his posse, some twelve men all told, rounded the bend and moved to surround the cabin, guns at the ready. Once he'd advanced far enough to see that it was Hettie standing on the porch, he approached a little closer and politely removed his hat.

"Miss Heloise, are the men in there?"

Hettie scanned the forest for those briars, but couldn't see them, even though she could almost feel the demon's breath. It was near, but where?

"You can tell them boys they're better off turning themselves in. Coming peacefully right now is the difference between jail and a hanging."

Behind her, in the cabin, she heard what must have been the pleading of her twin brother. At only sixteen, he could hope for a life once he'd served his sentence.

She heard it for only a moment before Hector's rifle seared the air with his definitive answer, and a cloud of dust blossomed at the sheriff's feet. Hettie's vision went red and the demon's breath coursed through her hair.

In that moment, surrounded by grown men who had no need to listen to her, in a situation she had never had any power over at all, she started to tally up her memories. How many times had she tried? How many tears had she wasted trying to fix everything about her life that she hated, trying to save her family members as, one by one, they proved not to care? There was absolutely nothing this half of her could do but watch it all burn.

The men reacted, first to the gunshot, then to the emergence of the demon from the forest. At the sight of it, their careful formation broke, and rifles fell to the forest floor, and a litany of terrified curses spread all around and through the cabin.

Hettie turned around. From the weathered porch, with the help of those antlers, she could climb onto its back, and the thought became an irresistible impulse. The thorns growing from its brows cut into her hands. She didn't care. Pain was irrelevant until she found herself astride its broad back, leaned forward until her whole body was wreathed in black smoke, and clung fast to its neck.

All her doubts, her weaknesses, her brief flickers of pity and hope disappeared into smoke and embers. The half of her that walked on two legs had tried and failed to change her life, but now she was whole.

Hettie looked down at her elder brother, who was terrified of her, as he always should have been. Hettie and the demon stepped up onto the porch together and watched the way the old building started to erupt into sympathetic smoke and flame just from their presence. They leaned forward and kicked out behind at the front door, reducing it to embers in an instant. They watched the sparks catch fire, and they loved the sight.

Together with her hatred, she reared up and, with hooves as huge and heavy as bricks, kicked at her damn brother until he fell to the ground and the blood started to pool around him and give off steam in the heat. She felt a bullet strike her somewhere in the back, but didn't have to care anymore.

Anderson, who looked just like the person she was before she was whole, stared up at her, trembling so fiercely that he seemed blurry. Once, she and this pitiful little creature had been virtually identical, except that he'd had the power to prevent all of this, and she'd had nothing but hatred.

But their eyes met, and her weaker half wanted to try one more time to save him.

So, they turned and left. Hettie, who no longer knew if she was one or two, turned away from the safe house as the fire spread to the roof, and ran, trampling over those of the sheriff's men slow enough to be in her way. Neither she nor her stronger self cared anymore what happened to them or anyone else. They felt bone give way under their feet, and they broke into a gallop, along the road leading past the farmhouse, to the crossroads where her strong self had been born, and out of Richter Hollow, westward, to anywhere else.

We Us You

Andrew Bourelle

He was taking her to the rodeo, so he wore jeans and a tucked-in long-sleeved shirt, with cowboy boots and a cowboy hat. He regretted how he dressed as soon as he saw her. Nicole answered the door in a dress, not a fancy one like girls might wear to a dance, but a summer dress, a light green color that flowed out around her legs, past her knees. Her sandy blond hair was pulled back in a short ponytail, tied with a red ribbon. She wore no makeup, but didn't need it. Patrick thought she was the prettiest girl he'd ever seen. Even years later, after all that happened that night, he remembered this moment. The door swinging open. The sight of her in her dress. Her smile. Her big, expressive eyes, green as a spring field. He felt a happiness he hadn't experienced before. This girl was going out with *him*.

She explained that her parents wanted to meet him. He walked in, his boots clicking on the hardwood floor. In the living room, her parents sat reading. The TV was off. He'd never seen his own parents reading instead of watching TV.

"Oh," Nicole's mom said, as she saw him, then she hid her surprise with a smile. "How are you doing, cowboy?"

Patrick regretted how he had dressed even more. Nicole and her family were from Las Vegas, new to the community and new to Montana. Why hadn't he thought that they might be put off by his boots and hat?

"Good, ma'am. Thank you." He removed his hat and held it.

Nicole's mother looked like her, older but still pretty; her father had a long gray ponytail, glasses that seemed to perch at the end of his nose. He eyed Patrick above the lenses, his face welcoming and friendly. Patrick sat with Nicole on a couch, and the four of them spoke briefly. Her parents asked Patrick questions, but he mostly answered "Yes, ma'am" or "No, sir" instead of giving them the sentences and paragraphs they were probably hoping for. He knew he should talk more but he was nervous and therefore quiet. Nicole grinned at him, her dimples showing.

"You're so polite, Patrick," her mother said.

"You can call us Greg and Tanya," her father said.

"Yes, sir," Patrick said.

Nicole and her parents began laughing, and then, a second later, Patrick did too.

When he and Nicole left, he regretted wearing a pair of jeans that showed off the ring from snuff cans he carried in his back pocket. Having a ring like that was a badge of esteem usually, but he didn't like Nicole's parents seeing it as he walked out the door. His boots clapped self-consciously against the floor as he left. He told himself to stop worrying about these things, it was too late now.

He opened the door of the truck for Nicole, and she climbed in. He came around and started the engine.

"What's this?" she said, pointing to the back window.

"A gun rack," Patrick said. "This is my dad's truck," he added, as if to distance himself from hunting, even though he was eager for the season to begin.

"Oh." Her voice held no judgment, only curiosity.

It was Saturday, and school had only started on Monday. The talk of the school the very first day had been the new girl from Las Vegas. He was seated next to her in English class. They'd exchanged glances right away, and smiles. She was beautiful, but not in what he expected to be a stereotypically Las Vegas way, bleach-blond hair and lots of makeup. She felt more down to earth, pretty in a cute way, not trashy. But she dressed differently than the other girls, wearing sundresses and blouses that girls couldn't get around here.

She was smart, too. She could answer all the questions the English teacher asked. They'd only had to write one paper so far, but for that she received a big red A+. He glanced at her score out of the corner of his eye. When the teacher called his name and he went to her desk to get his paper, the teacher had pointed to one of the sentences he wrote and asked him to read it aloud. He spoke softly, "I told my mom I'll get good grades this year," only he pronounced "I'll" as "all." He knew his mistake, but was helpless to stop what was happening.

"Do you mean '*I'll*?'" the teacher said. "As in 'I will'?"

"Yes, ma'am."

"Do you mean to tell me you've made it all the way to your junior year of high school and you think 'I'll' is spelled A-L-L?"

She didn't wait for a response, thrusting his paper at him as if it was a poisonous weed she no longer wanted to touch. He walked back to his seat, feeling the blood rushing to his head, knowing his face was sunburn red. He avoided looking at the new girl. She whispered to him, "Don't worry about it. It's only the first week."

On Friday, during group work when they were supposed to discuss the night's reading of several poems by Emily Dickinson, Patrick asked if Nicole planned on going to the rodeo that weekend. She said no and explained she didn't have any friends close enough to go with.

"Well, you should go with me," he said, surprising himself with his own boldness.

"Okay," Nicole said. "When do you want to go?"

They agreed on Saturday night and as he left class, his friend Alex saw him in the hall and asked, "What the hell are you smiling about?"

For dinner, he took Nicole to a local restaurant. It wasn't the fanciest restaurant in town, but he thought the food was the best. He asked about where she was from. His older brother had told him to do this: ask questions. She explained that Las Vegas wasn't as glamorous as the TV shows and movies made it seem—all gangsters and high-stakes poker players—mostly it was middle-class tourists, families even. The city had some seedy characters, she said, but mostly these were gambling addicts on a swing of bad luck.

"It's pretty big, though," Nicole said. "I think almost as many people live in Las Vegas as in the whole state of Montana."

"Wow," he said.

"Vegas isn't nearly as cool as Seattle or Chicago," she said. "Have you ever been to either one?"

Patrick shook his head. He didn't want to admit that Missoula was the biggest city he'd been to, with a population you could fit into some college football stadiums.

"They made a big fuss here," he said, "when we got the second stoplight."

She explained that her parents moved her to Montana so they could start a wild-horse rescue ranch.

"In Nevada, they capture horses from overpopulated areas, and break and tame them for adoption," she said. "We want to make a refuge where they can stay wild."

Nicole's family had bought one of the biggest ranches in the county.

"We don't have any horses yet," Nicole said, "but once things get up and going, we hope the whole place will be teeming with wild horses."

He asked what her parents did for work.

"Well, in Vegas, they were performers at one of the casinos. I guess now they're just going to be ranchers."

Patrick nodded, trying to imagine Nicole's parents working a ranch the way he and his parents did. He couldn't picture it.

"Have you ever ridden a horse?" Patrick asked.

"No," she said.

"You can ride my horse some time," Patrick said. He wanted to tell her how much he loved horses, how riding was the only time he ever felt truly happy, a way for him to escape and forget about his parents' fighting or his teacher teasing him about spelling words wrong. He felt giddy about the prospect of sharing this love with Nicole—no one else really knew about it.

But she just shrugged at the offer and said, "We don't plan to ride our horses, just, you know, keep them safe."

Deflated, Patrick said nothing more about horses.

When their meal arrived, Nicole began asking Patrick questions: about his parents, about his siblings, about life on the ranch. He tried to answer articulately between bites of his bison burger. Nicole had ordered a salad, explaining that she was a vegetarian, and she picked at it as he talked.

As they left the restaurant, he asked if Las Vegas had any good rodeos.

"Nevada has rodeos," she said, "but I've never been to one."

"You've never been to a rodeo before?"

She shook her head, looking embarrassed.

"Well," he said, opening the door to his truck for her, "you're in for a real treat."

As they walked through the dirt parking lot, they could hear the announcer talking about the contestants and kids laughing over at the fair. A Ferris wheel stood above the other structures, and Patrick imagined the two of them riding it, him working the courage up to kiss her. Behind the big wheel, the clouds were bathed in scarlet from the setting sun, giving everything around them a reddish tint.

"There's something about the sunsets here," Nicole said. "They're so beautiful. I've never seen anything like them."

Patrick said, "Thank you," as if she'd been complimenting him. He didn't know what else to say—he didn't have much to compare the sunsets to.

They were quiet for a moment. Then Patrick said, "Watch out for the cow shit."

Nicole maneuvered around a flattened brown pancake nearly the size of a manhole cover.

"I guess I shouldn't have worn these shoes," she said, pointing to her white sandals. Her toes were already covered in a layer of dirt.

"We'll be up on the bleachers most of the time," Patrick said. "Just watch where you step."

Inside, no one was dressed like Nicole. The crowd was all jeans and boots and ball caps and cowboy hats. Some people even stared at her but she seemed not to notice, and Patrick felt proud to be walking next to her. She was pretty and out of the ordinary, and she was with him. Patrick felt desperate for something different. When he was out riding, the feeling wasn't there. But other times, sitting in class, making hay on the ranch, or even at a party with friends, he felt he didn't belong. He wanted to be somewhere else, but he didn't know where.

Nicole seemed to embody a somewhere-else-ness.

As they climbed into the stands a friend of his, Jimmy, called his name and waved.

"Come over here," he shouted.

"Do you want to go sit with them?" Patrick said, secretly hoping that he and Nicole would have more time alone together.

"Sure," she said, and they climbed up the metal bleachers to where Patrick's friends sat.

"Have y'all met Nicole?" he asked.

Five of his friends were there, three guys and two girls: Jimmy, Toby, and Alex; Jeannine and Alicia. Patrick sat next to them, with Nicole on the aisle. Patrick leaned in close to her, pointing down into the arena, explaining the rules. A bareback rider came out of the chute with the horse kicking so hard that the rider's back crashed down into its hindquarters again and again, his head whipping back. The eight-second horn sounded, and the two standby riders came in to rescue the guy from the horse. Nicole's mouth was an O.

"How could he stay on?" she said. "It seems like that would give him whiplash."

"It's a tough sport," Patrick said. "I told you this would be fun."

A trick roper came into the center of the arena, swinging a lasso around his body like magic. He made the loop go up and down his body, like he was inside a tornado, then he made it even bigger, swinging it parallel to his body, and jumped back and forth through it while his arm swung the rope in a blur. Nicole clapped vigorously along with the rest of the crowd.

When team roping began, Nicole couldn't believe that someone could lasso the hind legs of a running calf.

"How can they do that?" she said, genuine bewilderment in her voice.

"I can do that," he said. "But not very well."

When the next duo came out, the first cowboy lassoed the calf's neck right away. The second shot his lasso but only captured one hind leg, so instead of falling into the dirt, the calf was pulled between the cowboys, one leg stretched out behind it like it was caught in some kind of torture trap.

"Oh," Nicole said. "That poor calf."

"They're resilient," Patrick said. "This don't hurt 'em."

He didn't know if this was true or not. He hadn't thought about it before.

More kids from high school showed up, and Patrick introduced Nicole.

"Come sit with us over here for a minute," Jeannine said to Nicole, gesturing to where the girls sat.

"Okay," Nicole said.

Patrick was glad for her. He knew she was new to town and hadn't made many—or any—friends yet. But once she was gone, sitting one row up and a few seats down, he ached to have her back.

"Going after the new girl, huh?" Johnny whispered, sitting down next to him and bumping his shoulder.

"Shhh," Patrick said.

"I'm just kidding. She's cute. I'd let her slob my cob."

Patrick didn't know how to respond, and so he didn't.

Johnny had a backpack of beer and offered everyone a can. His friends took them discreetly, sneaking drinks and hiding the cans out of sight. The bleachers were filled with neighbors, parents, teachers, but everyone expected high schoolers to sneak beer into the rodeo.

Patrick looked at Nicole and asked—he almost had to shout now—if she wanted one. She mouthed the words "No." He accepted one hesitantly.

Now that he was in the presence of his friends, and not alone with Nicole, he felt himself changing. He took on all the old manners he always had with his friends, slapping their backs, teasing them just as they teased him. He finished his beer and bummed a dip off Toby. He spit into his empty can. He knew this wasn't how he'd been acting around Nicole, in class or tonight, but he was unable to stop.

Later, even just a few years later, he attributed it to growing up. As a teenager, he assumed a pose—what he thought he should be—because he didn't yet know who he actually was. But that night, he felt like he was watching someone else in a TV show, a character in someone else's story.

He looked periodically back at Nicole. She seemed to be enjoying her conversation with the girls but time had skipped by since they'd been separated, like someone had fast-forwarded the video he was watching, and now the announcer was saying that bull-riding was up next.

"Oh, this is the last event," he heard Jessica tell Nicole. "It's the best."

Patrick looked back at her and she smiled sweetly, giving him a small wave. He smiled, conscious of the chew in his bottom lip. He wanted to stand up and go sit next to her but not with the snuff in his mouth. He stayed where he was, turning his back to her to spit the last of the grains out. For once, his entire group of friends was quiet, watching the rodeo with their full attention.

The first rider came out and was quickly thrown. The standby riders came in, lassoing the bull's horns and directing it toward the exit chute.

"My God," Nicole said. "It's so big."

She was right. Everything about it was big, its head, its horns, its broad and bulked shoulders. The bull was all muscle and madness, pure force, as big as a bear and probably just as strong. It took several minutes for the two cowboys to get the bull under control and out of the arena.

The next rider came out. He was thrown immediately.

Finally, a few riders came out who finished their eight seconds. One couldn't get loose once the horn had sounded, and the cowboys had to chase the bull around the ring until he grabbed one of them and jumped off. Other riders followed with similar outcomes, finishing and then squirming to be away from the bull. Another almost finished but was bucked off just as the horn sounded. The bull thrashed around, looking as if he was right on top of the rider. The clown ran in to distract it. When the bull was gone, the man stood up and limped to the side, climbing up and out.

"He's okay," the announcer said through the loudspeaker. "He's a real cowboy."

He looked back at Nicole. He'd succeeded most of the night in reading her expression, but now he was unsure. He hoped she was probably just captivated by what was happening, this being her first rodeo.

The final rider of the night was up. The bull's name was "Cannibal." When the chute opened he charged out, thrashing madly. The rider lasted a few seconds and then he was catapulted, twisting in the air. He landed on his head, with the rest of his body pile-driving him into the dirt, limbs flopping in ways that it seemed a person shouldn't bend. The crowd gasped. Patrick too. But the bull wasn't done. It jumped up, slamming its front legs down, then its rear, trampling the man.

The cowboys rushed in to drive it away. It ran to the other side of the arena. One of the standby riders lassoed its horns, and then the other. Still, the bull fought, struggling against the ropes.

Finally, it jumped, both sets of legs rising into the air, its body twisting—looking like a fish caught on a fisherman's line, a great marlin jumping out of the water and struggling fruitlessly against the cord, suspended in the air for a moment, just long enough for Patrick to remember the image in his mind like a photograph. Instead of landing, the bull crashed down on its side, creating a cloud of dust. It struggled up, but now it was beaten. It allowed itself to be pulled toward the chute.

Paramedics rushed out to help the cowboy, who lay unmoving in the dirt. Patrick looked back at Nicole and saw a look of horror on her face.

"They should kill that bull," Jessica said.

"It's not his fault—he's just doing his job," Alex said.

Nicole's skin was pale, as if she was sick. People started to leave the stands. Patrick stood and asked Nicole if she wanted to go. She nodded without saying anything.

"It was so nice hanging out with you," Jessica said.

"Yes," Nicole said softly, although it seemed like her thoughts had taken her far, far away.

Once off the bleachers, Patrick asked if Nicole wanted to walk around the fair for a while.

"No thanks."

Now he started to get angry. Back in the truck, as they waited for a line of cars to move and she was still silent, he said, "Nicole, you can't just come in here and start judging people."

As the truck crept forward, she said nothing, so he filled the silence with his own words. "People around here are ranchers. They work with cows and horses, and this is their entertainment. They're not vegetarians from big exotic cities who…" he trailed off.

Nicole let out a laugh. "Las Vegas is *not* exotic."

"People here," he said, "they eat meat and they don't think the cows are being abused and they like it when the bull-riders get kicked around a bit. It's like Nascar—it ain't worth watching unless there's a crash. That's what they think. The people here, they don't need your judgment."

The cars in front of them crept out of the parking lot. The interior of the truck was bathed in red from the brake lights.

Patrick said, "I had a great time with you tonight, Nicole, but the people around here, they don't need you looking down on them just because they do things differently. They ain't like you. They'd do just fine without you being here altogether."

"You're using the wrong pronoun," she said.

The traffic was at a stand-still again, and he turned to look at her.

In the glow of the brake lights, her face was colored a harsh red, more vivid and jarring than the subtle sunset shine from a few hours ago. But still, even red and angry, she was like no girl he'd ever seen, and his own anger dissolved.

"What's a pronoun?" he said modestly, trying to show her that he wasn't upset anymore, that they should move past this and remember how good the evening had started.

"You should be saying 'we.'"

He thought she was saying "we," as in the two of them, Patrick and Nicole. He was silent for a moment, trying to make sense of what she was saying, feeling pleased despite this recent conflict to think of the two of them as a "we."

"Don't say '*they* think this' or '*they* do that,'" she said.

Patrick heard the hurt in her voice and realized he'd misunderstood.

"You mean 'we'—you *and* them," Nicole said. "*You* ain't like me. *You'd* do just fine without me being here. You mean *you*, don't you, Patrick?"

"Yeah," he snapped. "So what?"

She didn't reply. He opened his mouth to speak but then stopped. He kept telling himself that he should apologize, that he didn't mean what he said, that he was confused and didn't really even understand what he was saying. But he couldn't form the words for the apology in his mind. Then the silence grew between them like distance and time, and then speaking seemed impossible.

When he pulled into her driveway, he grabbed his door handle to walk her to the door, but she stopped him.

"It's okay," she said, and then, politely, added, "Thanks for taking me out."

He watched her walk away, her shoulders bent, her head down.

She didn't go into the house. Instead, she skirted its edge and headed toward the barn out back.

Patrick put the truck in drive and headed down the driveway. He hit the brakes abruptly, and dust from the gravel wafted through his headlight beams. He imagined Nicole inside the barn, sitting on the floor, her knees pulled to her chest, crying.

He had to make this right. It wasn't too late.

He swung the truck around and went back. He shut off the engine and walked through the yard. The air was cool, the sky so clear he could see the Milky Way among the endless stars. The silence was ferocious—there was no sound but his own breath.

Then a thundering clap of hooves burst out of the barn and into the field behind it. Patrick jerked, his heart pounding. The horse galloped up a hill, moving with a playfulness that seemed more like dancing than running. It was a magnificent animal, Patrick could see that, even by starlight. Its fur looked chestnut, its body lean, muscular and something about it—its energy—made him think it was young. He guessed it was a filly.

Patrick laughed at how startled he'd been. This would be something funny to tell Nicole once he'd patched things up.

"Nicole," he called, as he entered through the barn door.

The building was dark except for an electric lantern at the other end. Patrick walked toward it, past empty horse stalls. He'd been in dozens of barns in his life, and none had ever smelled like this. Instead of the dusty smell of hay or the pungent odor of horse shit, the barn smelled like the deep forest: pine needles, rich soil, flora.

He stopped when he was a few feet from the lantern. Hanging on a hook on a four-by-four beam was a dress that looked like the one Nicole had worn tonight, with the red ribbon from her hair draped over it. Her sandals were lying on the floorboards next to her purse.

"Nicole," he called again, louder, to be sure she heard him before he stumbled upon her in the nude.

But she wasn't there at all.

He stepped out of the back of the barn into the pasture and looked around. The horse, barely visible in the dark, galloped in a wide arc. It headed in the direction of the barn, and then it came to a sudden, urgent stop and stood looking at him.

At this distance and with the darkness, Patrick had trouble making out the animal with much detail. But he could see its chest inflating with each quick breath, hear its snorts. Its eyes glinted in the starlight and, even this far away, Patrick thought he could see a wild, fearful look in its expression.

He wanted to walk forward, run his hand along its nose, put his face against the hair on its ribcage. It was a beautiful animal, but he was afraid of it—one of the wild horses Nicole's family hoped to keep wild.

He steeled himself to step forward, but then he noticed something else about the horse. He knew his mind was playing tricks on him, brought on by the darkness and his own adrenaline, but it looked like there was a horn protruding from the horse's forehead. At first, it was barely visible in the gloom, but the more he looked the more he could see it clearly: a pale protrusion, about a foot long, rising into a point.

He had a feeling that he was at an important threshold in his life. He had a choice, and depending on if he walked out and tried to touch the horse or he retreated back into the barn, different versions of who he could be would emerge. One Patrick or the other would wake up tomorrow, but they couldn't both go on and the Patrick he was right now would cease to exist. He had already gone too far.

Over the years, Patrick thought of this moment often and tried to convince himself that he'd seen some sort of optical illusion. Everyone looked back with a longing—a *what if?*—for someone from their past: the one who got away. For everyone, there is a person, once real, who over time becomes mythical, unattainable—a unicorn. So it wasn't beyond belief that Patrick's mind would manufacture a memory that made Nicole just that.

But late at night, when he has insomnia and flips through the TV channels, or lies in bed next to one woman or another, Patrick knows what he saw that night. He knows he lives in a different world than he would if he'd possessed the courage to step out of the shadows and approach the animal on the hill. To touch her and say, "I'm with you. We are a *we*."

But he didn't.

He backed into the barn, hurried through to the other side, his boots clunking loudly against the floorboards, and ran through the damp grass to his truck. He sped away as if he was being pursued by a ghost.

When he saw Nicole at school on Monday, he didn't make eye contact with her. She attended classes for only a few months before she and her family moved away. The rumor went around that her parents didn't make a single payment on their property. They just squatted there and then disappeared.

Patrick never talked to Nicole again. Once, before she left, he did make eye contact. He came around a corner in the crowded school hallway and almost collided with her. He jumped, startled, and she smiled at him—a sad, sympathetic smile that made him ache whenever he thought of it. The smile said, *We scared each other once before, didn't we? But we're past that now, aren't we?*

He walked away without a word.

Sometimes, in his dreams, he relives the encounter in the hallway, and this time he does speak.

He says, "I will look for you for the rest of my life."

Her smile falters, and she says, "You will never find me."

And then he wakes up, as he always does, in his world, not hers.

SCATTER THE FOALS TO THE WIND

Chadwick Ginther

My mom always said, "Michelle, never trust a short man. They've always got something to prove."

Most of her advice hadn't stuck, but that tidbit had; one reason most of the guys I'd dated had been the size of vikings. The latest was a bruiser of a redhead named Ted. More tattoos than a biker. Mouth like a sailor. Smoked like a chimney. Mom would've hated him, 6'4" or not.

We'd had a few dates. I'm sure he'd made the same plans for tonight I had.

He'd come over to my condo and made me dinner. We were having a toke on my balcony, the air was brisk, but warm for a Winnipeg November. He had one arm around me and the other pointed up at the stars, toward the constellation of Orion.

"So there was this giant, name of Veggbyggir," he said. "And he had this horse, big strong bastard went by Svaðilfari. Could tow a fucking mountain."

The story of the myth behind the stars had a practiced feel, as if this was something he said to all the girls. It was also wrong. The "horse" constellation he'd pointed to had been Taurus.

"Veggbyggir and Svaðilfari were tasked with building a wall around Asgard—that's the home of the Norse gods—in only three seasons or they won Freyja, the most beautiful goddess in Odin's court, *and* the sun and moon besides. And they'd almost done it. So Loki had to stop them."

Practiced or not, wrong or not, it was working. I wanted to hear where his story went. "Wait? Isn't Loki a bad guy?"

"You know Loki?" Ted's eyes caught the starlight and he laughed.

"Not personally," I said. "Who won?"

"Not the giant," Ted said. "And not Loki."

I took a deep toke, held the smoke in my lungs for a three count, and passed the joint back to Ted as I exhaled. "How'd Loki manage to stop them?"

"He turned into a mare and lured the stallion away."

"Classic honey pot," I said.

Ted laughed. "Right?"

"So why'd you say Loki lost? Sounds like he had the last laugh."

Ted shrugged. "He came back pregnant with an eight-legged horse son."

"Bummer," I said. "Which constellation is Loki? Where's he hiding?"

He stopped pointing at the stars to pull me close, and I figured he was going to kiss me, so I closed my eyes, leaned in, and over the balcony I went. As I tumbled ass over tits, his grin flashed; a crescent that glowed bright as the moon.

The last thing I saw before I clenched my eyes shut and waited for the impact was that *smile*. Wind whipped through my hair. I counted the seconds. One. Two. Three. We'd been on the 16th floor but I definitely should've hit the ground by now.

I opened my eyes. I was only two floors down from my balcony. Ted looked smaller but his smile looked bigger. The cherry of his joint glowed bright orange after a toke. I smelled the pot. His cologne. His…overwhelming pleasure with himself.

I looked down. I didn't want to, but I needed to see. The ground seemed so far away. So did the balcony. How could I get there? How could I get back? How could I be hanging in the air?

This was madness. It made no sense. None.

"I suppose you're wondering what's going on?" Ted called down from the balcony. "I suppose you also want to know why you're a horse?"

"What?"

The word didn't come out. Just an angry whinny.

I craned my neck around and the fucker was right. I *was* a horse. My hooves rested on air as if it were asphalt. The wind whipped through a mane and tail, not a head of hair.

Ted leapt over the balcony railing, joint still between his lips, and hurtled toward me. I spun, trying to get away, but he landed on my back.

"Didn't think we'd be going bareback tonight," he said, grabbing a handful of my mane and patted my flank.

The jokes.

I used to love his jokes. I used to think he was funny. Now, I just thought he was an asshole, and I wanted him gone.

I spun. Whirled. Bucked. He held on fast. Each leap shot me higher into the air, and I landed as if it were solid ground. He hung on. I tried something else. I tucked my legs tight to my body, and we plummeted like a rock.

"*Woooooo!*" he yelled. From his enthusiasm, I could only assume if he'd owned a cowboy hat, he'd be waving it.

Two storeys from the ground, I untucked my legs and ran on the air, gradually changing the angle of my descent. My hooves touched the ground and turned back to bare feet. Ted tumbled off my back and onto the grass. I whirled and kicked him right between the legs. My skin prickled with the cold, and I realized my clothes must've torn off when I'd transformed.

Perfect.

I'd loved that dress. And the lingerie beneath it had been *expensive.*

I was torn between trying to cover myself, or kicking the jerk again.

He moaned, and struggled weakly when I pulled off his now ridiculously-baggy t-shirt to cover myself.

"Okay, prick," I said. "Explain yourself."

"I'm not the one who's a horse," he said.

I kicked him again.

When Ted was done cradling his plums and whining, he started talking. And what he said made no sense.

"First off," he said, exhaling a cloud of weed, "my name's not Ted. I'm Loki."

"You're *Loki?*" I asked. "Norse god, Loki?"

"Yup."

I snorted a laugh, before realizing he was serious. "God of lies and trickery and questionable romantic partners?"

"And you're trying to decide if Loki would lie about his own name?" He raised and lowered his eyebrows like one of the Marx Brothers.

"No, I wonder why he *wouldn't* lie about being a horse fucker."

He smiled that shit-eating grin and I wanted to turn back into a horse so I could kick him even harder. "Also, don't be so hard on yourself about the 'questionable romantic partners' thing. You're great, but I'm not into you that way."

"Loki? You're serious? *Loki?*"

"Why would I lie?"

"It's what you *do.*"

He pouted. He actually pouted. "It's not *all* I do."

"So what am I? Your descendant from when you were a lady horse?"

He tapped his nose with his index finger and then pointed it at me. "Right in one."

"That's ridiculous."

"You're the one who's a horse."

"You're the one creeping on their descendant." I shuddered.

Ewww. I can't believe we were going to…just…I shuddered again. "*Ewww.*"

"We should go inside," Loki said, glancing at my chest. "It's cold outside."

I crossed my arms. "I don't have my keys. Thanks to you."

"Leave it to me." He gestured toward the door. I didn't move. "Trust me."

Loki didn't pick the lock to my building's front door. He just walked over and opened it. He bowed, gesturing for me to enter first. I did, and grabbed the door, pulling it shut behind me. I don't know how Loki slithered his way in, but when the door slammed shut, he was behind me. I screamed. More in frustration than terror. The elevator door *dinged* open as we walked across the lobby. It was empty. Loki's grin told me he'd done it. Somehow.

I didn't argue. We got in the elevator and headed up to my condo. He hummed a song…might've been *Genie in a Bottle*, the whole way up.

"Why?" I asked as Loki opened the door to the condo as easily as he'd got us into the building.

"They always ask 'why?'" he said with a chuckle.

I wanted to protest. Ask who "they" were. I was oddly disappointed Loki fucked with other peoples' lives. I shouldn't be surprised though. Disappointed, but not surprised. I guess we'd never said we were exclusive.

Nothing should surprise me anymore, since apparently, I was a werehorse.

"You're not a werehorse," Loki said as we went back inside. "If that's what you were thinking."

I closed the door behind me hoping he wasn't really a mind reader. Locked it. Latched it. Not that I believed a thin chain would impede Loki if he wanted to leave.

"Why—?"

Loki chuckled again. "Why?" he muttered, shaking his head.

"Let me finish, you interrupting bastard." I sighed. "Not 'why me?' *Why now?*"

"Oh." He smiled. "That *is* different. I suppose."

"I haven't heard an answer."

"Demanding little filly, aren't you?"

"If my building didn't have a no-pets clause, I'd turn into a horse and give you *such a kicking.*"

"Fine," Loki said. "Fine. Magic is coming back into the world. Hard. There's your 'now.' As for the 'why,' you can probably imagine, I have enemies."

"Really?" I said, voice dripping with sarcasm. "You?"

Loki waved off the remark. "So after I saved Asgard from itself, *again*, Odin stole my first kid."

"The eight-legged one?" I asked with a heavy dollop of sarcasm. He struck me as the type who had more than one bastard in his past.

"Yes." Loki's lips twitched in irritation. "Sleipnir could run on the air and water as well as over land."

"Useful trick, that," I said.

Loki nodded. "Odin thought so. Used my son as his mount. That wasn't enough for the one-eyed prick. Then he bred Sleipnir to make flying horses for his valkyries."

There was something in the way he'd spoken, a hurt still raw, genuine, which made me want to believe him. I'd almost certainly regret it.

"Valkyries are real too?" I asked.

"Everything's real, hon. Except the stuff that isn't."

That was *no* help. "They're coming for me, aren't they?"

He nodded. "To them, you're nothing but a beast of burden, something to be ridden. Not a person. A *thing*."

"*Hmph.*" That was not an attitude to which I was unaccustomed. "What if I don't want to be their ride?"

"They'll either bind you in your other form, or they'll kill you."

I rubbed at my eyes. "Jesus."

"Yeah, he's not going to help you with this. Sorry."

The wine bottle was still half full. I grabbed it and slugged back a couple swallows. I could've used something stronger. "I'm going to change."

"Not sure there's room in there for a horse," Loki said, smirking.

"Clothes." *Ass.*

Loki snatched the wine and had a pull. "I'll be waiting."

I closed the door behind me, even though Loki had already seen me in my all-together. This wasn't how I saw tonight going. Okay. It was sort of how I'd thought the date would go. Nudity? Hell yes. Horse transformation, shapeshifting date, and surprise family reunion? Hell no.

I pulled on a fresh pair of underwear, yoga pants and a sports bra and hoodie. I packed a bag with a few spare undies and shirts and sweats too, just in case.

Loki seemed disappointed with my practical attire.

I didn't care.

I tucked my phone into my bag. "I'm ready."

"Now you sound like my great-great-great—" he kept going, I lost track of how many greats he actually spoke, but I presumed he was being accurate and not snarky, because accuracy in this instance would irritate me more. "—Granddaughter," he finished.

"I'll take that as a compliment, I guess."

"Oh it is."

I asked. "Are we running or fighting?"

"We run," Loki said. "You're not ready to fight them."

I looked over my shoulder as we left the condo building. I'd forgotten to turn my lights off. I hated having to leave my home behind. Especially without knowing where we were going, or when I'd be home. I had tenderloin thawing in the fridge. What would I tell work? Would they believe me?

Of course they won't believe you're a magic horse. Don't be fucking ridiculous.

I sighed. It'd been a good job while it'd lasted. If Loki went on making my life "interesting" too long, I'd be sure to lose it. And default on my condo mortgage. I did *not* want to move back in with my parents. They already thought I was weird.

"Since we're running, where do we run to?"

Loki smiled. There was that Cheshire grin again. "I know the perfect place."

That did not make me feel better.

Loki led me toward the river, and not my car.

He watched the sky nervously. "The sooner you master your body the better."

That made sense. I just…*hated* agreeing with him. "Fine," I muttered. "Whatever you say."

He raised an eyebrow as if he were a cartoon character. "You should probably be more careful with your phrasing in the future."

I scowled, and Loki turned into a falcon, screeching with delight.

I wondered how he did it. The falcon's eyes glittered, as if he was reading my mind. I considered my carefully chosen clothes. They wouldn't survive the transformation—assuming I *could* make myself change. I stripped, stuffing the clothes into my side bag as I hopped, foot to foot, on the cold asphalt at the edge of the parking lot. I willed myself to change.

Nothing happened.

Last time the change had come when I'd been afraid.

Change. Change. Change.

A car's engine revved as it came into the parking lot, not slowing. The lights turned as the driver sought their spot. For now, I was hidden by a transformer box, but that wouldn't last.

Change.

C'mon.

I looked up at the sky, the damned falcon still circled.

I hopped into the air.

Change.

I landed, wincing at the impact, and stamped my feet against the cold. Huddled with my arms across my torso. The cold wasn't helping either.

There was a sound like rain slamming on a tin roof, and I looked up. Three horses, complete with riders, ran on the air, as if hurtling down the side of a mountain toward my building. The horses stopped next to my balcony, and their riders—all women in white— hopped off. Glass shattered and they entered my apartment.

Holy shit. The valkyries. I looked at the horses tied off to my balcony as if it were a hitching post. I was going to die.

Or worse.

I thought I heard someone call my name. I could barely hear from the pounding in my temples.

"Michelle?"

Shit. The driver was Veronica. My nosy neighbour across the hall.

"Are you okay, Michelle? Should I call—Oh my God!"

I hadn't felt the change, same as the first time, one moment I was a woman, the next I was a horse. My hooves rang off the asphalt. She backed away, hands up as if trying to ward off attack and she ran. She'd seen me turn into a horse. There was no going back from that. My life, as I'd known it, was *definitely* over.

I heard crashes from my apartment. The valkyries must be upset I wasn't home. My "I don't want to die" instincts fought with my "I *just* got my kitchen the way I liked it" anger.

"Time to go," Loki said.

I ran into the air, and into the night.

I think every kid grows up wanting a magic horse, but how many kids want to *be* a magic horse?

This "gift" wasn't something I'd asked for, but it was all I wanted anymore.

To run. To fly.

Nothing compared to this.

Not work. Not food. Not sex.

I could fly.

It's hard to describe the exhilaration of flying. High in the sky, north wind slapping against my body, I didn't feel its chill, only the rush, as I ducked, and dived, and climbed and plummeted.

In that tiny moment, all my troubles were forgotten.

We landed in the Assiniboine Forest, a popular hiker's destination, right inside the city, but fortunately not so popular at this time of night.

"They won't look for us here," Loki said.

"Why not?"

He twirled around, fingers pointing at nothing. "Because it's lousy with elves."

"*Right*," I said. "Because of the *elves*."

I sighed. Elves being real would be the least weird thing about tonight, so I shut up and dressed. Loki was in clothes the moment he landed. Not the dark jeans and dress shirt he'd been wearing as "Ted" but a rumpled suit that looked tailored for a much larger man.

I stared at Loki. "How come your clothes don't get shredded when you change shape?"

He shrugged, and smiled. "I'm more magic than you, I guess."

"Typical," I muttered.

Loki motioned for me to follow him deeper into the trees.

I lost track of how long we walked in the stillness of wood, dead leaves crunching under our feet, and misted breath drifting to join the clouds.

Loki broke the silence. "So…are you freaked out?"

A little. I didn't want to admit it, and ultimately, what I felt above all, was *awesome.* "I'm great," I said. And I meant it.

"You should keep practicing," Loki said, out of nowhere. "'Til the change is second nature."

There was room on the foot path, and the cool night air didn't bother me. It was the in-between step that was the problem.

"You just want to see me strip, you perv."

"It is our third date," he said, winking.

I gave him a shove, and he staggered. "Give it a rest. It's not going to happen. It was never going to happen. *Grandma.*"

His smirk told me he knew the lie in my words, but, at the very least, he did shut up.

For a while.

"How could you *not* suspect you're at least part horse?" Loki asked.

My eyes narrowed. "You need to tread very carefully, god or no."

Loki's voice was shiny as a new penny. "You're long of limb. Long of face. You don't eat meat. Like shoes."

"Oh yeah, *so* obvious now that you point it out."

He shrugged. "It was all there."

I hurled my side bag at him and made the change.

Changing shape was exhausting. My stomach growled, and my body was slick with sweat. I made the change standing in place, I made it running. I made it jumping, and I made it backing up. Learning to speak in my horse body had been the biggest challenge. My mouth and tongue didn't want to form the human words. By the time Loki was satisfied, I felt as if I'd been running all night.

"You'll need to eat to keep up your strength," Loki said, reaching into my bag and passing me an apple.

I bit into it gratefully. It tasted amazing. Juicy, fresh. I'd been so worried about having enough clothing to survive any accidental transformations, I hadn't thought about food. I had been full from dinner, and flushed with the excitement and terror of my new crazy life.

"Eat," Loki said, passing me a protein bar.

I wondered where he was getting the food, because it sure hadn't come from my kitchen.

"You need to eat more," he said.

My eyes narrowed. I felt like he was leading up to something...

"Like a horse!" he hollered, slapping his thigh.

I should've slapped him, but it only reminded me of our—my—predicament. "They'll never stop, will they?"

"No."

My eyes fell. That single simple word felt so damned defeating. Loki nudged my chin up. I didn't see any mischief in his eyes. No sass. Nothing but the truth when he said, "But I'll never stop either."

"Shit." I didn't know if I found Loki's promise comforting.

"We'll get you trained up, and keep you on the run. I'll play interference for you when I can. You'll be fine. You're a sharp little filly."

I bristled at the "compliment." All that was missing was him patting me on the head, like a pet. Maybe that's all I was to him. "If you were so good at interference, those flying bitches would be shy three horses."

His eyes dropped. I wasn't sure if it was embarrassment, or if I'd hurt his feelings. I didn't feel great about either result. Regardless of what had got me in this scenario, Loki was my only ally, my only way out of it. And he was *trying* to help. But I also needed to help myself. I couldn't run forever.

"I'm sorry," I said. "What I said…it was cruel, and unnecessary."

"But true," he said. "I do mourn the loss of any of my children. No matter the time or generations between us."

"We've got to teach the valkyries not to come at me," I said.

"That means fighting, not running," Loki said. "You up for that?"

"I'll have to be."

"Look," I hissed. "They're up there."

Backlit against clouds, glowing with moonlight, were the valkyries. At least, I assumed it was them. Unless I was suddenly in a Johnny Cash song, who else could it be? Riding horses. In the air.

"Are you out of your damned mind?" Loki jerked me under a branch.

"You think they see us?"

"I wouldn't put it past them." He shook his head. "I wouldn't put anything past them."

"How can we…"

"Kill them?"

It sounded so permanent when he said it, but I was glad he did. To be able to say the words out loud made them real. Made it a real thing that I believed I could do. I didn't like to think I could actually kill.

I asked, "Can we bribe them?"

Loki shook his head. "You're the only thing they want."

I ground my teeth. He wasn't helping. "Can I outrun them?"

"Probably in a straight shot, but their horses are more used to being horses than you so they'll be able to outmaneuver you, whether they have armed ladies on them or not."

When I turned around, a tall, muscular woman stood in Loki's place. The woman wore a white-feathered cloak, white leathers. With her pale skin, and white-gold hair, she looked like an apparition more than a real lady. I jumped back, stifling a scream. She glowered, holding a spear across her thighs with both hands. Then she winked.

Bloody Loki.

"This is what they'll look like," the woman said in Loki's voice. "The cloaks will allow them to glide. Their spears will kill anything they scratch, and let me tell you, it's not a fun way to go."

"Seriously?"

"Ayup."

"How do they control their..." What to say? Horses? Mounts? Slaves?"

"How will they control you?" Loki asked. "Is that what you mean?"

"Yeah."

"They have bridles woven from the hair of my son," he said. "Like a lasso. If they get that around your neck, you're done. And worse, while you're bound, you won't care."

There was something we could use... "Without the bridles?"

"You'll still be you."

I breathed a sigh of relief, so naturally, Loki had to ruin things. "Assuming they haven't broken you."

"If we lose the bridles, the horses will lose them."

"I'm listening."

"If they don't have...air superiority, they can't outrun me. The cloaks let them glide, not fly, and I run on air. Get the horses away from them, and they can't catch me. And if they're captured..." I needed to know what to call them—what to call *myself.*

"Vindafolöld?" he offered. "It means wind foals."

More poetic than I expected from the likes of him. "If we scatter the...vindafolöld, they'll never get all of us. With luck, the valkyries leave with nothing."

Loki smiled. "I'm glad to be a part of this plan."

"What plan?"

Loki laughed maniacally. "Exactly."

The ground whizzed by below us. If I concentrated on the movement of the ground, and not that I had a mythical god riding my back, I could pretend I was looking out the window of an airplane.

The moment never lasted.

I *did* have a god riding me.

"Tally ho!" Loki yelled.

I shook my head. The salvation he promised couldn't be worth the irritation.

"There they are," Loki called, gesturing with his spear.

The valkyries circled the forest, lingering over the river. Moonlight cast their shadows over the water, making it seem as if there were more of them. As if they had shadowy followers waiting to help bring me down.

I wanted to turn back. I wanted to run forever. Loki must've felt my hesitation. He uttered a yipping war cry that would've put Xena to shame and could've been heard in Saskatoon.

The valkyries stopped their circling, and swung around to face us. It was mildly interesting to note how they did so, they didn't turn in a wide arc like flying birds would have, instead they wheeled as if the air were solid, and charged in a v-shape, straight at us.

"I really don't like this plan anymore."

"It's *your* plan," Loki said.

I had nothing to say to that. I hated that he was correct. I hated being in this situation. But the only way out was through. Through three murderous goddesses who could kill me with a scratch. The only things stopping them were that they'd prefer to enslave me, my horny ultimate great grandmother, and a horse body I was still learning to use.

Loki patted my neck, and offered me a knife by the blade. I bit down on the hilt, trying not to think of how ridiculous I must look.

The valkyries were silent, other than the clatter of their steeds' hooves against the sky. Silent. Grim. Implacable. We barrelled toward one another. The timing would be hard to judge.

"Almost…almost…almost…" Loki's whispered.

Now.

Loki leapt from my back, screaming, "This one is *mine!*"

I barely heard him. I changed. It came, not effortlessly, but immediately.

My galloping hooves lost their purchase on the air. My legs ran against nothing and my arms pinwheeled as I struggled for balance I didn't have time to retain. The knife that'd felt so tiny and delicate a moment before suddenly felt huge, and the handle pained my jaw to contain.

I grabbed the valkyrie's bridle. My shoulder wrenched as my fingers closed around the braided horse hair. My momentum swung me against the horse's flank. I almost dropped the knife getting it in hand, but I held on.

"What in Hel?" the valkyrie cried.

She raised her spear. I had no time to cut. No time to think.

I was going to die. Just a scratch, Loki had warned. Only a scratch. The valkyrie looked a lot more stabby than scratchy.

I raised my knife, and she laughed. She didn't stab. *She laughed.*

The valkyrie's laugh ended when I slid the knife blade behind the bridle and slashed outward. I fell, taking the bridle with me. She had enough time to reach for the horse's mane before my momentum dragged her off its back and into the air.

Her feathered cloak unfurled, and her descent slowed as her horse galloped away. She stared death at me and reeled me in by wrapping the braid around the wrist of her free arm. Christ, she was strong. It felt like she could pull my arm clean off. The spear, she kept leveled.

I raised my knife and she laughed again. Until I severed the braid and dropped.

I bit the knife handle again, willing myself to change.

The transformation came more easily now, as if each time I did it, this unnatural thing became a more natural part of my body. Which concerned me. What if it meant someday I'd transform and forget what it meant to be human? Loki never forgot to be an asshole regardless of his form, so hopefully I'd be okay.

I ran as the valkyrie drifted to the ground, scanning the air for the rest of them. The freed horse ran in the opposite direction of me as fast as possible. Which probably made it the smartest horse in this race.

Two valkyries fought atop the back of a second flying horse. I had to assume one of them was Loki. At least he was still on plan. The third...where was the third?

I felt a shudder. A sensation you'd describe as someone stepping on your grave. But I wasn't in the grave. Yet. A shadow passed over a cloud beneath me. I looked up and saw a horse flying away.

An explosion hit my back. I'd spotted the third horse. But not the valkyrie, and now she was on my back.

"Not so clever now, are you beastie?" she hissed.

Her fingers tightened in my mane. She jerked my head back. Instinctively, I stopped running. I didn't want to, I wanted to bolt. But I couldn't. I reared as the valkyrie's heels dug into my flanks.

I cried out, and as the neigh of protest escaped, so did my knife.

"I should kill you," she said. "But we're already down two steeds. I will settle for breaking you."

"Go ahead and try."

The loop of a bridle passed over my neck. Shit. That was a good try. Without hands I couldn't get it off of me. With hands I'd start falling, and hang myself.

Loki hadn't said I could turn into anything other than a horse, but he was a shapeshifter, and assuming the god of lies had told the truth this time, his blood was in my veins as much as my horse grandfather's. Maybe I *could* do something.

I changed. I fell.

My hands came back first. I slipped them under the loop just before it choked me.

The valkyrie laughed as I swung at the end of her line. My human feet kicking feebly as I gasped and danced on the air.

"Michelle!" Loki cried from somewhere. Somewhere distant, and growing more so.

My vision greyed, and tunneled. My world shrank. I needed my hooves back. If I changed, would my front legs get caught in the noose? Would it kill me? Or break the bridle? It was magic. My heart thudded in my ears as grey turned black.

My first change had come when I was afraid.

I was plenty afraid now.

Afraid to change.

But I needed to.

My feet hit purchase. I stepped up as if climbing a ladder, and felt the braid go slack. Slack enough to loop it over my head and turn around to face the valkyrie. Human arms tugged and jerked. My torso hadn't changed, just my lower body. The valkyrie was much stronger than me. Without the added mass of being a horse there was no way I could overpower her. I dug my hooved feet in. It slowed the process, but didn't stop it.

The first valkyrie we'd kicked off her horse glided toward us, spear arm cocked back. She threw.

I looped the braid around one arm and changed to a horse again. I ran down, jerking the valkyrie into the path of the spear.

She cried out and the line went slack. When I whirled around, the valkyrie was gone. Her foggy afterimage glared at me before the wind caught it and dissipated her to nothing.

The valkyrie who threw the spear screamed in protest. She scanned the sky for her last sister. I looked too. I saw Loki, I assumed it was Loki, flying as a hawk beside one of the horses.

"You're outnumbered, lady," he said. "Go back to Hel."

"I'll be back for you, trickster," the valkyrie snarled. "And your little horse too."

The valkyrie faded into the clouds the same way her shishkabobbed sister had, and was gone.

"Wow," Loki said. "I can't believe that worked."

I shook my head, panting. "I think you're *exactly* the man my mother warned me about."

LIGHTLESS

K.T. Ivanrest

From the balcony of his prison, Fulsa watched the chariots streak through the sky. At this distance it was impossible to distinguish one from another or guess who might be winning—in fact, it was impossible to see chariots at all. Only balls of light trailing across the darkness, gliding into accidental constellations as teams pulled ahead and fell behind, collided and swerved. It was a simple training run, preparation for the upcoming race, but even so he could sense the energy, the starfire streaming off the horses, the anticipation.

Two days until the festival. He, too, ought to have been out there patterning galaxies with the other drivers. And instead—

"Your Highness?" Phaios' quiet voice drifted from the shadows, as insubstantial as the speaker. "The empress has arrived."

Already Fulsa was halfway across the room, nerves coursing around his stomach while he unbuttoned his shirt and tossed it on a nearby chair. Immediately the room grew lighter, and desperate hope fired in his heart. Perhaps he was brightening after all. Perhaps his nightmare was finally over.

He slid a sheer coat across his shoulders and then studied his hands, but could discern no difference in their glow. Here in this secluded tower with only Phaios for company, he had no way to determine whether there had been any further dimming. Beside the lightless slave he always looked radiant, so bright he could almost forget what was happening, and then the empress would visit and he'd see just how quickly his dignity and worth were seeping out of his skin.

A last glance out the window while he clenched his fists and tried to calm his heartbeat. Another last glance toward Phaios, whose silent nod spoke more clearly than any words.

Then he knelt before the door and waited.

Aithra's footsteps were mere *tps* on the polished stone, her presence announced instead by the brilliance which preceded her up the staircase, pressing away the shadows with proud disdain and careless ease.

"Your Majesty."

Her gossamer coat rustled softly, scattering specks of light like jewels for the less fortunate. Even knowing how much of it was unnatural, he envied her splendor. To have so much to shed...

"Fulsa."

Using only his name, his mother wove an intricate knot of shame, disinterest, and approval, three threads he could always perceive despite their incompatibility, each tightening or loosening at a moment's notice. He hated how it bound him, the possibility of that last thread, the enduring hope that one day she would look at him with pride.

But when he rose, it was to meet a face painted with practiced neutrality. Her blue eyes examined him a long moment and then she stepped into the room, striding between Fulsa and Phaios and snapping her riding crop at the slave as she passed. Fulsa winced, watched his attendant retreat from her aura, and kept his usual silence—now more than ever he could not afford the empress' ire, and when she caught him watching Phaios he rolled his shoulders back and raised his chin instinctively.

"And still," his mother said without preamble, "no improvement. I daresay it's worse than ever."

His stomach lurched, his proud posture collapsed, and the last of his foolish, nervous hope trailed away like the very glow that was abandoning him. Worse than ever, less than ever... He swallowed and tried to think of something brave to say, but instead rasped, "Doctor Candas?"

"Nothing." The empress pulled a small, cream-colored pendant from around her neck and held it out. "She continues to insist there is no explanation. Nor yet," she added, frown deepening when he did not accept the necklace, "a cure."

He took it at last, forcing himself not to look at Phaios nor think about the source of the light within the charm. Not a cure, just a temporary solution until the doctor—until *anyone*—could fix him. Between his fingers the smooth stone grew warm, and a searing heat spread through his limbs. His aura widened into the darkness.

As always, he watched his mother's face hungrily, hating himself for his weakness, but there it was: that flash in her eyes, the smoothing of her skin as her frown dissipated. Not quite pride, but recognition. For a beautiful moment everything held promise—the beads woven into his coat threw a glimmering dance across the room, Phaios' reading lamp seemed absurd again, and even the chill in the air was swallowed up in silver splendor. He was radiant Prince Fulsa once more.

And then Aithra's carefully schooled composure returned and Fulsa's heart sank beneath the weight of the truth and the ephemerality of his restored light.

If the empress saw his dismay, she said nothing; instead she nodded like a craftsman satisfied with her work, reclaimed the pendant, and turned.

"I cannot stay." She never stayed. She came herself only because she trusted no one else with the secret. "I must oversee the final festival preparations."

"Of course. Thank you, as always, for coming."

Fulsa bowed to her retreating back, and by the time he rose she was already gone. Trembling all over yet hollow within, he took a single, involuntary step after her. How long before he would accompany her down those stairs?

The race was finished by the time she was gone, and so the only thing left to do was cry.

But Fulsa couldn't make himself do even that, so instead he returned to the balcony and the darkness, to the pure and absolute silence that filled so much of the desolate northern coast. An abandoned watchtower, an abandoned prince…

High above, a wild horse streaked through the sky, its wings outstretched, radiance in its wake that put even Aithra's to shame. Further and further it climbed, away from the island and its tame kin, goaded on by nothing more than the joy of flying.

What he wouldn't give to join it.

Phaios came to stand at his side, as always, and said nothing, as often. Out of the corner of Fulsa's eye he was merely a dark blur crested with starlight-pale hair, fading into the shadows unless Fulsa looked directly at him. To the Celest nobility, this near-invisibility was the appeal of the lightless, but here in this prison locked only by disgrace, the empress come and gone without a solution yet again, it was no more than another ominous whisper of Fulsa's fate. For a moment he felt his mother's shame, and then he simply felt desperate and lost.

"What's it like?" he whispered, though he wasn't sure he wanted to know.

Behind the deferential tilt of his head, Phaios' gaze was as penetrating as ever. "Losing yourself," he asked, "or being lightless? Your Highness."

"The second. The…both." Fulsa slouched against the railing and sighed. Was there a difference?

His attendant traced a dull finger through the air, following the island's edge where it met the endless span of space. Somewhere beyond lay other islands, other cities and thousands of Celest, bright spots in the sky of Aithra's domain.

How far he felt from it all.

At last Phaios finished his outline and swept his fingers gracefully through the darkness, balling his hand into a fist as though attempting to contain it. "Like falling into the sky."

It was so like Phaios, that answer, at once poetic and dangerously real. Fulsa had struggled not to think about what the empress might do to him if he truly lost all of his light, but for a moment he saw himself hurled from the island's edge, clawing at blackness until he was dragging it within him, the distinction between his body and the sky vanishing, and no matter how loudly he screamed, no one could see him or hear him or save him—

He threw himself back from the railing with a gasp and shoved his sleeve up to his elbow, certain it was already too late, and when a dark spot appeared upon his shoulder he nearly panicked before realizing it was merely Phaios' hand.

"There has to be something." He couldn't let it happen. Three months in this tower and he couldn't endure another day of waiting. "Anything."

Everything he wanted was in the city and everything he might become hovered at his side, so instead he sought the sky for the horse. Far in the distance he caught its stream of starfire, and though it was leaving him behind, he felt a breath of comfort. Once, said the legends, everyone had been lightless, but then the horses had come. His people had called them the selphoroi, the light-bringers. They'd filled the sky and islands with their brilliant glow, and in the end, gifted it to those they'd deemed—

"The race!" He whirled and grabbed Phaios' shirt, pulling him closer and grinning into his startled face. "Phai, I have an idea."

Fulsa slid the bit into the mare's mouth and waited for Phaios to question his judgment again.

It was amazing, really, how the slave could say absolutely nothing and still convey a sky of meaning. He'd spent their harried journey to the city filling a vast expanse of starry darkness with nothing, and now he stood guard outside the stall, attempting a galaxy.

It was supremely irritating, but to be fair, everything was a disaster.

Shaking with nerves, Fulsa surveyed his progress, confident he'd done Lun's bridle properly but at a complete loss regarding the rest. It didn't matter that he'd already harnessed Sona—he had no idea whether it was correct and still less how to repeat the process. For all he knew, he'd used too many straps on Sona and would not have enough left for Lun. Was there really a line trailing down the horse's back? How had he never noticed?

Again he cursed their timing. The Right of Eos allowed anyone to vie for light by completing the annual race, but required that he or she drive the imperial horses, and so the plan had seemed simple: hide in the royal stables while Aithra performed the opening ceremony, wait until she returned with her chariot, then intercept it from the stablehands once she'd gone. One pair of selphoroi, harnessed and ready to race.

Instead they'd shouldered their way through a city bustling with festival-goers of every rank and brightness to find the ceremony complete, Aithra's mares already unharnessed, and the race looming scant hours away.

Their only luck was that the stables were deserted. A horse's soft glow marked each occupied stall; the rest sat lightless like Fulsa, who'd disguised himself in Phaios' thick-woven clothing and was trying not to think about the day he'd no longer have any aura to conceal. The empress had been right—it was getting worse. Already the pendant's store was nearly gone, and their progress through the city, past so many lighted in their cheerful gauzes and glittering robes, had left him more frantic than ever.

With trembling hands, he snatched one of the straps from the pile at his feet; the buckles clinked with every anxious jolt, then clattered loudly as the entire thing slithered from his grip and hit the sand with a defeated *thud*.

"Shut up," he snapped at Phaios, who'd said nothing and continued to do so. "Useless…"

The retort died on his lips—he couldn't berate a lightless for keeping well away from the selphoroi, not when his own hands were already throbbing. Even a brush against Lun's star-white coat sent heat searing through his skin, and her beautifully soft forelock all but singed his fingers when he pulled it over the browband. And this from a tame selphoros, far paler than her wild kin owing to the gift of light she'd given long ago.

Just one more horrible reminder how far he'd faded, and one more reason to abandon this plan before it killed him.

But he couldn't. Every time he considered quitting, the consequences seemed worse, the loss more devastating. He *would* regain his worth, and this was the only answer he had.

Retrieving the strap, he brushed it clean and took a deep, steadying breath, catching scents of hay and manure, leather oil and freshly groomed horses. Through the bars at the back of Lun's stall he could see one of the city's many statues honoring the selphoroi, mounted high on a pedestal at the far end of the arena—some artist's representation of a horse in flight, its surface tiled over with the same shimmering white stones that lined the island's shores. Fulsa remembered hurling them from the edge as a child and shouting "Shooting star!" until his voice grew hoarse. He recalled time and again threatening to shove Phaios over the edge, too, and how with each threat his attendant had looked a little less alarmed and a little more quietly amused.

The memories sustained him strap after strap, until at last Lun stood in full harness, or so he hoped. He slid the stall door back, wincing when it rumbled into the silence, and thrust the reins at

Phaios, guilty but more nervous and impatient than ever. So far, so good, but who knew how long it would take to harness them to the chariot...

"Hold her while I get Sona."

Phaios raised his eyebrows.

"I know. Look, just half a minute, all right?"

His attendant compressed a great deal of silence into the next moment, then took several steps back, withdrew his hands inside his sleeves, and accepted the very end of the reins between two misshapen pads of dark fabric, as if afraid Lun's heat might somehow work its way to him through her tack. Ears lazing back, the mare dipped her head and eyed her reluctant handler without concern. Well-trained, everyone said. Fulsa suspected otherwise, but he didn't have time for that right now.

"What *exactly* do you think you're doing?"

He leapt and collided with Sona—he knew that voice, as well as the unnaturally bright blur approaching down the aisle. Terror shot through him, then a vivid image of himself lightless, then worse terror.

"Go!" he hissed at Phaios, urging Sona toward the arena without a single idea what they'd do when they reached it or why they were bothering to run. But if they could get there, maybe—

"Not. Another. Step."

The empress' tone was as icy as the deepest sky, the fury in her light rivaled by that in her expression. Stomach roiling, Fulsa squared his shoulders and turned, looping his hands behind his back so he could wring Sona's reins unseen. Behind him both mares stood quietly, Phaios a conspicuous non-presence beside their gentle glow. A strange entourage, but enough to give him the courage to step forward.

"Your Maj—"

"What," she snapped, "is the meaning of this?"

"I'm here for the race."

She stilled, dark lips parted, and mouthed the words once before speaking them aloud. "The race." Her eyes narrowed. "You left the tower, you risked showing *this*—" she flourished a hand at him "—to the *entire city*, for a *race?*"

This. His face burned while his stomach continued to churn. She never named it, never acknowledged the nature of what was happening, and some part of him knew there was more to *this* than just his fading.

"And on top of that you're stealing my team. Dare I ask why?" From beneath her ceremonial headdress she scowled at the horses as though about to accuse them of treason, then tensed abruptly and turned incredulous eyes back on Fulsa. "Unless... You *cannot* be serious."

He clenched his fists and cursed his heart again for the way it faltered beneath her derision. Like she was giving up on him. Like she already had. But determination beat within him, too, stronger than disappointment. *Not this time.* This time they feared the same thing, wanted the same thing. He had to make her understand.

"Mother, no one knows why this is happening. I'm not getting better; you bring me light but I'm...I'm fading faster than ever. Why not the Right?"

"Why n—don't be a child! The Right of Eos was a ridiculous concession made to those low-lights presumptuous enough to seek a place amidst the nobility. You cannot honestly believe that three laps around the island will do a starspeck of good? That *they*—" She threw a luminous arm toward Lun, who flattened her ears and ruffled her massive wings. "—will simply judge you worthy and restore your light?"

"I *have* to believe it!" Even when she voiced the doubts he'd been trying so hard to ignore. "And if there's even a chance it could work... Mother, at least let me *try*."

"Absolutely not."

Sona's twisted reins bit into his palms. "Why not? I'll be wearing a mask, no one will recognize m—"

"That has nothing to do with it." But that was a lie and they both knew it. "How many Celest have attempted this and perished in starfire? You are a member of the royal family, and I'll not have you endangering yourself in some ritual that's guaranteed to fail."

"Guaranteed to fail?" Bitter laughter scratched his throat at her false concern for his safety. "Why, Mother? Because it's me?" The firstborn who'd failed to be a daughter. The prince who failed to be worthy no matter how hard he tried. Behind him Sona stomped a hoof and he jabbed a finger at her. "Or perhaps I'm not the problem this time. Perhaps if you stopped stealing light from them, I'd have a chance!"

He reveled in the taunt for as long as it took her to reach Phaios, and by the time he realized what he'd done she'd dragged the slave toward Sona, tangled a hand in his hair, and thrust his face dangerously close to the mare's gleaming coat. Phaios sucked in a ragged breath; Fulsa's caught in his throat.

"You heard *nothing*," the empress hissed.

"I heard nothing." Phaios' voice was calm but his body trembled and his chest heaved with each short, panting breath. Trapped between Sona and the empress, he seemed to fade beyond lightless, his silvery hair a feeble struggle in a lost battle.

"You will tell no one of this."

"I will not betray Her Majesty's secret." The slightest shake of his head while Fulsa watched them in mute horror, swallowing a plea that would only make her angrier.

"Swear it." And before he could speak, she pressed the slave's cheek against Sona's neck.

His vow rose on a gasp of pain and a desperate wail. "I swear, I swear!"

As quickly as it had happened, she jerked him back and steered him before Fulsa, the glass beads on her sleeves clattering harshly. The lightless swayed in her grasp, one hand caressing his scorched face, tears welling in his dark eyes. With a jolt of nausea, Fulsa realized far too late what "losing yourself" meant to someone like Phaios.

Aithra's cool voice cut into his guilt. "So determined to be rid of one secret that you would expose another."

He wrenched his gaze from the slave and glared at his mother, prepared to meet her wrath, but though her features were sharp, there was something else—recognition again. Anger, but acknowledgment. Finally she appreciated his resolve, and he found he no longer cared.

"I *will* have my light back." But not for her. For himself. And now, for Phaios.

She held him in a hard, unblinking stare, as though she could drain his remaining aura with no more than her will and be done with it. At last she tilted her head toward Phaios. "Reveal your identity, and he'll be only the first thing you lose."

By the time he'd bowed in thanks she was halfway down the aisle, Phaios trailing along at her unspoken command. As they rounded the corner the lightless turned and looked back at Fulsa, and for once his silence was empty.

He'd raced so many times it didn't occur to him to be nervous, not until they pulled up to the starting line and he faced the reality of what he was about to do.

Drivers on either side glanced at him, eyes curious behind their ceremonial masks. Even the brightest of the Celest nobility wore racing armor to guard against the horses' intense heat at high speeds, yet there stood Fulsa, bare from the waist up, pale beside their gleam. No one had witnessed it in years, but he could tell from the murmurs—some sharper than others—that everyone knew why he was there.

The mares jostled one another and he jerked from his reverie to gather the reins. Aithra was careful never to sap too much light at once, always waited until they'd regained their usual luster before taking more, and even subdued by the subtle theft, the team had power and purpose. Whatever the legends said, whether there was any truth to the Right or not, he felt tested in the empress' chariot, judged by the luminous selphoroi shifting eagerly ahead of him.

He could only hope their judgment was kinder than hers.

"Drivers, on your marks!"

There was no arena; instead, a towering semicircle of seats faced out into the vast, star-studded darkness, decorated for the festival with pennants and banners. Through its center ran a track just wide enough to accommodate the teams, just long enough for a running start and a leap.

He'd hardly processed the thought when a gong sounded and they careened forward, twenty-two chariots and twice as many shining horses all bearing madly toward the edge of the island. Fulsa crouched in the car, feet spread wide across the platform as it rattled beneath him. Soon, soon, a few more lengths, already he could feel starfire streaming off the horses, one moment to wonder whether he was mad to do this, and then they vaulted into the darkness.

His stomach lurched as it always did, and for several thunderous heartbeats he was lost in the thrilling nausea of rising wildly into space, caught amidst darkest black and dizzying streaks of white and the sensation of falling even as they flew. The sky rang with the shouts of drivers and thousands of cheers and the crackling of applause, then a rush of air as a chariot tore so close he could have touched it. Above it all he shouted encouragement, first to the mares, then to himself.

His hope returned and he let it blaze.

They banked a hard left and sailed past the empress' box, perched at the highest point in the stands beneath another mosaicked statue. From here the imperial seat was merely light, a court of unbroken splendor and a beacon for the drivers.

Fulsa's finish line.

The stands vanished and they shot off along the curved southern arm of the island. Below ran the shoreline, as full of spectators as the stands—cut off from view as they pulled past a stocky man in a yellow mask and chariot to match, then a woman in red with horsehair braided into her own. With every advance the knot in his stomach eased. At least half the teams were still ahead of them, but that meant the other half was behind. The Right did not require him to win, only finish, but the fewer teams ahead, the less starfire he'd have to endure.

It was worst in his hands, thrust forward and gripping the reins so tightly his arms throbbed. Since his first days of racing he'd been foolishly afraid that dropping the reins would somehow free the horses and send his chariot tumbling into space, but now he clutched them as much to distract from the heat as anything. It snaked up his arms and down his chest, a searing taunt that he was fading, an urgent reminder how much was at stake. His light, his attendant, his whole life—

"Out of the way, low-light!"

The woman he'd passed flew by, her laughter swallowed by the roar of the crowd and a sweltering burst off her team's wings which caught in his throat and sent him reeling.

By the time he finished coughing they'd turned at the southern point and passed three more pairs, then another and another, just blurs now through a cloud of tears. Any moment his hands might catch fire; he shifted the reins into one and let the other dangle behind the wall of the chariot, thinking of Phaios and his scorched face, the empress' threat, and everything he so desperately needed to fix.

"Come on," he whispered to his hands, or the horses, or himself. Three laps. Just three laps and everything would be right.

The world was a haze of brilliant starfire, flashes of light off nearby chariots and spreading wings, scorching wind filling his eyes with more tears and his ears with its roar, the leather blistering his hands, and still he felt no different. Tradition required him to finish the race, but how long before he would sense a change?

How long before he knew if there would even be one?

Please, please...

They arced at the northern point. Fulsa steered high and outside, pulling from the pack seconds before two teams below collided in a burst of silver and shrieks and the clatter of metal. He flinched and the mares' ears flicked, but on they flew, manes streaming as they tore into the stretch.

Heat and pain and no new light.

One lap, complete. The stands were a blur come and gone, the shore a gleaming batik of color and luster. If he squinted he could almost see individuals waving, children jumping up and down in excitement, banners bearing the names and crests of the drivers. Their cheers were a buzz in his ears caught up in the rush of starfire and the heartbeat pounding its way through his head and the inner voice chanting something like *my light my light* that never quite made it to his lips.

The teams stretched out along the southern arm, and the crowds thinned and then vanished as level ground gave way to jagged cliffs. Ahead a selphoros balked and the chariot pitched—Sona and Lun darted around it, and as they banked clear, Fulsa spotted two glowing balls at the base of the cliffs, near the very edge of the island.

His throat constricted. No one came this far south, not willingly, and it rattled him to imagine someone being flung to his death in the midst of the festivities.

One ball of light was a team hitched to an empty chariot. The second split into two as Lun and Sona thundered nearer—two guards.

Two guards and a dark figure between them.

Two guards and Phaios.

He didn't realize he'd jerked on the reins until the team lurched in response, jostling one another as they tried to respond to their driver's unexpected command. He slammed into the side of the chariot and scrambled to maintain both balance and control, but his eyes remained on the figures, squinting and blinking and squinting again, and every time, the same sight.

Phaios, perilously close to that endless expanse of sky.

Guilt and horror gnawed through him. Why? The lightless had sworn his silence and the empress had well and truly seared it into him. Was this a test? Some cruel distraction? Mockery?

Or simply Aithra, whose ancestors had tamed the selphoroi, whose grandmother had united the islands at last, disposing of a threat to her light and rule and legacy while the only person who cared a starspeck about the slave was occupied with something more—

No. He tightened the leather in his sweaty hands—and faltered. There were his arms, a gut-wrenching reminder of his unaccomplished goal, throbbing and paler than ever.

Or were they? A closer look, daring hope. Was it the mares' glow, or his own? Was the pain less severe, or was he growing numb?

No, they *were* brighter. Not by much, but it was there, and that meant—

He loosened his hold and the horses surged back into the pack. They blazed past another team and banked north while his mind thundered ahead, mapping out a plan, weaving in between the remaining chariots with renewed determination. Another lap and a half to reclaim his light, then back to this spot to find Phaios in the sky. Not long, not far. He could do it, save Phaios *and* himself. He had to—it was working, and if he left the race now…what good would he be without his light?

But then, what good had he ever been *with* it? In what galaxy had radiant Prince Fulsa ever stood up for anyone, so long as Aithra's displeasure and the far-off hope of her favor held him in such sway?

His heart wrenched and so did his hands.

The mares snorted, tossing their heads and beating their wings with increased vigor as the chariot's furious momentum tried to pull them off their sudden new course. Someone screamed; four pairs of hooves and two wheels sailed directly over his head while the driver shouted obscenities and threats that Fulsa hardly heard.

"Go!" he cried, staring beyond their starry manes to the point ahead where three figures were about to become two. So close but so impossibly far. How could their speed of moments ago now be so insufficient, their powerful wing-strokes so sluggish?

"Go!"

Faster they surged, closer and closer—and then they folded their wings and dove.

His stomach heaved and he seized the edge of the car as they plummeted, still on course but falling faster by the second. Everything hurt, his hands and arms and chest and his throat when he screamed. Their light enveloped him in a blistering embrace and he squeezed his eyes shut and gave up all hope of steering, and just when he was certain he'd burst into flame and leave Phaios to die, the chariot struck the ground and skidded along the stone-strewn shore. Somewhere beyond rose a shout and a clatter, then an indignant whuff when he dragged on the reins. At long last they shuddered to a halt.

Raw and throbbing but somehow alive, Fulsa hauled himself to his feet to see two shining figures prone on the ground and one blurred shape staring in utter disbelief.

"Get in!"

Phaios staggered into the car and reluctantly allowed Fulsa to embrace him before sliding to the floor and slumping against the curved wall, shielded from the guards and the horses' heat. His body quivered and the side of his face was red, blotched darker here and there and blistered along his cheekbone, but when he raised his eyes they were clear, full of relief and a silent thank-you. Fulsa nodded, a hundred apologies and a single promise. He deserved every bit of astonishment in the lightless' expression, and he knew it.

"Phai, I—"

"Stop right there!"

Lun shied before he even saw the guard lunge. She collided with Sona and the chariot jerked backward, forward, then up as they lurched into the sky. Somewhere below the guards were shouting, but Fulsa was too busy clinging to the rail to care what they were saying. The sensation of falling returned, Phaios yelped and grabbed his leg—and then they rounded the point and a massive mosaicked statue rose up to meet them.

He screamed and yanked on the reins, but already it was too close, too late—the horses were still scrambling to recover from their sudden launch, and even if they swerved they'd still—

The chariot slammed into the statue and all around was noise and debris, sharp stones and pain and Phaios screaming and light light light. Far away echoed a shriek that might have been a whinny, and the heat of the starfire vanished abruptly.

When at last he opened his eyes, his heart stopped.

Swirls of white poured from the remains of the statue and streaked in every direction, like the brilliance from a thousand of Aithra's pendants swelling into a tempest. Some collided with his team, some sailed toward the pack of chariots peeling northward, and some crashed over the guards who'd risen to pursue them. But no longer—brimming with new light and energy, their horses balked and threw their heads, tore the reins from the driver's hands, and dragged the chariot and its occupants into the sky, further and further from the island and those who'd stolen far more than Fulsa had ever realized.

Not just Lun and Sona. Not just occasional draughts of light.

Heart thundering, he watched a moment more, horrified by the truth and dreading the moment his team, too, would careen into the darkness with their helpless passengers in tow. He'd deserve *that* as well, though poor Phaios would not.

But the mares had stopped. Wings folded, they perched atop the cliffs, huffing quietly, brighter now than any tame selphoroi he'd ever seen yet radiating serenity. Hardly daring to hope, Fulsa gave the reins a cautious twitch and watched with relief as two sets of ears flicked in response. Attentive, listening. And maybe it was simply years of experience hearing resonance in Phaios' silence, but somehow he felt they were not just listening, but offering.

He pictured the island, its hundreds of horses and dozens of statues. *Erected in honor of the selphoroi*, said a voice in his head. *They gifted their light to those they deemed worthy.* The ready explanation for why tame selphoroi were so much paler than wild. Had it ever been true? Had the horses' gift prompted theft, or had his people—his *family*—never given them a chance to bestow light in the first place?

His aura had not returned, and for the first time it didn't matter. He snatched the mask from his face and locked eyes with Phaios. "How many more collisions do you think this thing can survive?"

The lightless regarded him with surprise, then thoughtfulness, then determination, and all the while he said nothing.

It was a very proud sort of nothing.

At last he nodded. "Enough."

"Enough" set every horse on the island shining like their wild kin. Rays of light darted again and again through the sky as teams tore free from chariots and horses broke from their stalls. Others remained, like Sona and Lun, over-bright spheres on the streets and in the fields. Whatever the intended purpose of the stolen light, whatever Aithra was doing about the revelation at this moment, no one could be ignorant now.

By some miracle both the chariot and its passengers were still intact. Fulsa held the reins for no other reason than that they were there—like the wild horse he'd watched from atop the tower, the mares seemed to be soaring for the joy of it, their coats so white they were blinding, new grace shimmering in every wing-stroke. Their starstream was a gentle breath against his raw skin, pure and effortless and full, no longer burning as they strained to preserve what light they'd been left, to make up for what had been stolen. So long as they wanted to press on, he wouldn't stop them.

Phaios stood at his side. It had taken a fierce staring contest and several more silent indictments against Fulsa's judgment, but at last he'd accepted that the horses' light was safe and climbed to his feet. Now he leaned confidently against the rail, squinting into the starfire and overflowing with astonishment. After a long, breathless silence he raised a dim hand and swiped it through the silver air.

"This is impossible."

Fulsa shook his head. "Not any more." This was *right*.

Up ahead, Sona tossed her head and snorted as though amused, and a moment later Lun whickered in echo.

"And what now?" Phaios asked.

Fulsa gestured into the black expanse, toward other islands and horses and lightless, everyone who needed Prince Fulsa, radiant or not. Needed him to speak, to act, to finally fill his own silence with more than just excuses.

Suddenly losing himself didn't seem so terrible, not when there was someone else he could become.

"Now, we keep going. Share a few more secrets." He raised his eyebrows. "Fall into another sky."

Phaios' mouth quirked. Stretching out a hand, he took the reins from Fulsa and gave them an experimental flick. "With all respect, Your Highness—if that's your plan, perhaps I ought to drive."

A GLORY OF UNICORNS

Jane Yolen

A group, a troop, a morning's glory.
A poem, a song, a pretty story.
A sentiment, a monument,
A moment meant,
And gone.

A tapestry, a tempest, we
Have nothing sentimental. See
That herd of odd-shaped stallions cross
The valley, sort of, kind of horse
With horn.

A dreaming, seeming, equus kin,
A shudder where the air is thin,
A blush of moment, pearl of day.
The eye goes inward, and away.
Curtain drawn.

ABOUT THE AUTHORS

J.G. Formato is a writer and elementary school teacher from North Florida. She lives in a little house at the edge of the woods with her beautiful family. You can find her work in *Persistent Visions, Luna Station Quarterly, The Colored Lens, freeze frame fiction*, and elsewhere.

Diana Hurlburt is a writer and librarian in Florida. Some of her short works can be found at *The Toast, The Prompt, witchsong, Kaaterskill Basin*, and *Body Parts*, and in the anthologies *Beyond the Pillars* and *The Queen's Readers*. Connect with her on Twitter and Tumblr.

Approximately 70% of **Tamsin Showbrook** is composed of strong tea and coffee. If you want to see her cry, tell her the kettle's broken. (Don't worry though, she'll pull herself together and heat water in a pan on the stove.) She isn't lucky enough—yet, at least—to write for a living, but keeps producing flash fiction, short stories and novels because she loves doing so. A qualified English teacher, she currently works as a private tutor. She has two young children and lives in Manchester UK. If you'd like to get in touch, you can at: tamsin.showbrook@gmail.com.

M. L. D. Curelas lives in Calgary, Canada, with two humans and a varying number of guinea pigs. Raised on a diet of Victorian literature and Stephen King, it's unsurprising that she now writes and edits fantasy and science fiction. Her most recent short fiction can be found in the anthology *Corvidae*, also edited by Rhonda Parrish. Margaret is also the owner of Tyche Books, a Canadian small-press which publishes science fiction and fantasy.

Laura VanArendonk Baugh overcame the dubious challenge of having been born without teeth or developed motor skills to become an award-winning writer of speculative fiction, mystery, and non-fiction. Her works have earned numerous accolades, including 3-star (the highest possible) ratings on Tangent's "Recommended Reading" list. Laura speaks professionally on a variety of topics throughout the year, including writing, fan costuming, and her day job as a professional animal trainer and behavior consultant. Find her at www.LauraVAB.com.

V. F. LeSann is a co-writing team presently living in Lethbridge, Alberta, Canada, comprised of Leslie Van Zwol and Megan Fennell. Court clerks by day and writers of myriad strange tales by night, they enjoying adding a touch of grit to imaginary worlds. Being lifelong prairie-dwellers, it was initially tricky to think of horses as fantastical, but the chance to riff on the legend of the Ghost Riders was far too fun to pass up.

Dan Koboldt is a genetics researcher and fantasy/science fiction author. His debut novel *The Rogue Retrieval*, about a Vegas magician in a medieval world, was published by Harper Voyager in January 2016. As a working geneticist, he has co-authored more than 70 publications in *Nature, Science, The New England Journal of Medicine*, and other scientific journals. Dan is also an avid deer hunter and outdoorsman. He lives with his wife and children in Ohio, where the deer take their revenge by eating the flowers in his backyard. You can find him online at dankoboldt.com.

J. J. Roth lawyers at a tech company, parents her two school-aged sons, and writes literary speculative fiction in the interstices. Her work is forthcoming in *Podcastle* and has appeared in *Nature, Urban Fantasy Magazine*, and various semi-pro and small press venues. For publication information and updates, please visit J. J.'s web site at www.jjroth.net, follow her on Twitter (@wrothroth), or find her on

Facebook (JJ Roth).

Susan MacGregor is the author of *The Tattooed Witch* trilogy, published through Five Rivers Publishing, the first book of which was short-listed for a Canadian Science Fiction and Fantasy Association Aurora Award. Her story "Ladies Day" reflects a similar world in her current work-in-progress. Her short fiction has been featured in *On Spec Magazine* and other anthologies. A prior editor with *On Spec*, her book *The ABC's of How Not to Write Speculative Fiction* is based on her 20+ years' editorial experience. She has also edited two anthologies, *Tesseracts Fifteen: A Case of Quite Curious Tales* (Edge Books) and *Divine Realms* (Ravenstone Books). Susan lives and works in Edmonton.

Pat Flewwelling is a novelist and short-story author from Oshawa, Ontario. By day, she is a senior business analyst at a major telecommunications company; on her weekends and evenings, she runs Myth Hawker Travelling Bookstore, and is a co-editor at ID Press. Please send more coffee to www.mythhawker.ca or www.patflewwelling.com.

Angela Rega is a belly dancing school librarian with a passion for folklore, fairy tales and furry creatures. She was raised in a multi-lingual household where nobody finished a sentence in the same language and still struggles with syntax. Her work has appeared in publications including *The Year's Best Australian Fantasy and Horror, Crossed Genres*, Fablecroft Press, Belladonna Publishing and PS Publications. She keeps a small website here: angierega.webs.com

Michael Leonberger is a writer and teacher from Virginia, where he currently lives with his girlfriend and their pet turtle. He graduated from VCU with a degree in Cinema and has worked jobs as disparate as a horror make-up effects artist for Kings Dominion's Halloween

Haunt to being an extra in the Steven Spielberg film, *Lincoln*. In 2014, his first feature film, *Goodish*, was an official selection in the VA Film Festival in Charlottesville, VA. That same year he published his first book, *Halloween Sweets*. He has since had several short stories published. He writes a monthly column for the online journal *Digital America*.

Sandra Wickham lives in Vancouver, Canada with her husband, toddler son and two cats. Her friends call her a needle crafting aficionado, health guru and ninja-in-training. Sandra's short stories have appeared in *Evolve: Vampires of the New Undead*, *Evolve: Vampires of the Future Undead*, *Chronicles of the Order*, *Crossed Genres* magazine, *LocoThology: Tales of Fantasy & Science Fiction*, *The Urban Green Man*, *Luna Station Quarterly* and *Sirens*. She slush reads for *Lightspeed Magazine* and promotes the Creative Ink Festival for writers and readers.

Stephanie A. Cain writes epic & urban fantasy. She grew up in Indiana, where much of her urban fantasy is set. She spends her work time at a small museum giving tours of a Victorian mancave and serving as a one-woman IT department. A proud crazy cat lady, she is happily owned by Eowyn, Strider, and Eustace Clarence Scrubb. In her free time, she enjoys hiking (except for the spiders), bird-watching, and reading. She's a World of Warcraft addict and visits office supply stores for fun. She owns way more movie scores and fountain pens than she can actually afford.

Cat McDonald lives on the eighth floor and can see all of Edmonton from here. She has a formal detective education and is currently enrolled in witch school as well. Her short stories can be found in *Sirens*, *Tesseracts 15*, and *Here Be Monsters: Tongues and Teeth*.

Andrew Bourelle is the author of the novel *Heavy Metal*, winner of the 2016 Autumn House Fiction Prize. His short stories have been published widely in literary journals and fiction anthologies, including the *Best American Mystery Stories, D is for Dinosaur,* and *Swords & Steam Short Stories.*

Chadwick Ginther is the Prix Aurora Award nominated author of the *Thunder Road* Trilogy (Ravenstone Books) and *Graveyard Mind* (forthcoming from ChiZine Publications). His short fiction has appeared recently in *Tesseracts, Those Who Make Us* and *Grimdark Magazine.* He lives and writes in Winnipeg, Canada, spinning sagas set in the wild spaces of Canada's western wilderness where surely monsters must exist.

K.T. Ivanrest wanted to be a cat or horse when she grew up, but after failing to metamorphose into either, she began writing stories about them instead. Soon the horses became unicorns and the cats sprouted wings, and once the dragons arrived, there was no turning back. When not writing, K.T. can be found sewing and drinking decaf coffee. She has a PhD in Classical Studies, which will come in handy when aliens finally make contact and it turns out they speak Latin. K.T. would like to not dedicate her story to Santa, who never brought her a pony for Christmas.

Jane Yolen, often called "the Hans Christian Andersen of America" (Newsweek) is the author of well over 350 books, including OWL MOON, THE DEVIL'S ARITHMETIC, and HOW DO DINOSAURS SAY GOODNIGHT. Her books and stories have won an assortment of awards—two Nebulas, a World Fantasy Award, a Caldecott, the Golden Kite Award, three Mythopoeic awards, two Christopher Medals, a nomination for the National Book Award, and the Jewish Book Award, among many others. She has been nominated three times for the Pushcart Prize in Poetry. She is also the winner (for body of work) of the World Fantasy Association Lifetime

Achievement Award, Science Fiction Poetry Association Grand Master Award, Catholic Library's Regina Medal, Kerlan Medal from the University of Minnesota, the du Grummond Medal from the University of Southern Missisippi, the Smith College Alumnae Medal, and New England Public Radio Arts and Humanities Award. Six colleges and universities have given her honorary doctorates. Her website is: www.janeyolen.com

ABOUT THE ANTHOLOGIST

Rhonda Parrish is driven by a desire to do All The Things. She founded and ran Niteblade Magazine, is an Assistant Editor at World Weaver Press and is the editor of several anthologies including, most recently, *Equus* and *D is for Dinosaur*.

In addition, Rhonda is a writer whose work has been in publications such as *Tesseracts 17: Speculating Canada from Coast to Coast* and *Imaginarium: The Best Canadian Speculative Writing* (2012 & 2015) and the paranormal non-fiction title, *Haunted Hospitals* (co-written with Mark Leslie).

Her website, updated weekly, is at http://www.rhondaparrish.com

MORE MAGICAL MENAGERIES
ANTHOLOGIES FROM RHONDA PARRISH

FAE
Rhonda Parrish's Magical Menageries, Volume One

Meet Robin Goodfellow as you've never seen him before, watch damsels in distress rescue themselves, get swept away with the selkies and enjoy tales of hobs, green men, pixies and phookas. One thing is for certain, these are not your grandmother's fairy tales.

CORVIDAE
Rhonda Parrish's Magical Menageries, Volume Two

In Corvidae birds are born of blood and pain, trickster ravens live up to their names, magpies take human form, blue jays battle evil forces, and choughs become prisoners of war. These stories will take you to the Great War, research facilities, frozen mountaintops, steam-powered worlds, remote forest homes, and deep into fairy tales. One thing is for certain, after reading this anthology, you'll never look the same way at the corvid outside your window.

SCARECROW
Rhonda Parrish's Magical Menageries, Volume Three

Within these pages, ancient enemies join together to destroy a mad mommet, a scarecrow who is a crow protects solar fields and stores long-lost family secrets, a woman falls in love with a scarecrow, and another becomes one. Encounter scarecrows made of straw, imagination, memory, and robotics while being spirited to Oz, mythological Japan, other planets, and a neighbor's back garden. After experiencing this book, you'll never look at a hay-man the same.

SIRENS
Rhonda Parrish's Magical Menageries, Volume Four

Sirens are beautiful, dangerous, and musical, whether they come from the sea or the sky. Greek sirens were described as part-bird, part-woman, and Roman sirens more like mermaids, but both had a voice that could captivate and destroy the strongest man. The pages of this book contain the stories of the Sirens of old, but also allow for modern re-imaginings, plucking the sirens out of their natural elements and placing them at a high school football game, or in wartime London, or even into outer space.

Featuring stories by Kelly Sandoval, Amanda Kespohl, L.S. Johnson, Pat Flewwelling, Gabriel F. Cuellar, Randall G. Arnold, Michael Leonberger, V. F. LeSann, Tamsin Showbrook, Simon Kewin, Cat McDonald, Sandra Wickham, K.T. Ivanrest, Adam L. Bealby, Eliza Chan, and Tabitha Lord, these siren songs will both exemplify and defy your expectations.

DISCUSSION QUESTIONS

Stars, Wings, and Knitting Things

1. In "Stars, Wings, and Knitting Things" Annie says that slippers are pretentious while her husband asserts that they are not pretentious but are, in fact, useful. What do you think? Are slippers pretentious? Are some slippers more or less pretentious than others?

2. Annie and Marcus are two very different types of people who want very different things from life. Which one of them can you relate to the most strongly? How do you suppose they met and became a couple in the first place? Was their relationship doomed from the start or do you think it could have worked out somehow?

3. Would you rather attend a Marcus-people party or an Annie-people party? Why? Is there some middle ground that could be found between the two types of party? What would that look like?

4. In the middle of a party, Annie accidentally lets her inside voice become her outside voice. Has this ever happened to you? How did the people around you respond? Did you cover it up better than Annie did?

5. Annie's favourite constellation is Pegasus, for reasons that become apparent pretty quickly in the story. Do you have a favourite constellation? What is it and why does it speak to you?

6. When Annie punctures her pillow with the knitting needles that were a gift from her husband the description is "Little bits of white fluff welled up from beneath the black satin pillowcase and bled through." Later in that scene, she goes out into the backyard to look at the stars and the story says, "The stars shone down, through the velvet cover of night. Wayward beams forced their ways through the

pinholes in the night sky." Obviously these two descriptions play off one another—can you think of any other similar juxtapositions in this story?

Eel and Bloom

1. If you were given the choice, would you choose to ride a normal, warmblooded horse, or a limerunner? Why? Would your decision change based on where you were riding it?

2. Have you ever smelled a corpse flower? Would you, if you were given the chance?

3. There's a whole host of supporting characters in "Eel and Bloom." Which ones intrigued you most? Who would you like to read more about?

4. Bea doesn't speak at all—at what point in the story did you realise that was going to be the case? Did it surprise you? How do you think her lack of verbal communication impacted how the author chose to tell this story?

5. Have you ever been to, or watched a horse race? How did it compare to the limerunner race in this story? What other kinds of no-holds-barred competitions did this story remind you of?

6. Bea's mother was willing to gamble her away in a bet, but she broke her pattern to come to the racetrack and learn the results first hand. What do you think drove her there? Did her showing up at the track change how you felt about her?

7. At the end of the story, Bea compares the way her mother used her to how she used Tim. Do you think that's a fair comparison?

8. The ending of this story leaves us with several unanswered questions, but Bea says she finds the only answer she needs when Tim opened his eyes once more. Do you feel the same?

A Complete Mare

1. In "A Complete Mare" Vez claims that family is overrated. Do you agree with her? How do you think your opinion might change if you were to discover that you were descended from a god?

2. If you were descended from a deity, which one would you want it to be? What kind of powers would you hope to acquire from your godly ancestry?

3. When Vez grows four heads she struggles to figure out how to work with them. What do you think the biggest obstacle to learning how to use the superpower you picked out in the previous question would be? How would you overcome it?

4. In the end, Odin offers Vez and her sister a safe place to say but she refuses, choosing instead to stay at the devastated Hall. Do you think she made the right decision? What would you have done in her place?

Neither Snow, nor Rain, nor Heat-Ray

1. "Neither Snow, nor Rain, nor Heat-Ray" begins with the line, "No one had been alarmed when the first Martian vessels had landed, pocking the ground like open sores." How do you think the world would react if Martian vessels were to land here today?

2. Emma and Beezus make a great team—they understand and complement each other and can anticipate what the other is going to do before they do it. Have you ever felt that kind of connection with another creature? Was it human or a different kind of animal?

3. Henry Fletcher is a Moreauvian—the result of cross-species experimentation by the fictional, but famous, Dr. Moreau. If you were going to be crossed with an animal, which kind of animal would you choose? What animal-like traits would you want to be gifted with? Which would you least want to gain?

Rue the Day

1. "Rue the Day" includes several different unicorns, each of which is distinct in appearance as well as personality. If you were to ride a unicorn, what would you want it to look like? What temperament do you think would suit you best?

2. Rue is supposed to be a guard for Galyne, but turns out to be an enemy spy. At what point in the story did you begin to suspect he was up to no good?

3. Galyne's unicorn, Nova, was injured by a spear long before this story takes place. She is left alive and able to fight but with an "ugly knot of scar tissue." Given what happens to Galyne, do you think this is foreshadowing, or does Nova's injury serve another purpose in the story?

4. In "Rue the Day," unicorns only consent to work with virgins and so the main character, Galyne, is frequently called upon to defend or explain trainers' decisions to remain virgins in order to work with unicorns. How do you feel about the questions Rue asks and the responses Galyne gives? Would you choose to remain a virgin in order to work with war unicorns?

5. "You are what you do. You are not what is done to you." This is the core idea behind "Rue the Day." Do you agree with this sentiment? Is it always true?

Riders in the Sky

1. The name of the horse in this story is Peregrine, like the bird of prey. Why do you suppose the authors chose to name him that? Does it suit him?

2. Setting and atmosphere are given a great deal of attention in "Riders in the Sky." Which sensory details stuck with you most vividly? What senses did you feel were focused on the most?

3. The Rider named herself Hennessy after the label on a bottle. How does her choice of name impact how you feel about her? Would you feel differently if she'd called herself Brandy, for example? How so? If you were going to call yourself something off a bottle of alcohol what would it be? Why?

4. Father Monaghan is far from a stereotypical priest—what about him surprised you the most?

5. Peregrine's vanity is used for comedic effect in this story, but the primary antagonist's name is Vayne. Do you think this was intentional on the part of the authors? What purpose does that serve? Is it effective?

Above the Silver Sky

1. Neshka is drawn to the magical horses in much the same way that young girls are often drawn to horses (though perhaps even more so because her mother disappeared on the back of one). Were you drawn to horses when you were younger? Are you still?

2. In "Above the Silver Sky" the rain stops, endangering everyone who dwells there. As the story says, "Our sky was broken, but we could not leave." Does this type of catastrophic environmental

change mimic, in a dramatic way, what is occurring in our own world? What should we do to prevent our sky from breaking? And if we cannot, what then? Can we fly away like the winged horses or are we trapped like Neshka's father?

3. Neshka's grandmother provides not only encouragement for her to mount a magical horse and fly away, but a physical tool—a bridle—to help her with that. What do you think motivates the grandmother to help Neshka escape? How long has she been working on the bridle, waiting to press it into her granddaughter's hands?

4. Despite repeatedly asking her to forget about the horses, in the end, Neshka's father puts her on the mare's back and watches her ride away from their valley. Did that decision surprise you? Why or why not?

5. When her father sets her on the horse and encourages her to leave, Neshka promises to come back to him after she fixes the rain, but in the end of the story she chooses not to do that. How does that make you feel? Did she make the right decision?

A Mother Unicorn's Advice to Her Daughter

1. What did you think about this advice? Did the mother miss anything important? What was your favourite advice?

2. Do you think this advice is unicorn-specific?

Ladies Day

1. What do the characters' names reveal about them? Lord Henry Dinglecrumb? Sissy Sutherland? Charles Cavendish? Duchess Ragnhild? Cassandra?

2. A multitude of details, from language choice to designer names,

work together to establish the setting of this story. Which bits had the biggest impact on your impression of it?

3. The glyphs on Cassanda's tunic translate to "There is no one who deceives who is not deceived, no one who does wrong who prospers at great length." Do you agree with that sentiment? Can you think of a time in your life when it has been proven to be right? What about a time when it has been shown to be wrong?

4. The idea of destiny is important in this story, especially to Cassandra. Do you believe there is such a thing as destiny? If so, can it be changed?

The Boys from Witless Bay

1. Jimmie and Paul have very colourful personalities (to say the least). Are they the kind of guys you'd want to hang out with?

2. What's the best prank you've ever pulled, or had pulled on you? Can it compete with what Jimmie and Paul did to Berton Blake?

3. This story includes plenty of local flavour in the dialog, from words like "b'y" to the phrase "I handy 'bout died" which is something you're unlikely to hear outside of Newfoundland. What phrases or slang terms are local to where you live?

4. Paul essentially plays a game of Twenty Questions with the kelpie at Dunker's Pond. If you could ask any mythological creature twenty yes/no questions, what creature would you choose to talk to? What would you ask it?

5. How do you feel about the people from Ecobay being left in the pond until it's cleaned up? Does that seem fair and reasonable to you?

6. At the conclusion of this story, Jimmie suggests that this will become just one of many ghost stories coming out of Newfoundland. What's your favourite local ghost story?

The Horse Witch

1. Do you believe in magic?

2. Lillian Jones is set up at the beginning of the story as an antagonist for Wendy, but before the story ends Wendy has made some peace with her. Was there ever a time in your life when you thought someone was your adversary/enemy and it turns out they weren't?

3. Lillian is big on pumpkins and cooks them in a couple different ways over the course of this story. What is your favourite pumpkin recipe?

4. When was the last time you rode a carousel?

5. Devon says, "Everything is temporary, Wendy." Is that true, do you think? Or can you think of something that isn't?

6. This story deals with the cull of wild animals. How do you feel about animal culls in general? Are there times when they are appropriate? Are there times when they are not?

7. Have you ever had occasion to deal with someone as unpleasant as Clive? How did that go?

Eli the Hideous Horse Boy

1. The very first line of this story is "Taryn escaped from home whenever she could..." Have you ever felt the need to escape from your own home? Did you act on it? Where did you go? How did you get there?

2. Derrel stalks Taryn because he's obsessed with a version of her that only exists in his own mind and Eli is thought to be stupid until he was hit hard enough that he could speak. Have you ever been confronted with the fact your impression of someone was completely inaccurate? How did you react and process that?

3. Have you ever been to a carnival? When was your most recent visit? What made it memorable?

4. "She saw a policeman working security and understood something when Derrel called her a bitch and the officer only chuckled." Have you had this same understanding? What was the situation that lead you to that understanding? How did/does that make you feel?

Different

1. In "Different" the main character is torn between wanting her daughter to have an easier/better/safer life and accepting her just as she is. Have you ever felt like that toward someone or something?

2. If you could ask a unicorn to grant you one wish, what would it be? What would you pay to have it come true?

3. "No creature should live restricted, defined by others." This is the advice Kyra's mother offers the unicorn. Can you share a time when you've felt like you were living restricted, defined by others? How did you overcome that feeling, or have you?

4. In the end, Kyra's mother chooses to not have the unicorn make Kyra "like everyone else." Do you think she made the right decision? Is it the same one you would have made?

To Ride a Steel Horse

1. Have you ever had a relationship with a non-living object like the one Demy has with her motorcycle? What was it, and what made you feel so strongly about it?

2. Did you undergo a quarter-life crisis when you turned 25 (assuming you have)? What form did that take?

3. When she was younger, Demy had read every horse-related book she could find. What was your favourite horse-related book when you were a child?

The Last Ride of Hettie Richter

1. At the beginning of this story, Hettie feels powerless, unable to stop her family from making poor decisions. Have you ever felt that way? How did you cope with that?

2. Hettie resents being compared to her brother Hector, but given what you know about the two of them from this story, do you think the comparison is an accurate one?

3. If you were ever to throw up your feelings at a crossroads and they would then take some sort of physical form, what shape do you think that would be?

4. If you were given the ability to separate your emotions from yourself and only feel them when you chose to, would you?

We Us You

1. Have you ever been to a rodeo? How was that? Do you think they are exciting entertainment, animal abuse or something in between?

2. Patrick mistakenly spells the word I'll the way he pronounces it

(all). Have you ever made a similar error?

3. When Patrick asks Nicole out he surprises himself with his own boldness. Have you ever surprised yourself with your own boldness? Was it a good thing?

4. At the rodeo Nicole is in unfamiliar territory but is she or Patrick the most uncomfortable with that? Have you ever been in Nicole's position? What about Patrick's?

5. Years later, Patrick looks back on his decision to run from the unicorn in the barn and knows that had he done something different his life would have been a lot different. Is there a moment like that in your past? Are you happy or sad that you made the decision you did? Given a choice and a chance to do things over, would you do something different?

Scatter the Foals to the Wind

1. In "Scatter the Foals to the Wind" Loki talks about one of his questionable romantic partners. Everyone has made some regrettable choices in the past, but at least most of us didn't end up pregnant with a six-legged horse, right?

2. "Scatter the Foals to the Wind" and "A Complete Mare" both deal with magic returning to the world and causing the descendants of gods to manifest unusual powers, but Loki's ancestors' powers show up quite differently in each story. If you were given a choice, would you rather have the abilities of Loki's descendant in "Scatter the Foals to the Wind" or "A Complete Mate"?

3. When Michelle's nosey neighbour sees her transform into a horse, she knows her life as it was is over. Have you ever experienced a moment like that, where you knew it was the end of one thing and

the start of something new?

4. "How could you *not* suspect you're at least part horse?" Loki asks Michelle. If you were to discover you were and animal/human hybrid, what animal would that be? How does that manifest in your personality or physique?

Lightless

1. At the beginning of "Lightless" Fulsa wants nothing more than to earn his mother's approval. Has there ever been someone whose approval you wanted above all others?

2. Phaios describes being lightless and losing himself as "falling into the sky." Have you ever felt that way? What inspired those feelings?

3. Though "Lightless" has many layers and hidden depths, on its surface it is a story about a boy's rebellion against his mother. How did you rebel when you were younger? Were there chariots and starfire involved?

4. Fulsa endures physical pain in order to try and achieve his goal in "Lightless." What would you be willing to endure to achieve your ultimate goal? What is that goal?

A Glory of Unicorns

1. Read this poem silently in your head. Now read it aloud. Does that change your experience of it? How?

2. How does the rhythm of this poem complement or contradict its subject?

World Weaver Press, LLC
Publishing fantasy, paranormal, and science fiction.
We believe in great storytelling.
WorldWeaverPress.com

Made in the USA
Lexington, KY
19 July 2017